REGENCY MISS

Regency Miss

A Regency Romance

Alix Melbourne

OPEN ROAD
INTEGRATED MEDIA
NEW YORK

Copyright © 1978 by Alix Melbourne

ISBN: 978-1-5040-9433-7

This edition published in 2024 by Open Road Integrated Media, Inc.
180 Maiden Lane
New York, NY 10038
www.openroadmedia.com

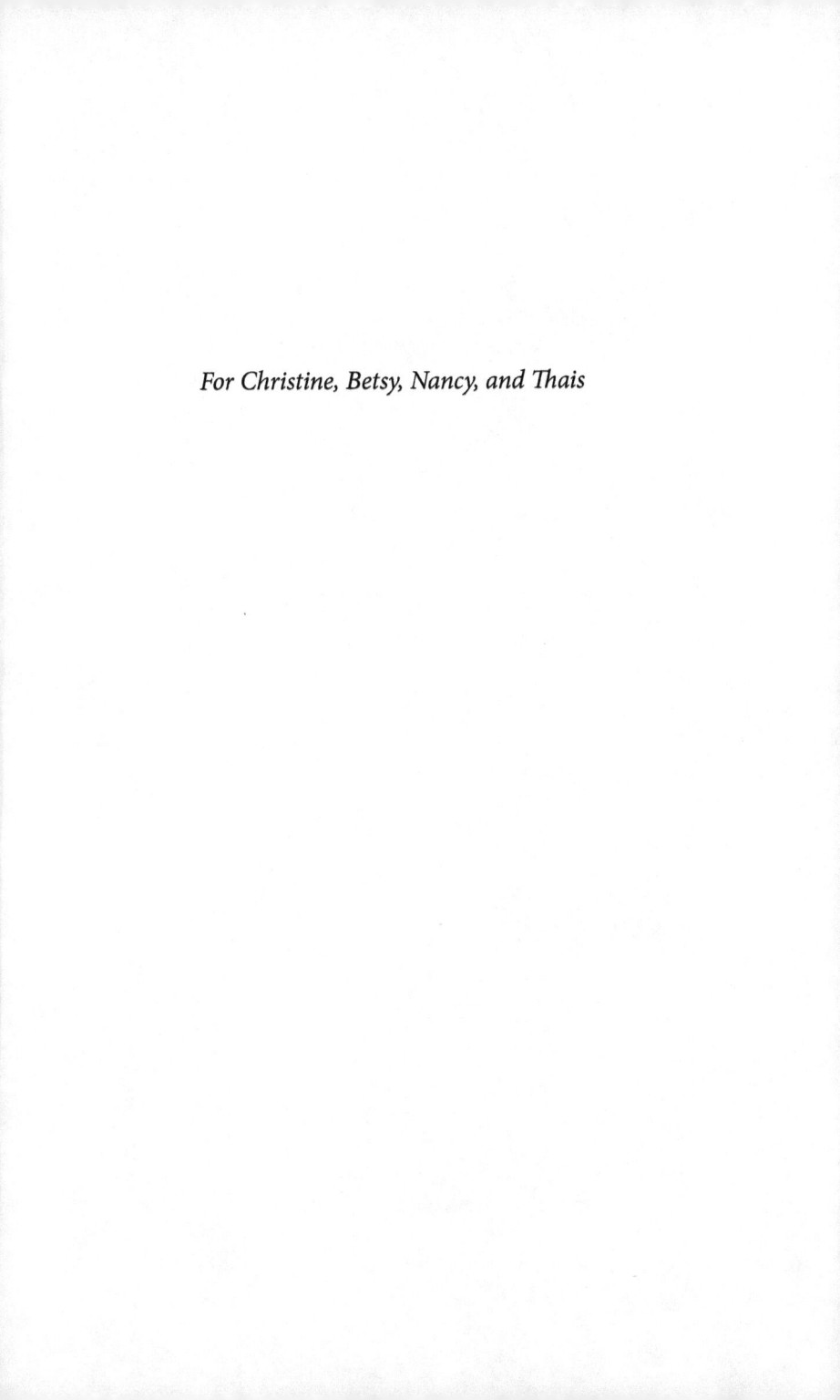

For Christine, Betsy, Nancy, and Thais

REGENCY MISS

PROLOGUE
1806—THE MAN IN THE INN

He had been drinking since the afternoon, but the oblivion he sought eluded him. He was drunk, but he could not forget the events of the morning, the sight of his friend's body on the dueling ground.

All he had left of him now was the heavy ring, with its rough uncut emerald; nothing else remained of the young rakehell who had laughed and drunk with him since they had been boys. . . . And the man who had killed him had been a friend as well. Now he was gone to take the first boat to America, possibly never to see England again.

He rubbed the ring mechanically and drained the last bottle. He sat in a daze, not thinking, not feeling—perhaps the wine was taking effect at last. He let the fire die down to a few embers, and was soothed by the darkness in the room.

At first he could not make out what the noise was, or where it came from, but then it occurred to him that it was someone tapping very lightly on the door.

"Come in, although what you can want at this time of night, I can't imagine."

The door opened, and a figure wrapped in a hooded cape could be seen in the dim light.

"I don't require anything more."

"I am not a servant, sir." It was a female voice. A young lady who was annoyed at being taken for a servant, he guessed.

"And who the devil are then, then?"

"That is none of your concern. I have come to ask a favor of you, but there is no need for you to know my name."

She moved closer to the dim light of the fire. She seemed very young.

"I do not grant favors to those I am not acquainted with, as a rule. But you may ask."

"I wish you to make love to me," she said as calmly as if she were asking directions to Brighton.

He laughed harshly. "You sound too young to even know what that means. I have no taste for children. Why should I do such a thing?"

"Again, I do not wish to be ill-mannered, but it is no concern of yours. It can make little difference to a man who paid the chambermaid to sleep in his bed last night—tonight you will not have to pay. And I am not as young as I seem."

"I do not find virgins of great interest," he drawled. "And even less the seducing of a lady of quality, which your voice reveals you to be. What of your family?"

Her voice was very cold. "Doubtless you will think yourself preferable to the ostler downstairs."

"So it's come to that—myself or an ostler," he murmured, almost smiling. The wine was clouding his brain, but he knew that he should tell her to leave. However, the girl knew what she was dealing with, and came closer still. She opened her cloak, revealing a gown that concealed very little.

He tried again, knowing his resolve was slipping as he

imagined her body under his. "You do not really wish me to do this. Once done it cannot be undone, and I doubt you will enjoy it overmuch the first time."

She was annoyed by his speech. "I know rather more than you may imagine. You are my only opportunity; I must make the best of it. Do not make me go down to that foul-smelling boy." This was said in the tone of a governess dealing with a rather unsatisfactory pupil.

This speech and her calmness provoked him, and he was driven to call her bluff. He stretched out his hand and placed it firmly on the curve of her breast. She did not move at all, but he could feel that her breathing had quickened.

"Well, then," he said consideringly, "I will do as a gentleman should, and give the lady what must please her."

She turned and smothered the remaining coals under the ashes.

"I do not wish you to see me," she explained.

"That is not what interests me," he said, pulling her to him. In the pale moonlight he saw that she would not turn her face to him.

"You must be brave," he said, lifting her chin.

"I am."

"Kiss me then, or am I to teach you that as well?"

Stung, she kissed him as expertly as she knew how.

The kiss changed matters for him, and he drew her to the bed and lay her down on it. She said nothing as he took off her cloak and then her gown. When he took his place beside her, he felt her body stiffen.

"I have made a mistake . . ." she whispered.

He did not answer, but kissed the hollow of her neck tenderly. She tried to push him away.

"Can you not see that it is already too late?" he said gently, smoothing her hair back from her face.

***

She rose from the bed five hours later and searched for her clothes in the darkened room. He heard her, and without opening his eyes, asked sleepily, "Why did you do this?"

She stood at the door, wrapped again in the cloak.

"Because I did not wish to be like the other women of my class: a virgin before marriage and a whore afterwards."

With that she left him.

PART ONE
SEPTEMBER 1813

1

A RASH ACTION

The letter from London had come at precisely the moment that Alicia Tierney was desperately trying to find a way to leave Tierney Chase. In the letter, an unknown solicitor, one Alexander St. Clair, had requested an interview with the only daughter of Isabel Latham Tierney, on a matter of extreme importance. Alicia had no idea of what this matter could be, or why her mother, who had been dead for twelve years, should be mentioned; but she had every intention of finding out. She had planned to order some suitable clothes, since she had none, write her godmother, Lady Mary, and leave for London in a month. But a nasty quarrel with her brother and sister-in-law made her lose her temper and decide to leave hastily and without preparation.

Her brother William had come to live at Tierney Chase after their father had died, and had brought with him his wife, Amelia, a delicate blonde who had disliked Alicia immediately. Alicia, long used to running the estate for her father, was forced to calmly accept the manner in which her brother and Amelia made her feel that she was a burden to them. But it was not until she rejected the hand of James Lanyon that a serious quarrel developed. Her brother warned her that she would never do better. James was wealthy and kind. He had dangled after her for years. Alicia agreed that he was all those things, but that she had not the slightest desire to marry him.

"I am past twenty-one, William, and I shall not brook your interference in my affairs!"

He turned a choleric red. "As long as you are under my roof—" Alicia, white with anger, did not stay to hear the rest of his tirade. The letter was in her pocket, and she had an excuse to go to London. She would sell the few jewels she had if Lady Mary would not house her, but she would go.

Her maid, Jellicoe, who had known her since her birth, tried to remonstrate.

"Do not pretend you wish to stay, Jelly! They have been worse to you than to me. . . .

"Red-haired temper, that's what it is," muttered Jellicoe.

"I am twenty-five, not twelve, and I am leaving. When my father was alive, this place meant something to me, but now it is no home to me at all. You may stay if you wish."

Seeing that Alicia would not even discuss this rash action, never mind change her decision, Jellicoe gave in and went to find a coachman. No one from the estate could be expected to drive them, and it took her the rest of the afternoon to find someone who would agree to the journey. She returned with the news that the blacksmith's son, Jim Taylor was willing. He was to have gone to London in a week's time to visit his uncle.

"Of course, I could have driven," Alicia said innocently. "Cousin Freddy taught me, you know."

Jellicoe stiffened. "Don't be thinking of it, Alicia! What's allowed on country roads isn't seemly on the turnpikes. You'd get some nice treatment from the ostlers, I'll be bound."

Alicia started to laugh. "Jelly, you didn't think I was serious!"

"Any young woman who would go off to London without a full day's notice, would count on imposing on a great lady without even sending a letter ahead—"

"Is capable of driving her own coach. Yes, yes, I daresay you are right."

The next morning the chaise, which had been surreptitiously loaded the night before, was waiting in the woods near the main road. Alicia found that she was unprepared for her feelings as she looked back at the house in which she had spent her life. Jellicoe unabashedly shed a few tears.

"No, no, Jelly, don't cry. Life will be exciting. No more Amelia, no more William. You'll see, we'll be happier than we've been in years!" Alicia wondered why her own words sounded so unconvincing.

Several hours later, Alicia was forced to admit that things were hardly promising.

"I do hope we won't have an accident. The boy is very young," Jellicoe had been fretting since the rain had started. The combination of the rain, the young driver, and the bumpy road had made her anxious.

"We won't have an accident. Jim is very good. You will feel better when we stop, which should be soon." Alicia said this with a cheerfulness she was far from feeling. It had been raining since they left Lincolnshire, and the muddy roads had slowed them down. Now they were outside of Bedford, and she had hoped they might reach London late that night. But now it seemed that they would have to spend the night in an inn. The money she had in her possession was just enough to pay for the changes of horses and one night in an inn. But if there were some accident, some unforeseen contingency, she would be unable to deal with it.

It was with relief that Alicia heard Jim Taylor call out that they were stopping at the next inn. Jim had never been away from Grantham, but he found the best inn in Bedford for them.

The Bridge was an imposing edifice, and the innkeeper's wife greeted them warmly. There was roast beef and mutton for dinner, news which cheered them greatly.

The room to which Alicia was led was both comfortable and elegant. The mahogany bed with the painted cornice and dainty curtains promised a good night's sleep. Examining the blue Staffordshire jug and basin and the sash windows, which had both blinds and curtains, Alicia felt she could happily stay in this room forever.

When it was time to go down to the private dining room, Jellicoe announced that she was too tired to get dressed again— she would have a tray brought up to her room. Alicia had no objections to this, she had wished to be alone after the enforced sociability in the chaise.

The dinner she was served seemed wonderful. She was brought beef, fruit pie, and Cheshire cheese. Only after she had satisfied her hunger did she take the trouble to examine the other diners.

Two officers, who had obviously been drinking for some time, sat in the near corner, and two gentlemen, whose clothes, even from a distance proclaimed London, sat in the far corner, reading newspapers.

As Alicia was finishing her cheese, she heard the officers quarrelling and cursing loud enough for her to hear. The younger one said that the other should not speak so in the presence of a lady. The second officer turned and looked in Alicia's direction.

"But perhaps she is no lady at all: let us discover the truth of the matter."

He approached Alicia's table.

"Do continue eating, madam. I merely wish to see if you are a drab or a duchess."

"Whether I am a lady or not can be no concern of yours, but it is clear that you are no gentleman."

The officer disliked her answer and was moved to assert himself. He wrenched her out of her chair, and bent her arm behind her back. She was about to kick him when she felt herself suddenly freed. The soldier and one of the men from the other table exchanged blows. But his opponent proved to be unusually adept with his fists, and the soldier was quickly floored.

Her rescuer returned to his table without so much as a glance in her direction and began to read his paper again. His former companion had left, probably just prior to the fight. Despite his forbidding air, she resolved to thank him. She made her way past the officer, whose friend was reviving him, and approached the gentleman's table.

"Excuse me, sir, but I must thank you for saving me from an unpleasant situation," she said with a charming smile.

But her display of good manners did not even cause the man to look up from his paper.

"I have always had a horror of being a hero in scenes," he said languidly, "and a greater antipathy to ladies in distress. Please say no more about it. You are quite welcome." Observing for the first time his starched linen neckcloth, rigidly perfect in its arrangement, the spotless blue coat with its creaseless fit, and the shining Hessian boots, it dawned on Alicia that this man must be a member of the dandy set. This no doubt explained his foppish air and dislike of gratitude. She was about to walk away, but then stopped.

"Of course," she said with a little laugh, "it was very silly of me to thank you. *You* can have no need of the world's approval when your own opinion of yourself is so high." She smiled gaily and had the satisfaction of seeing him look up at last. He appeared disconcerted, but only for a moment. His face was not as remarkable as his height; he had clear gray eyes which were rendered more intense by what seemed permanently tanned skin—he had been in a southern climate, perhaps—but the mouth was proud, the smile mocking. He looked to be about thirty-five, and as if he had never done a day's labor, despite his physique. She continued to regard him with the air of a visitor to an animal menagerie until he spoke.

"There was something else you wished to say, Miss—"

"Tierney. Yes. I wished to inform you that you may find me at my godmother's, Lady Terbury, 12 Grosvenor Square, London; I will be glad to replace your waistcoat, which is clearly important to you. Since it is my fault, I feel it is the least I can do to—express my gratitude."

Her emphasis on the last word was ironic, and the ghost of a smile could be seen in the gentleman's eyes as he inclined his head, as if dismissing her.

He had undoubtedly been surprised at the address, Alicia thought. Later, as she undressed, she had to admit that she could not have looked very elegant in these old black things. If he could judge her by her clothes, she could do the same. He was a dandy—what her father had always called a tailor's dummy, a clothes-wearing man. Alicia had better reasons to be prejudiced against the dandies as a group. Their influence on the young men of her acquaintance had been pernicious. The true dandy might be elegant, controlled, lucid, and, above all, refined; but the young men of Grantham admired their other qualities of pride and indifference to emotion. Style was considered more important than ambition or passion; both romantics and merchants were to be despised, and politicians were not even to be mentioned.

Her rescuer's insulting indifference, his assumption of superiority, conformed exactly to Alicia's conception of dandy behavior. She could laugh at his pretensions, but she dearly hoped that this was not a foretaste of London society.

The next day was sunny and clear, and Alicia arose in the best of moods, remembering that she would not have to see either her brother or his wife. She was having her coffee when Jellicoe burst in with the news that Jim had taken sick.

"What exactly is wrong with him?"

"Something he ate, or drank. Perhaps a kind of influenza. He feels weak and he could not keep his breakfast down. Could have been the mutton. Smelled odd to me. I *told* him—"

"All right, I shall go and see him. You try and see if there is anyone else to drive the coach."

Alicia saw that Jim was too weak to drive, but she did not think there was anything seriously wrong with him. It had most likely been something in the food.

When Jelly returned with the information that every man who could drive had already been engaged, Alicia made up her mind. The sight of Jim's coat on his chair had given her an idea. She would wear the long coat and the conical coachman's hat and would drive them the rest of the way herself. She was tall, she could disguise her voice, her hair was already cropped, and the hat would cover it anyway. All that was needed was a pair of boots, and Jelly could purchase them for her.

The scene Jellicoe made at this suggestion was brief but intense. Having no other choice, she finally agreed, but she warned darkly that Alicia would be quite ruined if anyone were ever to hear of it.

"No one would believe it," said Alicia. "I have always been just what a young lady should be. And I am tired of it—bored to death, in fact."

They finally left the inn before noon, with Jim driving until they were a mile or so out of sight. Alicia, who was already wearing pantaloons and a shirt under her dress and cloak, changed places with him. Jim said she looked like a proper coachman and settled in beside Jellicoe, who was fearfully afraid she would contract what she persisted in referring to as his "disease."

Alicia took the reins and started the horses. After ten minutes, she decided that she had missed her calling: surely a coachman was the happiest of men! She felt an increasing sense of exhilaration as she felt the wind against her face, and the painful memories of her father's death and her last months in the house she had loved were softened. There was life beyond Grantham, and now she was part of it—part of the landscape with the neat white fenced cottages, the beautifully enclosed estates, the striking church spires.

They had made good time and stopped only to change horses. They were less than an hour from London when Jellicoe decided she was coming down with the "disease." Alicia knew that the lunch basket was empty and realized that Jellicoe must simply be hungry. She stopped at the nearest tavern and went inside to get some sandwiches and tea for her two passengers.

The woman behind the counter was very friendly. She would have a hamper sent out to the chaise while the young gentleman had a drink in the front parlor, if he wished. This idea immediately attracted Alicia. She knew it was risky, but her curiosity was strong. What were men like when they drank together, without their wives or sweethearts? She nodded to the counter-woman and went in.

The room was almost full, and the serving girls were doing a brisk trade in gin and water and brandy. As she looked over her companions, Alicia spotted a familiar blue coat. The idea of eavesdropping on this man appealed to her, and she took a chair at the table next to his, her back to him. She ordered a brandy and settled down to listen. It was as if she were in the theater, watching the men around her. The snatches of conversation she could hear from different parts of the room indicated that men were not terribly amusing when they were in their cups, and that animadversions on the perfidy of the female sex occupied only part of their time; the rest was devoted to sport. The table next to her proved to be no exception. Her dandy and his friend had apparently just finished buying some horses and were going on to visit some women Alicia thought were quite definitely not ladies. Her dandy began to give his friend, whose name was apparently Jack, a lecture on the evils of marriage.

"Marriage, as Lyttleton said, is a species of traffic, as much a matter of commerce as any warehouse commodity. One exchanges passion for passion, beauty for titles, titles for money. Or youth for age, as some we know have done. In the end it is usually not profitable—for either side."

But his friend did not completely agree, which made Alicia like him much the better.

"You're being much too hard on the ladies, old fellow! I still say that if I could find the right woman—I'd settle down in a flash. Of course I'd like her to be rich, make my family happy, but it's not the main thing. Easy for you to make these statements—you have money, and Sibylla to amuse you—you don't need marriage!"

"But Sibylla is precisely what you have said: amusement. And I hope neither she nor I have any illusions about love entering into it—I like her very well, but that is all . . . I would never marry her. . . . There is someone else, however, who strikes me as someone I would marry. I may surprise you yet."

Alicia was getting up to leave when she heard the name Terbury mentioned.

"Doubt it," her dandy was answering to some question. "She was dressed like a country nobody."

Alicia was grateful that he could not see her face. She was flushing with humiliation, quite sure that the phrase referred to her. She did not notice the man with the limp whom she brushed past on the way out, but he noticed her, and he went to the window to observe her departure.

As she drove the last hour to London, Alicia comforted herself with the thought that she would never see this man again.

The number of vehicles on the road had greatly increased, now that they were close to London, and she had to concentrate on avoiding swerving coaches and reckless youngbloods who took the blind curves too fast.

Gradually the villages turned into rows of buildings, the crowds swelled, and the noise increased. Her last visit to the city had been ten years earlier, and much had changed. The gaslights which were now installed on many of the main streets seemed wonderful to her, as did the remembered beauty of the bridges, streets, and squares. She would try to see as much of the city as she could in her week, she decided. Even at night London was astir with life, as people traveled to and from the opera and the taverns; some shops were even open.

When Alicia stopped in Oxford Street to ask directions, she discovered that she was only ten minutes from Grosvenor Square. She and Jim exchanged places once again, and Alicia managed to change back into her clothes in the chaise, but only with the grumbling Jellicoe's help.

They all knew a moment's anxiety when they saw the severely magnificent facade of No. 12, Grosvenor Square, but Alicia took a deep breath and ran up the steps.

Her knock was answered by Cranmer, the Terburys' dignified butler. Jellicoe, who normally preserved a haughty demeanor when meeting other servants, thawed as she took in this person's imposing appearance.

Cranmer was looking at them with an inquiring air. The chaise was of the first quality, as was the maid. But the young woman did not look like anyone who had ever come to the front door of No. 12. Her accent, however, showed her to be a member of the quality, even if her clothes did not.

"Cranmer, I know I look a sight, but I had nothing else, I assure you. I daresay you don't remember me, but I remember *you*. I was a child then, and you called me Allie T."

"Miss Alicia!" he said, his face dissolving into a smile. "Her ladyship *will* be pleased! But we did not know—"

"Oh course you didn't. I had a special reason for not writing. Come in, Jellicoe, this is Cranmer." Alicia paid Jim and told him she would be in touch.

Jim protested that he did not want the money, that his father had been wrong, and that it had been the best time of his life. Alicia smiled charmingly and said that she had never had such a good coachman.

Cranmer reported all these events to the cook and expressed the hope that Alicia would cheer up Her Ladyship. Lady Terbury had not been her usual cheerful self since her son, who had gone to fight in France, had not been heard of for three months.

Any doubts Alicia had had about her reception were

immediately removed by the warmth of her godmother's greeting. When they were settled down at the tea table, she made Alicia tell her everything that had happened in the year since her father's funeral, which Lady Terbury had attended. Even from Alicia's very understated account, Lady Mary deduced a great deal, since she knew the parties involved. She was an energetic woman of middle age, and she did not hesitate to speak her mind.

"My dear, I knew that wretched woman would make your life miserable. Your brother is a simple dolt who needs a good beating, but she is the one who has made all these charming plans for your future. Amelia was not improved by marriage—it only strengthened her most unpleasant characteristics. . . . Well, you have done very well to come to me . . . I shall think of something. Now you are to go straight to bed—you must be exhausted."

Giving herself up to this stronger will, Alicia went to her room. The driving had indeed worn her out, and she thought she would sleep for days. She was so happy to be at her godmother's that she fell asleep immediately.

Lady Mary herself did not fall asleep for some time. Her husband was at his club, and she meant to take the matter up with him the next day. She was moved by the resemblance of Alicia to her mother. Isabel, her dear friend, had died much too young. Her death had been a tragedy for her daughter and husband. Alastair Tierney had never really recovered, but it was Alicia who had suffered the most. The girl seemed to have her mother's quiet temperament and her father's interests—books, riding, and cards. This was no doubt due to the fact that he had brought her up very like a son, or a best friend. It was understandable, under the circumstances, but perhaps not the best thing for Alicia. Alicia's appearance had shocked Lady Mary.

She was very pale, very tired-looking, huge circles were under her eyes—the same unusual dark blue eyes Isabel had had. And her clothes were impossible—that would have to be taken care of before the rest. Lady Mary had decided that no matter what Alicia thought, she was to stay much longer than a week. Perhaps a match might be arranged—twenty-five was old, of course, but Alicia was unusual and just might attract someone suitable. But Lady Mary knew she would not be able to bring Alicia up to the mark, help her choose clothes, tell her how everything was done. For that she needed someone closer to her own age.

When Lady Mary brought up the subject of Alicia with her husband the next morning at breakfast, he yawned and said that the solution was surely obvious: "Your cousin's daughter Harriet would do very well. If there was ever a female who knew more of clothes and hair, I don't remember it."

"The very thing, Henry! Thank you. And Lord knows the child needs to get away from that harpy."

"I take it you are referring to your cousin. Yes, do the child well to get away from the mother's sickness."

"Pooh! My cousin Edith hasn't ever known what sickness is! She just wants everyone waiting on her hand and foot. I'll send Gordie with the carriage—that way Edith won't resist—a free ride to London, even for her daughter, would be hard for her to give up."

2
LAURENCE AND NICK

Two months earlier, Lord Nicholas Fane, late of Wellington's army, had discovered Laurence Terbury lying in a cottage on the road to Madrid. He had been delirious with fever for weeks, and the family caring for him knew no English. It was by pure chance that Fane had recognized the trappings on the horse tethered outside an unprepossessing cottage as being of Scott's regiment. Inquiries produced the information that there was a young Englishman lying ill. Another man might have left him, sending help back after reaching Madrid. But Fane had imperturbably paid off all concerned and had taken him back in a carriage to Madrid, where they made arrangements to get to England. Laurence had gradually recovered, and by the time they reached the boat for England he was quite well. His companion interested him intensely. Here was a man who had probably saved his life, but who would accept no thanks and indifferently shrugged the whole matter off with a joke. Whether waging high stakes at the card table, or flirting with a voluptuous lady, nothing seemed to disturb his calm exterior. And he was most cynical about women.

"I have noticed that Spanish women are much like those of England and France. Money will purchase their affection, whether they be ladies or street girls. And when it does not, it merely means that the lady herself is rich. Oh, yes, I will allow them to have affections—but it is so rarely for their husbands and so often for their lovers. I daresay I know of precious few virtuous ladies left in English society. And if they are virtuous, one sees straightaway the reason—upon their faces."

"I cannot allow you to joke so, my dear Fane. I have seen love—between my parents, of all things. Natural affection does exist. You are merely to be pitied for never having seen it."

"Ah, but I *have* seen it, and have seen it degenerate into something quite different. At any rate, I know what women wish in a man—a coxcomb like this fellow Byron, someone to titillate their fancies. It is too boring, my dear fellow, to be constantly conterfeiting interesting sufferings, so that one may become a challenge."

Laurence laughed in agreement, but was much interested by this terrible view of womankind. Had his friend suffered so at the hands of women himself, or was this just prejudiced observation?

That Fane held a fascination for the opposite sex, despite his refusal to be a Byronic type was proven many times over on their journey. The Spanish women found this apparently indifferent milord to be an interesting challenge—and a certain contrast to their own fiery men.

They were most happy to reach England that September. Here Laurence saw a transformation take place in his friend. The rough soldier became the complete dandy, elegance itself, equipped even with a silver-handled walking stick.

"'Pon rep, Nick! What is this? I had not thought to be with a tulip of the *ton*! Why such a change in your skin?"

"In England it is easier to be a man of fashion than to explain to the quizzes why one is not. At any rate, I find it amusing. And I can tell you, Laurence, you in your soldier's clothes will be more noticeable than I in this rig!"

It was with real regret that Laurence parted from his new friend in Dover. Laurence was going to London but Fane was to go to visit his mother before coming to town.

Laurence found that his illness had left him weaker than formerly, and he had to rest periodically along the way, but by four o'clock in the morning he was in Grosvenor Square, saying hello to a most surprised Cranmer.

Cranmer's surprise was nothing in comparison to Lady Mary's.

"You should have written us, you young puppy! We thought you would never return!"

"And so I might not have, if Nick Fane hadn't found me. I was delirious, you see, and could not write."

Lord Terbury was stunned.

"Nick Fane, that gambler, that macaroni? My God, I doubt he would rescue a—a—cat, never mind yourself. Most unexpected! A man who refused to ride at Melton because he didn't wish to dirty his clothes! As bad as that tailor's dummy Brummell!"

Laurence laughed softly.

"Yes, he is a bit of a dandy . . . but he is a bruising rider, I assure you—when he has on clothes he does not care about. We had a good journey home."

Laurence restrained himself in his narration. He felt that some of the episodes he and Nick had shared would be best not mentioned to his mother.

"Well, I have always thought him unpleasantly *proud*," said Lady Mary, "but I am now ready to pronounce him the most wonderful fellow in the world!"

Laurence was put to bed, after being told the most important news of the past month. He was happy to hear that Alicia had come to town—he had not seen her in years.

This remark gave Lady Mary food for thought, and she mentioned at breakfast the next morning that it might be a very good idea if Laurence and Alicia were to see a great deal of each other.

"My dear," said her husband from behind his gazette, "I would not encourage it. Alicia is twenty-five, Laurence, twenty-two. But Alicia is far older than her years, and Laurence . . . is not the sort of man to interest her."

Lady Mary bridled at this. Wasn't her child a handsome blond Adonis? Had his experiences not matured him?

"As to that, I can't say. But I know they won't suit. Let them be friends, Mary! Other girls will be found for Laurence."

Lady Mary said she would take his advice, an assurance which did not deceive her husband in the slightest.

Everyone was so absorbed in the excitement of Laurence's return, that the invitation to Harriet Stornaway was virtually forgotten. It was not until the girl was actually being shown into the sewing room that Lady Mary remembered.

"My word! Alicia, this is my cousin's child. She is to be your friend—shopping, balls, and so on. She shall show you how to go on—she came out last year, but has had *no* pleasure, due to my wretched cousin."

Alicia thought this friendship a little sudden and the explanation a bit unclear, but by now she was used to Lady Mary's manner.

Any doubts there might have been disappeared as soon as Harriet arrived. The girl was obviously very shy, and her huge hazel eyes seemed to beseech everyone's forgiveness for anything she might do wrong.

Alicia immediately put forth her best efforts to put this child at ease. After she had told them all the news of her family, she seemed to relax. But it was not until Laurence looked in that she showed animation. He asked his mother to be introduced to the young lady.

"This is your cousin Harriet! I fail to see why an introduction is necessary when you have known her since birth!"

Harriet blushed and Laurence tendered his apologies.

"But you have changed so—in three years, is it? I hardly know you," Lawrence explained with a winning smile.

"You yourself have changed considerably," said Harriet in confusion.

Lady Mary regarded them dispassionately. "Such dull conversation one hears from the young, nowadays. . . ."

As she left, Lady Mary instructed the girls to become friends. Despite this sort of encouragement, which, as Harriet said later, positively made one wish to loathe the other person, after a few days Alicia thought they might very well become friends.

Alicia began to understand what Lady Mary had meant about Harriet having no pleasure. It was apparent that she was taken advantage of by her family. She felt guilty for having left her mother in the care of her elder sister, Julia. When Alicia said that Mrs. Stomaway would undoubtedly be just as happy with her sister as nurse, Harriet shook her head.

"No, I am afraid not. My sister does not take her headaches and palpitations seriously, and when one is feeling so ill, it is quite lowering to have someone telling you it is only your imagination."

Alicia could make no answer to this, since she strongly suspected that Julia was quite right. From what she could discover, Mrs. Stornaway was rarely ill when she was in London.

Lady Mary was also skeptical. "Strong as a horse! Outlive us all!" was all she said.

Harriet declared that helping Alicia buy clothes was the most enjoyable prospect she could imagine, and they began long discussions of what a lady in society would need. But Alicia did not see where the money was to come from: Lady Mary had persuaded her to stay, at least for a month or two. Since the mysterious Alexander St. Clair was still reportedly in Scotland, there was no sense in leaving—and, indeed, where could she go? But Alicia could not let her godmother pay for her new clothes. Her recent scene with her brother was too fresh—she would not be a charity case!

Alicia consulted Jellicoe, who had charge of her belongings.

"What is there that could be sold, to bring a fairly high profit—I do not wish to sell the books my father left me."

"Well, there is the jewelry. It isn't much, but the pearls might be worth something . . ."

Alicia did not think the pearls and garnets would bring very much, but she set out the next day with Harriet. They were going to visit Jeffrey's, the most exclusive jeweler in London, the shop that catered to the Prince Regent.

When she saw the showroom, with its Turkey carpets and satinwood cases, Alicia was a little daunted. The gentlemen who ran the shop (for one could never have called them shop-keepers) were as dignified as their surroundings.

She decided to be direct. She approached one of the gentlemen, and stated her problem. The very discreet Mr. Wain led her to a small room, more suited to such a discussion. Alicia told him that Lady Terbury, her godmother, had sent her to Jeffrey's. The gentleman across from her relaxed. Now he knew where he was—Grosvenor Square.

He examined the pearls first, and Alicia saw a fleeting

expression of surprise cross his face. The garnets received only the most cursory examination, but Mr. Wain's eyes seemed to return to the pearls again. He named a sum which Alicia would have been prepared to accept had she not been observing his face carefully.

"I am sorry, Mr. Wain. I think I had better go on to Rundell and Bridge, who are next on my list. I believe these pearls to be of greater value than you place on them." She stood up, her jewel case tucked under her arm.

"Please sit down, Miss Tierney. Perhaps I missed something in my appraisal. Do let me see the pearls again."

Alicia sat down again, sure that the price would be agreeable.

When she returned to the showroom, she saw that Harriet was talking to another young lady, clearly an old friend. Rather than interrupt, Alicia decided to look at the brooches at the other end of the store. There were a number of clients wandering through the cases, but the other end of the room was almost empty.

Alicia was examining some fine filigree work when she became aware that someone was looking at her. Looking up, she saw a strikingly handsome man surveying her critically.

"What *did* you do to old Wain? He looked positively *bitter*," said the man as if they were old friends. His frank curiosity amused Alicia.

"I am afraid that he paid more than he expected for something."

The gentleman seemed to understand her situation.

"Been under the hatches myself—had to sacrifice the family ring to get some of the ready. But I tell you, Wain is usually all smiles. You must have won a great victory!"

Other clients came to look at the brooches, and Alicia moved to the other end of the table, aware that she should not be talking to a completely unknown man, no matter how nice he seemed.

She was examining an opal brooch when he approached her again.

"No, that's not for you. This butterfly is much nicer."

She looked up at him, a sharp rebuff on her lips, but his smile was singularly charming. She could not bring herself to utter the set-down that would send him on his way. She looked at the butterfly.

"Perhaps you are right, but I have no money for either. Do you always talk to ladies in Jeffrey's? Is it a fashionable rendezvous?"

"No. Only if they are very pretty. Do I shock you? Pray forgive me."

"Oh I am not shocked by insincerity," said Alicia. "If I were, I should have left London long since."

"A most surprising lady. But I must introduce myself. I am Robert St. Clair, man about town, do-nothing, at your service." There was a slight tinge of bitterness in his self-mockery which caught her interest.

"Alicia Tierney. But I must go—my friend is looking around for me . . . I imagine that we shall see each other somewhere—"

"Almack's. I am sure you will receive a voucher." He took her unresisting hand and raised it to his lips, as she watched, amused by his boldness. The dark eyes remained fixed on hers as he pressed her hand to his lips.

Alicia calmly withdrew it. "I feel that in the past you have had entirely too much success with women, Mr. St. Clair."

"It is not the past that matters, but the future," he murmured.

Harriet demanded to know who the gentleman was.

"Ah, a slight acquaintance . . . rather handsome, isn't he?"

"Oh yes! He puts me in mind of a gypsy."

"Yes, he does rather. I wonder if he is related to *my* Mr. St. Clair . . ."

"Have you formed a . . . *tendre* for him?" Harriet asked expectantly.

"You are such a romantic, Harriet! Of course I have not. But I do like his shoulders . . . so broad. . . . Perhaps I should conceive a *tendre* for a man with shoulders like that. I think I shall *try*."

Harriet thought Alicia quite the most unromantic person she'd ever met. St. Clair, however, was a different matter: he looked like a perfect hero out of Lord Byron: a dissipated face, commanding dark brows. . . . She was sure that Alicia must have been more impressed by him than she had wished to show.

3
FASHION

Monsieur Romain was not happy. He knew that Alicia's hair needed something, but he could not discover what it was.

The little Frenchman circled around her, muttering to himself in French. Finally he spoke to Lady Mary as if Alicia were not there.

"So. *Très intéressant*. Lady Terbury, I do not think the so charming pictures you have show me will be right for her. She has need of something else, *ça se voit*. Such white skin . . . no, no rouge, never! It could be *épatant* with these hairs if I can do this—here we cut, here curls around the face."

Lady Mary nodded and he began to cut and then to curl. Alicia sat in the chair for what seemed like hours, terrified to look in the mirror to see what was being done to her. The hairdressers in Grantham had always made her look ridiculous, and she expected nothing better from this little man.

When Lady Mary and Harriet informed her that she looked wonderful in the new style she did not believe them.

She believed her own eyes, however, when she saw the new

person in the mirror. Her curls had been artfully arranged to look becomingly disheveled, and a dark blue ribbon running through them set off her eyes.

Monsieur Romain proudly pointed out all the clever things he had done.

"But the hairs," he said importantly, "this is only the beginning! Mademoiselle must go to Désirée—my cousin, by the way—few know of this—for clothes. This dress is not correct for her, she is too tall. Désirée, she will *know*."

Alicia could not take any of this seriously.

"I am twenty-five, after all, not twenty, like Harriet. I am not making my debut! I think I look perfectly well in this dress and wish for none better. It is a waste of time and money to trick me out in clothes from Désirée—although I am sure she is quite marvelous—"

"Do stop being such a bore, Alicia." Lady Mary had decided. "I see that Monsieur Romain is right. You need something unusual. You will go to Désirée's."

Alicia commented that there were more important things in life than clothes.

"Of course there are, but not, I think, when one is about to go out into society. Would you wish everyone to comment on the dowdiness of my godchild? Do think of me, dear. Or to assume that we have suffered financial reverses and are unable to dress you? You cannot imagine how these little things are viewed in the *ton*. And finally, if you are to spend money—mine or yours—why not spend it well, on clothes that are right for you?"

Lady Mary was triumphant, as if the whole plan were hers, not Monsieur Romain's. The little man looked at the older woman with admiration.

"Well, Alicia, what have you to say?"

"You have left me with nothing to say, ma'am," said Alicia meekly.

"And don't call me *ma'am*!" said Lady Mary with a shudder.

Several days later Alicia and Harriet visited Madame Désirée's exclusive shop. It was located in a charming house just off Mount Street, and as soon as she saw the exquisitely decorated main room, Alicia suspected that the money from the sale of the pearls would not go very far. Madame Désirée calmed her fears a little when she mentioned that she was making special reductions this entire month. Madame Désirée, who looked a good ten years younger than her actual fifty, was very shrewd, and she had her orders from Lady Mary. No prices were to be quoted; all bills were to be sent to Grosvenor Square.

At first Madame Désirée could not find the right style for her client. But when she saw how Alicia looked in the severely cut black velvet riding habit, she realized what was needed. This girl's unfashionable looks and figure must be emphasized, not camouflaged. Her gowns should be plainer, and perhaps a little more revealing than the current modes. The pale, translucent skin would be her chief accessory.

After two hours of fittings, Alicia requested some tea and suggested that Harriet herself try on a new gown for Almack's. Harriet thought this a wonderful idea, and Alicia was free to leave the overheated fitting room. She sat in the showroom, looking through *La Belle Assemblée*. She looked up when a couple was led into the room. The woman was so striking that at first Alicia did not even notice the gentleman with her. Her clothes were lavishly trimmed with fur, her pelisse was of pink velvet, and she had improbably golden hair, sparkling green eyes, and a flawless figure. It was difficult to guess her age, but

Alicia thought she was older than herself—her assurance was that of a woman, not a girl. After taking in this rather theatrical beauty, Alicia turned her eyes to the escort. He nodded to her, and she recognized Robert St. Clair.

She was conscious of a slight feeling of disappointment. He was the escort to such a beautiful woman . . . but of course such a man would never have lack of them. . . .

Madame Désirée came out to greet "Mrs. Crawford," and Mr. St. Clair was free to talk to Alicia. He was as charming as before, and this time she had more leisure to examine him. He was most certainly dashing, but not at all a dandy. His clothes showed a bit of the sporting blood. They were looser than Mr. Brummell decreed, more casual.

He told her that he regarded this second meeting as proof.

"Of what?"

"That we are meant to always meet. I should tell you that Sibylla Crawford is a friend—a platonic friend—like a sister, in fact."

This was so transparent that Alicia began to laugh. He was graceful enough to laugh at himself.

"Of course, it matters not a jot to you *what* she is to me. Forgive me—whenever I am talking to beautiful women, I tend to be nonsensical."

"Why is that?"

"Too busy concealing my thoughts."

"But why should you conceal anything?" asked Alicia with an air of innocence.

"I think I had better have some tea. I cannot continue *this* without nourishment!"

"I am sorry," said Alicia, "but you must be the most shocking flirt in London, and I do not yet know how to do it!"

St. Clair pretended to choke on his tea, which made them

both laugh. He looked at her thoughtfully, and then said, as if to himself: "Yes, you are in need of a little gaiety."

If she was startled by this sudden turn, which could not be described as flirtatious, she did not show it.

"Yes, I am. It is just since my father died, it has not been possible . . . and here in London I spend my time being made into a fashionable woman—but I never get to *be* one. . . ."

He was sympathetic, and asked her all about her father. She was sorry when Harriet came to get her for more fittings, but she knew they would meet again.

Madame Désirée had saved the best for last. On the stand was a beautiful satin dress, the color of seafoam, cut low on the bodice, with an overdress of gauze, the whole embroidered in tiny leaves.

Alicia thought it beautiful, but she began to worry about the cost. She had noticed that no prices had been given for anything, but she had assumed that they would be before the fittings were over. When she inquired about the bill, Harriet gave madame an imploring look.

"Ah, I see. Lady Mary at work," said Alicia. "I am sorry, Harriet, but I cannot allow myself to become a charge on my godmother!"

Harriet took a deep breath.

"Well, I think it very selfish of you, Alicia."

"It is just after taking charity from my brother, I cannot bear it—"

"That is the point. You are saying that Lady Mary is like your brother. Lady Mary derives pleasure from giving to you, and you would deny her that."

Alicia tried to convince Harriet, but her friend proved to be surprisingly adamant.

In the end Harriet succeeded in making Alicia feel that she

was being churlish. It was settled that the bills would be sent to Lady Mary, and Alicia would pay her back at some future time.

"When you are married, your husband will do it," explained Harriet.

"Absurd child! I shall never be married, I am practically an old maid now!"

But Harriet had seen St. Clair in the showroom, and said that it was fate. Something exciting was bound to happen when they met again at Almack's.

"Harriet, you amaze me! You will have me married to every chance acquaintance."

Harriet was tempted to say that not every chance acquaintance seemed to lift Alicia's mood as St. Clair did, but she wisely decided to hold her tongue.

4
ALMACK'S

The rooms on King Street, just off St. James's Street, were not particularly elegant, nor the refreshments particularly good—the cakes were stale, the lemonade weak—but mothers had been known to threaten suicide when they and their daughters were refused vouchers to the Wednesday balls in these rooms. Indeed, Wednesday during the season was so given up to this particular place that no one in the *ton* would have dreamed of giving a private ball on that day—for no one would have come. This was the holy of holies, presided over by women who were compared to the gods on Mount Olympus (or the tyrants of Rome, depending on the speaker); the place to which one could only be invited by the permission of these ladies, who viewed fortune and beauty as nothing: one must have that certain gloss, that town bronze which was called *ton*. And if one were an enemy of these ladies, if one did not qualify in some minute particular, one would never dance at the Temple of Exclusivism, the Marriage Mart, the only place a girl of high birth might meet a suitable husband—in a word, Almack's.

Lady Mary was to be forgiven for having congratulated herself on her victory: she had managed to procure vouchers for her two protégées, despite the personal animosity of the haughty Princess de Lieven, who had been quite against it. Nor was this the only problem: Harriet's mother, Edith Stornaway, was considered quite unsuitable, and Alicia's family was unknown to all but one of the powerful patronesses.

But Lady Jersey had carried the day, along with Emily Cowper. Emily Cowper was universally considered to be the most charming of these ladies, but Lady Jersey was not. Lady Terbury had explained to Alicia and Harriet about Lady Jersey:

"She is considered rude and arrogant by some, but she has a thoroughly good heart and an understanding that is not inferior to it. Do not be deceived by Sally's prattle—she has helped you, and you must show your gratitude."

Lady Terbury had been a little worried about Alicia, who seemed to have a prejudice against the exclusivism of Almack's, but now that she saw her goddaughter dancing down a set with none other than the Duke of Kendalford, she felt that all her fears had been groundless. The girl was doing her proud and making Princess de Lieven look foolish in the bargain.

Harriet was with Laurence in the same set, and it was obvious, Lady Terbury thought, that they were by far the best-looking couple in the place . . .

Harriet's expression of joy made her beautiful, which was perhaps more due to the identity of her partner than to the atmosphere of Almack's.

Lady Mary pointed out to her husband that the Princess de Lieven had not taken her eyes off Alicia and Kendalford since they had begun dancing.

"Is it not marvelous, Henry? Alicia comes to Almack's for the first time and catches the most eligible man present!"

Lady Mary and the princess were not the only ones present

to be watching Alicia and Kendalford: the dowagers who had come to see, be seen, and to gossip, were buzzing. Public opinion had labeled Alicia too unusual, a bit farouche, a bit of a bluestocking, when she arrived. Madame Désirée and Monsieur Romain had done their best, and it was true that Alicia took the eye in the blinding white muslin gown trimmed in green satin, a matching ribbon threaded through her curls. Her flaming red hair and alabaster skin, her height, and the fact that no one had ever heard of her family, made it impossible that she would be a raging success. But now Kendalford had changed the odds. He was in his forties, a wealthy man who had never married. He had seldom shown interest in any of the ladies at Almack's, although it was rumored that he was on good terms with several fair cyprians who would never be seen in the fashionable world.

Until the duke was introduced to her by Lord Terbury, Alicia had been heartily bored. Almack's was not interesting if one knew none of the people. Obviously the game here was one of gossip, and she could not play. The young men she danced with were pleasant, but uninteresting, and she found them all too young.

The duke, however, had been charming. He knew how to talk and told her stories about those present—stories which actually entertained her. She thought him quite distinguished looking, with the touches of gray in his brown hair and moustache. He seemed to enjoy her stories of society in Grantham, which she contrasted to what she saw at Almack's, humorously insisting that Grantham's assembly rooms were actually far more attractive.

"But you do not understand, Miss Tierney. The point is that Almack's is in no way beautiful—but it is more exclusive than any palace ballroom! This is what our ladies wished to emphasize."

"And do you approve of such an enterprise?" she asked, not sure of what his real attitude might be.

"I approve of it when it gives the opportunity of dancing with an interesting young woman—"

"A very interesting way of not answering my question, my lord."

He did not continue this discussion, but led her back to Harriet, saying that he must really go over and talk to his Aunt Adelina.

Alicia and Harriet had not been talking for more than five minutes when a young woman joined them. Harriet seemed to lose some of her high spirits.

The woman was introduced as Miranda Drayton. Miss Drayton nodded in Alicia's direction and then began to talk to Harriet, virtually ignoring Alicia. Alicia disliked Miranda almost immediately and sensed that Miss Drayton reciprocated.

A few minutes later another unwelcome visitor came to join them—Miss Drayton's brother Babcock. Harriet's lack of warmth was even more pronounced as she made this introduction. Looking at Babcock Alicia thought it understandable. Miranda herself was actually quite pretty, in a very conventional way. Her hair was blonde, her complexion pink, her eyes blue—and she put Alicia in mind of nothing so much as a china doll. Her neckline was high (chosen no doubt to cover the defects in her figure, rather than to demonstrate her moral tone). But her brother was at the other extreme. Babcock was dressed like a tulip of the *ton*, his shoulders padded to absurdity, his neck cloth starched so high that he could not look down at his shoes. His narrow face had somewhat the look of a ferret, and he was most certainly not what one would have expected as a brother for the proper Miss Drayton. Sisterly affection seemed to have blinded Miranda to his sartorial excesses, and she treated him as if he were a dashing breaker of hearts.

But it was Harriet who suffered most from this visit. Miranda pretended that Babcock and Harriet had been carrying on a flirtation, and kept "warning" Harriet not to lose her heart.

"He will be haunting Grosvenor Square, now that you are back, dear Harriet! You must not encourage him! He is far too young to lose his heart!" she tittered.

With great relief Alicia saw that Kendalford was once again making his way toward her chair, and she welcomed him warmly. Miranda paused in the middle of a sentence and asked Kendalford how long he had been here.

"Ah! Cousin Miranda, how charming. Why I just came an hour or so ago. Best one I've been to," he said smiling down at Alicia, who saw that Miranda was not pleasantly surprised by her cousin's choice of partner. She took up her conversation with Harriet again, but her eyes remained fixed on Alicia and the duke as they danced.

When they returned after the dance, the Terburys and Laurence had taken up their places. Miranda was clearly surprised to discover that Alicia was Lady Terbury's goddaughter, and this information produced a remarkable change in the lady's manner toward Alicia.

It was getting near eleven o'clock, after which time no one—not even Wellington himself—could be admitted. The rooms were filling with people, and very soon there would be no room to dance, Alicia observed to Kendalford. He assured her that there was nothing society liked better than a shocking squeeze, where ladies fainted—that would mean that it had been a successful evening.

"Nick! Over here!" Laurence suddenly shouted. "I had not thought to see you for weeks—this is a surprise!"

Alicia turned to look at the famous Nick Fane and suffered a shock. It was the despicable dandy who had come to her aid, the man who had labeled her a country nobody. She turned away to compose herself. She would pretend not to remember him—she had changed greatly, he had not looked at her for very long—but her hair! She was planning how to move away from this uncomfortable situation when Laurence introduced them. She assumed an air of friendliness. His gray eyes widened just a fraction, it seemed to her, but then she wondered if she had only imagined it.

"I am most happy to make the acquaintance of one who has so earned the regard of this family," she said automatically, noting that his clothes made every other man in the room seem badly dressed.

He smiled blandly, and was perfectly polite, just as if she were a stranger. After some conversation with the Terburys, in which he refused to accept their gratitude and said that it was just what anyone would have done, he turned to her and politely requested the next country dance. She would have refused, but she saw the rest of the company was watching them with interest. She accepted, rather than seem gauche, but it was with a marked lack of enthusiasm.

"I see I have some prejudices to overcome," he said as they went to take their places.

"Your prejudices or mine, my lord?"

"Yours, of course. *I* have none. I hope that you had no further adventures on the road. . . ."

The movements of the dance separated them then. Of course he danced beautifully.

Alicia decided to be just as rude as he was.

"It is puzzling," she said, "that you were on that road when Laurence was sure that you were going to visit your family—in Kent, I believe? Surely that was a little out of your way. . . ."

There was no reaction; indeed, he did not miss a step in the dance.

"Kind of you to take an interest in my affairs, Miss Tierney," he said firmly. "But I would not advise you to continue in this interest. I fancy you might find yourself at point-non-plus in a very short time."

She looked at him coolly. "Of course it is not my business, no doubt you were involved in an *affaire du coeur*. I merely wished to answer one impertinent question with another." She was controlling her temper with difficulty. How dare he use a threatening tone to her!

But he confused her completely by laughing, and then begging her pardon.

"Pray do not lose your temper on my account! I did not mean to put your back up, but I am very sensitive about my . . . *affaires du coeur*, as you call them."

This apology was accompanied by what seemed a genuine smile. Alicia told herself that he was merely exerting his charm on her, practicing on a country nobody, but it was very difficult to remain unresponsive.

"Come, Miss Tierney, let us start again. I have, I admit, been quite unlikable, and you were right to bite my head off; but now let us at least be friendly acquaintances!" His mobile face now expressed such deep regret that she had to laugh. He brightened, and began to tell her funny tales of life at Almack's.

"And why do you come?" she inquired. "Is it not too tame for you?"

"Has no one told you? I am a slave of fashion, and Almack's is fashion. Why, the Beau himself comes here!"

"And you are, of course, a follower of Brummell's."

"Not a follower, precisely. It is just that I agree with much of his opinion." He was smiling provokingly at her, as if he knew exactly how she felt about Brummell.

Fane found her obvious disapproval more interesting than the usual vapid chatter of the Almack's damsels, and decided that he would tease her further. When they returned to their seats, he made an elaborate ritual of abstracting his gold and enamel snuffbox from his pocket. He dipped his index finger and thumb into the powder and then delicately shook off the excess. Alicia was hypnotized by the affected manner in which he held it to one nostril.

"Ah, you are admiring my snuffbox. French work, you know. I also like a cigar, but it's gone sadly out of fashion. Snuff is all the crack now. I expect you wonder where my sort is to be found—lovely smell, is it not?—well, I shall tell you. At the Old Snuff House, in the Haymarket. One may meet everyone there—including the Beau—and they stock my sort—'Fane's' it is called. I can see by your face that you do not like snuff—but it keeps away the colds and throat troubles the cigar men were always subject to. . . ."

Alicia looked at him and wondered if he could possibly be making fun of her.

"Miss Tierney," he said indifferently, "you would do well to learn the art of dissimulation; it does not do to have one's thoughts written on one's face—"

"And what do you read there?"

"I am far too charming a fellow to tell you."

"Very good!" she said objectively. "I thought I had you, but you have regained the advantage. Now that you have entertained me with gossip and snuff taking, not to mention playacting, I feel that my evening was not wasted. Thank you, Lord Fane. And now I will go and talk to Lady Mary."

Lord Fane was interested to find that he was surprised by this speech. She was certainly the most unusual female he had ever met, and she clearly thought him not worth a second glance. Lord Fane was enough of a sportsman to relish a challenge, and in Alicia Tierney he perceived he had found one.

He was watching her converse animatedly with Lady Mary and Harriet when his friend Worthing came over.

Worthing, who would never make a dandy because he had a marked weakness for the fair sex, begged to know what could have been so interesting at Almack's, well known to be more soporific than a session of Parliament.

"The redhead over there, Alicia Tierney. Staying with the Terburys. Going to have a taste of London before going back to the provinces. She's taken me in dislike. Thinks I'm a frippery fellow."

"Ah," said his friend, comprehension dawning. "And you intend to break her heart. . . .

"No, what a vulgar idea! No, I merely wish to make her regret it, a *little*."

Worthing did not think this a very exciting prospect.

"You do not understand, dear fellow. She loathes me now. If I can make her even tolerate such an insufferable dandy as I, I have won. She is no peaches-and-cream child who will change her opinions easily. She is, I think, quite stubborn."

"More sport to make her fall in love with you, Nick."

"Very well, perhaps you are right. Harder to do, but then, everything worth attempting is. Have it your way, Jack. We shall go to White's and enter the bet now. You will of course accept it—my word of honor, she detests me."

Alicia was just asking Lady Mary about Lord Fane's manners when that lady hissed a warning. "Miranda's coming, and they are friends—I'll tell you later."

Alicia thought it most amusing that the two people she disliked most were friends, and she derived a kind of comfort from this.

Miranda was trying to be gracious to Alicia, but this, if anything, was worse than open dislike. Her last words to Alicia that evening were that she hoped town life would not be too fatiguing for one used to Grantham.

"I do not find it fatiguing," replied Alicia, fanning herself. "Although the inhabitants sometimes are."

"Oh, you should not have," said Harriet as they watched Miranda and Babcock leave the rooms.

"Do you think she even understood? I doubt it. Her self-consequence would protect her from it . . . She dislikes me in any case. A rather nasty little doll."

Later Lady Mary said that the children could hardly overcome the parents.

"The Draytons! The stories I could tell! They are forever invoking the deity to sanction their least desire. Miranda is a pious prig, just like the rest of the family. I have always suspected them of being hypocrites; but you must be careful, Alicia. Miranda's reputation is of the highest. They are considered to be one of the best families, in all ways."

"I wonder why this paragon is not yet married? She cannot be more than two or so years younger than I."

"Miranda has had . . . dreadful luck."

"Yes, Trevor married that other girl," said Harriet innocently.

"Yes, Cherry Littleton was quite bad luck—she stole him away from Miranda in the space of a week, just before the engagement was to be announced! And that Friday-faced creature, Lavinia Drayton, maintained that there had never been an understanding to begin with. When Miranda went around with her eyes red for weeks after, Lavinia claimed it was the London air!"

"Well, I cannot help feeling sorry for her if she was in love with him," said tenderhearted Harriet.

Lady Mary snorted at the idea. "In love with his fortune, dear Harriet, not with him! The Draytons have a vast fortune, but they intend only to have her marry into just such another one. No doubt that is why Fane is now being considered, though I doubt she'll get him up to the mark."

"Is Fane so very wealthy, then?"

"Yes, and he is also considered a great catch because of his family. His grandmother has some of the best blood in the country running through her veins."

"I think," said Alicia thoughtfully, "that you are wrong, godmother. Fane and Miranda will deal excellently. They are well suited."

"That may be. But you must remember that no one has yet caught Fane—he has not been engaged once, and he must be all of five-and-thirty."

"Five-and-thirty," repeated Alicia in wonder. "To be such a trifling fellow, a dandy with nothing to do but dress and dance—at that age! Why should her family wish such a connection, if they are so very pious?"

"He is far better than most," replied Lady Mary dryly. "And of course there is the money."

"He can be quite charming," Lady Mary continued. "But on the other hand, there is Lady Anne Dunstan."

Her listeners demanded to know what this meant.

"Well, I really should not be talking like this, but since we have already begun. Remember that I consider him quite a hero—he saved Laurence, or have you already forgotten? But his behavior with Lady Anne is most peculiar, although everyone long ago gave up being amazed at it. . . . Many years ago, after being friends with her and her family, he stopped speaking to her—he does not even seem to know she exists, even if they are placed side by side at a dinner—which of course they very seldom *are*. He has never explained why, or indeed made any reference to it, but there are many theories, most of them not fit for the ears of young ladies."

"I daresay," said Alicia yawning, "that he didn't like the color of her dress. Dandies are known to be absurd about such things—did not Brummell break off with a woman because she ate cabbage?"

When the Terbury party left, it was three in the morning, and Almack's had begun to be thin of company. Around the corner in St. James's Street, however, the crowds were forming around the play tables. The gentlemen who had left Almack's had arrived at White's. There the leatherbound betting book was requested, and the bet entered.

> *Lord Fane bets Lord Worthing 300 g. that a certain lady understood between them, will change her opinion of a certain party before nine months are up.*

5

THE PARK

Lord Fane did not expect to make rapid progress in overcoming Alicia's aversion to him, but neither did he expect to find a lack of interest so complete as to make civil conversation difficult. She laughed at his attempts to flirt with her and regarded him with a gay suspicion that forced him to conclude that he was about to lose 300 guineas to Worthing.

Alicia did not wonder at this sudden attention, but put it down to the dandies' style, their love of paradoxical behavior. In any case, she was not thinking of why Fane was paying her court, but rather why St. Clair had not. Discreet inquiry produced the information that Robert St. Clair was something of a gambler, and rather more of a rake. This, of course, made her all the more interested. She had never known a rake, although many gambling men had come and played with her father at Tierney Chase.

Her exposure to the young—and old—men of the *ton* had increased her interest in St. Clair. The Duke of Kendalford and numerous others had paid their respects, sat next to her at dinners, flirted in the blue saloon of Grosvenor Square, and all, without exception, had bored her, although the Duke of Kendalford was at least intelligent.

By Saturday the hope that she would see the very unsuitable Mr. St. Clair had died, but she was not unhappy, for she and Harriet were to go riding in the park.

When she was mounted upon Lord Terbury's spirited black, Douro, Alicia knew what she had been missing all these weeks in London.

As this first ride in the park revealed, most of the inhabitants were *not* there to ride. Lovely carriages, containing lovelier women, were driven slowly past what appeared to be a line of dandies. These last boldly surveyed each passing vehicle and discussed the merits of carriage and owner in an insufferable manner. Elder members of the *ton* stopped for hours on end, sitting in their landaus, gossiping and calling to each new arrival. These handsome people were there to show themselves, Alicia decided, to be admired and possibly to admire.

The park itself, despite its proximity to Piccadilly and Oxford Street, gave the impression of being deep in the countryside. The shining waters, groves of trees, and running deer all provided a perfect setting for riding, and in the distance Alicia saw the misty hills of Surrey, the green glades of Kensington. . . .

Harriet sighed with pleasure. "*Now* I feel that I am in London!" she said happily.

They rode past the dandies, too absorbed in the view before them to notice the viewers beside them.

"On a day like this," said Alicia, "I wish that my life might be nothing but reading in the Terbury library and riding in the park."

"What, no husband, no children?" asked Harriet mischievously.

"Ah, yes: unfaithful husbands, whining children—someday

you will remember this day in the park as the acme of your existence, Harriet!"

"But all children do not whine, and I believe that when they are one's own . . . it can be quite nice."

"Oh, I have no doubt of it! I am no child hater, it is just that the idea of the marriage mart, like Almack's—it is like so much horseflesh being judged. No, I am wrong! These men spend more time choosing their horses than their wives!"

"And love? Does that have no significance?" Harriet looked genuinely concerned.

"I have never been in love, and most likely I never shall be. My understanding of it is based only on what I have read and seen among my friends. . . . It seems a very impractical state. . . . Don't look at me like that, Harriet! I cannot help it—I shall undoubtedly be an old maid, an ape-leader, you know—but I'm quite sure you will be married."

"I don't think that an ape-leader would be seen in that hat in Hyde Park!" said Harriet.

Alicia had to admit that it was true—her appearance today was not precisely what one would associate with an old maid. Her new riding habit was of hunter-green cloth, with epaulettes and braiding of dull gold. It was drawn tight about her figure, and set off her waist. This toilette was completed by green kid boots and a tall crowned hat with a feather.

As they were riding down a path, two other riders rode toward them. Alicia looked up and met the dark eyes of Robert St. Clair. He smiled, but did not seem at all surprised to have met her in the park. He introduced his companion as Sir Reginald Warren. He was a man of fifty-five or so, rather strangely dressed, and obviously wearing a corset; his pale cheeks were enlivened by what was most certainly rouge. His manner was no better than his appearance. He professed to know both the Tierneys and

Stornaways and began to talk to Harriet about her parents. St. Clair maneuvered his horse so that he and Alicia were partially behind a tree, thus affording them some privacy.

"Do not take Sir Reginald in too much dislike. He has some important connections, which is why I cultivate him, of course."

"You are rather open about yourself, are you not? This can only mean you are concealing even worse traitsl" teased Alicia.

"Before this conversation turns to my other defects, let me tell you that you are looking lovely—Madame Désirée has done you proud."

"Yes, she has. But the money from Jeffrey's did not go very far, I am afraid."

"But Lady Terbury—"

"Yes, she wished to take care of my bills, but you know, I have the most absurd desire to pay my own way."

"I see, but I do not agree with it. I myself am only too glad to have anyone else pay for anything!"

"I expect so," said Alicia understanding, "but you are a rake and I am not. You are *supposed* to waste money, are you not?"

"And you disapprove of rakes . . ."

"Of course. But not of you—you are a rake only because no one has taken any trouble with you."

He began laughing, and begged her pardon.

"If I have heard women say that once, I have heard it a thousand times!"

"How very lowering," said Alicia despondently. "I quite enjoy the idea of saving you and making you—look after an estate somewhere, do good works. . . ."

"I must admit that I thought you were serious. Now please have mercy, Miss Tierney. I was most sorry to miss Almack's last week, I heard the lovely Miss Tierney made her appearance. Will you grant me a dance next week?"

"Who can say, sir? It may be that no more suitable partner will present himself. In that case—yes."

He took her hand in his and looked at her intently, a wicked smile in his eyes.

"As to that, I wager you will find the others more suitable, Miss Tierney." Here he pulled off her riding glove and kissed her hand. "But not," he continued, "more exciting."

Alicia was brought back to her senses by this impertinence. "Harriet," she called without looking at this provoking man. "We must be going."

"Coward!" murmured St. Clair as she rode past him.

As they were passing out of the park, they were greeted by Miranda Drayton and Lord Fane, who were both unexpectedly friendly. Alicia was glad to see that Fane had so quickly found another to receive his attentions—it was perfectly plain that Miss Drayton intended to demonstrate her ownership of Fane. Harriet began asking Fane about the latest indiscretions of the Prince Regent (just had from Sir Reginald). Miranda, pleasant until then, could not keep from trying to teach the girl a lesson.

"I'm afraid I was taught that one should never speak of a person at all, if one could not say anything good. Such a want of delicacy is implied by doing otherwise—and I know you are really not such a gossip, Harriet!"

Alicia thought it was very like Miranda to spoil even such a lovely day as this.

"I feel that those who think as you do, Miss Drayton, should simply leave such discussions instead of lending them your countenance. I am sure if you were to do so, gossip would cease altogether—in your vicinity at least," said Alicia.

Miss Drayton would have answered, but just then Jack Worthing rode up and demanded to be introduced to the two beautiful ladies, seen by him at Almack's. Since Miranda disliked

Worthing, she managed to detach herself and Fane from the group, saying she needed to let her horse get some exercise. As she was leaving, she looked closely at Miss Tierney's black horse and recognized it with some surprise.

"It is Douro! I wonder that Lord Terbury lets you ride him—he is—he must be—too strong for you, Miss Tierney. I'll wager that you were not galloping before when I saw you, but he had run away from you—is that not it?" A sweet smile accompanied this remark.

"No, I am afraid I was galloping. I could not make such a high-spirited horse keep to a sedate canter. As for his being too strong, he is exactly what I like—a horse with spirit. Otherwise I do not call it riding."

Since Miss Drayton's horse was a staid mare, perfect for a lady, there was nothing else to be said about this—at least to Miss Tierney. But as soon as they were out of earshot, Miranda began to express anxiety about ladies who galloped in the park on horses that were most certainly too strong for them.

Fane looked with approval at the delicate blonde beauty beside him, and said that Miss Tierney looked to be almost as strong as a man and that Miranda should not worry so.

Alicia and Harriet gave Miranda no further thought, absorbed as they were in the amusing stories that the incorrigible Jack Worthing was telling them.

In the next week, Worthing was often Alicia's riding companion. She and Harriet went to the park almost every day, determined to enjoy these last warm days to the full.

Laurence accompanied them regularly and by unspoken agreement Alicia let the lovers ride a little behind so that they might talk in privacy, a thing impossible at home.

Alicia enjoyed Worthing's company for many reasons: he was charming, good-looking, and it drove Miranda Drayton mad to see them together. Worthing's remarks about Miranda were most ungentlemanly, and he told Alicia that if ever he wanted to do penance, he would marry Miranda: "Better than a hair shirt, two years with that girl."

"But Fane is your friend—do you not wish to save him from her?"

"Nick is quite a different matter. I daresay *he* could handle her, and she's quite nice to *him*, you know. All sweetness and light. Of course Fane is a high-stickler—and Miranda's well-bred. I'll give her that. She's probably the only girl who would get past Fane's grandmother!"

"But what has that to say to anything?"

"Nick's parents are dead, no other close family—stands to reason, wants to please his grandmother. . . ."

Although the look of disapproval on Miranda's face whenever she saw Worthing riding with Alicia was enjoyable, other reactions were not. Lady Mary disliked this friendship, and was not at all sure that it was merely that. Worthing's reputation had been made in the course of two serious divorce scandals. When this was mentioned to her, Alicia said that she could not see that Jack was any worse than his friend Fane.

"Child, you mistake the matter," said an impatient Lady Mary. "Fane is, to be sure, a dandy, but he is also perfectly respectable. His name has never been connected to . . . the sorts of scandals that Worthing has been involved with. Worthing is a charming fellow, but he insists on conducting his affairs with women of good family—and he caused his first divorce at twenty-one."

"But he is now thirty-one, and the lady was not above reproach herself," objected Alicia.

"I see that you resent this, and I am sorry for it. But the man is a legend—his inconstancy, for example—and I would not wish you—"

Alicia found this amusing. "Godmamma, I have no intention of conceiving a *tendre*, as Harriet would say. He is a friend to me, and I like him very well."

It was true that Alicia felt nothing but friendship for Worthing. He was too practiced, too perfect in his role of lover, and Alicia could not take him seriously. After his first half hour of flirtatious conversation with her, he gave a sigh and said that there was nothing for it: they were destined to be friends, not romantic partners.

"Friends are far harder to come by than flirts are," said Alicia who found that she thoroughly liked this disreputable fellow. She teased him about his reputation, but he defended himself:

"True, all of it. But I have never been responsible for the ruin of an unmarried girl—part of their dowry is their purity, after all, and I would not do such a thing as to deprive them of it. But married women! One is so much safer there—it is so much more amusing, and their men neglect them shamefully!"

"I had no idea purity was of such value in our circles," said Alicia drily.

"Anything in short supply is—and, of course, men are such hypocrites."

"I am with you *there*," said Alicia.

Alicia wondered if St. Clair held these opinions. Although he was often to be found in the park, Alicia kept him at a distance now, not wishing to give him the opportunity to establish the kind of intimacy he was so adept at, the intimacy which she could not deal with. She admitted to herself that she liked to see him there; she would have been disappointed if he had not come.

But Worthing was a thoroughly undisturbing man, and their friendship was such that they could talk about almost anything. Worthing on love was not to be taken seriously, but Worthing on any other subject was quite intelligent, full of common sense and an understanding of the realities of life.

One afternoon they were talking of a popular novel, and Alicia asked him what he thought of the happy ending.

"The marriage? Not very good, never be like that in life—not that a novel has to be, but this isn't consistent with the hero's personality. No earl is ever going to marry a girl already ruined by someone else—unless she's as rich as Golden Ball! The chit should have just kept her mouth closed. In London she'd be one of Harriette Wilson's set, selling her favors to the highest bidder. Or an old maid."

"I suppose you are right. The author obviously has a romantic view of what a nobleman would do. . . . Alicia said slowly.

6
REVELATIONS

The alehouse in Southwark was not a place gentlemen usually patronized, but since it was the time of day when there were few drinking, the two men in the corner were in no danger of interruption by anyone but the waiter who brought them the ale.

The elder of the two men seemed to enjoy his ale and cheese, but his companion drank virtually nothing, contenting himself with a malodorous cigar.

After he had slaked his thirst, the elder man began.

"I have been reading the reports of our correspondents, and I can't say that I like it at all. This man Mercier is once again in England—and we have had no news at all of him. He is the man who provided the very useful information about our movements to Soult—I am sure of it. We got out of it well anyway, but what of the next time? And it is almost certain that he received this information in London. He has got to be caught this time, and I'm asking you to look into the matter. I do not believe it to be a very dangerous assignment—to our knowledge, Mercier has never killed a man."

The other gentleman stretched his legs and blew smoke rings, seemingly uninterested in this affair.

"Well, I should like to know how you are so sure he is here—no one has ever seen him—that is, to be sure of."

"Our men on the other side, of course. Little lady in Paris has a way with Buonaparte's officers. They are delighted with Mercier and talk of his exploits openly. One of her lovers told her that he had to leave Paris—to make arrangements for Mercier."

"And what is the port he used?"

"Lisbon, she thought. Damned strange."

"Most peculiar."

"Here is the entire packet on him. Be very careful with it, and drop it off at the usual place when you are done. As you will see, our people have almost found him from time to time, but the fellow is very, very good. Never in one place too long, of course."

His companion nodded and seemed to fall into a reverie until the elder man was finished with his drink.

They left by the front door and were observed by a young man lounging in the doorway of the next building. After they had passed him and gone off in different directions, the young man wrote a note and entrusted it to an urchin who appeared out of nowhere. He did not have to worry that the child would read the note: it was in French.

7

ALEXANDER ST. CLAIR

Alicia looked out at the rain in the square and sighed. Of all days to visit Alexander St. Clair, whose note requesting an interview had been sent upon his return to London. She was curious about his business with her, but not enough to enjoy the prospect of driving through the rain.

As Alicia and Jellicoe were getting ready to leave, Laurence came in the front door, looking so low that Alicia stopped her preparations and instructed Jellicoe to wait for her while she talked to Laurence.

She followed him into the sitting room that he used as his study.

"Laurence, why are you looking so blue-deviled? Have you lost your fortune at faro?" She was teasing, but she saw him look up, amazed.

"No, but what makes you ask that?"

"You are like a thundercloud, and rarely home, and one is always hearing of young men who land in dun territory."

Laurence laughed, but there was not a particle of mirth in his laughter.

"I wish I could tell you, but I must deal with Geor—*it*, myself."

Alicia regarded him sympathetically. He was really so very young, despite having been a soldier.?

"Let me guess, is it a woman—Georgiana, or a man—George?"

Laurence was struggling with himself, torn between the desire to share his misery with company, and his determination to keep it to himself.

"It sometimes helps to tell someone, Laurence, and you know that I would never break a confidence."

"It is the most dreadful mess!" he said finally, with great relief. "It is a girl, no a woman—well, she is a cyprian, most likely. And now she has some letters I wrote almost a year ago."

Gradually the story came out, though not very coherently at first. The girl was one Georgiana Porter, who worked in a Pall Mall gambling hell. The daughter of the proprietress of The Silver Tree, she looked to be an innocent and lovely sixteen. With visions of taking her away from her mother's house, Laurence fell in love. The letters had been written from abroad, and were not such as to reflect credit on the sender. The romance ended when one of his friends informed him that his true love was twenty-six, not sixteen, and an experienced member of the demimonde. Now that he was twenty-one and about to receive his inheritance, she had conceived the idea of blackmailing him. If he did not pay her a rather considerable sum, now, she would publish the letters of the young Viscount Terbury to a cyprian.

"The thing is, Alicia, I've no guarantee that she won't come here and make a scene—she's the most unpredictable girl! And with Harriet here . . . and her mother and sister due to arrive in a week . . . you can see that it just won't do! I must do something. She wants the money before the end of the month, and I don't have it—obviously she's in some kind of trouble herself or she'd wait."

Alicia thought of offering to lend him the money herself, but she knew that he would find such an offer insulting. She would stay out of this and let the boy turn to his father, or even to his friend Fane.

"I don't see that it would matter so very much if she did publish them."

Laurence looked at her as if she were mad.

"My dear Alicia! What can you be thinking of? I plan on a political career, and this is exactly the sort of thing which would make me look ridiculous. And Georgiana looks just like a child—she would appear somewhere and I should be branded forever—no one would believe *I* hadn't wronged *her*. And my father! I don't even want to consider how he would react."

Alicia saw his point. The amiable, if slightly distracted Lord Terbury positively beamed every time his eyes happened to light on his son—his son who had won praise in the dispatches from the Peninsula. For him to hear of this banal, vulgar affair would be most unfortunate.

And the effect on Harriet! Harriet was probably incapable of imagining that the blond officer she loved could have gotten involved with such a woman.

"What of Nick Fane—could he not help in some way?"

Laurence looked embarrassed.

"Fool thing to have given a woman a piece of paper with my name on it—that's what he'd say. I suppose I might ask him . . . but I'd look like a flat! But I shall manage something. I have some things that might bring in some money. . . ."

Alicia said a few comforting words and then joined an impatient Jellicoe in the carriage. All the way down Oxford Street, Alicia turned the problem over in her mind. There seemed to be no way she could help without hurting.

Laurence's pride. And perhaps he would manage to get out of this mess on his own. . . .

Oxford Street turned into Holbom, and then they were near Newgate Prison, a building which seemed to dominate the entire area, giving it the tinge of hopelessness, or so it seemed to Alicia. After the Old Bailey, St. Paul's and the other famed landmarks, they came at last to Cornhill and the Royal Exchange.

Alicia could feel the energy here, the fast pace of the men who traded goods, backed entrepreneurs, and dealt with citizens of a hundred nations, all dressed in varying national costumes. John Bull could always be seen in the center of each transaction.

Jellicoe smiled approvingly as they made their way to the offices of St. Clair and Crewe, on Fenchurch.

"Very nice it is. Nice buildings, Miss Alicia. Not made of that plaster stuff the Prince Regent likes! These men are for the stone, you see, something that *lasts.*"

Alicia thought the buildings done by Nash for the Regent were very lovely, but she had to admit that the architecture of the City was very impressive.

Their destination turned out to be a simple gray building, severe in facade, but made of excellent materials, giving one confidence in the prosperity of the firm that could afford offices there.

Alexander St. Clair was a courtly old gentleman, tall and thin. He bore no resemblance to the other St. Clair. He was very energetic, and Alicia liked him at once.

"Well, my dear, I am very happy that you have come to London. I have had a rather difficult time with your money."

Alicia had no idea of what he referred to, but she nodded intelligently, wondering if he was a little mad.

"Now, Richard Drake did very well by you, and I've tried to do just as well, but now we must fill out the required documents—"

"But who is Richard Drake, and what has he done for me?"

He looked at her in some bewilderment.

"Do you mean—you don't know? I *am* sorry! I should have known that you would not know yet . . .

He seemed quite upset, and Alicia tried to soothe him.

"Well, you know I have been positively buried in the country, I daresay that your office was supposed to—"

"No my dear, my office was not responsible—it was Drake's lawyer who obviously forgot about contacting you, or perhaps the letter went astray. At any raté, I shall do it now."

He took some tea which had been brought in, and smiled warmly at her. Alicia chose this opportunity to ask him if Robert St. Clair was a relation of his.

"So you've met Robbie? Quite a hand with the ladies, he is. Yes, he's my nephew—don't come around to see me till he's in the suds, however—like all the young bucks nowadays." Alexander St. Clair took another sip of his tea, and then opened a packet of papers which lay on the desk in front of him.

"Since you know nothing, I shall tell it to you as it happened. It all began when there was a dreadful row about the diamonds."

"Diamonds?"

"Your mother's. She sold them to help Richard Drake—known as Dickie Drake in the City—and so—"

"But who was Dickie Drake, and why should she have sold her diamonds? My father was not poor, after all."

He smiled at her reassuringly.

"Forgive an old man's ways, m'dear. I assume that what is known in the City is known everywhere. Dickie Drake met your mother at Bath, in the Pump Room. He was very young, and full of plans, though his family was aghast at his plans to go into trade. Your mother took to him right away, but your father never met him, and never wished to, either. She wanted to invest in Drake's new import-export company—India goods—but your father refused to let her. He thought the whole scheme completely mad, and he did not trust Drake to manage it well. He had been advised against it by some other friends who disliked Drake.

"The upshot of it all was that in order to avoid a serious quarrel with your father, Isabel sold the diamonds she had from her mother (she had always disliked them, or so she maintained), and had some good paste ones substituted. Your father never knew, but I am afraid your brother must by now—I imagine he would sell everything of that sort."

Alicia nodded dumbly. She could not believe what she was hearing. This headstrong young woman, Isabel, selling her diamonds without her husband's knowledge—this picture hardly agreed with what she had been told of her mother. . . .

"The point is, Miss Tierney, that Dickie Drake became one of the richest nabobs in the City. *And he never married.*"

Here he paused, looking at her expectantly.

"And why did he not marry?"

"Well . . . I should not be discussing this, of course. But it was so very long ago, and you are her daughter, after all. He loved Isabel Tierney, of course—not that there was ever a breath of scandal, mind you—and he wanted no second-bests if he could not have her."

Alicia found herself liking this nabob, and she began to suspect that the man in front of her might not have been indifferent to Isabel himself.

"And so," he continued, "he determined that her children would benefit—of course your father never knew—"

"Do you mean to say that my brother is also involved?"

"No, miss." Here he hesitated, obviously reluctant to elaborate. He sighed.

"He saw you both, you see, and after that he decided that it was to be you, only you."

"Whatever do you mean? How could he have seen us—when?"

"When you were both visiting your grandmother—may her soul rest in peace—he was a guest. It was the year before she died."

After an effort, Alicia succeeded in recalling that last visit, when she had been nineteen.

"Did he have a very red face and white hair?"

"Yes, that would be Mr. Drake. He said he didn't like the cut of your brother's jib, but that you had bottom. So there you are—the Drake heiress. Quite a decent sum of money, you know."

Alicia didn't know. Her dark-blue eyes—just like Isabel's the old man noticed—expressed amazement.

"Do you mean to say . . . that there are no charities, that I am the only beneficiary?"

"No, he thought only of Isabel, I'm afraid. This is how he paid her back for her belief in him—without that initial money he would have taken much longer to become a rich man."

Alicia's miiid refused to understand what was happening—it could not be real, it was too incredible. After a few minutes she had gained sufficient possession of herself and asked the exact amount of the inheritance.

Mr. St. Clair obviously found this direct request a little unnerving—he was used to more circumspection about money.

"The income from the principal will be approximately five thousand pounds a year." A little embarrassed, he cleared his throat and directed his gaze to the window.

Alicia felt an inclination to laugh at the absurdity of it all—one day she had nothing, the next she was an heiress—to a considerable fortune, by anyone's reckoning! But she did not laugh; she asked Alexander St. Clair what he advised her to do next.

He summoned his partner, Mr. Crewe, who carried in several documents which needed signing before the money could be banked for her. When they asked the name of her bankers, Alicia felt, for the first time, that it was all really happening.

"I have no idea who my bankers should be—I have none at the moment," she said candidly. "But I must ask your advice at first. Never having had a fortune, I am not at all sure of what to do with it. In time, of course, I shall understand it, but for now, you must help me—that is, if you are inclined to do so."

Since the two gentlemen wished nothing so much as the administration of the Drake-Tierney fortune, they were quick to express their inclination to help the young lady in any way she wished.

Mr. Crewe diffidently suggested that the news of her fortune be communicated only to those most directly concerned.

"I have known such news to attract undesirable attention," he said sagely. "And until you are settled somewhere, I see no reason for you to suffer the suits of the gazetted fortune hunters, as have other heiresses without families to protect them from such people."

Alicia quickly agreed, and it was settled that if questions arose, it should be hinted that she had inherited a competence from her great-aunt, recently deceased in Cumberland.

Jellicoe was full of questions on the way home, and when Alicia finally told her what she wished to know, that garrulous lady's maid was silent for once in her life.

"Well, I never!" was all she could say, her round brown eyes growing enormous. After fifteen minutes of unusual silence, Jellicoe's volubility returned. Miss must get a house—Curzon Street would be just the thing—and a landaulet, a good team of horses—Jim Taylor could help there—and of course, her own groom—

"Jelly," Alicia said wearily, "we will discuss all of that later. But now I must *think*. And on no account must you mention this in the servants' hall."

This last remark was so insulting that the maid did not talk again until they had arrived at Grosvenor Square.

As soon as she caught sight of Alicia's face, Lady Mary immediately began asking what the solicitor had said. Her curiosity had been thoroughly aroused. Alicia began to laugh like a child—it was all so funny, and her godmother would be so amazed.

"Provoking child! Do tell us what he said!"

"Well godmother, I believe that I am about to become a—a *social success!*"

Lady Mary immediately guessed that it was a matter of money, but when she was told the amount, she was dumbstruck. Harriet, however, was more calm.

"Alicia, just think—now you need never live with your brother again!"

"My first thought exactly, Harriet. And Jelly tells me we shall have a house in Curzon Street—and I can finally pay Madame Désirée everything I owe."

"No, I have already taken care of that," said Lady Mary, finally recovering. "You may buy me a nice little snuffbox instead."

The entire rest of the day was spent on the delicious business of spending the money in their imaginations.

"It is so much income that I am quite sure I shall never spend it all."

"That shall depend on your husband, miss. If you marry a gamester, for example, it will barely suffice," teased Lady Mary.

"But I have no intention of marrying—especially now," said Alicia, causing the others to exchange surprised looks. Alicia did not elaborate on this statement, but began to talk about cabinetmakers.

These conversations continued over the next few days, and Alicia, delighted to be finally independent of everyone, was in the most buoyant of spirits. Her own joy did not prevent her from perceiving that Harriet had become inattentive, and at times seemed almost despondent.

One afternoon Harriet asked if Alicia had seen Laurence. "No . . . why, is there something the matter?"

"He has not . . . you know, been at home very much. . . . I wonder . . ." here she stopped.

"What do you wonder?" prompted Alicia.

"It is just that these London girls are so very pretty, and I—do not think he likes me anymore, and I am sure I shall get over it . . . but now, it is so awful!" Alicia saw tears forming in her hazel eyes.

"Harriet, do not be such a ninny! You are more lovely than any of them—even you should know that! Young Johnson and Twynham are at daggers drawn over you, and I am sure that Laurence is just as much in love as ever."

"But sometimes people are just being nice to me, I know. My mother always said I was not as pretty as Julia, and I—"

"Fustian! Your mother must be blind, or something worse." Harriet looked at her friend, hope dawning in her eyes.

"Last night, after dinner, Laurence did not stay to play whist, but went off to White's. . . ."

Alicia debated whether to tell her why Laurence was not himself, but she decided it would be wrong to betray his confidence, even for a good reason.

"Harriet, I am sure there is a simple explanation, and I know the boy is mad about you. I do wish you could be brought to a realization of your own worth."

After this conversation, Alicia began to notice Laurence's comings and goings. He was coming home only to sleep—and sometimes not even that. When she managed to catch sight of him, he looked haggard and worried.

One morning, while riding, Worthing noticed Alicia's preoccupation, and he chided her.

She nodded ruefully and stopped her horse. Putting her hand on his arm, she looked up at him, a question in her eyes.

"Worthing, if by chance I should find myself needing help, may I count on you? It would be nothing dangerous, or illegal—at least I don't *think* so."

He kissed her hand. "My dear disaster, only too ready to be at your service. I sense something rather specific—no, do not tell me until it is necessary. My man Pickering will find me for you—day or night, prizefight or boudoir."

Alicia immediately felt better and began to devise a plan.

8
MERCIER GOES TO A BALL

Mercier had let the men follow him for several days, but now had come the time to get rid of these unsubtle bloodhounds. Turning down a malodorous alley, he quickly ducked into a small doorway. In three minutes, he had taken off his coat, lost his limp, and thrown away the white wig which had made him seem an older man.

Coley, the man following the suspicious old gentleman who had arrived from Ireland, looked in vain for his quarry. All he saw was a crowd of young men drinking gin. No white head among them. By the time he discovered the wig and the clothes, Mercier was on Half-Moon Street, answering an ad for a footman.

The housekeeper eyed him warily.

"*Est-ce que monsieur parle anglais?*"

"Of course. Both. I was in service one time to the Comte du Resnay, until his so unfortunate death. As footman to his lady."

The housekeeper lost some of her wariness. She knew of the comte.

"All right. You will be interviewed by Madame Rougemont herself. *Nous verrons, n'est-ce pas. . . .*"

Madame Rougemont was an elegantly slender lady with a queenly air to her. She was of an uncertain age and clearly wished it to remain so. A few of her remarks revealed to Mercier how to charm her: he talked of how unfeminine the English ladies were when compared to the French.

The lady dimpled.

"Monsieur was not born to be a servant—this is clear from his accent."

He lowered his eyes modestly.

"No. I have had a series of misfortunes, but then every *émigré* forced to leave by the usurper has had misfortune . . ."

"*Quant à ça*, I myself was forced to leave my rubies in the fat palms of a moneylender, just to get passage out! I was left with virtually nothing!"

Mercier had seen the exquisite furnishings of this house, and did not believe her for a moment. But if she wished to be seen as poor—

"Of course, for the honor of serving madame, I would not require as much remuneration as from one of the English. After all, the honor of serving such a family is itself worth something."

This woman, who spent more on one dress than she paid her footmen in a year, was entranced by the prospect of paying a new one—and such a handsome one—less. The man before her was not young—he must be near her own age—and the kind of admiration she saw in his eyes was far from undesirable, even in a servant.

She hired this Jean Latour immediately, and felt she had a bargain.

When she saw him in his livery a few days later, she knew she would have to take him to Lady Standen's ball with her.

***

Hélène Rougemont arrived at Lady Standen's a little later than most of the guests. Her new footman was remarked and approved by the ladies of her acquaintance, who gossiped behind their fans about the man in the perruke (so charming, if out of date) and scarlet and silver livery.

Lady Standen herself commented on the footman's maquillage.

"So unusual! A beauty mark as well!"

"Yes," said Hélène indolently. "I find I like to be reminded of the old days—before the Revolution."

Mercier was amused by all these conversations about his rouge, powder, and beauty mark—all conducted in his presence, as if he were a statue. This was just what he expected from such people—just what he had counted on, in fact. He looked around at the crowd, picking out familiar faces, faces from other trips. . . . The Draytons, the Terburys. And the girl talking with them—why was she familiar. He should have remembered the red hair, he thought, but it was the eyes that were familiar, not the hair. Where, where?

When madame dismissed him, Mercier managed to avoid going downstairs and placed himself instead near the refreshments. He was immediately rewarded by the conversation of two young men.

"Tommy's regiment goes in four days . . . no, not to Spain, to France . . . can't imagine . . . something's up, my father says."

He heard a score of such comments from the half-drunk young men who came and went at an increasing pace. Separately, these bits of information meant nothing, but put together, and with what he knew already, it was all quite useful. But the most important bit of information could come only from someone highly placed—a secret admirer of Napoleon who would give him what he had come for.

He was rehearsing what he had heard, putting it in a coherent form, when the redhead whirled past in the arms of Robert St. Clair. Fast company for her. Mercier was again sure that he had seen her—after a few moments of concentrated effort, he remembered. He had not seen the hair because it had not been visible. She had worn a coachman's hat and cape.

Looking at her now, in the elegant satin gown draped with net, he smiled. But a second later, his habitual caution made him reconsider. Of course it might have been a wager, a lark—but there were other reasons why a woman would be on that road, at that time. He felt a chill pass through him, like a knife. Suppose she was here for him. Suppose they were going to take him now, despite the powder and the wig . . .

But he looked around and saw nothing, no one approaching him. He talked to some of the other servants who were pouring the champagne and discovered the girl's name, and where she lived. Miss Tierney—Miss Alicia Tierney.

"You really must tell me, Alicia! What is your secret—why are you so gay tonight?"

Alicia, who had been teasing St. Clair unmercifully, hinting at all manner of mystery, relented.

"It is a very little thing, but one which changes everything for me. I have inherited, you see, from my great-aunt Ormond of Cumberland."

"Ah, and now you will marry a duke, I suppose."

"No, it is not enough for that—merely enough to purchase and furnish a house, and perhaps keep me in modest fashion."

"Sad, so sad," he said, revealing his very white teeth in a smile.

"Why sad?"

"I would rather see you kept in another fashion—such as you are wearing tonight."

Alicia knew she should not smile, but she could not help herself—he was always so impudent.

"You are most consistent, Mr. St. Clair," she murmured. "Consistently improper. I know I may always count upon you for *that*."

"You may always count upon me for anything."

"Pretty, very pretty."

"And did Lord Fane compliment you as prettily?"

Alicia lowered her eyes in a simulation of maidenly confusion. Then she smiled mischievously.

"No, rather the other way around. *I* complimented *him* on his new waistcoat, and he agreed that it was very nice. He told me he could not dance another country dance this evening."

"Why?"

"He said it was a sad romp and that he would become overheated." Her innocent air did not take in St. Clair. He laughed at this mocking of Fane.

"A complete coxcomb," he said contemptuously. "I do not understand why the Terburys court him—they never approved of the dandies."

"No, but he brought back Laurence to them, alive."

"Yes, as *anyone* might have done, and at no risk to himself, you may be sure. Simple luck."

"More puzzling to me," said Alicia thoughtfully, "is why the Draytons wish him as a son-in-law."

"Dearest Alicia," he said with a mirthless laugh, "you have not yet learned the great lesson of London: money is everything. That is why they wish him—they would take a monkey if the fortune were enough."

"I do not think I shall ever learn that lesson, Robert."

Saying his name was not very easy, she found, perhaps because this was the first time she had done so.

The dance ended and with regret Alicia returned to her place by Lady Mary. Her godmother disliked the friendship between St. Clair and Alicia, and the animation on Alicia's face during the dance had made her uneasy.

"I cannot like him," she told her husband.

Lord Terbury raised his quizzing glass and looked at the dark young man dancing by with Anne Milbanke.

"Yes, I quite see why. Handsome and thoroughly dangerous. Every young girl's dream, in fact."

9

AT THE SILVER TREE

The address in Pall Mall was a good one, and Farnsworth was impressed by the luxury to be seen in this gambling establishment.

The main room was lined with mirrors which reflected several magnificent chandeliers. The wallpapers were in the Chinese style, colored pink and blue; along the length of one side were blue velvet settees. Worthing led his friend to one of these and began to point out people of interest.

"That's young Jennings. He won over thirty thousand pounds at hazard last week—all in one night! Cardross, on the other hand, lost a fortune at whist."

"How could one get hard hit playing whist?"

"Play a hundred a trick, a thousand on the rub, lose steadily for five hours—that's how. . . . And there's another interesting fellow. The man from the Jockey Club who warned the prince off the Heath at Newmarket."

Farnsworth evinced great astonishment at this, and begged to know how anyone could do it to the Prince Regent.

"Well," said Worthing, taking a pinch of snuff, "his jockey,

Chifney, did some in-and-out riding one time too often. . . .
Here is Mrs. Porter—we shall have to circulate now."

Mrs. Porter, the proprietress of The Silver Tree, greeted
Worthing warmly and desired to know where he had been
keeping himself these many months. He complimented her on
the new decorations and said that he had been improving his
estates. Farnsworth was introduced, and warned not to play
hazard.

The two friends strolled through the other rooms, with their
lines of green baize tables, and stopped at the entrance to the
room devoted to roulette.

Here was one of the reasons for the Tree's continuing success.
Seated at the roulette table was a diminutive blonde, who looked
no older than sixteen. She was lovely indeed, and many of the
patrons felt that it added a certain piquancy to the game when
the wheel was tended by a girl who looked like a young angel.

"You may lose anything here but your nerve and temper,"
said Worthing.

Worthing and Farnsworth joined the others at the table and
began to play. Gradually the other gamblers drifted away, and
Worthing took the place nearest the croupier.

"Worthing, how nice to see you," she said in a perfectly indifferent voice. "What brings you back to the place you once loved
so well?"

"If that is a reproach, you are quite unkind. Did you think
I should like sharing your favors with young Ramsden and
who knows how many others? But that is now all in the past, a
lamentable episode . . .

She smiled engagingly. "'Tis a pity I can't blush—I never
learned how. . . . Of course I did not know why you no longer
came, Jack."

Worthing smiled and said there was someone who wished to

make her acquaintance—a young man up from the country, one of the Farnsworths of Devon.

Georgiana thought the young man quite charming. He looked to be a very pretty gentleman, with nice manners, and it would be no trouble at all to give him a little town bronze to oblige an old friend.

After a run of bad luck, Worthing moved away to the faro tables, but the young man stayed at the roulette table. Georgiana found it very touching that his eyes never left her face. The dear child was already infatuated; she could read the signs.

At one o'clock a supper of cold ham and lobster was served, accompanied by talk of Molyneux, Cribb, and the great fights seen by all those present. Georgiana saw that this talk bored the young man, who was drinking a great deal too much. After supper he stopped her and inquired whether the lady played piquet.

"Yes, I do. Rather well, too. And is that your game?"

Farnsworth said with a charming hesitancy that he felt he had some skill at the game. Georgiana was inclined to give him at least one game—he was so shy, so self-conscious, and this had an appeal for a woman used to self-assured rakes.

She led him to the corner alcove, where a sort of privacy was effected by drawing the velvet curtain across the opening.

He immediately pulled the curtain, saying he needed to shut out the noise of the play tables in the next room. Georgiana smiled at the ruse, but said nothing. She lit the candles and broke open a fresh pack of cards.

The first rubber was played in virtual silence. Georgiana won, and Farnsworth accepted it with good grace. She had half-expected some attempt to capture her hand or embrace her, but he was clearly too shy to undertake such actions.

An hour passed, and the young man's face grew flushed from

the wine they had been drinking steadily. She wondered when his play would start to suffer from it.

The second rubber was won by Farnsworth, who had been very lucky, she thought, and very judicious in his discards. Georgiana began to wonder if she herself had perhaps drunk a trifle too freely.

He saw her dissatisfaction.

"Are you surprised by my skill? It is just that I have played a great deal of piquet in my life—my uncle is mad for the game."

Georgiana was annoyed by this remark. This green boy thought he had won by skill? It was time to take him down a peg, luck or no luck. She smiled beguilingly at him, all the while thinking thoughts of manipulation.

"Shall we raise the stakes?" she asked.

"As you wish. Perhaps my lady would agree to a special wager?"

"Which would it be?"

"The best of five games. You would win what I have with me—five hundred pounds—and I would win something else— another sort of payment, well within your power to grant . . ."

Georgiana was stunned by the information that he had five hundred pounds with him. And she could keep it, without telling her mother. . . . As for the boy's request, she knew well what payment he desired, and she was amused. Not that there was any danger that she would lose.

She agreed to his proposition, but made it a condition that no one should ever know what the stakes were, even should it be her mother who entered unexpectedly. Once this was settled, she asked to be excused for five minutes—to refresh her toilette.

Farnsworth sat at the table, drumming idly on the green surface. His friend Worthing strolled by.

"This game goes well? I wish you luck, although luck often

has little enough to do with it. By the way, you should know that there are acquaintances of yours at the tables . . ."

Farnsworth inclined his head, but did not answer, and Worthing continued on his way. Georgiana reappeared, carrying several packs of fresh cards. As was the custom at White's, they threw the used pack on the floor after every rubber.

They played until the candles were half-gone, the advantage shifting from side to side, until it was two and two. During the last rubber Farnsworth seemed to suddenly gain the advantage. He had the odds figured to a fine point, and despite the quantity of wine drunk, he continued to be very sharp in his discards. It was at this point that Georgiana decided to place her trust in herself rather than in her luck.

She disliked cheating, but as her lover French Johnny had once said, when the odds are against you—you must change the odds.

She managed to spill some wine on her dress, and as she attempted to mop up the wine with her handkerchief, she began to slowly extract the card from her bodice.

Suddenly her hand was pressed to the table in a most painful manner.

"Sir! How dare you!"

"Most unfair of you, Miss Porter. Yes, the king you require. Let us agree that I have won, shall we?"

Georgiana was too surprised to make any calculations. The boy was not large, but he was quite a bit stronger than she was, and the expression in his eyes almost made her fear him.

"I think we shall go upstairs to your quarters—now."

He gathered up his cloak and hat.

She balked at this and refused to move until he pulled an elegant but deadly-looking pearl-handled pistol from his sleeve.

"It would be a dreadful shame to mar that beauty," he said softly.

She shuddered and rose to lead him upstairs. Once they were in her rooms, he locked the door. Deciding that there was only one way to deal with him—he must be mad—she tried to take his hand. He pushed her away.

"You mistake me, madam. I am come for the letters you have from Laurence Terbury. You will give them to me now, or I promise you, you will not wish to look in a mirror."

She knew a firm tone when she heard it, and she quickly pulled out the false drawer of the writing table.

"Here they are! And you are no gentleman. I might have surrendered them without this vulgar attempt—"

"No, you would not have. And of course, if they are not all here, you may expect another—less peaceful—visit."

It suddenly seemed to her that he was far older than she had thought. The hard look in his eyes frightened her. He did not see her as a woman, but as an enemy.

He made her sit down, and he began to bind and gag her with the bed linen.

"You should say that I refused to pay what I owed, that I jumped out the window that leads to the roof. This is by far the best course—mention of the letters will perhaps upset your mother, don't you agree?"

Since she knew that her mother would never forgive her behavior with Laurence, Georgiana was thankful that at least she would not know.

When the blindfold was placed over her eyes, Farnsworth went over to the window and opened it, but did not climb through it. Instead, he tiptoed to the door and quietly unlocked it. Pulling his hat low on his face, he turned left and headed for the servants' stairs. As he was about to take his first step someone reached out of the shadows to restrain him.

"I think you had better let me come with you," said the man in a whisper.

Farnsworth made no answer, but allowed the man to go down the stairs in front of him.

At the bottom of the stairs was the so-called porter, a man who had been in the foot guards.

"My lord! Good health to you!"

"Thank you, Browning. My young friend and I are rather tired—awfully stuffy in there."

"Aye, that's the way it be when the cards go against ye." They slowly made their way around the corner of the building. Farnsworth made as if to cross the street.

"No, you had much better come with me. Georgiana will have them looking for you very quickly—her mother was just on her way up when I left."

Farnsworth again said nothing, but allowed the other man to lead him to his coach. His protector made a number of trivial observations about gaming hells, but his young guest was not inclined to talk.

His first words were uttered when they were safely inside the house on Cavendish Square.

"Why have you insisted on helping me, sir? I did not ask it of you."

The boy was standing by the window, looking out onto the street, still in his hat and cloak.

"I assumed that if a person ties up Georgiana Porter, he has a good reason. And I did not wish to see you caught by the guard. It would have been most unpleasant for you, you know. As to how I found out—I was about to see Georgiana myself."

Comprehension dawned in Farnsworth's face.

"I have the letters—that was your errand as well?"

"Indeed it was. I do admire your way of dealing with problems, Farnsworth. For an amateur, you did rather well. I would have obtained them in due course, but I fear my methods would have been less—ah—colorful. Would you like me to return them to Laurence?"

Silently Farnsworth handed the packet over, never taking his eyes from the street below.

"You know, a gentleman does not leave his hat on," said his host, moving very close. "Do let me take a look at you." With that, Fane removed the offending hat and the wig that was under it.

"I don't believe I've ever held a gentleman in my arms before," murmured Fane as he kissed Alicia with great deliberation.

She did not struggle, but simply allowed him to kiss her. When he stopped, she slapped him as hard as she could. Without a moment's hesitation he bent her arm behind her back. He had rarely seen such anger in a woman.

"You must not forget, Alicia—you are not really a man—but *I am.*"

"Until now I was not sure," she said through her teeth. "Your airs have often cast it into doubt."

His answer to that was to kiss her again, deliberately forcing her lips open. Alicia was so angry she could not speak. But Fane remained calm—and amused.

"I seem to have been carried away, Miss Tierney. My temper is as bad as yours, I'm afraid. But you must see that women who dress as men leave themselves open to all manner of insult."

"From such as you, certainly."

"I am most heartily sorry, but I suppose your behavior tonight led me to believe—"

"That I was a doxy. A pretty compliment." Alicia tried to

mantain an offensive, but she felt embarrassed now. She was in his house, alone with him, and he had treated her like a Covent Garden woman. She would never forgive him—never—but she knew herself to be at fault. She had been so sure that she would get away with it.

She looked up at him frankly. "Let us forget this, Fane. I was stupid—an amateur, as you say. I did not think anyone I knew would be there—Worthing said—"

"I cannot credit it! Worthing knew?"

"Yes. I am supposed to be at Almeria Hunt's card party. I left early, Jack picked me up, and I changed clothes in his coach."

"You changed in Jack's coach?" he asked in amazement "Yes, but he wasn't in it. Don't be such a gudgeon, Fane!" She was irritated now, and wished that Worthing would come with her clothes—surely he must know by now that Farnsworth had left with Lord Fane—the porter would tell him . . .

Fane looked at her as if she were a rare sort of snake.

"My God, I pity the man who marries you," he said, almost to himself.

"Well, you can be quite sure it won't be *you*," she said sharply. "I would never marry a fop."

"Dandy, not fop. Fops are stupid," corrected Fane.

"Fop it was, fop it is."

Much to her annoyance he refused to take offense—she dearly wished a reason to slap that face again. But of course he would not hesitate to wrench her arm again, either.

But he surprised her by changing his tactics. As if nothing untoward had occurred, he began to treat her like a desired guest, offering her cheese and brandy, showing her the collection of snuffboxes in the corner. Almost against her will, she found herself responding to his politeness. He left her alone for a few minutes, and she began to examine the snuffboxes. An oval gold one, adorned with beautiful renditions of Bellevue, done by van Blarenberghe, particularly delighted her. When Fane returned, he told her a little about the box and its owner.

"I see that you admire the *vielle cour*," said Alicia.

"No, just their partronage of the arts. The Bourbons are a rather stupid lot, I think."

"And Napoleon?"

He laughed. "No, no, I am a patriot, I assure you. Buonaparte has a dreadfully bad style, and that I cannot admire!"

Exactly the sort of reason a dandy would give, Alicia thought, but it struck her as being false.

He looked at her and sighed.

"Really, I dislike sermons, Miss Tierney, but you simply cannot go on like this. Think of your reputation."

"That does not interest me, Lord Fane, and I'll thank you to have done with these earnest lectures. I am grateful for your concern, and I wish only Miss Drayton to arrive to make my joy complete!"

He smiled and said that Miss Drayton had never visited his house, but that Worthing was just now arriving in the front hall.

Fane poured his friend a glass.

"Jack, I drink the health of a remarkable girl—A. Tierney! Most girls I know cannot even dress themselves, and she can do it in a coach!"

Alicia did not find this amusing. She regarded him coolly, and with an air that would have done credit to the Princess de Lieven herself, she proceeded to thank him for his help.

At the door, Worthing went ahead to the coach, leaving them alone for a few seconds.

Fane apologized again for the kiss.

"Oh, *that*," said Alicia, "that was nothing. You merely thought that I deserved to be treated like a cyprian. I expect you cannot help your manners. I have noticed that persons who are toad eaten too much are like that."

Most provokingly, Fane did not react to this piece of calculated offense. He smiled enigmatically and wished her a good night.

Later, over another brandy, he meditated on the character of one Alicia Tierney and decided that he might win the wager after all. She disliked him far too much.

10
A VISIT FROM JAMES LAYNON

Fearing that Lord Fane would say something to Lady Mary, Alicia had several bad days. But as time went by, and no one showed the slightest interest in the reason for her early return from Almeria Hunt's card party, Alicia relaxed. To see Laurence and Harriet happy again was worth any worry, and with time she became convinced that Fane, whatever his faults, was not a man to carry tales.

Worthing was most apologetic about everything, amazed that Fane had seen through what had seemed to him an impenetrable disguise, and aghast that he had forgotten about the guard at the other entrance to The Silver Tree. Alicia laughingly told him that all was well that ended well, but she mentally resolved never to rely on anyone but herself for details.

As for Fane, she did not expect to see much of him in the future, which was certainly no hardship. She would do very well without his affected drawl and sleepy irony.

It was with some surprise, therefore, that one day she found his card in the bowl upon returning from a visit to her new house.

"Lord Fane will call upon Miss Tierney tomorrow afternoon," it read. So like him—to assume she would be there. So he was not going to avoid her—he was coming to scold instead.

The second card in the bowl was even more unlooked for: James Lanyon, her old suitor, had called.

"Cranmer, will Mr. Lanyon be calling tomorrow?"

"Yes, miss. He said in the afternoon. He can be reached at Grillon's if it is inconvenient."

Cranmer looked at her speculatively. He knew that both gentlemen were due at the same time, and from what he had seen, they would most definitely not suit.

Alicia decided that she did not wish to be alone with either of the gentlemen. She would leave things as they were.

She found Lady Mary in a taking over the impending visit of Edith Stomaway.

"I have gotten a letter—she is coming in two days! Henry says he will spend the week at his club, he can't abide her. Nor can I. She's announcing—not asking—that she's bringing her eldest, Julia."

"And what is Julia like?"

"I have no idea. But she is the favorite, so I have no very high expectations. Edith wishes to attend Almack's, which is a rather difficult feat to manage. I am afraid I shall have to presume on the good nature of Emily Cowper once again."

Laurence was nervous about the Stomaways' visit for other reasons. He and Harriet had come to an understanding, and now he was afraid that her mother might not approve.

"Only a mother not in her right mind would disapprove of you, Laurence," said Alicia firmly.

He was not convinced, however, and he conceived the idea of taking everyone to Vauxhall Gardens—he would stand the cost of a dinner, and in general be the host. This plan delighted everyone, including his parents, who resolved to be otherwise engaged that night so they would not have to be with Edith.

The next day Alicia became depressed at the prospect of seeing James. He was a perfectly decent man, but his very name brought back the bad times after her father's death, the arrival of William and Amelia to Tierney Chase, and her former, self, the deliberately dowdy, sullen Alicia, a girl who was afraid of the future because of the past. But in London, under the care of Lady Mary, she had flowered. And the unknown Dickie Drake, God bless his soul, had set her free from fears about the future. Now she was free, independent, happy. But she was not yet strong enough to resist the feelings James Lanyon called up.

When James actually arrived she was calm. He had not changed. Still good looking, still wooden, still humorless;

Harriet, who had expected him to be a country bumpkin was surprised by his air of fashion—conservative, to be sure, but quite *comme il faut*. Alicia, unhappy that Fane had not yet called, insisted that Harriet stay in the drawing room and work on her screen.

James began by begging Alicia to accept his mother's warmest regards. Alicia involuntarily began to smile. Mrs. Lanyon held that no woman on earth was good enough for her son, and certainly not Alicia Tierney! But she responded in kind and asked how Mrs. Lanyon was.

"She had a touch of catarrh this year," he said earnestly, "but Dr. Thennell has assured me that she is in no immediate danger. But she is so brave, you know. She smiles and says it is nothing, when she is suffering from a dreadful cold. . . . She maintains that tea and a mustard plaster can cure anything. Remarkable woman."

He gazed at Alicia and Harriet smugly, no doubt thinking that his mother was more remarkable than either of theirs.

"Are you in London for the auction at Tattersalls'?" asked Alicia.

This question seemed to discompose him, and he paused before answering.

"There are many matters which require my attention here. The auction is one, to be sure. But there are others—of even greater importance."

The glance he gave Harriet at this point indicated clearly that he wished her gone. She was unable to overcome her natural impulse to do whatever people wished her to do, and she excused herself, saying she needed a different kind of thread for her screen.

As soon as Harriet was gone, James began to renew his suit, pointing out that Alicia could not live here with Lady Mary forever.

"I do not intend to," said Alicia. "I am going to have a house in Curzon Street—I have already signed the papers, in fact."

James was astounded.

"Do not look so amazed, James. I have inherited something from my great-aunt Ormond. Do be happy for me."

He stiffly said that he was happy, but it was clear that he was not. The one thing he had to offer was financial security, and now even that had been taken care of.

"I suppose you will spend the money in a month," he said hopefully.

"No, Lord Terbury is giving me advice. I am sure that you must approve of the fact that I shall no longer depend on my brother for anything."

"Yes, yes, of course. William and Amelia continue their ways—sending to London for everything. William has taken to using a quizzing glass . . .

It was at this juncture that Cranmer announced Lord Fane.

He was wearing a maroon jacket, cream pantaloons, shining Hessians, and an outrageous striped waistcoat. His neckcloth had been coaxed into what was known as the "Waterfall."

James Lanyon looked at this apparition with disgust. He disliked dandies intensely—even noble ones.

Fane raised his quizzing glass and inquired in a supremely bored drawl if Miss Tierney had spent a pleasant weekend.

Alicia primly kept her eyes on the embroidery she had snatched up and said that they had spent the time restfully, answering letters and reading from Mr. Scott's new novel.

"Ah, Scott. I do not read him, I am afraid . . ."

"And why is that, sir," asked James, trying to be polite.

"Too long. I am sure it is quite bad for the eyes, straining to read anything that long . . .

James looked at him as if he were some incomprehensible insect.

It seemed to Alicia that Lord Fane was being deliberately provocative, and she shot him a reproachful look, receiving in return an amused one, which immediately caused her to remember that he had kissed her. She was grateful that James Lanyon was not looking at her.

Lanyon assumed that this affected fop was a suitor, and he resolved to find out what he could about him. He began to talk of hunting, hoping to draw the man out. But Lord Fane did not utter a word about hunting, and finally James asked him where he did his hunting.

Fane took some snuff with an elegant, if effeminate, gesture.

"I do not hunt. I do not enjoy it," he said indifferently.

"And may I inquire as to your reasons?"

"You may, and have. It is just . . ." Here he paused and flicked an invisible fleck from his sleeve. "Just that one becomes so heated, and one's clothes! I am sure it cannot be good for one's organism."

James ignored him after that and directed his remarks to Alicia. He told her how her acquaintances were and asked her about the people she had met in London.

"My mother is quite worried about you. She was afraid that you might fall in with the Carlton House set."

Alicia did not know whether to laugh or cry.

Lord Fane regarded James with an air of intense interest.

"And what is it that your mother has against them?" he asked James.

"Why, they are merely the most dissolute—the Prince of Wales himself is—"

"Pray, do be careful with your words, sir," said the ominously soft voice. "I should dislike having to call out an acquaintance of Miss Tierney's, but if you persist in this slander, I shall."

Lanyon looked at him in bewilderment.

"My dear fellow! Duels are outlawed, and I certainly should do no such thing!"

Fane looked at him satirically.

"I forgot. I thought I was dealing with a gentleman. . . . Don't look so upset, Miss Tierney. I shall go along and have a look at Miss Stornaway's screen."

He sauntered out, leaving James shaking with rage.

"My word," said James when they were alone, "I do believe that man-milliner must know the Regent."

"He is a member of the Carlton House set. And you should never animadvert on the Regent's character, you know, unless you are sure the opinion is shared."

James disliked this, coming as it did from Alicia.

"I regret to say that London has changed you. You were used

to think that the truth was the truth. The Regent is a débauché, and rank cannot blind one to that truth."

"But you do not even *know* the Regent, James, and he does. Surely you must see that it is like criticizing a friend—"

"No, it is quite different. But Alicia, this is not what I came to speak of."

There followed twenty very bad minutes as James pressed her to be his bride. After she insisted that she wished to marry no one at all, he took his leave, in no very good humor. He was convinced that she was interested in Fane—because of his rank.

Alicia stayed in the empty drawing-room for a while, enjoying the silence and trying to decide with whom she was most angry—Lord Fane or James Lanyon. There was a knock and Fane entered.

"I thought you had gone," she said.

"Do you wish I had? I am really very sorry for your Mr. Lanyon. He is far too boring for you to marry. And do not worry, I have no intention of pursuing the quarrel. The opinions of such a man are not worth thinking about."

"He is a human being, you know, and quite a decent man."

"In *that* coat? Never."

"Is that what makes a man? A coat and an autocratic manner to go with it?" Alicia felt her anger rising.

Fane met her hostile glance with one of mild surprise.

"My dear Miss Tierney! Surely you knew I was joking . . . ah, I see. You did not. What can I have done, I wonder, to deserve this very low opinion of my character. . . . I think I shall call you Alicia anyway. Our *acquaintance* has deepened since last week, I feel."

He meant to make her blush, but she did not. Instead she regarded him with cool contempt.

"Why did you affect that drawl when he was here?"

"All dandies must have affectations. The nature of the beast."

"But it seemed to me that you did it purposely. You *knew* what he thought of dandies!"

"I am so bored with this subject," he said with a plaintive sigh, "and you have not even told me what you think of this waistcoat. . . ."

Alicia would have dealt very summarily with the offensive garment if Harriet had not returned, bringing Laurence with her.

"Nick," said Laurence happily. "Just the fellow. We're going to Vauxhall next week—Harriet's mother and sister are coming. Why don't you come along?"

Much to Alicia's relief, Lord Fane said that he did not think he could.

11
SIBYLLA AND ROBERT

Sibylla Crawford was unhappy. She looked at the furnishings of her gold salon, and even the realization that they cost a small fortune could not comfort her. When Fane had first set her up in the house on Montague Square, she had been delighted. Presents, an allowance, and the affection of a truly elegant man had at first been enough. But now it all seemed as nothing: her best friend Sarah had married her lover, Edward Orrington-Smith, and was now Lady Smith. No amount of money could compete with *that*.

Sibylla had been a respectable widow when Fane had met her, and she did not see that it would be out of the question to marry him. True, he was a wealthy peer, but he admired her beauty, enjoyed her company, and knew that her manners were perfectly suited to the beau monde.

"Do you not think that Fane might marry me?" she asked Robert St. Clair one day in Regent's Park.

"He might. It has been done . . . but I have heard in the clubs that Miranda Drayton is set on him—or her mother is, I'm not sure which."

"Miranda Drayton!" sniffed Sibylla.

It was most unfortunate that she had not known about Miranda before this. That explained Fane's inexplicable absences. She would have to do something to regain his interest—perhaps stimulate his jealousy? Of course the handsome man beside her might help. St. Clair and she, it must be admitted, were actually far better suited to each other. But Robert had very little money, and money was a thing she could not do without.

Alicia found the opera of little interest and welcomed the intermission, during which she could look at the crowd. Among the couples moving out to where the refreshments were, she saw the woman who had been at Madame Désirée's.

"Laurence, do you know that woman there, in the gold dress?"

"Mrs. Crawford? Of course, she's Fane's—" Here he stopped, realizing that Alicia did not know.

"Oh, don't be so stuffy, Laurence. I knew about such things at twelve. So she is Fane's inamorata . . . how surprising. . . . One wouldn't believe he had the energy for such a woman. . . ."

Remembering Spain, Laurence remarked that Fane could conquer hearts when he wished to.

"I shouldn't think her heart the chief thing," said Alicia. "And that gold lamé gown, just the shade of her hair! Must have cost a fortune. Keeping her must cost him even more than his clothes—the true definition of love for a dandy."

Alicia watched with fascination as Lord Fane came face to face with Mrs. Crawford. This would not have been so interesting if Miranda and her parents had not been with him. Sibylla's face was worth the price of the ticket, Alicia thought. She looked at Miranda with an expression that said she did not think *her* so very much! Luckily, Miranda was talking to someone else and missed this entirely. Fane, admirably cool, gave a stiff little nod in Sibylla's direction—a nod which put her in place just as surely as one of his set-downs.

Alicia asked Laurence if he thought Sibylla would try to make a scene.

"No, never. Fane owns her house, after all."

"Owns her house? You mean she is totally dependent on him?"

"The usual arrangement," said Laurence, who felt uncomfortable discussing this with Alicia.

"How very nice for him. Anytime he wishes, he can send her packing. I feel sorry for her, being in his power like that."

"Well, I can tell you no one else does! The way of the world, you know."

After the opera, the Terbury party went to supper with the Duke of Kendalford, who had arranged to have an entire room of the Green Restaurant set aside for them. Once again Alicia was aware of what a perfect gentleman he was—so unlike Fane, for example. He was considerate, never overbearing, and he managed to make each member of the party feel at ease.

When he spoke to Alicia, Kendalford's voice took on an especial warmth which she found singularly pleasant. . . .

On the way home, Lady Mary wondered aloud what kind of husband Kendalford would make. Her husband commented that he was not aware that Kendalford was considering matrimony.

"He wasn't. But now he has met Alicia."

Lord Terbury looked at Alicia.

"He has said nothing to me," said Alicia, who now realized with dismay that it was very possible he might.

Lady Mary was intrigued by this response, and later asked her husband if he didn't think there was something wrong with Alicia's attitude towards marriage.

"I don't think she has any attitude."

"But that is precisely the point," said his wife, as if explaining to a child. "She hasn't. And that is quite unusual in such a young woman. It's as if she *never thinks about it!*"

Her husband was not interested. He told her that she should be worrying about Edith Stornaway, not Alicia.

Hoping to avoid the arrival of the Stomaways and the resulting chaos, Alicia left early the next morning, resolved to spend the day touring her new house, empty though it was.

Alexander St. Clair had sent a Mr. Scott to interview prospective servants, and he was the only inhabitant when she arrived.

"A very nice house, if I may say so, Miss Tierney."

"You may. To me, of course, it seems quite the most beautiful house in the world—because it is the first one I have ever owned."

Mr. Scott went back to the candidates in the kitchen, and Alicia wandered through the rooms, picturing them as they would be when they were decorated and furnished. She wrote down the things that needed fixing on one piece of paper, and ideas for colors on another. In this way several hours went by without her noticing it. Mr. Scott introduced her to Stilton, soon to be her butler. She liked him immediately. He was about thirty-five, dignified, and impressively tall. He had been a soldier, but his health, despite his robust looks, did not permit him to stay on in the Peninsula any longer. Alicia approved this hiring and left Mr. Scott to decide the rest.

As she opened the front door to leave, she found herself staring into the eyes of Robert St. Clair.

"How in the world did you find me?"

"Servants do talk. Are you going to invite me in?"

She smiled up at him, conscious of how glad she was to see him.

"No, it is empty, and I am on my way back to Grosvenor Square. Perhaps you might accompany Jellicoe and me?"

"Gladly, but may I not see the house, even empty?"

"No," she laughed. "A man is interviewing maids in the kitchen, and if they saw you they would think you were to be the master. And they would get quite the *wrong* ideal."

"It's dreadful, being misunderstood," he said gloomily. "All I ask for is a wife, children, some port, and Cheshire cheese—"

"Lord Rochester had all those things, and it was far from enough."

"Comparing me to a rake! A rake who wrote indecent poetry, at that."

"Of course I have never read his poetry," said Alicia with an innocent look.

"I can see you have read it. Shame on your father—he must have had it in his library. . . . Come, let us go. Your Jellicoe is impatient."

Alicia began to suffer from the sensation St. Clair almost invariably produced in her. He made her feel unsafe, that there was no protecting barrier of politeness or lack of understanding between them. She cast about for safe topics of conversation and settled on the proposed visit to Vauxhall with Harriet's mother and sister.

This caught his interest.

"Masque night And what color is your domino?"

"Black, with a green border. Will you be there? What color is yours?"

"That I will not tell you. Let it be a surprise."

When they reached the house, Jellicoe made a great show of going in, but Alicia remained on the steps a moment, enjoying the unusual sunshine and the presence of St. Clair beside her. He was looking at her and standing so close that she could easily have been in his arms.

"I have missed you," he said quietly.

After the artificiality she had grown used to, Alicia could not help but respond to this affecting simplicity.

"And I you," she said, not looking in his eyes.

He took her hand and kissed it, as he always did, his eyes never leaving her face.

How silly she had been to think she would avoid him. He was the only man she felt alive with.

"We shall have to see to it that it does not happen again," he said, and left.

Much exhilarated after this entirely improper encounter, Alicia was smiling as Cranmer opened the door to her. She asked him if the Stomaways had arrived.

"Yes, miss. They are in the drawing-room. But if I may be so bold, I would suggest going up to Miss Harriet first."

One look at the butler's face convinced her that Lady Mary's worst fears had been realized.

Outside Harriet's room she met Becky, Harriet's maid.

"Becky, why are you here? Is Miss Harriet ill?"

"No, miss. She's just terrible unhappy. Her ma says she can't go to Vauxhall, and the sister is just as bad!"

Inside, Harriet was sitting on her bed, her eyes red from weeping. She looked up at Alicia's entrance, an expression of fear in her eyes.

"Oh, I am so glad it is you! I was afraid Mamma had returned to lecture me. . . . Alicia, you cannot know how awful it has been! My mother does not approve of the match with Laurence! She had planned on something else, and I never knew!"

"But does not Lady Mary know how to handle her?"

"Yes, but Mamma is very careful not to say it to Lady Mary—she simply says that I am too young, and have seen too little of the world. She says in six months, if the attachment is still in force."

"And what is wrong with that?"

"Alicia, she will use the slightest pretext to end the possibility of an engagement! She wants me to be a marchioness—there is some old duke she has in mind—Camerly or some such name."

Alicia looked at her, deeply disturbed.

"My God, she means Richard Camerley—a man of fifty years! That is absurd!"

"It is not, Alicia. She will do what she wishes with me, she always has! And she wants me to visit the Camerleys the very day we are to go to Vauxhall. . . ."

Alicia made a decision.

"*Tranquille* yourself, as my governess used to say. I shall do something, all will be well, and you most certainly *will* go to Vauxhall. Let me meet them, then I will have a better idea of how to manage it."

Harriet looked gratefully at her friend, amazed that anyone could contemplate a battle with her parent. But as she looked at Alicia's determined face, she began to feel hope. This girl was strong, she would not give anyone a moment's peace until she had her way.

It was at dinner that Alicia got her first look at the enemy.

Mrs. Stornaway was a gaunt woman of fifty-five who dressed in the style of one who was some twenty years younger. She used the rouge pot a little too freely, Alicia thought, but she had undoubtedly been a beauty in her youth. Nothing to rival Harriet, however. Mrs. Stornaway affected a simpering style of discourse which often turned on her weak constitution and many illnesses, when it did not involve her numerous friends in the *ton* and how they had invited her to too many events.

Alicia was introduced, and then virtually ignored until Lady Mary said something which caused their guests to regard the unknown Miss Tierney in a new light.

"Alicia, I quite forgot to tell you. Kendalford visited today, and invited you to go riding tomorrow in the park. If you cannot we will send a note round."

"Of course I can, ma'am. He is an excellent rider, and it is a pleasure to ride with him any time."

Edith and Julia Stornaway stared at Alicia in astonishment.

"Have you known the duke long?" asked Edith.

"My dears, what a question! You will embarrass the girl. Kendalford," Lady Mary said confidentially, "has distinguished Alicia with such marks of attention as must leave no one in doubt as to his intentions. Alicia is the only woman he has invited to go riding with him, for example, in all the years I have known him."

This remark produced a remarkable change in the attitudes of Edith and Julia.

Julia herself was a good deal more intelligent than her mother, who was, Alicia had decided, dangerously silly. Julia, however, had a good deal of what could only be labeled slyness. The girl was quite pretty, had an excellent figure, and her manners were quite acceptable. But there was a predatory quality to her face which occasionally made her seem less attractive.

After dinner the ladies retired to the drawing room to play loo. Alicia did not choose to play, but sat reading a book instead. Julia came and sat down near her and began to ingratiate herself. She complimented Alicia's gown, flattered her outrageously, and asked a store of questions which finally exhausted Alicia's patience.

"I am afraid that I owe everything to my maid, Jellicoe. The secrets are hers, not mine. I find that I do not have the intense interest in beauty preparations that she has."

Julia immediately understood that this woman was not for conquering by flattery. At that very moment she became Alicia's sworn enemy.

Edith Stornaway continued to ask about Kendalford, even during the game of loo, causing her partners much irritation. As she listened, Alicia began to see how the visit to Vauxhall might be effected.

"Do you know, dearest godmamma, I am going to ask Kendalford if he can go with us on Friday . . ."

Lady Mary's cool gray eyes met the dark blue ones and showed complete comprehension.

"How very nice, dear. I wonder that I did not think of it. Lady Standen will be quite green—*she* has never succeeded in getting him there, though she has tried. Of course he will do it—for *you*. It makes me quite sad that I am not going. . . . And it is really too bad that Edith and Julia can't go—they would enjoy it so much. I suppose I shall have to ask Mrs. Selby to chaperone. . . ."

Edith Stornaway's brain was in a whirl. Of course they were supposed to sup with the Camerleys—but the Camerleys would be willing to put it off. And they would never have another opportunity to be in a private party with the Duke of Kendalford, one of the richest, most highly connected peers of the realm. It was too much. They would have to make new plans. She excused herself early, complaining that the food had been too rich for her digestion.

"If Edith hadn't had two servings of the sturgeon, she might feel more the thing," Lady Mary said dryly to Alicia. Alicia almost smiled, but realizing that Julia was still nearby, restrained herself.

When the gentlemen rejoined them, it was clear that Lord Terbury, who had stayed home despite his threat to eat at the club every night *that woman* was in his house, wished to continue the political discussion they had begun. The conversation grew quite lively. Lady Mary predicted a quick peace with France, and her husband seemed to agree.

"Wellington himself has said that he fears a peace that is too sudden, too ill-considered," said Alicia, who saw that her friends did not wish to consider the idea of another year or two of war.

Lord Terbury waved his hand and said any peace was desirable.

Julia seemed to find this conversation of little interest, and she and Lady Terbury were soon discussing common acquaintances. Alicia was listening with half an ear to both conversations and was startled to hear Julia pronounce the name of Robert St. Clair.

"Mother says many men are sadly unsteady in their twenties, but that they settle down. . . ."

The girl's remarks revealed that the Stomaways had met St. Clair at a country house and had been favorably impressed by him. Alicia almost chuckled. This girl, as Lady Mary had said, was looking for a husband, and Robert St. Clair was the most unmarrying man in London. The poor child, to be languishing after St. Clair. Although, it might be that she was not. Julia struck one as too cunning to waste her talents on only one possibility.

Edith made an unexpected reappearance near the end of the evening, saying that she felt much better. She took Lady Mary aside and said that she could not make her dear Harriet unhappy by preventing her from going to Vauxhall.

"And, dear Mary, if I can be of service to you, as a chaperone, I will go. And Julia would enjoy it as well, I am sure."

During this speech, Edith kept her eyes on Alicia. She saw a young woman who was too tall, too pale, and too old to compete with her Julia. And of course her girls were *heiresses*, too. There was no accounting for tastes, of course, but she would try and see if Kendalford could be interested in someone new. . . .

Lady Mary had seen everything on her cousin's face, and she was delighted. She wished she herself could go to Vauxhall and see Julia making up to Kendalford—and the duke ignoring her—in a nice way, of course. Thank heaven these women were leaving in a week.

Harriet, still looking a little despondent, was playing cards with Laurence in the corner. Lady Mary went over and whispered a few words in the girl's ear, and there was an immediate change in Harriet's expression.

When Lady Mary returned to her loo table, Mrs. Stornaway was favoring Alicia with her opinion of Nicholas Fane.

"His behavior to Anne Dunstan! And I have heard that he was at one time . . . not indifferent to her himself, if you read my meaning. I am glad to hear he has some reputation with the military, but it will be some time before I care to see him in my circle," said Edith.

"I have no such reservation," said Lady Mary coldly. "When he rescued my son, he lived down anything he may have done, as far as we are concerned."

Mrs. Stornaway could answer nothing to that, and she was quite unhappy that no one had thought fit to warn her that the disagreeable Lord Fane was quite high in the Terburys' estimation. Julia saved her mother, as she had done countless times, by tactfully asking Laurence all about Spain.

It was with a general feeling of relief that Alicia and Harriet retired to their rooms.

"I had forgotten what they are like," said Harriet thoughtfully. "Is it a sin to—not wish to be with one's family?"

Alicia laughed. "If you did not find such scenes tedious and upsetting I should think you a complete ninny. One cannot help one's family, or one's feelings about them."

"You do not like my sister, do you? I own I am not surprised. She is very different from you . . . but she is just a little spoiled, she will grow out of it."

Alica would not have cared to stake a fortune on that, but she passed over it. She was satisfied with the first skirmish in the war of Harriet and Laurence. To be sure, Vauxhall would not be so much fun with the Stornaways along, but at least Harriet could go now.

12

VAUXHALL

Vauxhall Gardens was one of the chief pleasure spots of London, and had been since its opening in 1732.

The eleven acres that had once belonged to the widow of a certain Baron Vaux were thickly planted with trees and criss-crossed by walks. In the clearings one came upon raised colonnades, theaters, temples, alcoves, orchestras, dancing pavilions, and fireworks exhibitions. With its trees festooned with thousands of lamps, Vauxhall had the appearance of a fairyland.

The Terbury party was very gay that evening. The older members of the party were delighted that they had arrived by water in a gondola-shaped barge, courtesy of the duke. It was quite the most beautiful water conveyance anyone had seen since the Prince of Wales had visited the previous summer. The younger members of the party liked the gondola very well, but their minds were on the intimate corners and benches of Vauxhall, so dear to the hearts of the young.

"And where is the masque to take place?" asked Mrs. Stornaway, who was tired of walking.

"In the pavilion on the other side of this grove," said

Laurence. "We shall be there presently. But the masquerade starts at ten."

"Well, I hope the girls will be circumspect," said Mrs. Stornaway, who had never been to Vauxhall before, but who had heard about the dark things that were supposed to take place during these masques.

They were shown to a supper box in the pavilion. At the duke's suggestion, Alicia examined the paintings which lined the pavilion. They were, in order, a northern chief with a princess and her swan in a sledge, all being drawn on ice by a horse; the play of hot cockles; a gypsy telling fortunes using coffee cups; cutting flour, a Christmas game; and playing cricket. Alicia laughed with delight and called Laurence and Harriet to come and see.

The party, consisting of Laurence, the duke, Harriet, Mrs. Stornaway, Julia, Alicia, and Frederick Phillips, a friend of Laurence's, sat down to the dinner he had ordered.

Laurence had outdone himself, and even Mrs. Stornaway was impressed by the array of dishes. There was lamb, chicken, tongue and ham (the last two ornamented); there were lobsters, raised pies and Savoy cakes; and to finish, ice cream, strawberries and cherries. All of this was accompanied by rare vintages, and Alicia found herself wondering where the money had come from. Laurence had not yet come into his principal—that would be next year; for the moment, he was existing on an allowance. Perhaps Mary had helped? She had her answer later, when they were listening to the singers. Laurence, frankly bored, took the seat beside Alicia, who was sitting farthest from the edge of the box.

"Tolerable supper, Alicia?"

"Wonderful. I wonder you can afford it."

He hesitated for a moment, then said:

"I can't. Kendalford sprang for it. Told him all about Harriet's mother, and he said he'd be glad to help, and that's how he chose to do it. Wonderful fellow, you know."

"I know." Alicia felt a rush of friendship for the duke. He was intelligent and charming, but in the *ton* it was more unusual to have a good heart, which he did. She tried to express her gratitude to him later, when they were dancing during the masquerade.

"No, you must not thank me. You make me feel like an old fairy godfather, which I dislike. Look around you, Miss Tierney—is this the place for serious conversation?"

Alicia looked at the pavilion, decorated in silver and scarlet streamers, filled with beautifully dressed people, some masked, some not.

"No, you are right. I am being too earnest."

"There is a place for that, too. But not here. This brings back my youth, Miss Tierney, and I don't want to be distracted from it All that's left to an old man, you know."

Alicia was about to tell him not to talk fustian, but she bit it back. One didn't talk to a duke that way—not to such a nice one, anyway.

Looking at her. Kendalford wished he were younger. This was exactly the sort of woman he had wanted when he was thirty-five, but had not found. Intelligent, mature, but not predictable. He knew she enjoyed his company, but he was sure she did not think of him as anything more than that: a companion.

Alicia was not unaware of the wistful looks he cast her way during the evening, and she thought about it. He would be nice, understanding, comfortable. But there would be no passion. But did she want passion? The one night of passion in her life had not been something she wanted to repeat. . . .

The party, which had been gay enough already, became

positively giddy when the orchestra struck up a waltz. Since the dance was not quite acceptable yet, although it had been danced at a number of *ton* parties, everyone wondered if it would be all right. It was Julia, dancing with Frederick Phillips, who decided the matter. She told her mother that it was quite all right, wasn't it, and without waiting for her answer, went out onto the floor. The rest of the young people, as well as the duke and Alicia, followed her lead, and were soon lost in the crowd—beyond the call of Mrs. Stornaway. After this, since the duke himself had taken part, she could say nothing.

During the dance, Alicia torn her gown and went to repair it, with Harriet to help. While they were gone, Mrs. Stornaway arranged matters so that the duke was virtually forced into dancing with Julia, who found ways to keep him by her side even when Alicia returned.

"Ah, successful in my absence," said Alicia to Harriet. "Well, if I do not mistake the matter, I am about to have another partner soon." A man in a red domino and black mask was staring at her, and he quickly came up and offered himself as a partner. Wishing to join in the next waltz, Alicia accepted with alacrity, and they were soon whirling gracefully. After the dance they found themselves on the other side of the pavilion, and her partner suggested a walk around the building, rather than dancing across it. Alicia, quite overheated, agreed, but with some misgivings. Her misgivings were justified less than five minutes later when her gallant clumsily tried to embrace her. She had assumed she was safe because there were so many other people in the gardens, but this man paid no attention to her protestations that she would scream. A moment later, Alicia screamed loudly, and a man in a green domino appeared from nowhere, knocked down her partner, and quickly took her down a path with him. A few seconds later, she was sitting on a bench with the green domino, while he fanned her and pressed her to sip some water.

"I am grateful to you, sir! I should very likely have had a sad ending to my story if you had not come just then."

He seemed to smile. "Have no fear, madam. Someone would have been sure to come after hearing such a scream." He spoke almost in a whisper, a ruse often adopted at masques when people did not wish their identities to be discovered.

He offered her some wine from the flask he carried on his person, and she felt much better after a few sips. He suggested that they rejoin the dancers, so that her party would not easily discover that she had left the pavilion. They swept into the dance not ten minutes after she had disappeared from the view of Mrs. Stornaway. The duke caught sight of her domino at the other side of the dance floor, and was relieved. Miss Tierney was perfectly safe.

Alicia, however, did not feel she was perfectly safe. The wine had been stronger than she had thought; that was the only explanation for what happened when she danced with the green domino. She felt an overwhelming impulse to lean against him, to rest her head on his chest. He seemed to notice the flushed face and the feverish eyes.

"I think you need some air. The wine and the dancing have been too much. Here, we shall dance out onto the walk for a bit"

"Yes," she said sleepily. "I want to dance until I swoon."

He led her back to the same bench and sat her down gently. He unloosened her mask and gently removed it, as well as the domino.

"You have drunk too much; that is all," he said soothingly. "It will be all right in a bit. You probably had a deal of wine at supper as well. . . ."

"Yes, I did . . . but I can manage," she said haughtily.

He found this amusing, and at first she was angry, but then, realizing that she must indeed be drunk, for perhaps the second time in her life, she began to laugh herself.

Her laughter was stopped only when the green domino took her in his arms and kissed her. She returned his kisses sleepily, not even thinking about it. He stroked her hair.

"My poor girl, you are dreadfully tired, aren't you?"

He held her encircled in his arms, the green domino draped over them both. She became aware of a pain in her left arm—something was pressing against it. She gently moved his hand and saw that it had been a ring. An unworked emerald ring. A flash of terror went through her. She became sober in an instant, her fear forcing her to think.

She gathered up her domino and replaced her mask.

"I must go, thank you, but I must go."

"Suddenly you are not drunk." He was puzzled. "Why must you go?"

"You do not remember sir, but we—have met before. Seven years ago, at the Carlton Arms, Grantham."

It was as though she was reciting a list of casualties, her voice was so dead and hard.

Then her words penetrated, and he became very still. All his gaiety drained away in an instant. Seeing him change so convinced Alicia that it was indeed the man.

She quickly ran to the steps of the pavilion and was soon lost in the crowd. The gentleman in the green domino sat gazing after her retreating figure. He made no attempt to follow her, a fact noted by the little boy dressed as a page, who had been sitting behind the hedge the entire time.

By the time she reached her party again, Alicia had been through the worst. She had felt a strong desire to cry, but had fought it. Then she saw Kendalford coming to meet her.

One look at her face was enough to tell him that she was upset, but he asked no questions. He walked her slowly around the perimeter of the dance floor, chatting about nothing, allowing her to recover. When they were almost to where their friends were sitting, she stopped and looked at him.

"You know, I think you are the kindest man I know. I thank you."

He smiled and patted her hand.

"Here we are, back to Laurence and the others. I will sit you down and bring you some lemonade. Just what you need. Had a bit of an attack from the heat, didn't you?"

She was grateful that he had suggested what line she should use. Mrs. Stornaway sympathized and related similar problems she suffered at church in the summer.

Alicia used her attack as an excuse to sit the rest of the evening, watching the dancers with Mrs. Stornaway.

She went over every moment of the meeting, every word the green domino had said. This man could blackmail her. But he had seemed surprised at her admission—that had been real. He had not known—or had he? It seemed so providential, his being so nearby to save her from the other man—but perhaps he had been watching, following. The more she thought of this, the more it seemed true. It was all too convenient.

At midnight a silver domino approached her and asked her to dance. She shook her head decisively, and he turned to Julia. Julia danced the next three dances with him, and as Alicia watched them, it seemed to her that they must know each other, the way they were talking and laughing. Perhaps Julia had drunk too much of the Vauxhall punch, too.

After a few dances with Mrs. Stornaway, and another with Harriet, Kendalford returned to Alicia's side and stayed there, despite numerous entreaties by Mrs. Stornaway to rescue her daughter from the silver domino.

"I do not think," said Kendalford to Alicia with a laugh, "that Julia wishes to be rescued *at all*. It is even possible that the gentleman is the one in need."

Alicia was much amused, she had never heard Kendalford say anything so pointed before.

Mrs. Stomaway was busy keeping an eye on Julia (the provoking child, ruining her chances with the duke like that) that she quite forgot to look for Laurence and Harriet, who were having quite the most unsupervised conversation of their entire acquaintance.

Alicia had not forgotten them, however, and watched from a box above the festivities, where the duke had taken her.

The crowd below them was beginning to disintegrate: the masks were now dangling, the dominos were unfastened, faces were flushed from wine and dancing. It was getting to be the hour of the bloods, the time when young ne'er-do-wells liked to frequent the gardens, with the sole aim of causing trouble. The duke gestured to Laurence and told him to gather the party together. He smiled down at Alicia.

"So, Alicia—may I call you that? You must call me Fitz. Have you had an amusing evening?"

"Yes . . . Fitz. It was one of the most memorable I have had in London, and you were everything that is kind and considerate."

"Some time you must tell me why you were upset—believe me when I tell you that I am sympathetic to all that concerns you."

She looked at him, doubt in her expression.

"And I am open-minded," he added, his instinct telling him that this was what she needed to hear.

For some reason Alicia felt relieved. She would never tell him, of course, but it was good to know that she could.

"You are too kind to me, Fitz."

On the boat ride home, Julia could not stop talking about the silver domino, and found a thousand ways to introduce him into the conversation.

"So exciting! And he seemed to know me, almost . . . but he never used my name. Do you think he knew me, mother?"

"Why should he, dear? Now do please stop . . . I believe I am getting a headache. It is that punch—I knew my digestion was too delicate for such stuff! Why did you let me drink it, Julia?"

"I don't see how I could have stopped you," snapped her daughter. "You were drinking it like a cat laps cream."

Since this rather crude simile was a very good description of the way in which Mrs. Stornaway had imbibed, the entire company was hard put not to laugh.

The only member of the party who seemed not to have had a wonderful evening was Frederick Phillips. This young man, who, Alicia thought, was the most boring person of her acquaintance—an acquaintance that included the likes of James Lanyon and Edith Stornaway—felt that he had been wronged by Julia. Julia had begun the evening flirting with him and dancing all the dances with him; then had come the fatal hour and the arrival of the silver domino, who might well have been some low person, a rowdy aping his betters. And in order to dance with this person she had sacrificed the dances promised to Frederick. Frederick knew what to think of such young ladies: flighty and insincere. The young man preserved an injured, but very noticeable silence the entire way home, which Alicia counted as a blessing. But Laurence felt that he was responsible for everyone's happiness, and he tried to cheer his friend. When they arrived at the other shore, Alicia took Laurence aside and advised him to ignore his friend's sulks.

"If no one pays any attention, he'll get tired of behaving like that. And if he doesn't, at least you haven't wasted your time."

"Yes, you're right. He's been tiresome all evening, anyway, and I can tell you, Alicia, I think it's all his own fault."

The duke had been listening to this advice, and he told Alicia she was a most unusual woman.

"Why do you say that?"

"Do you think any other woman would have put it quite that way? It was exactly the advice I myself would have given, but not what I expect from a woman."

The dark blue eyes looked at him evenly. "Do you wish to say that I am not feminine? What a terrible setdown, Fitz, I had not expected it from you."

"You know I did not mean that," here he took her hand, "quite the reverse. No, it is just that you are not at all what is expected."

She noticed that he did not surrender her hand until the carriage came to a stop at Grosvenor Square.

"Thank you," she said to him when they came to Grosvenor Square. "You have been very kind, and I am grateful."

"I only wish I could have done more," he said gently.

13

THE DRAYTON'S BALL

In the course of the next two months, it gradually became apparent to those interested that Alicia Tierney had virtually disappeared from the routs, dinners, and balls which made up the life of the *ton*. She no longer rode in the park, but it was rumored that the Duke of Kendalford was often invited to the house on Grosvenor Square for tea and informal suppers. But Alicia herself was nowhere in evidence in the great world.

When she was consulted. Lady Terbury smiled and said that her goddaughter had gone house-mad and that she was to be found in Curzon Street every day—morning, noon, and night. When delicate inquiries were made as to the source of funds which enabled Miss Tierney to purchase a house in such an exclusive area, the answers received were very vague. Miss Tierney had inherited a decent amount from her great-aunt Ormond, and attorneys had made some wise investments. . . . But it could not be expected that Lady Mary would be able to silence all questions with her story of the aunt. It was not very long before rumors drifted back from the City and the coffeehouses around the Stock Exchange: Miss Tierney was said to be an extremely wealthy woman. These rumors were not completely credited, however, and the end result was that society suspected that Alicia was wealthier than Lady Mary implied, but less than the informers from the City maintained.

There were those who were glad of Alicia's absence from social events and who put it down to quite other causes.

"I must say. I am glad that everyone has seen through her," Miranda Drayton said to her mother. "You may be sure *that* is the real reason she is no longer in evidence. Such manners could not fail to eventually disgust. . . ."

Her mother looked up at her beloved daughter.

"But you are going to invite her to the ball, dearest? Mary Terbury is not an enemy I wish to have, and she would not come if you did not invite Alicia."

"Oh, mother, as if I would be so petty! I do not hold grudges, you know that. I shall of course invite her, but I imagine that she will be unable to come."

Happily ignorant of the interest her absorption in her house was arousing, Alicia was busier than she had ever been in her life.

The house now shone, inside and out. The lovely red brick mansion had been thoroughly cleaned and refurbished, the marble fireplaces scoured, the brass fittings polished. She loved everything about her house, from the huge pantry to the willow-green salon, to the lion's head on the brass knocker.

It had been almost two months, and the work was finally at an end. The weeks of attending auctions, visiting cabinet-makers, consulting with drapers and carpet makers, choosing wallpapers and paint colors—it was all finished.

She walked around the house, which was now habitable, almost all of the furniture in its place. This would be her very first night spent in her own house.

She went happily to her room, the first one decorated and furnished by herself. She had combined the beautiful walnut winged armchair, an early eighteenth-century piece, with more modern pieces: a mahogany escritoire, some chairs from Sheraton, and a beautiful canopy bed, covered in light blue velvet. The carpet, an Axminster, was of blue and deep rose. The only picture in the room was a landscape by Richard Wilson. It was not fashionable, but she liked it for the peaceful mood it always induced in her. She went to bed in a very satisfied frame of mind.

When she awoke she discovered that she had slept for twelve hours.

"Jellicoe! Why did you let me sleep so long! There were things I should have done."

"You were that tired, dear. After all this work on the house, I couldn't wake you."

Alicia lay against the pillows and looked out the window. Another gray day. Images from her dreams came into her mind. She was aware that these were only parts of the whole, but these fragments were all that she could remember: she was in a maze, and could not find the way out. Above the maze was a jester, acting as guide. But he only laughed at her when she begged for his help. Then the scene changed, and she was with a gypsy woman who was reading coffee grounds, a scene familiar from somewhere, but at first she could not place it. The gypsy pointed to the bottom of the cup, but Alicia could make no sense of the design there. It seemed to be spelling out a name, but she could not read it, no matter how hard she tried.

She did not need a gypsy's help to understand these fragments. For two months she had thrown herself into the preparation of her house. This activity had made it possible for her to almost forget Vauxhall and the man with the emerald ring.

At first it had been very difficult to think of anything else. The man was in London and perhaps even knew her. He could easily start a rumor that would make her situation very unpleasant, the *ton* being what it was. These were her first reactions, but time brought her to see that the Drake inheritance was a great amelioration: she need not marry—at least, not for money— and society was reluctant to censure the rich—at least without evidence, which in this case would be rather hard to find. So for a time she had been calm. But then Kendalford had begun his visits to Grosvenor Square. Although he was careful never to say or do anything that would make her feel in any way pressured, she knew that he liked her, and she herself felt genuine affection for him. Suppose that one day she decided that she did not want to spend her life alone, and she accepted this entirely charming man? What would the man with the emerald ring do then?

Even after she came to terms with these fears, there were others that she could not reason away so easily. The incident at the Carlton Arms had happened seven years earlier. She had been a child of eighteen, and it seemed to her that it had happened to some other person. These memories had been safely locked away for years, but now the kiss at Vauxhall had suddenly brought them flooding back.

The man in the Carlton Arms had been drunk, but he had also been in a state of despair. Something terrible had happened to him, and she had become aware that he was attempting to drug himself with wine—and her body. He had been tender and considerate, at first, but as the hours went by, he had changed— as if he were taking revenge on her, as if she were someone else.

Alicia lay in her bed, in her new room, but all she could see was the darkened bedroom of the Carlton Arms. She had schooled herself to forget that night, to never recall the details.

She was a child no longer, and the things that had disturbed the girl of eighteen did not mystify the woman of twenty-five. But the idea that this forgotten, much-regretted incident could be resurrected in the person of the man himself, here in London, was frightening. He was a threat to her happiness—the happiness that was so close for the first time in years. But perhaps he meant her no harm. Perhaps she was being melodramatic. . . .

The maid came in with the first breakfast to be served from the kitchen downstairs, and the sight of the food brought Alicia back to reality.

She should not waste time on these memories, she decided. Nothing was to be gained by that. She must try and discover his identity before he discovered hers—although it was possible that he knew hers already.

When she visited Grosvenor Square, Lady Mary's first words were about the ball at the Draytons.

"And am I invited?" asked Alicia indifferently.

"Of course. And you really must go. Time to get back in the center of things."

Alicia's first thought was that St. Clair might be there. Like Worthing, he had been rusticating in the country, visiting friends, trying, he had claimed, to save the money of operating his town house.

Surely he would return when he got word of the Draytons' ball, the first one they had given in years.

"Do you think Miranda will allow such as Worthing and St. Clair, ma'am? It will be a sad bore if they are not there."

Lady Mary cast a comprehending eye. "I daresay it would. Can't say. Miranda's mother knew St. Clair's family rather well. But he does have a reputation. Of course the fact that he's a handsome devil will be in his favor. My feeling is that the Draytons will invite everyone—has to be crowded to show how popular an event it is."

"Why is it that they are giving it at all?" asked Harriet. "I always thought they frowned on such things?"

"Actually, it is rather interesting," said Lady Mary, happily in the position of being able to answer just this question, which was now being asked all over Mayfair. "It's really the silliest story! Lord Fane and Miranda are perilously close to being engaged, and there is a rumor sweeping the clubs to the effect that the Draytons had serious losses on the exchange! Untrue, of course, but now they must show that they can afford a ball as lavish as the Prince's!"

When the night came, Lady Mary was able to say that while decidedly not as original as the Prince's entertainments, the Draytons' ball was lavish by the normal Drayton standards.

"For once dear Fanny has enough champagne to go around," she observed to her husband. "I wonder Drayton himself agreed to it—he was ever tight-fisted. . . . Come, girls, let us go and sample some of the things he has paid so dearly for!"

It was wonderful, Lady Mary thought, to watch Miranda trying to be condescendingly charming to Harriet and Alicia.

Harriet, in a pink gown which suited her to perfection, was wearing the justly famous Terbury pearls, far and away the most lovely jewels in the room. Alicia, whose very appearance was undoubtedly a surprise to Miranda, was wearing a daringly cut French gown, of simple white, which revealed that she, unlike other redheads, had no freckles. She could not be called a beauty, but she undeniably took the eye, Lady Mary thought with satisfaction.

Miranda was visibly shocked by the French gown.

"My dear Alicia, you are looking so well! But are you not

afraid of catching a chill?" Miranda's large blue eyes were wide with innocent concern.

"No, I am overheated, actually. Too much dancing, I'm afraid." Alicia was determined to be polite.

"Yes, my brother Babcock has been making a perfect cake of himself! You must not take his attentions seriously—he is a mere boy," said Miranda with a tinkly laugh.

"I most certainly do not take him seriously," replied Alicia in an offhand manner.

It was with great relief that Alicia saw St. Clair making his way toward her. She smiled a welcome at him, but was conscious of a certain feeling of tension as they conversed with Miranda.

Finally they were able to get away from Miranda and went to join the dancers.

"I have not seen you since you were to go to Vauxhall," he said. "Did you enjoy it?"

"Yes, did you?"

He smiled mysteriously. "What makes you think I was there?"

She did not know what to make of this, but she was convinced he had been there.

He again asked her what she had been doing these many weeks.

"I am sure you know already—your sources of information are reliable," she teased.

"You mean the house in Curzon Street? Yes, I did hear something of the vigorous activity there. You worked like the very devil, and when it was done you slept for twelve hours. In a pink robe du soir which clashed, I am sure, with your hair."

She looked at him in amazement for a moment, and then began to laugh.

"You are the most impudent! Improper! Wretch!"

"Not really—you must get to know me better."

"Do you talk so to all women? Miranda would faint if you said such things to her. Tell me, is there anything you do not know about me?"

"A few things. A very few things."

She could not countenance the intensity of his gaze, and dropped her eyes.

He returned her to Lady Mary, where she found Worthing talking to Laurence. St. Clair excused himself and went to speak to some acquaintances across the room.

She felt relief as soon as he was gone. She had been so tense, waiting for a clue—but there had been very little that would help her know.

Worthing declared immediately that he had missed her dreadfully, and that he was sure *she* had missed *him*. In five minutes he had them all laughing at his descriptions of his uncle in Sussex who declared to all and sundry that Napoleon was the Antichrist come at last. He broke off his recital to raise his quizzing glass, in order to better examine an elegant and obviously French woman who was walking toward the door, followed by a strangely dressed footman . . .

"Ah, the Rougemont," he said, disappointed that it was not a new face. "Husband's always away. Strange rumors, don't you know. Dressing this footman up like a doll! Woman'll do anything for attention. Wonder the fellow don't quit. But he's probably a Frenchie, too. Don't know how to dress, anyway."

Later, at supper, Alicia surprised this bewigged footman looking at her. When she looked up again, he was studying the wall, and she dismissed him from her mind.

After the champagne and ices, dancing resumed with renewed energy. The older people were now sitting and fanning themselves, but the young couples were determined to make a night of it.

Alicia danced with a young lieutenant just back from France, who was full of interesting anecdotes. He worshiped Wellington and was firm in his belief that Boney would be beaten. His contempt for those Englishmen who admired Napoleon was great.

"There are a lot like that," he said. "They think it good *ton* or something! Let them see how they'd like Parliament shut down, some Frenchman telling them how to live. Change their tune then, Miss Tierney."

Alicia agreed, remembering how Lady Mary had said that her liberal Whig party was ruining itself by its antiwar stance.

The young lieutenant looked around at the room.

"I tell you, I feel guilty just being here, after what I saw at Bayonne. I know people need amusement, but . . .

"The war is real to you," said Alicia sympathetically. "But to us it is not—we have not seen and felt what you have."

"I don't suppose I'd really want you to," he said quietly. "But if I meet any more of those dandies who don't want to get their hands dirty, I think I'll call one of 'em out."

The young lieutenant's words came to mind when Lord Fane asked for his one duty dance, encouraged, undoubtedly, by Lady Mary. Alicia's evil genius prompted her to tell him of the lieutenant's views, and asked what he thought.

The dance had ended and they were by the french windows. Fane lounged against the wall and looked absently at the crowd.

"Fellow may be right," he drawled. "Damned if I know. Told you before, Boney has bad style. Politics don't interest me, you know. Like the war to be over, of course. Get some nice French fabrics to market again!"

Alicia was rendered almost speechless by this.

"I don't believe it! You deliberately—" she sputtered.

"State my opinions. Do try a little tolerance, Miss Tierney. Especially after I have not mentioned your own behavior tonight," he drawled.

"What of it?"

"You would do well to play the game and conceal your . . . er, *inclinations* a bit more successfully. But I suppose you don't care what the room is saying."

Alicia's eyes grew very bright and hard. "Well, you are right about one thing. I do not care what the room is saying, and I care even less what *you* think." She turned and walked away, almost running into Worthing, so blind was she with anger.

"Whatever is the matter, Alicia? You look mad as fire."

"Ask me to dance, Jack."

"What is it? I saw you and Nick—"

"I am too angry. Wait a moment and I will tell you.".

Gradually she regained control of her temper. "I have never had a man talk to me in such a tone. . . ." When she had told him everything, Worthing frowned.

"Very Strange, most unlike Nick. You must bring out something in him—"

"And he does in me. No, of course I was quite as bad as he, to answer in that way. It is because I will not toady to His Lordship, the wealthy peer! He is too used to what Miranda provides, unending agreement with all his views. Surely you cannot think what he said about the war was admirable."

"No, but he has a devilish sense of humor. Depend upon it, he Was taking you in."

That he had been laughing at her struck Alicia even less agreeable. What was there about Lord Fane that made her hackles rise?

Lady Mary assured her that his reproach has been the merest nonsense—no one had noticed anything about her and St. Clair.

"Except for Nick, of course." Lady Mary looked very pre-occupied. "It's rather strange, really . . ."

This incident put Alicia in a thoroughly bad mood. When St. Clair came to claim her for the last dance, she insisted he take a seat beside her instead. He hesitated, and she asked if he was afraid of what people might say.

"What a strange idea! No, of course not. It is just that your admirers will have my head for monopolizing you in this way."

"You really do not care?"

He sat down and looked at her seriously.

"I have come to the conclusion that it is useless," he said. "The incredible hypocrisy one meets with every day among these people—"

"You talk as if you were not one of them. . . . And what of your inamoratas? What if they talk of them?"

He did not seem shocked by this improper question, but merely shrugged.

"Unlike Lord Quakenberry, I do not pretend that they do not exist. I accept the fact that man is an animal—as our religious men do not." He looked directly into her eyes.

She lowered her eyes to her fan, unable again to withstand those intense dark eyes, which seemed to see into her mind.

You can be brave enough to at least *look*, Alicia."

"Aroused by this accusation of cowardice, she flashed him an angry look.

"Better. Your fearless look is very provocative. Makes one wish to teach you fear."

"A silly Byronism, St. Clair. And I would not wish to be the one to do it, if I were you. It might cost you far more than the pleasure would be worth."

He sighed comically.

"Just when I think I have you in full retreat, you return to the field."

14

MERCIER RECEIVES A MESSAGE

The gentleman who inquired if there were any letters for Mr. Quentin Bellcourt was dressed in a manner indistinguishable from that of the other clients of the Temple Bar Coffeehouse. The innkeeper looked through the letters in the box.

"Here we are, sir. A nice feminine sort of look to it."

Mercier took the letter, concealing his eagerness. It was only when he was alone at the corner table that he opened what appeared to be a billet-doux. He was not cheered by what it contained:

Tell me not, Sweet, I am unkind,
That from the nunnery
Of thy chaste breast and quiet mind
To war and arms I fly.

Mercier read it twice, to be sure, and then tossed it into the fireplace.

"So it's bad news is it?" asked the innkeeper.

He walked to the corner slowly, going over it in his mind. The message, the first stanza of Lovelace's "To Lucasta, on Going to the Wars," meant that there was great danger, and no one was in a position to help. He would have to change his disguise, and try to escape.

He started to sweat. British prisons . . . This message meant that someone knew where he was, and was almost sure of who he was.

At the corner, he hailed a hack and took it to Crescent Street. Once there, he slipped down an alley and entered an imposing house by the back door. He told the woman inside what he required, and then went to bed. It would be a long journey, and he would need his strength.

By late evening, he was in Dover. There he made arrangements with a Dutch captain, and settled down to a good dinner at the George.

There were times, he thought with satisfaction, when the best disguise was no disguise at all.

Madame de Rougement was inconsolable when she received the letter. Her so charming footman had returned to his sick mother, and how would she ever find another who would look so elegant in that livery?

15

A SUDDEN DEPARTURE

The courier arrived at the house on Cavendish Square at the end of the first week of December. The same week had already brought news of the great victories on the Continent: Leipzig had been taken, and the King of Saxony as well. London began to feel that Buonaparte was on the run, but rumor had it that Wellington did not feel it was over quite yet.

It was very early in the morning, but Lord Fane's factotum, Jerry Daws, quickly understood the urgency of the matter and went to wake his master.

Lord Fane came down in his dressing gown, but he seemed alert. He greeted the courier warmly.

"Williams! How are you? How's the old man?"

"Moving, at this moment. I can't stay long, sir. I must talk to you in private, right away."

They went into a room and stayed there less than thirty minutes. When the courier left, his lordship quickly dressed and went into consultation with his staff. Domestic matters taken care of, he then went to his club and had several important conversations.

***

Alicia was comfortably settled in Lord Terbury's library, and when she heard Lord Fane's voice in the drawing room, she resolved to stay there. This plan came to nothing, however, for he was shown into the library a moment later.

He stood at the door for a moment, as if hesitating.

"You wished to see me?"

"Yes, I did. May I come in?" He was uncharacteristically hesitant.

"I believe you already are. Please, do sit down."

He was the last man on earth she wished to see, and she was in the middle of reading a French novel—the sort one could not get at Hookham's Lending Library—but she was determined to be polite. She had not seen him alone since the Draytons' ball, for which good luck she was thankful.

He was dressed, she noticed, for traveling, in gleaming boots, impeccably cut buckskins, and a dark brown coat. The brown hair was carefully arranged, and the gray eyes watched her from behind a quizzing glass. The perfect dandy, save for his tanned skin. Spain had quite ruined the desirable pale complexion.

"I am most sorry to interrupt you, Miss Tierney, but since Laurence and I are leaving this evening—"

"Leaving?"

"I am sorry, you were not there when I told Lady Mary. Yes, for the Continent. Couriers are needed, and we are available, so . . ."

Alicia's thoughts immediately flew to Harriet who would be very upset Fane seemed to read her thoughts.

"I have heard that you are to go to Hansdown for a month or so. That is very near my own estate, Bayhall. I think it will provide a distraction for Miss Stomaway. It is lovely country."

"Yes, that may help a little. At least she won't have to see the scenes of their courtship . . ."

Alicia looked at him questioningly. Surely this was not his reason for coming to see her.

"You may have guessed why I am here," he drawled as he settled himself into a chair, legs stretched out in front of him.

"No, I have not"

This made him look up.

"I am come to make you an offer, of course."

"Make me an offer!"

Fane produced his box, and, with a graceful gesture, took some snuff. His expression was skeptical.

"Pray forgive me, Miss Tierney, but do you mean to say that you do not wish to marry me?"

"Of course I do not. And why you can wish it eludes me, to say the least. You cannot like me! I know you do not."

"Ah. I see that I have miscalculated. Do forgive me."

Alicia looked at him, suspicious of this sudden proposal.

"What are you trying to accomplish, Lord Fane?"

He sighed. "My grandmother is very sick, you see."

"What has that to do with it?"

"She wishes me married quickly, before she dies, and I wish it before I leave for the Continent"

"You are joking! It is not possible to marry on such short notice, so I know this is all a hum!"

"Here is the special license, I procured it this morning."

Alicia began to fear she was dealing with a madman.

"And what of Miranda?"

"Yes, there is Miranda, of course. But honor demands that I make up for the regrettable manner in which I took advantage of you after The Silver Tree—"

"I see. You wish to make an honest women of me. Very noble,

I'm sure. Lord Fane, will you stop this farce! Over a kiss! I am not a child, and I was certainly as much at fault as you yourself. This is nonsense! Obviously you do not wish to tell me the reason—not that it would matter. You know we should not suit. Agree, it is ridiculous."

"Perhaps it does seem so," he said stiffly. "But reflect. I do not propose marriage to women as a joke. I am quite serious about the matter, and you would do well to restrain your temper and think on it. I could make you very comfortable. I would demand . . . nothing—but discretion."

She looked at him, feeling nothing but contempt for this suggestion.

"You mean that you would continue with Sibylla Crawford and—"

"You with St. Clair."

She lifted her chin.

"Since I never began with St. Clair, I doubt I could continue! Such an arrangement would be repugnant to me. I shall not marry where my heart is not engaged."

He examined his nails with a great show of absorption.

"I had forgotten Kendalford, of course. A duke is a duke, after all."

"Why do you propose to me and then insult me?" She was making a great effort to control her temper. "Surely this is at cross-purposes to your intentions?"

He passed his hand over his eyes. "Very well, I have done my best. Let us end this comedy. Shall we say that it never happened?"

"By all means. I begin to wonder about your sanity, my lord."

Later that afternoon, they all assembled to say farewell to Laurence. Harriet was tearful, as she had been all afternoon.

Lady Mary managed to remain calm, but it was obvious that it cost her a great deal of self-control.

This scene was so painful that Alicia was almost glad to see Fane ride up to end it. He was cheerful and refused to let Harriet continue crying.

"I'll take care of him, Miss Stornaway, done it before. Our work is very safe, actually, just couriers. Safest job in the army."

Alicia, confused by the rush of events and the memory of Fane's proposal, was silent. Fane did not even seem to notice her until they were actually leaving. She and Harriet waited on the steps, and everyone else had gone upstairs to watch them from the upper windows as they rode away.

Fane kissed Harriet's cheek and then turned to Alicia.

"Come, my girl, let us forget and part friends." He smiled at her so frankly that she was betrayed into an answering smile. A moment later, he turned her face up to him and kissed her.

16

MERCIER DISAPPEARS

The elderly clubman was dissatisfied. The reports from Jem and Coley indicated that Mercier had left England, but the letter from France said that he was not there and was not expected. Once again Mercier had vanished into the waves.

There were some interesting aspects to the reports. One agent had seen him, he thought, but his hair had been black, not brown. And he had been in Dover, talking to a Dutch captain, de Hooch. The face had been nothing like Mercier's—it had been a particular way he had of moving his hands that had made the agent think it was Mercier. But the face had been nothing like. . . . The captain this man had talked to was somehow familiar to the elderly clubman. He had heard the name before, a long time ago, but he could not remember—no matter, it would come to him, he had no doubt of that.

The reports made him uneasy. Mercier was up to something new—he could feel it. Where was he? Why had the trail gone cold at Dover? . . .

He rang for the waiter and had him take the packet to the servant waiting across the room. Working at White's had its advantages—no one but himself would dream of conducting state business there. And one could always get a good meal afterward.

17
CARLTON HOUSE

The Prince's victory dinner at Carlton House was the last event before Christmas, and everyone agreed he had outdone himself. Carlton House was magnificent beyond anyone's imaginings.

Alicia did not agree with this general opinion; the house, like its master, seemed overdone to her. But she had been curious, and she was glad to be inside the two-storied mansion that had been transformed (through three architects) into the closest thing resembling Versailles to be found in England.

Lady Terbury had been determined that they should make an appearance at this final fete, despite the fact that Harriet, who had been in low spirits ever since Laurence's departure, did not wish to attend. It was all Lady Mary could do to get Harriet to take an interest in her dress and hair. She had needed no such persuasion with Alicia, who was looking quite her best.

She had told herself that it was silly and schoolgirlish, but Alicia had been unable to banish the thought from her mind that this might well be the last time she would see St. Clair for some months. She remembered that he disliked the Regent, but he was related to one of the Regent's cronies. . . . It had occurred to her that she might return from the country early after the holidays, but she immediately banished the thought: she would do nothing *especially* for him. It was stupid enough of her to be thinking of him as she dressed and had her hair arranged. Still unsure of whether he had been the green domino, she was determined not to be led into foolishness by her weakness for a shockingly unsteady rake.

Despite these worthy resolutions, she found herself looking everywhere for him, as their party was led through Carlton House by the Regent himself.

The Prince of Wales was just over fifty, but looked much older, Alicia thought. He was very fat, but he dressed like a young beau. She could see traces of his former charm: he knew a great deal about the arts, and he was quite likeable as he pointed out the beauties of his mansion. The other side of his personality was revealed when he thought a servant was staring at him. He turned to his aide.

"Want that man fired, Carstairs. Immediately."

She was amazed by this behavior, but later Lady Mary told her it was due to his self-consciousness—he knew he was fat, and he imagined that everyone was staring at him.

"Well, the way he chooses to dress would be reason enough. It is really too bad he broke with Brummell."

"Hush, child! Not here! And what do you think of the place, Harriet?"

Harriet's eyes were dancing. "It is the most incredible thing, ma'am. Don't you think the porphyry columns with the Etruscan grifiins on them a bit overwhelming for an entrance hall? And why did he purchase the dagger of Genghis Khan for his armory—I am persuaded it cannot be the real thing!" Harriet began to giggle contagiously, and Alicia joined in. Lady Mary told them she would send them home before dinner if they did not behave, although she was happy to see Harriet so cheered.

The girls tried to restrain themselves, but when Harriet and Alicia saw the throne room, which featured a canopy of helmets and ostrich plumes, and a fender which supported the eagle of Jupiter subduing prostrate dragons, it was too much for them, and they had to leave the room, on the pretext of a torn hem.

They met with Lord Worthing in the crimson drawing room and told him of their near disgrace.

"That's nothing," he said disdainfully. "*I* was at a dinner here when there was a stream running among the tables, with live fish in it."

When Lady Mary caught sight of her charges in animated conversation with the dangerously charming Lord Worthing, she hurried over.

"My dears, have you seen the Princess de Lieven? Black velvet, up to her throat, and long sleeves."

"The ruff looks a bit like Mary, Queen of Scots, and the diamond chains quite spoil the desired severity, I fear," said a voice behind Alicia.

Determined not to let St. Clair see how happy she was to see him, Alicia affected a cool little nod of recognition. He seemed not to notice her attitude, but made pleasant conversation until it was time to go in to dinner. He asked Alicia if he could be her partner at dinner, and despite the sure disapproval of her godmother, Alicia agreed. On the way to the conservatory, he walked very slowly and made certain to be at the end of the line, which afforded them a little privacy.

"Well, *cousin*," he said with peculiar emphasis, "I have been to see my uncle, and he has told me that you have become something of an heiress. I must congratulate you—have you informed your family of it?"

She was not sure of how much he knew, but she was certain that Alexander St. Clair would not have told him the entire truth.

"No, I have not. It is but a competence . . . but I fail to see why this news should be of interest." She looked him directly in the face.

"Come, Alicia, I was not born yesterday—the City talks of nothing else: Dickie Drake left his fortune to the Tierney girl!"

"Oh well! Since you know . . ." He had obviously expected her to be embarrassed, but she was not. She was offended by his attitude.

He stopped and took her hand, smiling in that familiar way.

"Do not be annoyed! It is merely that I was surprised that you trusted me so little, thinking, no doubt, that I was a fortune hunter."

"And are you not?"

"You know I am, but surely you also know that I found you attractive before I knew of the fortune."

"No, I do not know that!" she laughed. "You are such a shocking flirt that one could never be sure of anything of the sort. I am sorry, Robert, but the thing of it is that I have told very few people. I do not wish the sort of notoriety that comes with such news."

"You seem to have forgotten that you told me of Farnsworth! You—trying to avoid notoriety!"

"But I did," she said, nettled by this reminder. "No one ever knew!"

"Forgive me my churlishness. The fact of the matter is that I was hurt. . . . And speaking of Farnsworth, you never told me how you managed to pull it off."

"I do not think I wish to tell you, *cousin*."

"Very well. I shall not pursue this—you see how discreet I am. Am I forgiven?"

"I am not sure yet," she said mockingly.

"And when am I to see you without a hundred other persons present?"

"I do not know, but if we do not take our place soon, Lady Mary will come looking for me."

He led her to their seats in the conservatory, and remarked that he'd have more time alone with a convent girl than he did with her.

"And have you ever been involved with one?" she asked innocently.

"With one what?"

"Convent girl."

"Go ahead and tease me, my girl, I shall find ways of repaying you, never fear. You are very safe here, of course. . . ."

They were not to have much conversation during dinner: Worthing was to Alicia's left, and Mrs. Selby to St. Clair's right, and it seemed as if these two were conspiring to keep them occupied most of the time.

Now that Alicia had time to look at it, the conservatory itself was remarkable. It had been an addition to the palace, and seemed a miniature version of a Gothic cathedral, with some rather unusual finishing touches. Carved pillars, stained-glass windows, a ceiling adorned by glazed traceries—all as a background to an Olympian feast.

The Regent's cooks had clearly spent days in preparing this dinner. On the vast quantities of gold and silver plates, one counted several roasts, lobsters, quail, pineapples, grapes, and peaches. Surrounding them were many bottles of iced champagne and various wines. But the most remarkable dish was a huge recreation, in spun sugar, of an *Hermitage suedois*.

As she looked at the table and the antique draperies of pink and silver, the mirrored walls with the vases and candlesticks before them, Alicia was conscious of a feeling of exhilaration. No matter what one felt about the excesses of taste, it was impressive, and very regal.

She even began to feel friendlier toward the Regent himself. He had such zest for life and was clearly full of generous impulses. But it seemed he could be very petulant when he didn't get his way. Alicia continued to wonder what Worthing and Fane could see in him. St. Clair suggested that it was the simple fact that he was the Regent, and would become the king when the old king died.

"It is always the case with snobs, I believe," he said.

While her prejudice against him was very strong, Alicia could not believe this of Fane. He must have some other reason, and Worthing, too. They might be dandies, but they were not snobs on such a primitive level.

"No," she whispered, aware of Lady Mary's frown, "I think it must be something else. Perhaps he is better when among friends. And if you dislike him so, why did you come?"

He took a sip of his wine, his eyes never leaving her face.

"I think you know why I came."

Not trusting her ability to keep her countenance, Alicia turned to Worthing. Worthing was trying vainly to distract Harriet, whose low spirits had suddenly returned.

"What happened?" she asked Worthing.

"It's that boy Phillips. Went on and on about the number of casualties in the last battles in France. Doesn't seem to understand about Laurence and Harriet, and he's being most tactless. Here, I'll try again."

This time he was successful, and Alicia once again realized that the frivolous Lord Worthing had a very kind heart. As for

Frederick Phillips, he was simply a stupid young man who had not even noticed how downcast Harriet became when he talked of the wounded soldiers.

When supper ended, the many guests went in several directions, some to play at cards, some to listen to the singer, some to wander through the rooms of the palace. Alicia and St. Clair formed part of this last group, and were intending to look at the collection of oriental vases in the Blue Velvet Room.

"You do not think much of it, do you?" said St. Clair as they walked a little behind the others.

"No, I do not. I believe people should be comfortable, but this is far more than is necessary. . . ."

"So that is how you feel too? I wondered, so many of your friends are so close to this set, one of them is part of it. . . ."

"I suppose you mean Lord Fane. Yes, he is, but I do not think I wish to be called a friend of *his*." She felt she had been too sharp, and immediately tried to remedy matters. "That is, I am sure Lord Fane has reasons for liking the Regent . . . he undoubtedly has a side not shown here. . . ."

"You are most amusing when you are trying to be fair! But I suppose if we come and sup with a man, we must be tolerant. Here, let me show you the rose satin drawing-room. Many consider it superior to the blue velvet, or the golden, but I confess to a liking for it nonetheless."

He showed her the room and then led her in the general direction of the garden, a direction which seemed most uninhabited by other people.

Alicia knew what Lady Mary would have said, but she felt an overpowering desire to see what he would do when left to his own devices.

He showed her the peacocks that were strolling along the walk, even though the night was cold.

"Prinny goes all out, you see. The poor peacocks! But they are nothing to the peacock inside."

"It is a lovely garden, however. But close the window—it is terribly cold."

"And now I shall take you to one of the secret rooms few people ever see."

He led her down a small staircase which had been concealed behind a tapestry. Feeling she was in some Gothic romance, Alicia stifled all thoughts of propriety. She was certain she could manage him. . . .

"Here, do you like it?"

"How is it that you know such a convenient place, Robert? I imagine that if you were in a foreign country you would immediately discover them; you have that talent." He laughed softly but made no answer.

The room, with its cheery fire, was lovely. All the hangings were pale green, the carpet was an Aubusson gold, and there was no mistaking the room's purpose.

"You know, this looks very like a special room for the seduction of rather willing women. Do tell me, how did you know it was here? You are not a frequenter of the palace. . . ."

"What a statement. Have you no maidenly modesty?".

"Famsworth would have cured me of that—if I had ever had it. I have known of such places since I was fourteen, and in fact my cousin Freddy—"

"Taught you all about them. I would give much to meet this Freddy person, if he does in fact exist."

She remained composed. "Do not be cross because I am unafraid. We country girls are sometimes more used to being on our own, you know . . . and I have very little sensibility."

His answer to that was to pull her to him. She looked up at him, waiting.

He told himself that she was powerless, he could do anything with her; but at the same time he sensed that she herself wanted this embrace, this kiss, and that it was her doing as much as his. A moment later, all such considerations were forgotten.

He kissed her several times, with great intensity and unmistakable meaning. And she responded, despite herself. He began to gently kiss the hollow of her throat.

"Please do not," she said.

But he had no intention of stopping. Alicia made a strong effort to pull away. She was a strong woman, but she was unable to free herself—he was much larger and much stronger. Fane's words the night of The Silver Tree flashed through her mind: "You must not forget: you are not really a man—but I am."

Her struggles did finally succeed in making St. Clair stop for a moment. Without releasing her from his embrace, he turned her face to him.

"Do you really wish me to stop?" She looked at him steadily, but he thought he saw a flicker of fear in the dark blue eyes.

"I do not know," she said at last "But I feel we are in danger of discovery here, and surely ruining my reputation is not in your plans."

He gave a sneering laugh. "No, it was not my intention to seduce you in Carlton House, of all places. . . . I beg you to believe that I have let my emotions rule my head."

This was so patently insincere that she began to smile.

"Oh, do not blame only yourself. I am sure that I am quite as much to blame."

"How curious to hear a woman admit that. . . . I begin to think we will deal extremely together, Miss Tierney."

As they made their way back to the conservatory, she went over their conversation and found the last phrase interesting. It implied some kind of future arrangement, such as marriage. It was hard not to feel a kind of relief. If he was the man in the inn, he could have no objection to her past. But did she want to be married to a man who disturbed her so intensely. Did he know how much she had wanted him to continue to kiss her, despite her struggle to stop him.

They had been walking without even touching, but as they neared the main hall, St. Clair stopped and pulled her into an alcove. He kissed ruthlessly this time, making her know that he had been holding back before. He stopped suddenly, before she wanted him to.

His smile flashed like a knife. "*Now* I think we may return to the recital."

They entered the room separately and went in different directions—he to his friends, she to the Terburys.

When the recital was over, however, St. Clair managed to engage Mrs. Selby in conversation, just behind Alicia and Lady Mary.

She talked to her godmother for twenty minutes, and could not have told anyone later what they talked of. She was aware of him every moment, and found herself half-listening to his conversation while conducting her own. Finally the two groups became one, as Mrs. Selby, a vivacious lady who seemed to know a great deal about everyone, narrated the latest Caro Lamb-Byron story.

"I would not wish to criticize, you understand, I know that Byron is unfeeling, but the girl is really quite beyond the limits! Caro decided she would not waltz because Byron didn't wish her to—when they were still together, that is. (To my mind, it isn't that he don't approve, but that he can't, what with the foot.) At any rate, at Lady Heathcote's ball, Caro asked Byron to give her permission to waltz. Everyone heard his answer. He said that it was a matter of complete indifference to him whether she did or not. She said if his indifference was real, she did not want to live! His answer was, 'then take the knife.'

"Well, that evening, when everyone returned to bed, she went up with the ladies, broke a glass in her hand, and was very cut, of course. Then she got a knife from somewhere, put it up to her throat. They stopped her, but I can imagine how she'll end! Her family's in a fine taking over it, I can tell you!"

Mrs. Selby was satisfied with the effect she had produced. After some seconds of silence, the company began to discuss whether it was true, and what it augured if it were.

St. Clair asked Alicia what she thought of it.

"I think her a very poor creature! Why should his answer—or *any* answer—drive her to that? She is clearly deranged, if the tale is true."

"An unfeeling answer," said St. Clair. "I think you have much to learn about men and women still."

"Yes," said Mrs. Selby, "you are a little hard on the girl— although her behavior is such as to give good society disgust of her, I must own. But Byron—"

"No, I simply refuse to feel sorry for a woman who makes such a complete fool of herself over a man—and really we have better subjects for conversation than Caro and Byron."

This struck a responsive chord in Harriet, silent till now.

"Yes, as we enjoy ourselves here, Laurence and Nick are riding across France—into a battle, perhaps."

Alicia caught sight of a tear trembling on her friend's lashes.

"Yes, a very lowering thought. You know, I believe you are very tired, Harriet, and so am I. I shall go and find His Lordship; it must be almost time to go."

Lord Terbury needed no telling: he had seen Harriet's dejected looks and had ordered the carriage.

As she was waiting by the portico, St. Clair came to say goodbye.

"And so, farewell until after the holidays, Alicia. Your servant."

The familiar shock went through her as his lips caressed her hand. His dark eyes mocked as he uttered the most conventional phrases. Most delighted, most honored, it had been a marvelous dinner party.

"I have been most grateful for your company, sir," she answered in her best imitation of Miranda Drayton's haughty civility.

"I can only regret that you did not have even more to be grateful for . . . I fancy that one day you will understand Caroline Lamb a bit better."

PART TWO

18
HANSDOWN HOUSE

It was the greatest good luck, everyone agreed, that the letters from Laurence had arrived just as they were preparing to leave for the holidays. The journey down was spent in the reading and discussion of them.

The letter to his parents was full of interesting observations on his surroundings.

The letter to Harriet was much different, judging by the blushes which colored her cheeks as she read it. It was remarked that only half of the letter had been read aloud, and Lord Terbury teased her about the rest of the contents.

This gay mood continued most of the way to Sussex, as Alicia read *her* letter to them. Unlike Harriet's letter, this one had not been delivered by a soldier, and came from Tierney Chase rather than France. It was from her brother William, and it gave her hearers the strong impression that he loved his sister more than his life.

"I see what it is," said Lady Mary thoughtfully. "He has heard about the inheritance. That is why he is planning to come and visit London at the end of January—to see if he can have a little cream for himself. I do hope he can't."

"No, he can't, and I almost feel sorry for him. He's going to be so annoyed."

"Interesting thing, the way people behave when money is involved. I know men, gentlemen—you can trust them in affairs of the heart, politics, what you will, but if money is in it—they'll do *anything*," said Lord Terbury with an air of surprise, as if it were a fact he had just discovered.

This casual comment gave rise to a train of thought that Alicia found unpleasant. She knew that St. Clair needed money—he had never concealed it—but she did not want to think what she had felt between them at Carlton House could be explained so simply, so unpalatably. She had told herself before that it did not matter; but now it did, she discovered she did not want to be married for her money. Of course, she thought ruefully, some months ago there would have been no reason for anyone to marry her, and now at least there was the money. She began to understand the plight of the great heiresses, forever unsure of why their mates had really chosen them. One would never be sure. . . .

When she reviewed her various encounters with him, it struck her that he was very sure of her, certain in his expectations, or so it seemed in retrospect. While it was true that his kisses were able to almost cause her to forget herself, she had *not* done so. She had been able to conquer her physical response to him. . . . He had perhaps enjoyed too much success with women, and it did not seem to occur to him that she might be capable of resisting him in the end, no matter how attractive he might be.

But no matter how she tried to think of his defects, her thoughts kept returning to the little room in Carlton House, and the feel of his arms about her. Fleetingly, she tried to put his face on the body of the man in the inn, but it was so many years ago now, it could not make it seem real to her.

But Alicia knew where to find another view of Robert St. Clair, a view which might help her to be less overwhelmed by him.

"Tell me, godmamma, what do you think of Robert St. Clair? Your real opinion."

Lady Terbury recognized that this was no casual question, and she knew that she must be careful in her answer. Across from them her husband and Harriet were playing cards, and talking to each other.

"I think he is rather intelligent, actually. But he has been spoiled by having too little to do in life . . . his father would not surrender control of anything to him when he reached his majority. But I think that with the right woman—he must marry money—he might change, but I do not think it likely. He was brought up by women, all of whom acceded to his every whim. I can see that he is terribly attractive—fascinating, even, but would not wish my daughter, if I had one, to fall in love with him. He is not a man who would make a good husband."

Alicia mused on this. There were times when she herself did not wish to be married, not in the least, so it was not so terrible that St. Clair, in Lady Mary's opinion, would not make a good husband.

Alicia had been in London society long enough to see what marriage often came to. The ladies of the *ton* who were faithful were condemned to a lonely life with their children, while their husbands frequented their clubs, their gambling hells, their horse races and boxing matches—and their well-kept mistresses. The wives who were unfaithful fared somewhat better, although it was rare that they could divorce and remarry if they wished to. If they divorced, they often risked being cut out of polite society. In some ways spinsterhood might be preferable to either of these alternatives.

There were happy marriages, of course. Lady Mary had one, and Harriet and Laurence would most likely deal well together.

For many reasons, however, Robert St. Clair was her logical suitor; and if she did not marry him, he would quickly find someone else to marry, in order to have money. And then her only choice would be to have him as a lover, or not at all. Alicia found this idea faintly amusing. No, it would never do. She could not share him with anyone. She would always be thinking of his wife. . . .

Watching Alicia's pensive face, Lady Terbury was unhappy with herself. She had been too honest in her evaluation of St. Clair, she should have been subtle, and she should have tried to discover the exact extent of Alicia's feeling for him.

When she thought of Alicia's mother, Isabel, Lady Mary became a little disquieted. Isabel had always seemed to be such a proper young lady, but great daring had been hidden under that calm manner. If Alicia were like that, there was little one could do. She would be halfway to the altar before anyone knew about it. But surely the girl had common sense. Surely she could see that St. Clair was the most hardened fortune hunter. And what did it mean that Alicia had asked her what she really thought of St. Clair? Why should she wish to hear ill of him?

But what she really wished to know was whether St. Clair was the reason why Alicia had rejected Fane. This matter had been on her mind ever since Alicia had laughingly recounted the story of the "ridiculous proposal."

The two ladies were brought out of their reveries by Lord Terbury, who announced that they were nearing the neighborhood of Hansdown.

Alicia had not been told what to expect, and she was delighted by her first view of the house.

"I know it is all the crack nowadays to have stucco, and lowly brick is not at all the thing, but I love this mellow brick," said Lady Mary with pride. "Do you like it, Alicia?"

"It is lovely. The brick must be very old to be that color."

"The house was built some hundred years ago," said Lord Terbury. "See how they varied the brickwork on the trim. You don't see anything like that now."

The approach had been through a park full of plane and beech trees, and to the right, slightly behind the house, Alicia glimpsed a sickle-shaped lake. At the end of it was an exquisite summerhouse.

"I have a weakness for summerhouses," said Alicia. "It is really too bad that it is so cold."

"You will be down in spring, sometime. I was here in the summer once," said Harriet, "when I was a child. We had a marvelous time, especially tormenting Jakes, the gardener."

Lord Terbury looked grim. "I had forgotten about Jakes, thank heavens. The most exhausting bore in the world, goes on and on about illness and deaths in the neighborhood. Morbid fellow."

"But he is an excellent gardener," reminded Lady Mary, "and we couldn't do without him. The greenhouse alone—"

"Yes, yes, the man will be around our necks, an apt image, the rest of our lives, I have no doubt."

The housekeeper, who introduced herself as Mrs. Zachary Jones, immediately took to the young ladies and went up to help them get settled.

"I been housekeeper for thirty years here. And Lady Mary, she be a demanding sort of mistress, but fair, you could say. I expect you young ladies will be needing some gentlemen company—I was young once! Well there are a group of officers over near Tunbridge Wells, staying in a private house they are."

Harriet tried to assure Mrs. Jones that they were in no need of military company, but the merry old lady discounted their remarks as missishness. They would see, she nodded sagely. Yes, these gentlemen often rode nearby, and were allowed to hunt in the woods which ran with the Terbury estate. Alicia and Harriet protested in vain that they were not interested in these soldiers, but Mrs. Jones smiled knowingly.

The friends separated to unpack and then met in Harriet's room.

"Alicia, I had forgotten how nice Hansdown is! I thought it would be like my family's house, everything faded. But it is quite the reverse."

"Yes, I much prefer it to my father's house—we never had sufficent funds to maintain it. I always felt that one had a duty to take care of beautiful houses; they require it. And Hansdown is obviously carefully redecorated, without the gold leaf and gilt everywhere which goes beyond what was originally intended."

"I wonder what Bayhall is like. . . . Nick had it refurbished last year," said Harriet.

"I can imagine—miles of chinoiserie and perhaps a few remnants from the Egyptian craze."

"No, I don't think so. I have a very different opinion of him. I think he would do it very well."

Alicia looked at her friend in surprise. "I can see that he *has* charmed you after all. I suppose that only I am immune. . . ."

The friends spent the hours before dinner roaming through the house.

In the gallery which contained the family portraits, they found one lady who looked like Lady Mary herself: one Lady Jean Terbury, an imperious beauty of the seventeenth century.

"I believe there was a good deal of scandal about her," said

Harriet with a giggle. "She was shockingly wild, had lovers before her marriage and after as well!"

Lady Mary had ordered dinner served in the library, an idea all of them found charming.

"The fire in here is particularly good, and I thought we would enjoy it after those formal London meals. Cook did very well with the chicken, do you not think?"

Lord Terbury was too absorbed in opening a bottle of fine French wine from the Hansdown cellars to answer, but Alicia and Harriet proclaimed the tarragon chicken excellent.

"Ah, forgot," said Lord Henry vaguely.

"Forgot what, my dear?"

"Something. Let me think."

"Really, Henry, you have been here only several hours. How could you forget it already."

But his good-natured face was clearing.

"Met Major Trilling and the Marlowes. Invited them to dinner tomorrow."

There was a hint of exasperation in Lady Mary's voice as she asked him who Major Trilling was.

"You remember him, m'dear. Friend of Nick's. Served in the Peninsula and is now home on leave."

Harriet became excited.

"He may have news of them—did you ask?"

"No, I saw him only for a moment, as he was riding off. He's staying at Bayhall."

"I suppose I have nothing to say to it," said Lady Mary. "Since the matter is accomplished. So he's staying at Bayhall. . . . I thought Fane's grandmother was there."

"So she is, but she opens the house to any of his friends who wish to come."

"Rather a change from the past, I must say. After Quentin Fane died, she had no visitors for ten years."

It seemed to Alicia that Lord Terbury did not wish to talk about Quentin Fane, because he deftly changed the subject and did not return to it.

19
NEW ACQUAINTANCE

The only guest to arrive on time was Major Stephen Trilling, who was accustomed to military punctuality. He was in his late thirties, with the easy manners of a man used to traveling in diplomatic circles. His address was such that Harriet, usually shy with strangers, felt him an old friend after twenty minutes.

Lady Mary, who had been prepared to dislike him, pronounced him charming; much to the enjoyment of her protégées, she even began a light flirtation with him.

"I am thankful she is off the market," whispered Harriet. "She would easily cast us in the shade."

"Oh, yes! Imagine what she must have been as a girl. Quite above my touch," said Lord Henry, who had been listening. "Mary," he said, turning to his wife, "you have apparently been wasting away for want of military company. Perhaps we may find a house in a camp-town; then you might entertain men like the major every day!"

This sally did not disconcert his wife in the least.

"There are precious few military men such as Major Trilling," said Lady Mary. "He is quite out of the ordinary, I am surprised you do not see it."

"Hoist by my own petard," said His Lordship.

"Lady Mary," said the major with a slight smile, "I am thoroughly undeserving of this flattery you heap upon me. It is merely that your own charm brings out the best in me."

Lord Terbury turned the conversation to events in France, but the major's news, no matter how tactfully delivered, was not encouraging. The major had recently talked with an officer who was attached to Stewart.

"He had just returned from France, and he said a major battle was in the making at Bayonne. Only the weather conditions had prevented it, but the day he left, the weather was clearing. He did not see Fane and Terbury, but said he had heard they were there."

"So it is possible that the battle is taking place even now," said Lord Terbury unhappily.

"Perhaps . . . please, ladies, do not look so unhappy! They are quite safe, I am sure. Wellington does not mean to lose such men—and I would rather be in battle alongside Nick Fane than any man I know."

Harriet brightened at this. "Yes, I feel it is so. He will protect Laurence, won't he? Laurence is so young. . . ."

"That he will, Miss Harriet; you need have no fear if he's with Nick."

Alicia found the major's views on Fane surprising. Trilling seemed a levelheaded military man, very different in character and style from Lord Fane. But he had nothing but the highest praise for Fane, both as man and soldier.

Bustle in the hall indicated that the Marlowes had at last arrived. They entered, making profuse apologies for their lateness, caused by a lost necklace.

Mr. Marlowe, who had made his money when a piece of land

he owned was found to contain rich coal deposits, was a stout little man with very strong opinions. He was now immensely wealthy, but, as Lady Mary said, it was obvious that he could not forget his past. He had been born the ne'er-do-well younger son of an impoverished peer, and now he felt obliged to prove himself a success. Despite his manner, it became clear to Alicia that he was quite intelligent and essentially kind. His marriage to a merchant's daughter had scandalized his family, but it looked to be a happy one nonetheless.

His wife was overdressed and wore far too much jewelry, but she was a forthright woman, with no pretensions to being anything but what she was: the daughter of a merchant, a devoted wife and mother.

The parents were no preparation for the daughter: Charlotte Marlowe was a girl of great social poise and intelligence; Alicia saw that at once.

She had the large, innocent eyes of a child, but her wicked sense of humor had nothing in common with childhood. Her vitality made one forget to notice that she was not really pretty. A pair of sparkling gray eyes was her one asset, since she was too dark-complected for current ideas of beauty.

Like her mother, she was overdecorated with jewels, but Alicia became convinced that this was to please Mr. Marlowe, who was obviously proud of the quality of these stones.

The last member of the party was Stanford Lowell, introduced as Charlotte's fiancé. He appeared to be constantly meditating on something known only to him. When she later learned that he was an inventor, Alicia understood his distant civility. But after a conversation with him, she was at a loss to understand why the vivacious Charlotte was engaged to a man who was her opposite in every respect: thoroughly nice, but thoroughly uninterested in anything but machinery.

At dinner the major sat between Alicia and Mrs. Marlowe, but Charlotte, to Alicia's regret, was placed at the other end, near Lord Terbury, who clearly enjoyed her company.

All was amiability between the major and Mrs. Marlowe until she inquired where the major was staying.

"At Bayhall, some five miles from here in Kent."

"Near Tunbridge Wells, I know the place. Is Lady Fane there now? A charming woman, I believe."

"Yes, she is there, and she is very charming. Like her grandson, she has a gift for making people feel quite at home, even on short acquaintance."

"I am afraid we disagree *there*, major. We knew Nicholas as a young man, Mr. Marlowe and I. *Then* he was quite a wonderful boy. But when he came to his majority, the money spoiled him, I'm afraid. He became a patten-card dandy, wasting his fortune, cutting old friends! No, I don't mean us. But we were at an assembly in Bath, when he refused to acknowledge Lady Anne, now Lady Dunstan. And she had been part of his circle once—I don't know whether you know that tale. And he continues this inhuman coldness to this day! Absurd, as if *she* were responsible for what happened."

This speech was heard by the entire table, and an uncomfortable pause ensued.

Alicia found Mrs. Marlowe's remarks to be of great interest, and she did not think her far wrong in her estimate of Fane's character.

"I am sorry you think so of him," the major said finally, "but Nick Fane is my friend. And I rather think there is more to his dislike of Lady Dunstan than we may know. He is most certainly not the sort of man to do such things to merely demonstrate his consequence." The major was obviously very uncomfortable and clearly did not wish to discuss the matter further.

But Mrs. Marlowe did not leave it at that; she allowed that a friend could not be expected to be objective about Fane, and she asked Alicia if she did not find Fane "high in the instep."

Alicia looked at the major apologetically. "I must admit that he has sometimes seemed arrogant . . . but I suppose he has been spoiled by society and cannot help it—and I have seen him be kind, on occasion."

"Damning with faint praise, Miss Tierney." The major smiled, however. "I shall have to warn Nick that he is in your bad books."

Lady Mary effectively ended this line of discussion by asking if they had heard of the splendid dinner the Regent had just given the Russian delegation.

"Of course," she said dryly, "it was the least he could do, when you consider that their reason for coming was to convey the orders of Russian knighthood to the Regent, from the Emperor of Russia himself."

"I was told," said the major, "by a friend who was there, that there was a temple in the middle of the table. Decorated with basso relievos. And, can you image what they portrayed on the borders? The King, Queen, and the Regent himself, in their roles as patrons of the arts!"

Stanford Lowell, hitherto silent, was aroused to speech by this description.

"The man's a parasite! There are people suffering in this country, and the Regent's having himself immortalized on a dinner table!"

As Lord Terbury said later, this was quite true, but hardly the thing one said in polite society.

Charlotte chose this time to address her fiancé for the first and last time during the evening.

"I am sure your good heart does you credit, Lowell, but it

does not do to dwell on matters which neither you nor anyone else here is able to do anything about. A dinner party is no place for reforms."

It struck Alicia that her attitude was that of an adult speaking to a child. Why in the world were these two engaged?

After dinner, card tables were set up, but Alicia said she had no desire to play.

"Why, how very convenient," said the major, "since I did not wish to play either. This way the numbers will be even."

"Do you dislike cards, major?"

"No, I don't dislike them, but I cannot take them seriously enough. It is always a game to me, and real gamblers, like Lady Mary, find this annoying."

"I am uninterested," said Alicia, "unless there are wagers of some size. My father and I used to play piquet for hours—but always with something riding on the game. In any case, I would much rather hear of your adventures in the Peninsula than play whist."

"A soldier can never resist an invitation like that!"

The stories he told her were both funny and sad, and Alicia found herself liking him a great deal.

He began a story about regimental dandies who were in the habit of having their men actually hold umbrellas over them during the battle, so that their beautiful uniforms would not become soaked by the rain.

Alicia could not resist interrupting him.

"I must own that I should have thought that Lord Fane was such a dandy-soldier."

"How very odd. Of course he is a very well-turned-out fellow—no mistake about that. But whatever he does, he does well: when he is being a soldier, he is not being a dandy. It is really too bad that Nick has so ruined his chances with you."

It crossed Alicia's mind that the major might have heard about Fane's proposal.

"He never had any chances with me, major. I must admit that when you speak of him, I hardly recognize it as the same man. It seemed to me—wrongly, it appears—that he was playing at war as a way to defeat his ennui."

"Ah, I do not dispute that ennui may be the reason, but it in no way changes the fact that he is a fine soldier—and friend. He is a dandy, and I do not share his love of dress, but he is also able to laugh at himself, unlike others I have known. Surely, even with you, that must excuse a great deal."

Alicia shook her head. "You lead me to the unpleasant conclusion that I bring out the worst in him. Rather like this Lady Dunstan."

"No, no, it is quite a different matter, she—" Here he stopped, unwilling to finish his sentence. He laughed and continued smoothly. "I find myself talking to you as if to an old army comrade, Miss Tierney."

"Please call me Alicia, I don't in the least feel like a miss. You were saying, about Lady Anne?"

"No, I am not at liberty to discuss what I know of the lady. But you are very wrong about Nick—you must believe me. Of course I don't know how he is with women. . . ."

"He is a perfectly delightful fellow," said Charlotte, as she and Alicia watched the major take his leave.

"Yes, the kind of man who makes one feel *safe*."

Charlotte was surprised. "That is precisely what I was thinking myself!"

Alicia smiled at her. "You know what that means, don't you? It means that we should be friends, being kindred spirits."

"Oh, I knew that already," said Charlotte nonchalantly. "You are, after all, the only intelligent young woman who has ever visited my neighborhood. How could we *not* be friends!"

20

AN INEXPLICABLE GIFT

Christmas was made much of at Hansdown. Presents were piled under the tree a week in advance, money and food were sent to the poor of the village, and the mummers and the choirs came on Christmas Eve.

Neither Harriet nor Alicia had ever taken part in such a lavish Christmas. It appeared that the entire county had come to call at Hansdown House, and they were all offered some of the famous Terbury punch and tarts.

Christmas Day itself was celebrated with a goose and a baron of beef, and the ladies agreed that they would have to have their clothes let out if they continued to dine in this fashion. After this substantial afternoon meal, the presents were opened. They ranged from diamonds to saddles, but everyone seemed equally content.

Alicia had received a silk shawl and several sets of books, with which she was very happy, much to the surprise of Lady Mary.

"I don't consider books to be a gift," said Lady Mary, patting her new diamond necklace. "They are so colorless, so humdrum...."

"No," laughed Alicia, "I should certainly never give them to *you*, but I would rather have this set of Sterne and this edition of Pope than your necklace."

"Dearest Alicia, you have very narrow horizons. People will say you are a blue if you do not keep this quiet!"

"Well, I shan't read in public, then, but you know very well that you read constantly—and no one calls *you* a bluestocking."

"Yes," said Lady Mary, with a satisfied air, "but I am a marvelous dissembler. My beaux were always convinced, for example, that I was absolutely innocent of knowledge. They were surprised that I could point out London on a map, I am sure, so giddy did I seem."

Just when everyone thought that the last gift had been opened. Lord Terbury announced that there was one more, and handed Harriet an oblong box.

The box contained an exquisite antique ivory fan.

"It is from Laurence!" cried Harriet after reading the note. "He must have bought it that last day . . . with all he had to do . . . and I cannot send him anything."

"Perhaps the major will know a way to do that," said Alicia quickly, seeing that Harriet was near to tears.

"I think I will go up and lie down for a bit," said Harriet. "I will join you when the major and the Stapletons arrive."

Lady Mary and Alicia exchanged a knowing look. Harriet was undoubtedly going to have a good cry in peace.

Alicia went to the kitchen with Lady Mary. Every surface was covered with cakes, pies, and candies, all sent as presents by the villagers who had received Christmas money.

"My father used to give presents to the poor at Christmas," said Alicia. "But my brother has stopped the custom. Too wasteful, he says. It is most instructive, what different natures people of the same family may have."

"You have only to know Harriet's mother and sister to see the truth of *that*," said Lady Mary in a low tone. "You know, they will be coming here after New Year's. . . ."

Lady Mary caught Alicia's incredulous expression.

"You are wondering why I did not prevent it? There are many reasons. I wish my cousin Edith to have nothing but affection for me—at least until Laurence has married his Harriet, which will not be for some time."

"Do you really think the Stomaways would not consent, ma'am? Are they still for Camerley, or some other beau?"

"No, but Edith is quite capricious. She is capable of changing in a moment of pique, and I don't wish to give her any reason to prevent the match. Harriet is underage, you know, and without her parents' permission, she can do nothing but go to the Border for a runaway marriage—and that I will not permit!"

"I can't imagine that Harriet would ever entertain such an idea. Does not Mr. Stornaway have anything to say to the matter?"

"No, he is down in the country with his hunting and riding; he is run by Julia and her mother."

Lord Terbury came in to ask his wife if he might fire Jake, the gardener.

"What has he done now?"

"Spoiled my Christmas, that's what he's done! He told me just now, when he brought in the hothouse flowers, how his uncle chopped his finger off last Christmas while chopping wood. Then, as if that weren't enough, he insisted on describing the stages of his cousin's death from blood poisoning. All the colors the poor fellow turned, and so on. Mary, I cannot bear the fellow!"

"But he is such a good gardener, Henry."

"In some peculiar way," mused Alicia, who had also heard

some of Jakes's hair-raising tales, "he derives enjoyment from these narratives. Rather like Jellicoe describing her aches and pains."

"You show your youth, dear. When you are older, you will discover that Jellicoe is right: aches and pains are the most interesting subjects."

Harriet, who had just come down, protested.

"But aunt, I have never known you to talk of such things."

"Of course, I am made of sterner stuff. In conversation I prefer scandal, and if that is not to be had, I make do with a little simple gossip. But that does not mean that I do not find my own aches and pains to be of absorbing interest. My dresser Robbins and I talk of little else."

Lord Terbury told her that he thought she talked of them to make herself interesting; actually, she had nothing wrong with her at all.

"And now, young ladies, we must prepare for the charades and poetry recital. Our guests will soon be here, and you must find comic poems to recite."

Alicia suggested that she recite parts of "The Rape of the Lock," and His Lordship mimicked shock.

"Too racy, m'dear. Shock Harriet—and the Stapletons."

Harriet started to protest that it was not that kind of rape when she saw the glint in Lord Terbury's eyes.

"Oh, I am so stupid sometimes! But he has such a sober expression when he says these things—I can never tell if he's serious."

Alicia saw that Harriet felt left out at times, when everyone around her was laughing at something she didn't understand. Watching Harriet play with the little white kitten, a present from one of the farmers, Alicia wondered if this innocence were really its own protection. Would Harriet ever have to know about the other, less pleasant, side of life, or would Laurence's love serve to protect her from real misery?

And what of herself? St. Clair, for example, was not the man to protect one from anything, unlike Major Trilling. It was too bad that Major Trilling did not make her pulse race in the way St. Clair did. But, of course, she did not require protection in the same way that Harriet did.

Harriet and Alicia were going through the books of poetry in the library when Jellicoe came in to announce that a messenger had arrived from London.

"It's something for you, Miss Alicia. A present, I think!"

There was no return address, and interrogation of the messenger revealed only that a servant had brought it to the London office.

Alicia opened the outer box and found a smaller one inside, wrapped in silver paper.

"It is from Rundell and Bridge," said Lady Mary, who had been summoned by Jellicoe. "I recognize their silver paper and scarlet ribbons."

Inside the box, nestled on white satin, was a butterfly brooch, set with pearls and pinheads of enameled gold.

There was no name on the card, but in the upper right hand corner, written very small, were the words, "Give me more love, or more disdain."

Lady Mary looked at the brooch and then picked up the card.

"But what does it mean, and who is it from?"

"I am not *certain*," said Alicia, her eyes twinkling, "but I *think* it is from St. Clair. Carew is one of the poets he quotes to ladies."

Alicia's tone was ironical, but Lady Mary could see that she was delighted with the present. Lady Mary had the sudden conviction that matters between St. Clair and her goddaughter were threatening to become serious.

"Do you happen to know the rest of the quote?"

"Yes, I do—my father always liked Carew." A fact that St. Clair knew perfectly well, Alicia reflected, from their talk in the park one day.

> Give me more love, or more disdain;
>> The torrid or the frozen zone
>
> Bring equal ease unto my pain,
>> The temperate affords me none:
>
> Either extreme of love or hate
>> Is sweeter than a calm estate.

"Oh, Alicia! It is the most exciting thing! He thinks you have been too cold to him." Harriet was thrilled by this romantic gesture.

"It is quite an expensive bauble." Lady Mary said.

"Poor Robert," sighed Alicia, "wasting money on me. He should have paid some of his gambling debts instead."

Harriet was shocked by this attitude. "Alicia, it is the most romantic thing imaginable, and you are being so—so—"

"Lacking in sensitivity. Yes, I know. But really, he is the most accomplished flirt! He is afraid that I shall forget him while I am in the country—and this is the result."

Lady Mary knew that she should feel relieved that the girl had such a realistic view of St. Clair, but she did not. It crossed her mind that Alicia knew all of his sins but forgave him every one. How had this friendship sprung up so quickly . . . and what did Alicia expect from the man?

Lady Mary was given further food for thought later that evening when yet another, even more unexpected, gift was delivered.

It was unfortunate, everyone agreed afterwards, that young Mrs. Stapleton, an indefatigable gossip, was present when Major Trilling arrived with the package under his arm.

"I see you are about to begin a game of charades," said the major, "but let me deliver this present before you begin."

He walked over to Alicia's chair and dropped a small package into her lap.

"Perhaps it is from the same person?" Harriet theorized.

"No," said Alicia, unwrapping the oval snuffbox, "it is not from the same person."

"My dear!" exclaimed Lady Mary, "Von Blarenberghe scenes of Bellevue! A priceless object, in the most exquisite taste!"

"Most unfortunate that I don't take snuff," said Alicia. "The only place it will be seen is in my drawing room."

Harriet examined the box from all sides and then opened it.

"There is something else inside! A ring!"

Alicia lifted out an antique rose-cut diamond ring, which Lady Mary immediately pronounced to be Jacobean and quite lovely.

"But who can have sent you such shockingly valuable presents?"

Major Trilling, who had been sitting silently throughout this scene, spoke.

"They are from Nick Fane."

This announcement produced a sensation. Lady Mary, aware of the rejected proposal, was stunned, as was Harriet. Lord Terbury looked puzzled, and Mrs. Stapleton, feeling she would burst with the news, immediately began to think of whom she would tell the next day.

Alicia did not gratify anyone's curiosity about why Lord Fane should send her such presents and seemed to be the least surprised of anyone present. For the rest of the evening, she appeared completely taken up with the charades and poetry recital, and made no mention of the gifts to anyone.

When the major took his leave of them, Alicia managed to be alone with him for a few minutes in the hall.

"Major, you really must take back these presents. I cannot keep them—they are far too valuable. And I think you know why I am reluctant . . ."

"The rejected proposal? Yes, I heard of it, but not from Nick."

"Well, there you are. I cannot conceive of why he should do such a thing—unless it is to cause me embarrassment, and to throw all the other presents I have received into the shade!"

The major looked unhappy. "I had thought better of you, Alicia. Do these beautiful things really embarrass you? I don't believe it. You would find any present from Nick unpleasant, because you hold to such prejudice against him. He meant only to give you the ring he had bought for you when he proposed—he said it was your ring, whether you married him or not. He gave it to me just before he left, knowing I was going to Bayhall."

"You have read me a sermon, sir, and I am chastised. Lord Fane is lucky in his friends. Very well, to show that I am not an ungracious chit, I shall keep the presents. But only so that you will not think ill of me."

"I think you nothing but charming, and I envy the man who gets you."

"Major," said Alicia with mock severity, "you have spent too much of the evening flirting with Mrs. Stapleton. I shall answer you in her style: 'Oh, la, sir, I vow you are a breaker of hearts—and I just a country wife!'"

"A very good imitation. Tell me, it seemed to me that you knew that the presents were from Nick before I said it—did you?"

"Yes, I *had* seen the snuffbox before," said Alicia, remembering the night of The Silver Tree.

This answer left the major more puzzled than ever. Fane had never used that box; it had formed part of his permanent collection, never leaving his house. When could Alicia have seen it?

21

AN UNFORGETTABLE EPISODE

It surprised no one that the vivacious Miss Marlowe and the unconventional Miss Tierney found each other interesting. But few would have guessed at the degree of intimacy this friendship had reached in a short time. That they would become friends was due to their personalities and would have happened in any case; that their friendship would develop so quickly was due to Alicia's need to discuss St. Clair and his present, a subject that she was unwilling to bring up with either Lady Mary or Harriet, for reasons she herself did not quite acknowledge.

Alicia had rarely felt the need to confide in a friend. Indeed, other than her father, she had had very few friends in her life, but now she felt an overwhelming desire to talk about St. Clair, and Charlotte seemed by far the best person. She was old beyond her years, and very tolerant.

When Alicia described the presents of Christmas Day, Charlotte's reaction was unlooked for.

"Well, St. Clair certainly must have you on his mind," said Charlotte, "but I confess I am more intrigued by Nick Fane— such an unexpected thing! It does not fit in at all with what I have heard of him. Although I have never even seen him, he is quite well known in these parts, you know. They say he is a terribly proud, disagreeable person, although there are always men like the major, who say otherwise."

"Whatever his reason, he has certainly succeeded in putting me in the wrong," said Alicia, who wanted to talk of St. Clair, not Fane.

"I have it! He did it to draw attention to the fact that he is generous to you, despite your refusal of his suit! How very cunning of him."

"And the worst of it is that I *particularly* like that snuffbox, and I don't want to banish it to some dusty cupboard. I'm sure he counted on that."

"Oh, Alicia!" said Charlotte, pushing her brown curls back from her face with an impatient gesture. "Don't you see what you should have done? You should have been extremely gracious, as if it was just what you expected. Perhaps it is not too late. I doubt that the major can write and tell him. You must begin to tell everyone how *kind*, how *thoughtful* Fane is."

"Charlotte, you are a Machiavelli. Of course, I see now, that you say it, that I did precisely the wrong thing."

But Charlotte did not seem to be listening.

"And how did he know it?" she said suddenly.

"Know . . . what?"

"That you liked that snuffbox. He had shown it to you?"

Alicia looked at the snuffbox which lay on the table beside them. Should she tell Charlotte the truth, or should she lie? The intelligent brown eyes had a question in them, but Charlotte was already saying that of course it was none of her affair, that Alicia should forgive her impertinence.

"Mama has always told me that I shall someday fall into a dreadful scrape because of my curiosity," she finished.

"No, I don't think so," said Alicia with a warm smile. "You will, however, find out a great deal that is not to your liking."

Charlotte looked at her and said with great conviction that she did not think that she could dislike anything about Alicia.

Touched by this, Alicia took a deep breath and began the story of Farnsworth's visit to The Silver Tree.

At the end of the recital Charlotte was silent for a moment.

"Alicia, you terrify me," she said at last.

"Then I shan't tell you anything else."

"You mean to say there is more? Well, don't tell me now. First let me get used to the idea that you dressed as a man and went to a gambling club!"

It was not only Alicia who enjoyed the possibility of discussing things with a sympathetic friend. Some days later, when they were out riding, Alicia mentioned that she was beginning to miss London.

"I can imagine. I have only been there a few times, but I loved it! I do wish I could go with you," said Charlotte with longing.

"What prevents you from doing just that? You could stay with me in my new house."

"What prevents me? Stanford. My parents. My life."

This was obviously the time to ask Charlotte the question she had been longing to have answered.

"You are very much in love with Stanford, I suppose."

"He is very kind, very good," began Charlotte.

"Of course, these are not the qualities one wishes in one's beloved," said Alicia dryly.

"Exactly. He adores me—do you know how tedious it is to be adored? No matter how uncivil I am to him, he forgives me."

"That is, of course, a great defect . . . but if you feel this way, why are you engaged to this paragon of virtue?"

"My parents, of course. The best parents in the world, who have spoiled me dreadfully—and they wish me to marry this man. Our lands march together, our families have always been close . . . and they know that Stanford is kind and intelligent—but completely wrapped up in his work. Stanford needs a wife who would share his interests. I know myself a little. I am frivolous in many ways, and I need a very different sort of man—one who would entertain me."

Later, after they had changed from their riding clothes, they sat in Charlotte's room, having tea.

"And did you ever meet the sort of man who could entertain you?" asked Alicia.

"Yes, during my season in London two years ago. But I knew that I could not possibly interest him, so I made no effort. I am not pretty, and in London that is everything—especially with such men. Once men get to know me, they like me, even fall in love with me—but it is very hard to attract their notice."

It was true that Charlotte was not exactly pretty—her complexion was dark, and her hair was of the most unromantic medium brown. But her sparkling gray eyes, vivacity, and stylish figure were assets.

"I know someone in London who would make you very *noticeable*, if not beautiful. You have an elegant figure, and with the right gowns . . ." Alicia said, thinking of the transformation Madame Désirée had effected.

"But I'll never get to London," Charlotte said flatly.

"Charlotte, you must not sacrifice youself just because your parents love you! I am sure that they would much rather you be happy. Why don't you tell them that I have invited you for a few months—you must know how to get 'round them. As for Stanford, he deserves a better wife than you would be to him, and you should tell him so."

"You make it sound so simple, but it is not! You cannot understand how much they wish me to marry Stanford."

"That may be true—I am sure I do not understand. But it is my experience that when a person wants something badly enough, she can make it happen."

It was not boredom that made Alicia wish to return to London; there was quite enough of interest to her at Hansdown, especially now that her groom, Potts, a former soldier, was teaching her to shoot. No, her reasons for wishing to leave were directly related to the arrival of Edith Stornaway.

Harriet's mother had managed to infect Hansdown House with her own unpleasantness, criticizing everyone and everything, exasperating Lady Mary beyond words. But Lady Mary was forced to hold her tongue for fear of destroying her son's chances of marrying Harriet.

Edith knew that she had the whiphand, and occasionally pretended that there was another suitor she favored for Harriet.

Harriet herself seemed deaf to the mother's remarks, and spent as much time as she could with Major Trilling, who thought up new plans for her entertainment daily.

Edith was as disagreeable as ever, but Julia, everyone agreed, had changed. She had been pretty enough before, but now there was a kind of glow about her, a softness that was new. The sly expression and the air of calculation seemed to have disappeared as well.

Jellicoe's opinion was that Miss Julia was in love, and Harriet agreed. No other explanation seemed possible.

One evening when the young ladies read *Childe Harold*, there was further reason to suppose that this was indeed the case. When it was her turn to read aloud, Julia became quite impassioned.

"You read that with great feeling," remarked Harriet.

Her sister looked up from the page. "That is the way I think men should be! Unafraid to live—it must be wonderful to love like that, following one's feelings. And to love such a man, a man whose passions take him beyond the everyday conventions."

It was unpleasant, Alicia discovered, to hear something very like one's own views uttered by a person one considered inferior in intellect.

Harriet looked surprised.

"But Julia, how is this? You have always told me that I should marry the wealthiest man I could find—a marriage of convenience, in fact."

Julia's smile expressed a consciousness of her own superiority.

"That was . . . *before*. I have come to understand that passion is as important as wealth, perhaps more so."

Harriet could not keep from smiling a little.

"I see it—you are in love."

At first Julia denied it vehemently, but finally she admitted that it was true.

"And who is he?" asked Alicia, who really felt very little interest in the answer.

"Oh, I cannot tell you! It is too early yet. But he is very like *this* man," she said proudly, indicating the copy of *Childe Harold*.

Both Harriet and Alicia agreed that the change in Julia was all to the good. Lady Mary, however, took a different view.

"You may find her adoration of the Byronic harmless, but I do not. Such a girl as that is capable of very undesirable behavior when under the influence of such ideas."

The change for the better in the daughter could not make up for the mother, however. The only respite the Terburys could enjoy from Edith's ill temper were card parties or dinners, when she could be foisted off on some other guest who enjoyed talking of illness, or at least hearing of it.

As a result, Hansdown House saw an endless stream of evening entertainments, which, as a matter of course included the popular Major Trilling.

Alicia was as friendly as ever to him, but she was not inclined to speak to him alone, feeling that she had been put in the wrong with him.

"If only you will permit me to call on you before I leave," he said one evening, "I promise not to say another word about common acquaintances. I am leaving for France in a few days."

"Oh, I *am* sorry, I did not know! So soon . . . we shall miss you dreadfully, you know."

"Is tomorrow afternoon convenient?"

Alicia hesitated.

"What is it? Would the evening be better?"

"No, all these people . . . it is just that—" Here Alicia whispered. "I have been taking shooting lessons from Potts near the lake, and I can't let anyone know—Charlotte is the only one who does. Lady Mary does not think it is feminine, you know."

The major found her the next afternoon, dressed for riding, shooting at a wooden target with a small silver pistol.

"Is it not a lovely little pistol, Major? Potts found it for me. Much better than a rifle. I need never fear the footpads now!"

He watched her finish her practice and was impressed by her accuracy. He asked her why she had taken it up.

"Boredom. But now I like it for itself. It's like driving fast in a curricle, or dancing the waltz. A sensation of . . . freedom."

The major found this remark extremely interesting, coming as it did from a well-bred young woman.

They talked for a while of his plans, and he promised to visit Curzon Street when he returned to London again.

"Major," said Alicia constrainedly, "I must apologize for my behavior. I do not wish you to tell Nick Fane how unhandsomely

I accepted his gift. Let him think it was appreciated . . . and I do love the snulfbox, as he knows. And here, I have worn the ring today."

"Yes, but I see that you are also wearing St. Clair's butterfly. Beware—it is hard to serve two masters."

"But I serve no master; that is my secret. But please, do not tell him how it was. I would not want him to think me so small-minded . . . which, of course, I was."

"I had no intention of telling him in any case. I expect that he and Laurence will have moved on, actually, and it may be some time before I see them."

Major Trilling rode back to the house with her and said good-bye, having already taken his leave of everyone else.

"Here, a kiss on the cheek, Alicia. If ever I can be of help to you, let me know. We have a mutual acquaintance, you know, Jack Worthing. A dreadful gamester, always on the town, but a very good fellow all the same. He will know how to reach me once I am back in England."

Alicia was more touched by this offer than she cared to show.

"Very well, I shall ask him. Major, you have made my stay here far pleasanter than it would have been otherwise, and I thank you. Now go, before I start crying, like Harriet."

Still under the influence of this parting, she went back into the house, and looked in on Harriet, Charlotte, and Julia in the sewing room, where they were poring over the latest issue of *La Belle Assemblée*, just arrived from London.

"So you said good-bye to the major," said Charlotte. "And did he make you an offer? I often thought he wanted to."

"No, nothing of the sort. There was never anything but friendship between us."

"I shall miss him," said Harriet sadly. "Somehow it was a little like having Laurence home when he was here."

"Yes, it was. I must go and change. I am filthy from my ride."

"You do not at all look like you have ridden for an hour," said Julia admiringly. "Did the major give you that butterfly brooch?"

Alicia's hand went to her throat, where the brooch was pinned to her stock.

"No, he did not. I received it as a Christmas present."

Seeing that Alicia was not in the mood to talk, Charlotte attempted to distract Julia.

"Oh, my dear," she said brightly, "haven't you heard about the mysterious presents? This one is from Robert St. Clair, and came with the most killingly *romantical* lines of poetry. *Then* she received a snuffbox and ring frpm Lord Fane. Quite a Christmas Day!"

Julia seemed intensely interested. She asked Alicia if she had known St. Clair for very long.

"No, some four or five months—that is all."

"As to that," teased Charlotte, "it's not the length of time, it is the force of the attachment that counts. And any man who would send lines to the effect of 'give me more love or more disdain,' is hanging out for a wife, if you ask me."

"You mean he is courting you, Alicia?" asked Julia quietly.

"No, it is nothing so settled—whatever is the matter, child? You look quite white."

Charlotte saw the angry tears and gestured to Alicia to leave, but it was too late.

"I know what it is," said Julia with a bitter laugh. "It is the money. You are the Drake heiress, are you not? I wish you well of such a marriage, made for money!"

"What a peculiar thing to say," protested Harriet. "What can you be thinking of, talking to Alicia in such a way? As to money, you yourself always talked of nothing but a wealthy peer."

"That was before . . . before I knew Robert!" she said furiously. "He will never marry you. He loves me—I know it!"

Here the violently upset young girl ran from the room, crying. Charlotte was the first to recover.

"I am to blame. If I had not volunteered the information—but who could have known?"

"Do not blame yourself," said Alicia mechanically. "She was sure to discover it sooner or later. Obviously the child has had some kind of flirtation with St. Clair and has taken it seriously. I remember now that Mrs. Stornaway and she met him once, in the country, some time ago."

Alicia was inclined to feel sorry for the girl; she herself had taken many things too seriously when young. Of course St. Clair was capable of anything, even leading on such a young girl.

"It can be nothing," said Harriet. "My sister has magnified a few moments of flirtation out of all proportion."

Harriet seemed more disturbed than she should have been, and Alicia could not imagine what the cause was.

"Oh, I am not worried, Harriet. I know what a shocking flirt Robert is! He is thoroughly disreputable in these matters, which is why all the women in London are dying for him. I think your sister is the one in need of consolation; you had best go to her."

She left, and Charlotte and Alicia looked at each other.

"So this is why she was so happy—" began Charlotte.

"She was in love with him," finished Alicia, whose sense of humor was returning. "The wretched flirt! He undoubtedly led her to think he was passionately in love, and the poor little—"

"Fool thought he meant it. But I fail to see that she is either poor or little. I'm going to get myself some sherry. Would you like some?"

"Yes. We must think what this means. I think that now we have an excellent reason to return to London ahead of time!

After all, Edith will be angry, and my presence would contribute to a great deal of unpleasantness here."

"And Edith positively *loathes* me," said Charlotte with satisfaction. "She imagines that I am always making fun of her, and since she is right, I understand it."

"But how are you going to tell your parents?" asked Alicia.

"In a stroke of brilliance, I have decided to ask Lady Terbury to intercede. A wonder I had not thought of it earlier! They positively *grovel* before her magnificence (as they should), and regard her as an authority on everything."

"And why is that? Your father is a gentleman, and they did not strike me as the sort to toad-eat the nobility."

"Of couse they aren't. But Lady Mary, as you must know, is quite a shrewd businesswoman. She put them in the way of some shares of an Indian company, and they all made money. So my father regards her as slightly higher than the Deity. To be a peeress is noble, but to make your friends rich—is divine."

Alicia laughed, but she felt a little sorry for Charlotte. What must it be to love your parents, and at the same time to see them objectively.

Any lingering doubts as to the wisdom of returning to London were speedily erased by Mrs. Stornaway herself. She came into the room, a glacial stare in her protuberant eyes. She informed Alicia that she wished to speak to her and made it clear that Charlotte was not to stay. Charlotte chose to pretend that she did not understand this, and when Edith said that sherry was bad for the digestion and that young women should not be drinking it during the day, Charlotte only smiled vaguely.

Seeing that the incorrigible Miss Marlowe had no intention of leaving, Edith began in her presence.

"I have been informed by my daughter of a lamentable state of affairs. There has obviously been a serious misunderstanding.

Who is to blame I cannot say but I have my suspicions that certain parties have been *misled*. I hope you understand what you must do."

"I am afraid that I do not understand what you mean, Mrs. Stornaway," said Alicia, all amiability.

Mrs. Stornaway felt this was too much. She, a loving parent had received several shocks, her constitution—frail at the best of times—had been suffering from the overrich cuisine of Hansdown House. And now she, a woman of some standing and wealth, was being condescended to by a red-headed nobody!

"You understand me well enough! And I can tell you this! You—you—you spoiler of happiness! Harriet will not marry Laurence Terbury if you become engaged to St. Clair! I know your sort—you no doubt have a bag of tricks to use on him. My daughter is young, innocent, and pure—what chance would she have! But if you do, there will be no marriage between Laurence and Harriet! We will not ally ourselves with such a family."

Alicia tried to point out that she herself was not really related to Laurence, and that in any case Mrs. Stornaway was Lady Terbury's cousin and was therefore already allied with that family.

But Edith had worked herself into a fine fit of hysterics and had no interest in reason or logic.

"Hussies!" she spat at them. "And how will it be to be married for your money—"

"Robert can only marry for money," said Alicia, "so why shouldn't it be mine?"

Such equanimity only infuriated the lady further. She finally collapsed on the settee, claiming she was suffering an attack. Alicia called for the servants, who had been lurking just outside the door.

After this scene, it required very little to convince Lady Mary that Alicia should go back to town early and that Charlotte should accompany her.

"Well, I must say I shall be glad to go back to that dusty, odoriferous city. Spring is when I long to be in the country, but town is nice in the winter. But I have enjoyed this visit, godmamma, more than I can say. Such a lovely Christmas and New Year's!"

"Too bad that harridan had to arrive and spoil everything. Well, I daresay you two will find ways of amusing yourselves— you know there is the Frost Fair in London now. Everyone is on the ice, my friends write me."

"But do not look so unhappy, godmamma! You will come soon, won't you?"

"Yes, as soon as I can—just in time to find out what you two have been up to, so be careful!"

That night Lady Mary tossed and turned in her bed, her head filled with a thousand worries. She knew her cousin. Edith was capable of preventing the marriage at the last minute. And then there was the problem of Alicia. She was certainly not in love with St. Clair, but he seemed to be the only man who held her interest—a hundred ladies of the *ton* would understand that—and Lady Mary had the uneasy conviction that the girl was going to marry him if he asked. And that present meant something. And what of Fane's snuffbox and ring?

She debated the matter for an hour and then decided she could not let the matter rest there, depending on the little knowledge Alicia had of men in general, and of St. Clair in particular. She must take action. She wrote:

Dear Torrance,

I wish a special favour from you, dear friend. It will seem peculiar to you, but I have a good reason for it, and will explain when I return to London.

I wish you to discover what may be known at the clubs, as well as from your less respectable sources, about Alexander St. Clair's nephew, Robert. His amours, current, or recently ended, what manner of man he is held to be by those who are not his intimates as well as those who are.

It is most important that you tell *no one* why you are asking about these things. In general it would be better to elicit the information without seeming to ask for it.

I ask this of you in response to your promise of old—that you would do what I asked, no matter what it was, in return for that small service I rendered you so many years ago.

I shall be back at Grosvenor Square within the month.

I remain, your affectionate.
Mary Terbury.

22

A RESCUE

Old Crawley thought it the worst weather he had ever driven in. The unusually large amount of snow combined with one of the longest stretches of freezing weather in anyone's memory had caused a large number of accidents all along the post roads. As he drove around a curve, he came upon a coach with a wheel off. He slowed down to look and saw that two women were standing beside it, looking terribly cold, even in their furs. He stopped and talked to the coachman, who was trying to repair the wheel enough to allow them to drive to the inn which was only two miles away.

Crawley pulled up a little way from them, got down, and asked his mistress if she would mind two ladies in the coach with her, as far as The Swan.

"Of course not, the poor creatures! They must be quite frozen."

Old Crawley happily walked over to the coachman and offered to take the ladies off his hands.

The two ladies, despite the cold, seemed in the highest of spirits.

"What an adventure," said the dark one. "I do hope it is an interesting lady in the coach!"

"I don't care if she's the most tedious woman imaginable, Charlotte. I just want to get my feet warm!" said the other.

Alicia and Charlotte climbed into the coach, and discovered that the lady inside was far from uninteresting.

Even in the dim light of the coach, it could be seen that she was very fashionably turned out, and the interior of the coach proclaimed its owner as a wealthy member of the *ton*.

"We are most grateful, ma'am," began Charlotte. "We were just preparing to walk the two miles to the village."

"But you would have caught your death of cold," said the lady in a mellifluous voice. "No one should walk in such weather! Here, do take some hot bricks for your feet."

"Just what I was dreaming of," said Alicia. "These kid boots are very pretty, but give no Warmth at all, I'm afraid. Do let us know to whom we are indebted. I am Alicia Tierney, and this is Charlotte Marlowe."

The lady smiled charmingly and introduced herself as Lady Anne Dunstan.

Charlotte felt Alicia give a start when she heard the name, and then remembered that this was the same woman who had been discussed in connection with Lord Fane.

They rode to the inn in high spirits, and ordered a substantial dinner.

In the light of the inn, Anne Dunstan proved to be even more attractive than she had seemed to be in the coach. Fashionably slender and ethereally fair, she had the finely sculptured features that were considered the height of beauty by the portrait painters. Her conversation contributed to the impression of a warm and gracious lady.

Charlotte proposed a toast to their friends fighting in France.

"You have young men with Wellington?" asked Lady Anne.

"Yes, my godmother's son, Laurence Terbury."

"He is gone as an aide to Lord Fane," added Charlotte, without thinking.

The wineglass which was on its way up to the lady's mouth stopped in mid arc.

"Do you mean *Nick* Fane?"

"Yes, you know him?" Alicia had decided to pretend complete ignorance.

"Yes . . . once we were rather good friends . . . I am quite surprised that he is gone to France. He was always used to make fun of those who took the war seriously."

She did not say anything about him, but turned the conversation to literature. She disliked Byron, adored Scott, and had just purchased a rare edition of Cowper. Since Alicia shared these opinions, she began to ask what she knew of Mr. Scott—was he really as charming as everyone said?

Charlotte found literary conversations boring and excused herself, saying she was tired.

Lady Anne then invited Alicia to her room to examine the copy of Cowper. Cowper occuoied them for only a short time, however, and their conversation soon became more personal.

Anne mentioned her husband. Ferrar Dunstan, a wealthy man who had been some thirty years older than his bride when they married. Alicia asked sympathetically if she had been very young when she married.

"No, about twenty-four. I had been in love with someone else much earlier. But my family needed the money, and I was ready to sacrifice myself. But it wasn't really such a sacrifice. He was a perfectly nice man, and when he died five years ago, he left me very comfortably. I cannot say I regret it. It would have been

nice to marry a romantic young hussar, of course . . . but all that
is past, as is my youth."

Alicia protested that she looked no more than twenty-five,
which was the truth, to which Lady Anne answered that she was
thirty, and felt every day of it.

Lady Anne began to ask her about the Tierneys, and Alicia
found herself talking of her father's death, and the resultant
clash with her brother's wife, a woman she had always disliked.

"They wished me to marry a man I had nothing but contempt
for. But I feel that no marriage is better than the wrong one."

"Yes, you are right there," said Lady Anne with some warmth.
"But there are other things just as bad, and being a widow in
London is one of them! I do not mean a nice merchant's
widow—they receive respect in their circles—but in what are
conceived of as the highest circles in this country! My dear,
you cannot imagine the kind of proposals I have received, even
in the conservatory of Carlton House! The next time I marry,"
continued Lady Anne, "I shall marry for love, and nothing else!
And I must marry. Being a widow is the surest way to find out
which husbands are philandering. And sometimes turning away
a would-be lover can result in the most dreadful consequences
even if one is not a widow."

It seemed to Alicia that Anne had something quite specific
in mind.

"What sort of consequences?"

"Ah, I have drunk too much wine! But I can tell you this, it
was a *gentleman* long, long ago. . . . One day when I was home
alone, he came to visit. My maid left the room for a moment,
but I did not worry—this man was a friend, or so I thought.
He proceeded to make an indecent proposal, and before I knew
what was happening, he had taken me in his arms and was
taking familiarities which disgusted me. Of course I told him

in no uncertain terms that I wished nothing of the sort from him. Since that day we have not spoken. He did his best to cut me socially, but I rather think it has hurt his reputation more than mine. It is said that he will not disclose the reason why he is so implacable in his dislike of me. I alone understand why. His pride has not recovered from something that happened so many years ago. He will never forgive me for rejecting his advances."

It was easy enough for Alicia to supply the gentleman's name, and it remained only to hear it from Anne herself. When Alicia asked if the man might be Lord Fane, Anne acted very surprised.

"However did you guess? Please do not mention it to anyone! Few people know the true story . . . I suppose his anger is understandable—he thought no one could refuse him—but that is not what I hold against him. I hold him responsible for the death of my fiancé."

Here she turned away and looked into the fire. Alicia could see the tears forming in her eyes when she turned back.

"Perhaps we should not speak of it," said Alicia sympathetically.

"No, I have spoken of it to no one, and perhaps that is why the memory of that day is so fresh. The man who killed my fiancé insulted my honor, and that is why the duel took place. I have it on very good authority that Nick Fane is the man who put him up to it. Of course, they never thought that my fiancé would fight over such a remark—they did not guess at the depth of his love . . .

She put her hands up to her face, and a shiver seemed to run through her body.

"I have always known that Lord Fane was arrogant," began Alicia, "but I never thought him capable of quite so much baseness! I wonder that any people of feeling receive him!"

Anne was now in command of herself, and she smiled a bitter little smile.

"They do not know, most of them. You must remember, Alicia, that in our world rank and fortune count for everything. Even if they *did* know, it would hardly matter. You may be anything you like in the *ton* as long as you are not poor or without position. For example, Fane's mistress, Sibylla Crawford, is accepted in society because she is of good birth. And, of course. Fane undoubtedly tells *his* story well, even to you, I imagine!"

"No, he had never spoken of it to me. But I see that he is too well placed to feel the criticism due him for such conduct. There are many who dislike his behavior to you, but it goes further than that. . . ."

When Alicia had left Anne Dunstan late in the evening, she felt that she had made a very interesting acquaintance. There was something very sympathetic in Anne's manner that made one wish to confide in her, and Alicia thought that she might very well become a friend. They had promised to meet in London, and Alicia hoped they would. It was amusing to think of how Nick Fane would react if he came into her drawing room one day and found Lady Anne Dunstan sitting there.

The next morning. Charlotte had to shake Alicia several times before she would wake up.

"Alicia! We are leaving in twenty minutes! Potts will be very angry if we keep him waiting, and you haven't even had breakfast!"

Alicia seemed to wake up at once.

"Now, don't fly into the boughs! You go down and save me some bread—I'll eat it in the coach."

On the way to London, Alicia told Charlotte about Fane and Lady Anne.

Charlotte thought that Fane's behavior was monstrous and said she had very little doubt but it was true.

23
CURZON STREET

Great changes had been taking place in the house on Curzon Street while Alicia was at Hansdown. The new housekeeper, Melling, and the butler, Stilton, had seen to it that the last of the furniture was installed and all the servants' quarters repainted, down to the last scullery maid's room.

The result of all this activity was that when Alicia returned, her house seemed even nicer than she remembered, and Charlotte declared that it was the most perfect place imaginable.

Jim Taylor's news was that he had found a beautiful pair of matched bays for her, perfect to draw her carriage in the spring. Mellings had found a very good cook, she said, and miss would sample her fare this very evening. Even Stilton had his news: he had found a young girl who was suitable for the post of abigail, to help Jellicoe.

Alicia's first act was to go through the mail, which was in a large pile on the hall table.

"Is there something from St. Clair?" asked Charlotte, who was dying to meet him.

"No, nothing. But there is a letter from my brother, who

threatens to visit me—oh, good God, they are coming next week! It is too late to do anything about it," she said bitterly.

"We shall just make them very uncomfortable," said Charlotte with the confidence of one who had alienated Mrs. Stornaway. "It is your house, after all."

"Yes, but you don't know William and Amelia. He writes that they will introduce me to their friends, who will be able to help me to procure vouchers for Almack's! As if I had not gone there before! The person who will enjoy their visit is Jellicoe."

"She likes them?"

"No, she loathes them. Their servants always did their best to make her feel inferior. Jelly will find a nice way to put them into their places now."

The mail contained letters from Worthing, the Duke of Kendalford-and others, but not a line from St. Clair.

The next few days were spent pleasantly enough, seeing hairdressers and buying clothes for Charlotte, as well as attending the concerts and plays which that young woman had been longing for, but Alicia did not derive very much enjoyment from it.

"What is it, Alicia?" Charlotte asked one morning at breakfast.

"What do you mean?"

"Why are you so distracted? And you don't look at all well."

"I have not been sleeping well. Dreams . . ."

Charlotte looked very skeptical.

"But that is surely not the reason—"

"Oh, Charlotte," she sighed, "I am really as silly as Julia. I think that I am waiting for word from St. Clair, and that is what is wrong with me. I am not in love with him, nothing so ridiculous! But somehow—"

"Somehow not hearing from him gives you a fit of the blue megrims! And why is it not love?"

"I don't know, but isn't it foolish to think of loving someone like Robert St. Clair? A thoroughly disreputable character, a fortune hunter and gambler. I have never been in love, but I should imagine that it is more than just wanting to see someone. . . ."

Charlotte looked thoughtful. "Yes, it is a bit more than that, but if you have never been in love, it is quite possible that you will not know it when you see it."

Since this was just what she herself was afraid of, Alicia had no answer.

The next morning Alicia was awakened by the sound of someone crying. She got up and opened the window that gave onto the courtyard. The sound grew louder.

"Who is that crying?"

"Me. Eliza!" said a tearful voice.

Looking down, Alicia saw a tousled dark head. A young girl was sitting on the back steps, crying her eyes out.

"Aren't you the new abigail? Why are you out there?"

"Lost me job! *She* says I come too early, *she* says I was to come later, so now I lost me job. Won't let me in, she won't."

"And who is this she?"

"Cook. Awful mean, she is." Here the girl began to cry again.

Alicia rang for her maid and told her to let the girl in and give her some breakfast, after which she was to come to Alicia's room.

After breakfast Stilton asked if he might show in Miss Eliza Jones.

The young person who was ushered in seemed to be overwhelmed both by the room and Stilton himself. She fastened her eyes on the carpet and could not be made to raise them. When Stilton left, matters improved.

Inquiry produced the information that Eliza was just seventeen years old.

"Where is your family?" asked Alicia.

"Got none. I just come from the north; my relatives couldn't take care of me. A fine gentleman said as how he could find me work, but I found out right enough what kind of work he wanted. I seen Mr. Stilton in a tavern, and I seen he was a proper gentleman. He told me he would try and find me sumpn' here. Maybe I shouldn't be saying this?"

"Not to the other servants, no, but it is quite all right to tell me. Do you really think you could become a lady's maid? My Jellicoe is an excellent one, and I am sure she would enjoy teaching you. Are you good with hairdressing or cleaning clothes?"

"I can do anything, ma'am! Just try me. Working for a lady, I would be so happy, I'd learn everything right away!"

This was said with fervent desire and Alicia could not resist the pleading in the dark eyes. She had thought the girl too young at first, but now she thought she might do. And Stilton obviously approved of her, which meant a great deal.

"All right, you are engaged. But we shall have to get you some proper clothes."

"You'll never regret it, miss, never!" said the happy Eliza.

Alicia changed into her old black riding habit, and was just preparing to go out and look at the team of bays that Jim Taylor had found, when Stilton announced that Mr. St. Clair was waiting in the drawing room.

It occurred to her that she should run back upstairs and put on something more flattering, but she decided that a man who did not write or call on her after having sent her a most embarrassing Christmas present did not deserve to see her in anything more flattering than her old black habit.

She was very polite to him and asked him if he had enjoyed his Christmas. Just as politely, he answered that he had. She had the feeling that he was making fun of her, but when she looked at his face, she saw no sign of a smile.

"I must thank you for the lovely butterfly. It is very beautiful, but you really should not have given it to me."

He was standing very still, leaning against the mantel of the fireplace, and his eyes never left her face.

"And why should I not have given it to you, Alicia?"

"Because it put me in a terrible position, you wretch, and you knew it would!"

"It has been too long a separation," he said in his familiar mocking way. "I have been terribly bored by the women in town, and the gaming hells as well."

"A case of overfamiliarity on both counts, I should think." She regretted that she had not changed her clothes.

"You must excuse me," she said, "for being dressed in my old riding clothes, but I was going out to inspect a team of bays."

She suddenly felt uncomfortable sitting in the chair, and got up and pretended to straighten a picture.

"Oh, I quite like you in black," he said lazily. "Makes your skin even whiter and your hair redder."

She did not know what to do with herself. He was making her terribly self-conscious, the way he was staring at her.

"I thought I had taught you not to look away, my brave Alicia. Have I upset you?"

"I have forgotten how the London beaux flirt; you must forgive me."

"I would forgive you almost anything," he said with a slight emphasis on the "almost".

"All right, I shall stop." He told her all the latest news and then insisted on being shown the house. He admired precisely the right things and said he thought it all quite charming. They finished the tour in the library, where St. Clair affected a deep interest in her collection of history books.

"A different side to you," he commented when she disclosed that they were her own. "A bit blue, I think."

"I have always been fascinated by history, a taste my father encouraged."

She turned and found he was standing so close that they were almost touching. She looked at him, a question in her eyes, and he answered by taking her in his arms.

"*My* father, as you see, encouraged rather different tastes in me."

Alicia was about to warn him that the servants or Charlotte might enter the library at any moment, when he let her go, obviously annoyed.

"Don't you think it is time to announce our engagement? Or would you prefer a less formalized arrangement?"

"Does one decide engagements in this manner?" She was not convinced that he was serious.

"No, of course not, but we would not wish conventionality, would we? My relations would be *most* relieved. Going to have some of the ready at last, they'll say."

"How provoking of you to point out that you are interested only in my money."

"If you were poor, I would offer you *carte blanche*," he said promptly. "But you understand me; that is what I particularly like. Life should be beautiful and pleasant. Lack of money makes it far otherwise."

When she saw that he really meant it, Alicia collapsed onto the couch and began to laugh like a child, until she was near tears.

At first St. Clair looked to be offended, but then he too, began to smile, as if he knew what was going through her mind.

"This is . . . a most . . . ridiculous engagement . . . Alicia managed to get out, "and my brother won't like it . . . at *all*!"

"Ah. The brother. I expect you wanted it to be romantic, serious—but we are not like that, are we? I am forever kissing you in corners, but it really must stop. We have an obligation to make our nearest and dearest happy."

"I take it you are referring to your creditors."

"Unromantic creature!"

With an absurd expression on his face, meant to portray a love-struck condition, St. Clair dropped to his knees in front of her, and with one hand over his heart and the other grasping her hand, he proceeded to confess his love, saying he would die if he could not have her.

"And so, Lady Cecily, I, a poor, poor creature (you cannot imagine how poor), dare to offer you my love . . ."

It was at this very touching moment, as Alicia was giggling in a most unladylike fashion, that Charlotte walked into the library.

"Oh! Please excuse me!" said Charlotte in great confusion, as she quickly backed out the door.

"A friend of mine, Charlotte Marlowe," said Alicia to his questioning look. "I will introduce you after this—*scene* is ended. Are you actually serious, St. Clair? I have many flaws, you know."

"And I have mine. I have been spoiled, and have the most expensive habits . . . but I will *not* run through your fortune—I am not so stupid as that."

He drew her to him then and kissed her until she felt dazed.

"And are you quite sure *you* wish this engagement," he asked, scanning her face. "I am not, after all, unique; you may find many such in Pall Mall every night."

She could not explain to him that it was the way he looked at this very moment, the way he kissed without permission, his very honesty, which made him unique. She mentally sacrificed that ideal husband, the Duke of Kendalford, without a qualm.

"I do not pretend to understand myself," she said. "But I am sure that any other man would bore me to tears inside of a month."

"And to whom shall I pay my addresses? Your brother? Lord Terbury?"

"Both, I think. Lord Terbury will be here in a few days, and my brother next Monday. But I am not a minor, so it will be a mere formality. I would not let my brother's opinion weigh with me in any case."

"But it would not do to have them crying about it to everyone they know, however. I shall do my best to be acceptable."

"Since you are bent upon being a pattern card of respectability, you had best be leaving—the servants, as well as Charlotte, are sure to think the worst if we remain here alone."

She walked with him to the door.

"I shall be gone for a few days—I must pay a visit to my aunts. I will call upon you as soon as I return. Since we met first at Jeffrey's, I think we should remember to invite him to the wedding!"

After he left, Alicia went to her room to think. The remark about Jeffrey's would give her no peace: did it mean that St. Clair was *not* the man in the inn? Would he not have made reference to it today? Should she ask him about it? Of course, he might not wish to bring it up at all.

Charlotte was delighted with the news, and found Robert, seen only for a moment, to be one of the handsomest men she had ever seen.

24

A CONFESSION

Alicia arose the next day with a wrenching headache. All night long she had dreamed of mazes, dreams which were variations of the one she had had after Vauxhall. When she got up, her glass showed her that she looked as wretched as she felt.

Charlotte came in and inquired whether they were going to the Frost Fair.

"I don't think I am going today," said Alicia. "Perhaps tomorrow?"

"What is wrong, Alicia? You don't look at all like the happy fiancée."

Looking into the sympathetic and intelligent face of her friend, Alicia made her decision.

"There is something about you, Charlotte, that makes me want to tell you everything I shouldn't."

"Oh, secrets!" said Charlotte in happy anticipation. "Let me get settled in this chair. There. I hope it is excessively shocking."

"It is," said Alicia grimly, "and, as you will see, it is not a story that I would tell just anyone. You are the only other person besides myself who will know it."

"Of course I would tell no one," said Charlotte, with a look of gay expectation.

"When I was young, about sixteen, my brother, who is ten years my senior, married Amelia, about whom I have told you a little. She thought it her duty to prepare me for life as the wife of a wealthy man, and she told me stories of women who had married fortunes, and what their lives were like. But it was not only from Amelia that I heard stories of how great ladies lived—Amelia's friends would come and gossip with her, and I would hear everything. You cannot imagine how it affected me.

"What I heard sickened me. My father brought me up to expect something better from marriage than faithless wives and philandering husbands. All these women saw virginity as the main commodity a woman could offer, but they expected nothing but deception after marriage, especially if one married into the world of the *ton*. There, it seemed, ladies could have bastard children by all the lovers they pleased, if they only remembered to be discreet in public.

"I was exposed to these women for two years, and a little after my eighteenth birthday I resolved to do something that would prevent me from turning out like Amelia and the women she talked about. I climbed out of my window in the dead of night and rode to an inn which was nearby, determined to give myself to the first man I came upon. Needless to say, I did no such thing. The first man was an ostler who was much too unattractive to consider. But I went into the inn, wrapped in a hooded cloak so that anyone who knew me might not recognize me. I think that at that point I might have contented myself with my adventure so far—just running away, seeing the inn. But then, as luck would have it, the only person sitting in the taproom was one of the maids, and she, taking me for a disreputable character like herself, told me of the handsome nobleman upstairs, who had paid for her presence in his bed the night before. This man sounded much more suitable than the ostler, and I decided to go and accomplish my aim.

"At first he would not agree, but I finally convinced him. I thought better of my plan at one moment, but by then it was too late, and his chivalry was replaced by something quite different. I left him in the morning, just before sunrise. I had come to him in darkness, and I left him in darkness. I never really saw his face, nor he mine, thank God!"

Charlotte sat spellbound. It was an effort to marshal her thoughts.

"This is all quite shocking—wonderfully shocking—but why is it bothering you now? Surely what happened so long ago— there are other women who have done the same, or worse, surely."

"That is the part I have not gotten to yet. I have good reason to think that the man from the inn is now in London and that he knows my name."

Charlotte was amazed, and asked how she could be sure. Alicia told her of the masked dancer of Vauxhall and of the unworked emerald ring which had caught the light from the dying fire in the room at the inn.

Charlotte sighed.

"Of course this is a dreadful problem, but I envy you a little— such a romantic situation!"

"Oh, you *fribbet*," said Alicia with exasperation. "I need advice, and all you can think of is what a nice novel one could make of it!"

"How unjust—how ungracious of you. No, no, I shall think of something . . . and so you don't know whether to tell St. Clair, or even if he himself is the man . . ."

Charlotte sat perched in the wing chair, with a look of

concentration so intense that Alicia smiled. Somehow, just telling Charlotte had lifted a weight from her shoulders.

"First of all," said Charlotte after consideration, "I do not think the gentleman is the sort to make any kind of threat. But the only way to discover what manner of man he is—is to meet him. One could put a notice in the *Gentleman's Magazine*, mentioning Grantham, the inn, and the ring."

"But any number of men might answer the notice. No, it will not do."

"I see your point. You know, I can't imagine that St. Clair would care a rush, if it isn't him. After all, he is not precisely 'pure of mind and body' himself."

"Quite the last thing he would wish to be. But he might value precisely those qualities in his wife. These rakes, you know, are very moral in certain areas."

"I doubt that," said Charlotte sunnily, "but in any case, you should not tell him anything. Let him bring it up. As for the rest, I can't imagine a man wishing to blackmail a girl he seduced—a girl of good family, who was only eighteen at the time!"

These words, so confidently spoken, made Alicia feel a great deal better. She had been silly; she had let these shadows from her past overwhelm her. There was really very little to be afraid of. Perhaps it was not even the same ring—but no, the green domino had understood her—she had no doubt of that.

"I think that until this person reveals himself, which I doubt will ever happen, you should put the matter completely out of your mind. And now I am going to ask a personal question: are you in love with the dashing St. Clair?"

"I don't know. I remember you saying that I might not know love when I saw it, and that is how I feel. I am not sure, but I know that he excites me as no other man does, and I was very disappointed when there was no letter from him. I think that was when I knew how much I missed him . . . in some ways I think he understands me very well, but he himself is a genuine mystery."

"Which is of course what one likes in men," said Charlotte. "It is too tiresome when they are easy to read—like Stanford."

"Actually, my real fear is what Jellicoe will do when she finds out that I have gotten engaged without her advice!"

That this fear was well grounded became clear the following day, when the Terburys and Jellicoe returned to town.

Charlotte was just going out when Jellicoe arrived in Curzon Street. There was a certain rigid formality in that estimable lady's bearing which indicated that although she had nothing against Charlotte, she was not going to unbend for anyone on this day. Charlotte immediately surmised that the servants at Grosvenor Square had already informed Jellicoe of the engagement. So much the worse for Alicia—to hear of her mistress's engagement from other servants was most unforgiveable of all!

"Her royal highness is after having a snit," said Jim Taylor with satisfaction as he helped Charlotte into the carriage. "Wouldn't give a farthing for the mistress's peace of mind this week. As for the new girl, Eliza, she might just as well leave now."

But to everyone's amazement, Jellicoe was kind to Eliza from the first. The young girl approached Jellicoe with an air of worshipful attention, and she received the kindest of greetings.

Some below stairs said that this was due to a quick word from Stilton: others maintained that Jelly saw that she couldn't cut the girl out with Miss Alicia, so she had elected to charm her instead. Jim Taylor's answer to that was that Jelly couldn't charm anything.

Whatever the reason, Jellicoe's attitude toward the little

maid was motherly. The same could not be said of her attitude towards her mistress.

It began with subtle hints and remarks to the effect that one knew when one was no longer a valued employee, because one was Kept in the Dark About Certain Events. Alicia managed to ignore most of this for a day or two, but then the excessive servility that Jellicoe began to assume drove her mad. There were endless "Beg pardons," and "Please do not let me disturb yous." After a particularly trying scene over the smoking fireplace in the drawing room, she resolved to speak frankly to her maid.

"Jellicoe, I am aware you resented my sudden engagement and that you found it out in such a fashion, from the Terbury servants. But if you are going to continue in this vein, I shall have to ask you to find a place somewhere else. I am twenty-five now, and am not your child. If I wish to marry the man in the moon, I shall—and I will not have my personal maid punishing me for it."

This was said in a tone of voice that brooked no opposition. Jellicoe was shaken by the unexpected severity of Alicia's expression, but she was not about to give in so easily.

"Why, I never! I can't think what your father would say to hear you speak so to me!"

Alicia, afraid that she was about to say something even worse, turned on her heel and left the room.

Jellicoe, who dearly loved an argument, regarded this as inexcusable, and spent the rest of the day in a mood which ended in a battle royal with Mrs. Melling, the housekeeper, over bed linen.

"My God," said Charlotte who caught a few words of the scene between Melling and Jellicoe, "this is a battlefield! These women are out for blood!"

"It is my fault, I let Jelly incite me to the point of saying cruel things to her. I can't just send her packing—she is the closest thing I have to a family, the one person I have left over from my childhood, from my father's house. . . . I don't know how I could let myself lose my temper like that."

"I do. You need to get out. We've been doing nothing but getting me dressed and settled. It is time to have some fun."

Alicia replied that she was sure there was a great deal of self-interest in this observation, but that Charlotte was probably right. And what should they do? Social life was at a low ebb. Most of the *ton* was still away in the country . . .

"We shall go to the Frost Fair, of course," said Charlotte. "The simplest pleasures are the best ones, you know."

25

THE FROST FAIR

Once in a generation the Thames froze over, giving London an excuse to have a Frost Fair on the solidly frozen ice. For hundreds of years, since the time of Elizabeth I, the tradition had continued of roasting a whole oxen on the ice and operating booths which contained everything from books to gin. So it was with a sense of participating in an old tradition that all of London went out on the Thames, frozen in this year all the way from London Bridge to Blackfriars.

Charlotte became very excited and said that she had never seen anything so gay.

The sign in front of them, as they got out of the coach, proclaimed: "Safe to Cross the Ice." The central path across the ice, which cut right through the middle of the fair, was labeled Feezeland Street, and it was this street that they walked down, passing bakers, bookstalls, toyshops, and gin shops. Alicia was amazed to see a printing press operating, producing mementos which proclaimed that the bearer had been "At the Great Frost Fair of 1814, This Message Printed on the Ice."

Jim Taylor led them to the Wheel of Fortune, where Charlotte won a toy, and then on to the Pricking of the Garter.

They ate oysters and pies, bought brandy balls and ginger-bread to take back to Curzon Street for Eliza, and were in the highest of spirits.

The people of London, Alicia observed, seemed to think that anything on ice was more amusing than anything off the ice. There were skittle alleys, barbers shaving customers in full view of the pedestrians, butchers hard at work, and, of course, the most striking thing of all: the huge ox being roasted on the ice, which enterprise disturbed many who were afraid that the ice would be melted by such a fire.

Charlotte watched with satisfaction as Alicia gave herself up to the enjoyment of all these novelties. Perhaps she would be able to forget her problems here on the ice—at least for a day.

While Jim watched a skating race, Alicia and Charlotte wandered off to the largest bookstall.

"Pooh, nothing but a hundred copies of *Marmion!*" said Charlotte, who disliked the rage for Byron.

"There are other things as well," said Alicia, who had found a corner containing a small pile of books by Maria Edgeworth. She was looking through *The Absentee* when she heard a familiar voice pronounce her name. With displeasure she saw that it was Miranda Drayton and her brother Babcock.

Miranda was at her most patronizing, and Alicia was grateful when Charlotte came up to meet her. Charlotte immediately took Miranda's measure and resolved on a course of opposition.

Miranda was dressed in an obviously expensive walking suit, trimmed with ermine.

"Such a lovely muff," said Charlotte blandly. "My friend Sally Winter bought one just like it at Smith's Emporium."

Since Smith's was well known as the cheapest place in London for furs, Alicia expected Miranda to lose her temper.

But that young woman was so sure of her own consequence that she did not even recognize the insult. Miranda cast an appraising glance at Charlotte's costume.

"I daresay that *you* may shop there, Miss Marlowe, but I do not. I purchased this at Madame Fanchon's. Of course it cost a great deal, but mamma wishes it to *last*."

At that point Alicia would have said that the match had ended in Miranda's favor, but she had not counted on Charlotte's resiliency. As if she had not just been put firmly in her place, Charlotte spoke again, her gray eyes innocently wide.

"I knew father was wrong about London manners, Alicia. He always said it was vulgar to refer to the cost of things! But I find this London *openness* refreshing!"

Even Miranda understood the thrust of this remark, and there would have been quite a tense little scene if Babcock, completely unaware of what he was interrupting, had not begun to ask Alicia about her holidays.

"Babcock, why do you not show Miss Marlowe the travel book you found? I am sure she would be most interested."

When her brother favored her with an uncomprehending look, she made it clear to him that she wished a few moments alone with Alicia.

"It is quite providential that we chanced to meet here," began Miranda. "I happened to hear a bit of gossip yesterday, quite by chance—I do not listen to gossip as a rule—and it shocked me. It was said that you and Robert St. Clair are engaged."

"I cannot see why it would shock you—it is possible that we may become engaged."

"I beg you to think better of it, Miss Tierney! I know that Lady Mary cannot be happy about it! Think of how it will reflect on such a distinguished family if you contract such an unsuitable alliance."

Here Miranda touched on sensitive subjects. Lady Mary had been told, and although she said she was happy for her, Alicia knew this was not true. Lady Mary had been very restrained in her enthusiasm.

"Lady Mary has already given me her blessing," was all Alicia found to say.

"There are such rumors about him. Do you not see that it might very well damage the social standing of the Terbury family?"

"If it does, I am sure you will be able to restore it," said Alicia tartly. "All you need do is invite them to Drayton House for tea."

But Miranda was untouched by this sarcasm. "Miss Tierney," she continued, "you must understand that I am thinking of your welfare as well. Of course St. Clair is a dashing fellow, but his reputation—surely you cannot ignore that! And, as a final point, which I had hoped I might not have to mention, Lord Fane does not have a very high opinion of him, and his opinion must be more well-informed than ours."

"I imagine that you and Lord Fane will make a lovely couple," said Alicia through clenched teeth, "deciding who is worthy of your high opinion and who is not. I wish you very happy, if there is indeed to he a match."

Here Alicia had the satisfaction of seeing her opponent become angry. Miranda was most sensitive on this particular point: Lord Fane had not yet made the proposal everyone had been expecting.

"Why you ill-bred—began Miranda, but Alicia did not stay to hear the rest.

Charlotte and Babcock had wandered off and Alicia thought

she could make out Charlotte's rose-colored mantle in the crowd at the Wheel of Fortune.

She was walking along quickly when she heard a voice call to her. She turned and saw a tall slender form encased in buckskins which ended in a pair of dazzlingly polished Hessians.

"Worthing! How very fortunate! You shall cheer me up—I have just had the most unpleasant meeting with Miranda Drayton."

"A perfectly awful way to greet an old friend whom you haven't seen since before Christmas," he said reproachfully.

"Do not tell me you have missed me! I wonder how many of the mammas have now refused to let you near their darling daughters!"

But it turned out that the gregarious Worthing had had a very boring holiday with a bachelor uncle in Scotland.

When he was introduced to Charlotte, Worthing immediately assumed his professionally charming manner. Very subtly he flattered and showed interest. The velvety voice was used to great effect, as were the penetrating green eyes. He seemed to imply that Charlotte was the most fascinating woman he had ever met. Alicia had seen him do this many times, and she was interested in seeing what effect it would have on Charlotte.

Charlotte, looking charming in her Bivouac mantle and hat, exactly that shade of rose which made her skin seem golden, proved to be more than a match for him. Her vivacity was equal to his, and her humor pulled him up short several times when he was in the middle of some particularly elegant comparison. Alicia watched with enjoyment as he progressed from thinking that Charlotte was a dowdy who would easily be impressed by his style, to being puzzled, to finally understanding that she was making fun of him.

"Come, Miss Marlowe! It is not fair to make sport of new

acquaintances." Here he gave the smile which had charmed so many. "I might have thought you serious if Alicia were not smiling like that."

"Alicia, you must learn more self-control! You will give me away every time," said Charlotte with not a particle of discomfiture or remorse in her manner.

"No, but it is so funny," protested Alicia. "Your telling Jack that you would love to see the Tower and St. Paul's! Imagine this paragon of dandyism going to such places, with a provincial."

Worthing took it with his customary grace and insisted on walking them back to the coach.

"Well, what did you think of him?" Alicia asked when he had gone.

"A charming fellow who will never settle down. I imagine there are many who would enjoy a flirtation with him."

"I know it to be true, but I was never able to see him in that light," said Alicia.

"That is because you have something like a similar character. No, don't look like that! You are not at all like a rake, of course, but there is some quality you share—I don't know what, precisely, but I can see that you would never do as a couple."

Other than this, Charlotte had nothing more to say about Worthing. It looked as though Worthing had found one fair citadel he would not be able to storm.

26

A VISIT

As he later told Melling, Stilton was very much puzzled by the gentleman who all but demanded to see Miss Alicia at an hour of the morning when that young lady was still in bed. Stilton assumed his most freezing air and gave the gentleman to understand that Miss Tierney was not inclined to entertain callers before eleven. To which the gentleman, now red in the face, answered that he was William Tierney, Miss Tierney's brother, and would not, by God, be condescended to by some fool of a butler.

Jellicoe, who had been somewhat constrained since the battle of the engagement, was galvanized by the arrival of her old enemy and quickly forgot Alicia's past transgressions in her haste to warn her of this unwelcome visitor.

"Well, I knew he would come this week," said Alicia philosophically, "so it is just as well that we get it over with on a Monday."

She dressed in her most fashionable morning dress and took her time getting ready. It would do William no harm to wait for her.

She found him in the drawing room, examining a small case which contained several lovely pieces of china given her by Lady Mary.

She had the satisfaction of seeing that her appearance surprised him.

"Town life seems to suit you, sister. You are looking wonderfully."

"Thank you, William. Are you come to town for long?"

He answered at some length, and Alicia used this opportunity to study him.

She had once thought William a great dandy, with his padded shoulders and nipped-in waists; now she saw that he was nothing of the sort, but rather a crude imitation of the London exquisites. Fane and Worthing were the real thing, but her brother was a counterfeit—a man who did not have the taste to accomplish his aim.

They spent an agreeable few minutes discussing events at Tierney Chase and Grantham, and she managed to remain polite. But William's evil demon finally led him to bring up the matter of the inheritance.

"Of course I am very happy for you, very happy. A wonderful sort of security. I gather that it is a very *considerable* sum." He paused and looked at her expectantly.

"It is a respectable sum, yes."

Seeing that she was not going to favor him with any precise accounting, he went on. "Yes, and Amelia—who sends you her warmest regards of course—wants to hold a small rout at which you may meet some of the best people—old friends of ours. I am sure you would enjoy it."

"I am afraid I am rather busy at present, William. Very kind of her to offer—do thank her for me—but I really can't consider putting you to such expense at present."

This was a good approach—William had always disliked spending money on anyone but himself.

"Ah, yes, you are busy. . . . And I almost forgot: Amelia will send you over to her dressmaker, Burroughs. And I—" here he smiled warmly—"have a letter of reference for you."

"To whom?"

"To my banker. Just the fellow to help you invest your money wisely."

Alicia was so taken aback by this suggestion, following, as it did, on the offer of Amelia's dressmaker, that she could not think of how to answer him without insulting him at the same time.

William did not seem to think an answer was required, and he began to estimate the cost of the house and its contents.

"Of course," he said, looking at the china, "my friend Westerby has the best collection of china in London. Much better than this stuff—"

"William, I am sure that Mr. Westerby does indeed have a better collection, but I happen to like mine. I thank you for your various offers, but I am obliged to refuse them."

"Refuse them?" He did not seem to comprehend.

"I have already met the best people. I have a banker and a dressmaker as well!"

Here he lost his temper and brought up all the subjects they had so far managed to avoid: how she had refused James Lanyon, left his home under scandalous circumstances, and had always been the most ungrateful creature—after all he had done for her!

"I daresay," said Alicia tiredly, "but now I am twenty-five, and no longer a child. I must live my life as *I* choose, not as you wish. I have made friends in London. I am very happy here. You need not worry about me."

"Friends! Fine friends—they are friends to your money. You should ask yourself what the London dandies see in a redheaded hoyden! And living alone—"

"But she does not live alone," said a cool voice from the doorway. "She has *me*."

William gave Charlotte a look of exasperation, but was forced to be polite to this unknown as they were introduced.

"I am only concerned about your welfare, Alicia." Here he turned to Charlotte, as if beseeching her to be on his side. "After all, my poor young sister—"

"Oh surely not so young, and certainly not poor!" interrupted the irrepressible Charlotte.

William turned a bright red and said that Alicia had found the perfect companion—a girl as ramshackle as herself.

"Ramshackle," mused Charlotte after William's angry departure. "Yes, I suppose we are. Is it such a bad thing to be, do you think?"

"To William it is," said Alicia, who was feeling very tired. Charlotte took a closer look at her friend and then declared that she would tell Stilton to never let him have access to her again.

"He has depressed you horribly! Such an awful person. I know he's your brother, but it is the truth. And what malicious thing did he say that made you feel so low?"

"Oh, he catalogued my sins—many of which were true—and he told me that my friends were friends only because of my money."

"Absurd! Such jealousy. Of course, there are always people who are more interested in one's fortune than one's character, but not, I think among your intimate friends."

"No, I'm sure they aren't," said Alicia quietly.

***

Alicia had been feeling like a fairy princess these many months, but William's arrival seemed to presage unhappy events to come. Perhaps the princess would turn back into the unhappy girl she had been. And St. Clair—did he care at all for her, or was it really the money, the money they joked about, the money he needed? She had always thought she did not care if he was marrying her for money, but now she knew she did. She needed to know that it was not just her fortune. But it was already too late to find out.

It made her feel worse that St. Clair was away, not there to make her feel that it was all silly. It was as if William's remark had found a resonance somewhere in her mind—something she had felt all along, but had refused to acknowledge. And there was no one who could say what St. Clair's real reasons were, save St. Clair himself.

It was Eliza who finally cheered her up. Alicia found the little maid dusting her bedroom one afternoon, crying as if her heart would break. When she asked what the matter was, the girl said that she would never be able to marry Mr. Stilton.

"And why is that? I thought you went on very well together," said Alicia who had heard all about this romance from Jellicoe.

"Oh, miss, I would love to be his wife, I would. But I wouldn't wish to be always shaming him."

"But you have very pretty manners! What can he object to?"

"He doesn't object, miss. It's me. I won't marry a refined gentleman when I can't even read or write my own name!"

She began to sniffle again, and Alicia realized that the girl was serious. Her own pride would not allow the magnificent Stilton, some fifteen years her senior, to marry an illiterate girl.

"Well, you needn't put off the wedding. *I* can easily teach you to read—I taught several of the neighborhood children at Tierney Chase. It is not at all difficult, you know."

Eliza looked at her in wonderment. She was not so ignorant that she did not know that fine ladies did not generally concern themselves with the teaching of their servants; indeed, there were many ladies who believed it was an act of folly to teach servants—it made them "get above themselves."

They had their first lesson that very evening, and the proud look on Eliza's face at the end of it was payment enough for Alicia.

She could not say how it was exactly, but teaching Eliza made William seem unimportant. The next day she was quite her old self, as Charlotte immediately saw.

"Ah, you are back among the merry, Alicia! This is most convenient, since I have decided that we are to go and visit Tony."

"And who is Tony?"

"I did not tell you? Oh, you were out when the letter came. Well, I received a letter from my black-sheep cousin, Tony Wycherly. He's been in Italy studying painting these past years. I have a feeling that he was sent away, but be that as it may, he is back. He wrote to me at home, and my mother sent the letter on—only because she did not guess who had sent it! He is quite the most scandalous member of my family, and I am the only one still speaking to him. He actually has a studio, and invites me to come and see the pictures."

"But why does your family consider him so scandalous?"

"Well, he began his career by eloping with his eldest brother's wife. She left him, of course, and then he went on to worse and worse things, till finally the family refused to acknowledge him. But now he is no longer a boy, has been on his own for many years, and I expect he has changed greatly. I heard from some who saw his pictures in Rome that he has become a rather good portrait painter."

"It sounds very enjoyable—I have never been in an artist's studio. When shall we make the visit?"

"Next Tuesday. He has sittings all this week."

It began to be borne in on Alicia, as the days passed, that while she had been moping about William, something had been developing between Charlotte and Worthing.

Everywhere they went—shopping, sightseeing, dinners, card parties, and Venetian breakfasts—Worthing seemed to be there.

Close observation of Charlotte yielded nothing. The two seemed on perfectly friendly terms, but no more than that. Charlotte seemed surprised that Worthing always seemed to turn up at least once a day, and she welcomed him with unruffled courtesy, not at all like a woman who was under his spell.

Matters became clearer when Alicia and Charlotte finally paid their visit to the artist's studio in Queen Anne Street.

They arrived at teatime, and their host, a very romantic-looking figure, complete with scar and air of dissipation, welcomed them warmly and invited them to partake of a surprisingly lavish tea.

Alicia thought Tony Wycherly was a fascinating man who had interesting things to say about the Italian character, and she saw why he had so completely captured Charlotte's imagination when she had been young. Wycherly's manner was frank and open, his sense of humor highly original.

Halfway through tea, there was a knock at the door, and Worthing entered without waiting for a reply.

Alicia asked him suspiciously if he had followed them.

"What a peculiar idea! Why I came because I knew the fair

(though she is not fair, but dark) Charlotte would come today to see her cousin."

"Don't make a gudgeon of yourself, Jack," said Charlotte dispassionately. "Sit down and have some tea."

Even Mrs. Radcliffe could not have extracted romance from this remark, but by the end of tea, Alicia was almost certain that Charlotte and Worthing were involved in something more than friendship.

Not that either of them exchanged melting words or looks. No, it was the little things that Alicia saw—things which others might not have noticed. For example, Charlotte immediately indicated a chair near herself when he came to sit down; then she poured the tea for him herself, despite the fact that Alicia was closer to the teapot. This was all done almost automatically, as if it required no thought. During the conversation that followed, Charlotte looked at Worthing every time something interesting was said, as if to see his reaction. Alicia drew some disquieting conclusions.

After tea they looked at the paintings which were stacked about the room. The one on the easel, however, was draped, and Wycherly refused to let them see it.

"I am superstitious about this portrait. It is of someone I have not seen in years, so I am doing it from memory. In a way, my entire youth is in that picture. When it is completely finished, I will show it to you, but not until then."

Everyone was immediately curious. What kind of portrait could contain the artist's "entire youth"? Wycherly managed to get them off this subject by involving them in a heated discussion of Turner's provocative *Snowstorm*, which was currently shocking aesthetic tastes due to his painting of the violent sky.

During this discussion, which concerned things she knew nothing about, Alicia took the opportunity to wander about the studio. The large room was strewn with draperies, books, and an odd assortment of furniture—some of it very good, some of it looking as if it had come from a rubbish pile. Alicia found this disorder very attractive and just as unpretentious as the artist himself. She was examining a small landscape when she caught a snatch of the conversation between Wycherly and Worthing.

"Hard to believe that you remained friends after all that," Worthing was saying.

"Yes, the situation was a bit difficult. But he gave me help when I needed it. . . . Fane's a fine fellow when you're down . . .

Alicia's eyes met Charlotte's, and they exchanged surprised looks. It was odd enough that Tony knew Fane at all, but that they should actually be friends was very unexpected, despite the fact that as Lady Mary always said, everyone in the *ton* knew everyone else. But given Fane's pride, his concern with respectability, it would have been normal to expect him to cut a connection with the scandalous Wycherly.

When Alicia finished examining the pictures, she discovered that Charlotte and Worthing had found some pretext for going into the next room by themselves. Alicia, thinking that Charlotte might have done it without quite realizing it, walked to the door and was about to enter when she caught sight of them sitting on the window seat.

They were not even sitting very close, but the air of intensity as they looked at each other made it clear to Alicia that this was not the first time they had been alone. In that one moment she became afraid for Charlotte.

Alicia quickly turned and quietly went back to the tea table.

Wycherly was sitting in a comfortable sprawl, smoking a cheroot, for which he apologized.

"No, please do. I like the smell," said Alicia.

"A commendable taste," he said, smiling the boyish smile which was not quite in keeping with his hardened face.

"I have noticed," here he gestured in the direction of the other room, "that when couples wish to be alone together, they generally manage to pull it off. It is some law of science, I think."

"Yes, and high time it was registered with the Royal Society!"

He blew smoke rings into the air, and then regarded Alicia quizzically.

"Why, Miss Tierney, can it be that you are worried about my cousin?"

She looked at him steadily and answered that she was.

"But Charlotte was the most self-sufficient child, and she has become an equally self-sufficient woman. I think she can take care of her affairs very well."

"I don't know. I wish she may not find herself at point-non-plus too quickly. Jack is a friend of mine, and I love him dearly, but I cannot think it is quite the thing for him to be alone with an *engaged* woman—never mind that she is your cousin as well." As soon as the words were out, Alicia felt she had been a prig and that this experienced man of the world would laugh at her. But he did not.

"Of course, of course. But I do not think that it was only Jack's idea—and I am sure that her engagement is only to satisfy her parents, who are very good, but very limited people. Charlotte does not belong in Sussex with ten children and a husband who is always too busy for her."

Alicia could not help but agree with him there, but she said that there were many men who were unsuited to being husbands, and Worthing was one of them.

"You may be right there!" laughed Wycherly, "but that is his charm for the ladies—taming him, making him settle down. How seductive an idea! But somehow, I don't think Charlotte is thinking of that."

"Nor do I," said Alicia tartly. "I do not think she is thinking at all."

Tony took another puff of his cheroot and blew the smoke toward the ceiling. "If you wish to help," he said in a quiet tone, "you must not say anything to her. It will only put her back up. You must find some other way. But I know Charlotte. She has the flaw of the independent: she won't take advice. But believe me, she'll land on her feet. It takes more than a Jack Worthing to make her lose her balance."

But Alicia could not rid her mind of the sight of them sitting at the window. Thinking back over the weeks since they had been introduced at the Frost Fair, it occurred to her that there had been many times when Charlotte had gone out on errands alone, except for Jim Taylor. Could she have met Worthing, accidentally or on purpose? Thinking of her own willful past, Alicia could not help being worried. Charlotte did not know what it would be like to always be afraid of what people would find out.

When Charlotte came back to the table, she seemed so self-possessed that Alicia began to wonder if she had imagined the intimacy she had sensed. But when he said good-bye, Worthing kissed Charlotte's hand in a way that reminded Alicia of how St. Clair had kissed hers. No, she had not been mistaken.

27
PROBLEMS

The idea for the party came from Charlotte and Harriet who felt that since Alicia had not had a housewarming, the least she could do was to have a party to which they could invite their friends.

"But I want it to be only the younger set," said Charlotte. "I don't want the dragons and dowagers, thank you very much."

This appealed to Alicia, but she did not know whether she could exclude Lady Mary.

"If we make a very little, *inconsequential* party," said Harriet, "I shouldn't think she'd care. But who can be the chaperone?"

"Anne Dunstan would be perfect. She is thirty and a widow— what could be more respectable?" asked Alicia.

Harriet left, and Alicia began to make up the guest list.

"Shall we send Stanford an invitation, Charlotte? He said he might come to town this month anyway."

Charlotte looked half-ashamed, half-defiant. "No. I know it is shocking of me, Alicia, but I cannot realize that Stanford exists in the same world. I know I should write him and end the engagement, but I don't know if that is really what I want."

She sighed. "I am all at sixes and sevens. I don't know what I want from hour to hour. Don't laugh! I know Worthing is a fribble—no one knows it better than I—but he—he *understands* things."

"I am sure that of the many women who have played roles in Jack's life you are the only one attracted because of his understanding!"

Charlotte began to smile. "You are unfair, Alicia! Here you are, my example: engaged to a dashing ladies' man—"

"Who would leave me for a woman with a larger purse," said Alicia resolutely. "To be sure, I like him a great deal, but I have no illusions. I can afford none. Whereas you have a chance to marry a perfectly decent man who *loves* you."

"I am not so sure of even that. Stanford has never really known anyone else, you know, and he has utterly no imagination where women are concerned. Whatever woman is in the vicinity will do nicely. All his passion is reserved for his work. But you mustn't worry about me, Alicia. I know what Worthing is."

Alicia did not find this at all reassuring, but remembering what Wycherly had advised, she gave no more advice.

Before the guest list was settled upon, there was much discussion of whether Miranda Drayton must be invited. The rumors of an engagement between that young woman and Lord Fane continued as strong as ever, and this made Harriet think that they would have to invite her.

"Laurence has just written me, you know, saying that Fane has saved him time and again from all sorts of disasters! I would not wish to offend Miranda if she is to indeed marry Nick . . ."

"No, not Miranda!" protested Alicia. "Sour-faced prig. Her moral education does not permit her to be frivolous, you know. No, if that simpering miss comes, she will ruin everyone else's enjoyment."

Seeing that Alicia would not be moved from this position, Harriet gave in, but she warned that the party must be kept as secret as possible.

"For even though it is such a small, intimate gathering, Miranda and her set have all been excluded. If word gets out, they will take their revenge."

"I, for one, would be glad to miss Miranda's next rout," said Charlotte. "But the person I take exception to is Frederick Phillips. He is positively the most boring young man of my acquaintance, which is saying a great deal!"

"No, he must come," said Alicia. "There will be cards, you know, and a little gambling. Which means that we need someone who knows all the rules, which Frederick does. And his personality makes him ideally suited to arbitrate disputed points."

The final list contained the names of the couples who had entertained them from time to time, Worthing, Anne Dunstan, Frederick Phillips, and St. Clair. Wycherly had declined, saying he had a dislike of parties, as had the Duke of Kendalford, who would be away.

A further addition was made when Anne Dunstan paid a visit and begged permission to bring along a Frenchman of her acquaintance as her escort.

"The most personable man, Alicia. Such manners! His family emigrated some years ago, after the most incredible adventures!"

"Well then we must have him, by all means."

Jellicoe had other opinions.

"Don't know why we need a Frenchy at our party, Miss Alicia. They all claim to be émigrés, but I have heard that some of them are no such thing!"

"And what are they then?" Alicia knew of her maid's dislike of the French, but enjoyed inciting her.

"Spies!"

"And what would they expect to find out at my card party? That my servants don't serve well?"

Jellicoe went off in high dudgeon to sulk in the kitchen and give her opinion of the Frenchies to anyone who would listen. Eliza would not agree, however. She was thrilled that she would be waiting on a foreigner.

In general the staff viewed this relatively small card-party as a test which they must pass with flying colors. Alicia had never done any formal entertaining in her new house, and half of the servants had never worked in such a fashionable establishment. It would require a great deal of work to see that all went smoothly.

Jellicoe felt it incumbent on herself to make sure that everyone knew how to bow and scrape and phrase things prettily. Since Stilton regarded this as his province, there was a good deal of stress and strain in the week before the party. Charlotte, who heard some of the details from her maid, advised Alicia to stay well out of this dispute. Alicia was unable to pretend deafness, however, when Jellicoe complained that a Certain Person Was Getting Above Himself. Since she did not want another scene like the one she'd endured over the engagement, Alicia was determined to remain calm this time.

"Of course, Jelly, I understand your feelings. But I do think Stilton feels that he is the one to prepare the servants. You must remember that this is very important to him, and he knows that you have many other duties to attend to." Seeing that this would not answer, Jellicoe's frown being just as firmly in place, Alicia tried to think of another approach. "Jelly, the thing is, to *you*, this can mean nothing. You have been present during the grand entertainments at Tierney Chase. For Stilton, however, who has not half of your experience in fashionable society, it is all very different. You really should let him have his way—your position here is unassailable, while he must still prove himself."

Jellicoe was much soothed by this speech. She sensed that there was perhaps something in it that she had not grasped, but it made her feel quite happy to hear her mistress take this line. She went downstairs in a new mood, exuding regal condescension and affability.

Just as Alicia was feeling that things were smoothed over, the cook began to insist that she would not prepare the menu Alicia had decided upon. Cook felt that to prepare these French delicacies was unpatriotic. Alicia said she quite understood and would send for Lord Worthing's *French* chef to come and manage the supper preparations. After this no more was heard from the mistress of the kitchen about the *gateaux de feuilletage praliné* and the *huîtres au gratin*.

All of this was early in the week; as the day drew nearer, nerves began to stretch to the breaking point, and Charlotte and Alicia began to take refuge in Wycherly's studio, since that gentleman had no objection to it.

The first visits were made without the appearance of Worthing, and Alicia understood that Charlotte was trying to be discreet so that Alicia should not worry. But when he was not there, Charlotte seemed to be in a daze, not hearing remarks addresssed to her and spending a great deal of time gazing out of the window. After a few such experiences, Alicia told her she should invite Worthing and have done with it.

"It is true," said Charlotte happily, "that when he is not here I miss him. I cannot help it—I enjoy things more when he is there to share them with me."

Alicia had been hoping that time would eventually lead Worthing to pursue some other interest, but when she saw them together it was clear that the romance was continuing as before.

"Do you think Jack is serious about her, Tony?" She and Wycherly were talking in the studio while the lovers sat on the window seat in the other room.

"Jack is always serious," laughed Tony. "He does not say anything to me one way or another. But I can tell you this; he knows enough not to trifle with girls of the quality."

"And you think that Charlotte is still able to take care of herself?"

"I do not know. But you may be sure that Worthing does. Perhaps one should look upon it as an enjoyable romance, something Charlotte can remember when she is safely married to her Stanford."

"But I thought you told me that she didn't belong in Sussex with ten children."

"Yes, but that is preferable to being Jack's mistress, I imagine. Who knows—another party more suitable than Stanford may come along."

"Well, I shall be looking for one—you may be sure of that So you do not think Jack is thinking of marriage?"

He was sketching her profile, but when she asked this question, his pencil stopped moving.

"No, I do not."

"And is there a specific reason?"

"Yes, but are you sure you wish to know it?"

Alicia looked at him evenly. "I imagine that I can bear it, yes."

The pencil was moving again, and Wycherly's voice expressed no particular emotion as he told her that Jack had been seeing a lot of Caroline Parr, a young lady of the highest connections to the royal house.

"I see. A very good match, as opposed to Charlotte, whose

grandfather on the maternal side was in trade . . . but I find it hard to believe, Tony. Jack is not the fellow to mislead a girl like Charlotte—he has some honor, after all!"

The artist smiled sardonically. "And I thought you knew a bit of the world, Alicia. Have you never noticed that most people find a way to justify doing what is in their interest, even when it conflicts with the moral values they have been taught?"

"Yes, I have seen it sometimes, but never with someone I liked. I think you are overly cynical. I do not believe that Jack is thinking of giving up Charlotte for Caroline Parr, either."

"Oh, he is not *thinking*—that is not the way it is done! No, one morning he will wake up and realize that it is time to get the nasty business over with, and he'll write a letter to Charlotte—a noble letter, to be sure—and then go off and get married in the Abbey."

"So you don't believe in ideals or honor."

The pencil was laid down this time, and he looked at her, something very serious in his hard eyes.

"No, I don't I don't know what those things mean when it comes down to a specific instance. If you had ever seen what men are capable of doing in battle, or what they may have to do afterward, just to stay alive, you would not talk of ideals, either. I believe in being as decent as one can be, given the situation, but I don't believe in noble causes and noble actions. In the end we will all crawl for a piece of bread when we're starving, and we'll crawl over the other bodies if it's necessary."

"That may be true, and from what I've heard, it probably is. But even you say you believe in being as decent as you can. Why not simply be as evil as you can?"

"But I don't believe in evil either. I simply believe that people do what they have to, to obtain what they feel they need. And when it is a matter of survival, people will do anything."

"But for Worthing it is not a matter of survival—"

"Ah, but it may be. It depends on how he views it. Marriage is an important thing in the Worthing family, and don't mistake the matter: Jack may run wild through all the fair Cyprians, but when it comes to family feelings, he's very traditional in his views."

"Well, you have a very convincing way of explaining it, but I think that you are leaving out the one thing that can change everything—love."

Wycherly looked at her with a smile in his eyes.

"And what do you know about love, Alicia?"

She was annoyed at this.

"Why do you ask? Don't you believe that I know anything about it?"

He took her hand and turned the palm up. After a minute's examination he said that she had certainly not been in love yet.

"You know very well that palmistry is the utmost nonsense!"

"Yes, but I thought you might believe that more readily than the truth, which is that I can tell whether someone has ever really been in love or not."

"But whether I have been in love does not matter," said Alicia, recovering from this attack, "because I have heard and read about it. And from what I know, it is very possible that if Jack loves Charlotte, he will not behave as you predict."

"That is what I love about the English! To believe in the force of something which one has never experienced oneself—now, that is faith!"

"I take it the Italians are different?" Alicia wished to get him onto another subject.

"Yes, they believe in nothing but enjoying life as much as one can, and they always expect the worst. Which is why they want to wring every drop of pleasure from things while they can."

"What my father used to say was that if people expected the worst, they often got just that."

Wycherly was very struck by this and said that there might just be something to it.

28
THE DAY BEFORE

The willow salon looked exquisite, Alicia saw with satisfaction. It was the day before the party, and the house was ready, all polished and scrubbed. But the salon, filled with flowers and candles, positively gleamed.

She was standing in the middle of the room, admiring the way the paintings looked against the Chinese wallpaper when she heard the door open behind her.

"Eliza?"

"Yes, mum," said a very unconvincing falsetto. Alicia turned and was wrapped in a warm embrace.

"St. Clair . . ." she murmured happily into his waistcoat.

"You could at least call me Robert."

"But I think of you as St. Clair."

"As long as you think of me, I don't give a damn which name you use."

He held her away and looked at her. It seemed to her that his eyes were unnaturally bright.

"And how have you been? What is this about a card party? Were you going to have it without your devoted fiancé?"

"No, you'll find the invitation at home. . . . Robert, have you been drinking?"

This was a mistake, since St. Clair disliked the idea that he might not be in complete control of himself. He immediately became elaborately formal, as if to show he wasn't inebriated. He said that he had had a few brandies with some friends, but nothing was wrong with that, was there?

"You are foxed, cherished fiancé, and I think I shall ring for coffee to be brought."

"I don't need coffee. I need *this*," he said, and kissed her so forcefully that her mouth hurt.

"It is not a compliment when you kiss me like that, drunk as you are."

"There are women who would not mind it." He looked very angry.

"Perhaps you had best go and find some, then," she said coolly.

He walked over to the window and opened it, taking deep breaths of the icy air. He called her over to him, but she did not move.

"No, you won't do as you're told, will you, Alicia? You're not malleable clay."

It seemed to her that the space separating them was much more than the length of the carpet that lay between them, but a moment later he was kissing her again, this time very differently. Now he seemed completely sober, and he looked at her as if he were really seeing her.

"You looked as if you wanted to slap me, Alicia."

"I did. You reminded me of my brother, who used to get drunk every night when he was younger. The only way to deal with him and his friends was to be very angry."

"And are you still angry?"

They were sitting on the sofa, and he had his arm around her. He was gently tapping his fingers against her throat, in the hollow, and she found this very distracting.

"No, I am not angry."

"I have missed you, but it was all for a good cause. My family has been told that there will soon be an announcement of the engagement, and are delighted. The black sheep is about to redeem himself."

His fingers continued their caresses, and Alicia found herself wishing and fearing that they might move lower. She both willed and forbade someone to enter the room; she was horrified at herself, and simultaneously absolved herself of all blame. She leaned her head against the back of the sofa, against his outstretched arm.

He told her to open her eyes, but she had not realized that she had closed them. He looked at her intently for a moment and then bent his head down to kiss her throat. She felt completely within his power for that moment, and he seemed to sense it. It was almost with a feeling of disappointment that she felt him move away. He stood up and took some sherry from the sideboard.

"It is fortunate that you are to be my bride, because otherwise I should have to seduce you."

There was a hint of contempt in his tone, but she could not say whether it was for her or himself. She made every effort to regain her composure, but she was breathless.

"Perhaps it would be I who would seduce *you*," she said. "Did you ever think of that?"

He was momentarily stunned, but then began to smile. "No, I didn't A very attractive idea, however."

She rang for Stilton, and when he came they were on different sides of the room, looking at books.

After St. Clair left. Alicia found it very difficult to settle down to the various tasks that remained. Charlotte was out with Harriet, and there was no one to talk to. Feeling suddenly tired, she went to take a nap.

An hour later she awoke with a start from a frightening dream. The man in a green domino had been choking her while her friends danced past.

When Charlotte returned, Alicia told her the dream.

"You are still afraid that the man from the inn will come back and interfere with your marriage. But it is only a dream, Alicia, it is not prophecy."

"No, it is all my own mind. I know it. I kept asking his name, and the answer was always 'not what you think.' A very unhelpful dream . . ."

29
THE PARTY

The gods were smiling down on 16 Curzon Street that Saturday. The provisions had arrived in the early afternoon, the various foodstuffs unspoiled, the bottles unbroken. Miss Alicia had risen at noon in the best of humors, well-rested. Miss Charlotte had complimented every member of the staff on the way the house looked. The only possible problem, everyone agreed, was the hairdresser. As reported by Jellicoe, Miss Alicia was tired of the style she had been wearing and had recklessly requested the services of the famed Lemoine. It was feared that this gentleman would either arrive late or do something hideous to Miss Alicia's beautiful, if unfashionable, red hair.

Charlotte was the first to descend the staircase at nine o'clock, her appearance timed to coincide with Worthing's arrival in the front hall.

She was wearing ruby-red velvet, cut to display the back, bosom and shoulders as much as possible. A topaz necklace and earrings set off her dark skin. Worthing watched her float down the staircase, a gratifying expression on his face.

When Alicia made her entrance, there was no one to watch

her, no eye to indicate admiration, but she did not feel the lack of it. She felt a wonderful sense of buoyancy, very much like what she had felt when driving the coach on the road to London. It was her first party at her own house, and everything was beautiful.

Monsieur Lemoine had deserved his reputation. He agreed that the style given her by Monsieur Romain was perfectly charming, but said that one did not always wish to be charming: sometimes one wished to be beautiful, *n'est-ce pas*?

He kept the curls, but took them a little off her face, partially revealing for the first time the beautiful forehead which had been hidden. This small change made her look quite different. After long consideration, he put the emerald laurel sprigs in her hair instead of on her dress.

The dress itself was cut very simply, made of foam-green sarsenet trimmed with lace. The sleeves were worn off the shoulders, contributing to the impression that a vast amount of skin was revealed. Monsieur Lemoine had declared the general effect to be stunning, and quite original.

The guests, understanding that this was something more than the usual card-party and supper, had also dressed far more elegantly than was expected. Of the women, the most striking was Anne Dunstan, in a brown velvet which matched her eyes and emphasized her blondeness. Her escort, the suavely charming Lucien de Rohant, was equally elegant, and he won Alicia's heart by the kindnesses he showed to Harriet, who was always shy at parties.

The elegant company and the equally elegant surroundings made Alicia feel so happy that she did not even mind the fact that St. Clair was late.

They were deep in play when he arrived. Normally quite undistinguished in his dress, St. Clair had made an effort:

his blue coat was perfectly cut, the formal black pantaloons, buttoned tight to the ankles, ended above striped silk stockings and oval-toed pumps. All of this perfection was completed by his dazzlingly white brocade waistcoat. Alicia thought she had never seen him look so handsome.

She went to meet him and had the satisfaction of seeing his eyes widen in surprise.

"I thought I would stun you," he said, "but it is you who are stunning."

"It is all the doing of a new hairdresser, nothing more."

"He may have done the hair, but you have produced the glow. You are looking very beautiful."

Alicia led him over to Charlotte, who was very absorbed in a game of deep basset. When she caught sight of St. Clair, however, she gave a sigh and turned to her partner.

"That man is sinfully handsome! Worthing, you'd best prevent me meeting him."

Worthing moodily suggested that perhaps she should just go into supper with that gypsy instead of himself. Undisturbed by this churlishness, Charlotte smiled graciously at St. Clair.

Alicia wanted them to get to know each other, and she mentioned some friends she knew they had in common. While they were safely discussing the lamentable affairs of this family, Alicia went to the kitchen to check on the preparations.

Cook was putting the final touches on the *petites pommes souffles*, complaining the entire time about how all this food was going to waste on a lot of Frenchmen.

"Cook, there is only one Frenchman, and he is quite nice. Of course he is used to the very best, having eaten the food of the great Carême, for example."

This was the wrong thing to say. Carême had recently become

the chef for the Regent, so this was an obvious insult to English cooks.

Still smiling to herself, Alicia went out into the hallway to speak to Stilton when she heard him letting someone in the front door.

She watched in astonishment as Laurence Terbury and Nick Fane walked into the hall. Laurence rushed to give her a hug.

"What a wonderful surprise! When did you return?"

"Just today," said Laurence, "a few hours ago. My mother said we would be a nice surprise for your card party!"

She told them they were both looking well, which was not the truth. They both looked exhausted, the kind of exhaustion that has accumulated over weeks and is not to be dissipated by a few days' rest Fane held his left arm very stiffly, she noticed, and looked much older. Laurence too, who had left a boy, was now a man. These observations rushed through her mind as she led them into the salon. She wondered if Harriet would faint, and whether Fane would cut Lady Anne Dunstan in some particularly awful way.

Fane said very little, but a smile was continually playing about his mouth. Other than that, his manner was irreproachably correct as he greeted everyone.

Harriet did not faint, and a look of unalloyed joy came over her face when she caught sight of Laurence. They begged permission to leave the party, to which Alicia immediately agreed.

"And do you wish to run off, too, Nick?"

"No, I am very well here, and half in love with Miss Marlowe. I must congratulate you on your party. With one or two exceptions, they are very amiable."

"I cannot quarrel with a man just returned from France, so I shall obligingly pretend that I do not know what you mean."

"The farouche Alicia is gone, I see, replaced by something

that actually resembles a society hostess!" He smiled more charmingly than she remembered he could.

"But what has happened to me must be far less interesting than what has happened to you—did you have many adventures?"

But he did not choose to answer this, asking instead about the guests he did not know. He appeared especially interested in de Rohant.

"Ah, like Jellicoe, you think he is a spy!"

"No, but he is somehow familiar to me . . . perhaps I have met him before."

As she watched Fane talk to Charlotte, Alicia was struck by the subtle changes in him. Somehow the dandified clothes did not suit him as well as they had, and he seemed more phlegmatic than ever. Tired, she supposed. She was grateful that he chose to avoid coming into contact with either Anne or St. Clair, but so discreetly that it was not apparent to anyone else.

Supper went off beautifully, everyone thought, and cook was much mollified when Eliza reported that the guests were praising her dishes.

After the champagne, Alicia sought out Charlotte, who was in very high spirits.

"My dear, you never did Fane justice! He may be all the things you say, but he is also most amusing. It is well that Worthing was at the Frost Fair, or I should certainly succumb to the sleepy dandy. And the elegant way he takes his snuff! I have never seen the like."

"Nor have I," said Alicia dryly. "And what did you think of my Robert?"

"The handsomest man I ever saw in my life—but poor Fane, I hear that Miranda Drayton's going to get him. A dreadful shame, isn't it."

Alicia began to think that perhaps a romance between Fane

and Charlotte was a possibility. He was not the man to encourage a woman and then marry someone else. But Charlotte was still engaged to Stanford, and that problem would have to be dealt with first. However, it would be awful to have her friend married to a man she did not like herself.

But when she saw Worthing and Charlotte laughing together, she knew that Charlotte would not really become interested in anyone else.

Alicia was sitting at one end of the room, thinking about all of these things, when she became aware that St. Clair was staring at her from the other end. She sat waiting for him, curiously passive, as he stopped and talked to various people. Even as he talked, he continued to look at her. The sensation of being desired became so strong that she finally closed her eyes.

"You are being a very odd hostess, sitting at one end of the room this way," His voice was low and caressing, and it seemed to be carrying a message of its own, separate from what he was saying. She opened her eyes and saw him sitting opposite her. She felt that even if she closed her eyes again, she would not be able to get away from that intense glance.

"Why do you look at me that way?"

"Because I am remembering," he said softly, "how soft your skin felt against my lips."

Alicia smiled involuntarily.

"I am sorry," she said, "but you do it so well—*too well.*"

"Always, when I think I have you, you slip away like a fish."

"An unflattering simile. Can you be trying to call me a gudgeon, I wonder?" She was gay again; she had escaped his spell once more.

"Someday you will not be able to laugh your way out of it, my girl. There are some things that should not be treated humorously."

"I am afraid we disagree. There are very few things that I cannot laugh at."

"You are still young; you will learn."

"No, I will never learn. There is nothing more ridiculous than a person who does not perceive the ridiculous."

St. Clair was puzzled and slightly annoyed by her sudden change in attitude, and he left the party with the first guests to leave.

Charlotte and Alicia went into the library to get out the sherry; the champagne had been exhausted. Alicia was in the middle of telling Charlotte about St. Clair's bad mood as they walked into the room.

"Well, I do see his point, Alicia. The man was being terribly romantic, and you ruined it! Now, confess: were you or were you not fascinated by him when he was staring at you from across the room like that?"

"Of course I was. I had the feeling that he could come and carry me off right there, and I would let him . . . but when he said that about my skin being soft under his lips—"

"This of course inspires the question of how he knew it was soft, and where, exactly, this skin was."

Alicia started to laugh at Charlotte's censorious tone.

"That I shall never tell! Disgusting mind you have! At any rate, when he said that, I suddenly saw it all as being like one of those Gothic romances, one of his usual speeches to women, and I couldn't take it seriously."

Charlotte said nothing until they had assembled the bottles on a tray.

"No, Alicia," she said finally, "I think you were afraid of him, and laughing is your protection against him."

Alicia was so surprised by this thought that she could not answer. Charlotte, who had no wish to upset her, immediately took it all back, saying it was probably nothing of the sort.

"No, no, you may be quite right, Charlotte. I never thought of that—but why would I be afraid, I am afraid of very little. And I am ready to marry him."

"My dear, there are scores of women married to men who scare them. It is nothing new."

"But I have no reason to fear him."

A few minutes after the door had closed, Nick Fane got up from the wing chair in which he'd been sitting during the entire conversation.

He had been about to reveal his presence, but the conversation had been so personal from the first that he saw it would be embarrassing for them. He had never eavesdropped before, and he was very uncomfortable during the entire conversation, but he had found it interesting. And very enlightening.

PART THREE

30

DISASTER AND RECOVERY

Lady Mary Terbury did not know what to do. This was such a rare occurrence that her husband offered to stay home from Tattersall's and his club. Lady Mary, much touched by this concern, told him that there was no need for both of them to be miserable: he should go and enjoy himself, but he should try and think of a way out of The Problem.

It was always the way, she reflected. Laurence was home safely, Alicia was established in her new house, and Harriet was happier than anyone had ever seen her.

But now these two letters had come, both of them bringing very bad news for everyone. She looked at them again.

The letter from Torrance revealed that Robert St. Clair was said to be secretly engaged to a young heiress, name unknown. Lady Mary had no difficulty in deducing that it was poor Julia Stornaway. The rumors had not caught up with the new engagement to Alicia, but Lady Mary knew it would not be long. And then Alicia would find out about the first engagement.

The second letter was worse. Edith Stornaway wrote her cousin Mary Terbury that she categorically refused to allow any marriage between Laurence and Harriet so long as Alicia Tierney was engaged to Robert St. Clair.

It took her breath away. Edith had always favored Julia, and she had no intention of letting the much-disliked Alicia take her daughter's fiancé away. Probably the mother did not even know that Julia was secretly engaged—and neither of them cared that they were destroying Harriet's happiness. Lady Mary had not thought Edith would do it, but here it was.

Since Laurence did not know when and if he would be called back into action, he wished to marry his Harriet with all possible speed. But no one could consider a border elopement, the only way they could marry if Harriet did not have her parents' permission, since she was underage.

Lady Mary quickly saw that these two letters were connected, that the problems were actually one large problem—a disaster, in fact.

Her first action was to summon Charlotte Marlowe and acquaint her with the contents of both letters, under a strict vow of secrecy concerning the letter about St. Clair.

"Well, Lady Mary, you can never show that letter to Alicia. She would refuse to believe it, and she would think you had been—"

"Meddling. I know. I shan't show it to her. Now what do you think of this St. Clair fellow, apart from what we have read?"

Charlotte hesitated and then spoke frankly, feeling that it was too important a matter to ignore. "I cannot like him. But he has a great power over women, much experience, and I think Alicia is genuinely attracted to him, and he to her. Although even she says that he would go with any heiress who had enough money."

"She says that? This is very bad. She might forgive him the engagement to Julia . . . I must think. . . ."

"But there is one thing I am certain of. She does not really love him. He fascinates her, but that is all."

Lady Mary brightened at this. "Well, then, we may be able to do something."

Charlotte was conscious of the desire to tell Lady Mary about the incident from her past which made Alicia reluctant to consider anyone but St. Clair—but she could not.

They sat silent until tea was served. Food always made Lady Mary think better, and she began to conceive of a plan.

"Suppose we have Alicia pretend to give up the engagement to St. Clair—" she began.

"—and get engaged to someone else to make it look real! And then after Harriet and Laurence are married, everyone can do what they like! Very good, but who? And how can we make Edith believe it?"

Lady Mary took another scone and ate it thoughtfully.

"I have the man!" Charlotte was excited. "And it will take care of all the problems! Fane!"

Lady Mary looked at her in admiration. "Really, my dear, you are almost as resourceful as I. The perfect choice. Already offered for her once, sent the present, everyone knows about it. . . . And he is Laurence's friend, and I think would agree. Besides he has rank and fortune, so everyone would understand her throwing over St. Clair."

"But Miranda," Charlotte said unhappily. "Miranda will ruin everything."

"Oh, I think Fane can manage her," said Lady Mary. "The thing is to get him to agree, and the rest will follow. I think I know how to present it to him. Of course, if he won't, he won't. But is there no other gentleman who would do?"

"Wouldn't be convincing. He sent her the ring, proposed . . . and he is perfect in other ways, as well."

Lady Mary did not bother to ask what these ways were; her mind was already on other things.

"And what of Alicia and St. Clair? How do we stop that?"

"Lady Mary, we really can't do anything there! It is Alicia's affair. If she wishes him, she will have him, and it is none of our business—but I fancy he won't like this plan much."

"I'm surprised at you, Charlotte. What is this reluctance to help end a totally unsuitable connection. There are times one *must* interfere!"

But Charlotte was adamant. St. Clair was Alicia's business. The two schemers spent an hour discussing the details of the plan and then separated, ready to initiate action.

Lady Mary's first order of business was to write an indignant letter to Edith Stornaway, which maintained that St. Clair and Alicia were not engaged—no announcement had been published yet—and announced that Alicia was on the verge of getting engaged to Nick Fane, who, as Edith must have heard, had offered for her before Christmas.

For her part, Charlotte hurried home and presented the problem to Alicia, and then the solution.

At first Alicia raised a storm of objections, but Charlotte was able to convince her that this was the only way that Harriet and Laurence would be able to marry.

"I am willing to do this for Harriet," Alicia said at last, "but I doubt that Fane will be persuaded."

"And do you think St. Clair will agree?"

"Oh, he will understand," said Alicia with certainty. Substantially the same scene was repeated when Lady Mary spoke to Fane.

"I doubt that St. Clair will agree," he said to her. "He needs the credit the engagement will give him."

"You will have to explain it all to Miranda, of course," said Lady Mary.

"Oh, she has a good heart; she will understand. And, after all, she did not wish the announcement to be made of our engagement until her family is out of mourning for her grandfather."

It was a time of disillusionment for both Alicia and Nick. Neither Miranda nor St. Clair proved admirers of the plan.

"It is most improper!" said Miranda. "I am surprised that you wish me to agree to such a thing!"

She and Lord Fane were sitting in the music room of the Draytons' Hanover Square house, under the watchful eye of Mrs. Drayton, who seemed to find something to do in the music room every ten minutes. A disagreeably proud woman and stern mother, she did not believe that well-bred daughters should be left alone for long periods with gentlemen.

Nick had done everything he could to persuade Miranda, but she did not see it as her duty: it was not her business if Laurence and Harriet did not know how to convince Mrs. Stornaway.

Fane looked around the room which was furnished in perfect taste, but which was a little colorless despite the expense which had been lavished on it, and inspiration struck.

"If we were to wait," he said casually, "Prinny himself would give us an engagement party. He is far too busy entertaining the allies at the moment, but in a few months he'd be able to manage something rather nice—perhaps in the Brighton Pavilion itself."

Miranda quickly saw that this would be a triumph: she, dancing at the Pavilion, surrounded by the cream of European as well as English society. Yes, that would be something that the other girls of her set would envy. Nick mentioned that Prinny gave presents on such occasions—the last engaged couple had received a very nice country house as a gift—and the more he talked, the more Miranda knew that this was what she wanted, and she understood that the false engagement was the price.

"But, dear Nicholas, I cannot like you being thrown together with that woman! What will people say?"

Nick was very grateful that Miranda did not know of the marriage proposal he had made to Alicia.

"She is less of a hoyden that she used to be," he said, thinking of how Alicia had looked the night of her card party, "and we can tell people that my grandmother wishes the match. I'll write her—she'll help us. Alicia was down at Hansdown for a month around Christmas time—my grandmother could have met her then and liked her."

"Not very credible, Nicholas, given Alicia's character, but I suppose it will have to do. We can let it be known that it is against your will, that of course you are not interested in her, but wish to please your sick grandmother . . . Miranda began to see the ways in which even this false engagement could be turned into a triumph for herself. Alicia, the Drake heiress, would ultimately lose Fane to Miranda. . . .

As for Fane, he could not help feeling a little contemptuous of Miranda, so easily persuaded when the Prince was mentioned. But she was certainly no worse than the rest of her sex, he reflected cynically.

St. Clair turned out to be even more difficult to manage. "Just because a silly child I hardly know has convinced her mother that I am hers! Alicia, it will be the devil to pay with me if I don't have the engagement announced soon—my creditors, dear girl! It is an unpleasant aspect, but it must be dealt with!"

Alicia was worn down by what had been almost an hour of disagreement, and she finally saw what she must offer.

"All right, I have the solution. Send your most pressing bills to me and I will settle them. I'll have to do it sooner or later, so it makes no difference."

St. Clair hesitated, and then agreed. She saw that things must be very bad with him if he would let her pay his bills now.

"And then you would agree to the scheme?"

"Yes, of course. But I still don't like it, your going about with Fane, of all people . . . and I shall pay you back, Alicia," he said somewhat constrainedly, "when my estates are in better order."

"Of course," she said, feeling guilty that she had so much money, and he had none. She had hardly seen him since the card party, and now she began to think it was because he was worrying so about his debts.

When she told Charlotte about it, she did not mention the payment of debts, but she did say it had been difficult.

"Well, I imagine that Nick had a bad time of it, too! Miranda could not have liked the idea of you replacing her!"

"No, you may be sure she did not."

A few days later all was settled and the announcement of Alicia Tierney and Lord Fane was sent to *The Gazette*, and was read with interest by many, not the least of whom was the Duke of Kendalford, who found it not at all to his taste.

The first public appearance of the newly engaged couple was to be at a concert of the Philharmonic Society. Charlotte disliked Haydn, but she said she would go to see what people said when they saw Nick and Alicia together. Worthing would accompany her, and they would arrive after Alicia and Nick, so as to observe everything from the back of the hall.

Fane and Alicia arrived at the concert in surprisingly good spirits, due to the fact that they had hit upon the pleasant subject of Major Trilling.

The Philharmonic had been established only a year earlier,

and was meant to compete with the Concert of Ancient Music. It was run by professionals, rather than enthusiastic amateurs of aristocratic means. Because of this, one could expect an unusually mixed audience, drawing its members from all levels of society. Alicia saw many acquaintances, such as Mrs. Selby, who would be sure to tell everyone she saw the next day that Lord Fane and Miss Tierney had been seen together. In the crowd Alicia also recognized Cranmer, Lady Terbury's butler, and Alexander St. Clair, who waved to her from across the room.

Nick's face grew wooden, and following the direction of his gaze, she saw Anne Dunstan and Lucien de Rohant sitting several rows ahead of them. Nick, who had been very pleasant until then, became silent and withdrawn.

Alicia found herself growing irritated with him, and she meditated on all of his past sins as the orchestra played one of the Salomon symphonies. Anne Dunstan's story came back to her, and she found that she could very easily believe that the proud and disdainful dandy sitting beside her could do such a thing. She admitted to herself that it would be easier to like him if he had not rescued her several times, putting her in his debt.

When the concert was over, he seemed to become friendly once more, but she was not, and welcomed a chance to talk to Alexander St. Clair, who was approaching them.

Mrs. Selby caught Nick and congratulated him on his engagement.

"A most unusual girl, an original," she said fanning herself. She was dying to tell someone about the engagement, but she felt that she should first try to obtain a little more information from the bridegroom-to-be.

"Yes," drawled the dandy, lazily smiling, "I find her a continual challenge. But of course anything worth having is worth exerting oneself for, at least a *little*."

Sure that this remark would create a sensation in the Drayton camp, Mrs. Selby hurried off to confer with a dowager in a hideous purple turban.

Much to her discomfort, Alicia was congratulated by Alexander St. Clair.

"There was talk you were thinking of marrying my nephew, Miss Tierney, but he's not a husband I would wish on anyone— too much like his father, you see, run through the money, and other things as well. Got yourself a fine fellow in Lord Fane. Very happy for you." He patted her avuncularly, but Alicia felt anything but happy.

Worthing saw her face and asked what had cast her down. When she told him, he laughed and said it was to be expected.

"Think of poor Nick, hearing about Miranda. Can't be helped, given the situation, but don't pay too much attention. Society always finds enough to dislike in any match."

"Yes, I suppose I shall hear a stream of criticism when Fane and I dissolve this match," she said, cheered by this idea.

"I daresay. That's the ticket! A nice smile, no stormy looks." Worthing genuinely disliked seeing a woman unhappy. As a true lover of the female sex, he felt that they should have anything that would make them happy. The problem, Alicia saw, came when two of them wanted the same thing. Himself, for example.

Alicia took his arm and told him to walk her around the room a bit.

"You know, Charlotte likes you very much," she began.

"Yes, I know I amuse her."

"I don't mean that. I think she may be in love with you."

"Oh, I don't think so. Women always like me well enough, but they don't fall in love with me. But she might have . . . I suppose I haven't thought about it very much. . . ."

"Do you suppose that you might before her fiancé arrives?" asked Alicia tartly.

"Fiancé?"

Alicia saw that he really knew nothing about it. She told him about Stanford, stressing his good qualities, his fortune, the lands that marched side by side, the historical connections between the families, and finally, how he adored Charlotte.

Worthing seemed bewildered by all of this information.

"And what do you have to offer her, Jack?"

"I must confess—I simply enjoyed being with her. I suppose it never occurred to me—that she might be engaged, although such a girl would of course . . .

"Yes, yes," said Alicia, "but the point is, she has no real desire to marry Stanford. But she needs more than vague promises if she is to break off with him."

They walked back to the door, unaware that Fane was watching them. Worthing was very distracted and hardly heard Alicia say good-bye.

"He seems rather upset about something," remarked Fane.

Feeling that it was none of his business, Alicia made no answer to this, but said that she thought Mrs. Selby was enjoying their engagement.

"Yes, I expect she is. I have the feeling that this is going to be more difficult than Lady Mary envisioned. What have you told your servants?"

"Oh, I did not tell them the truth—that would be trusting things too far, and word would immediately get back to the Stomaways."

He took a pinch of snuff and said that it looked to be rather fatiguing, being an engaged man, going out every night.

"But we shan't do it that often," said Alicia, feeling guilty that he was giving up more than she. "We don't have to be seen more than twice a week, I should think. The rest of the time no one can really know whether we see each other or not. Of course we shall have to be careful about seeing our real fiancés."

"Yes," he agreed, "Mrs. Selby would wonder at my seeing Miranda, or you, St. Clair. Tell me, Alicia, how were you persuaded to do this thing? I felt it a small price to pay for Laurence's happiness, but it involves greater sacrifice on your part."

Alicia thought this a rather odd statement. Why should he think it easier for himself to put off Miranda than she, St. Clair?

"I cannot imagine that our motives are so very different. Harriet is a close friend of mine, I owe her debts I can never repay . . . and she cannot oppose her mother and win—that I know. I felt I had to help her—it cost me so little, really."

He looked faintly surprised, and she felt that she had been correct in her earlier evaluation—he did not think women capable of real acts of friendship. Where could he have gotten this contempt for the sex? Perhaps his mother had been one of those fashionable women with a pincushion where her heart should be.

31
UNPLEASANT ENCOUNTERS

For a few weeks, the *ton* found the engagement of Lord Fane and the Drake heiress, Alicia Tierney, to be of interest. After that, the appearance of Byron's *Corsair* (selling a brisk 13,000 a month), the news of Wellington's victories in France, and finally, Napoleon's abdication in early March, overshadowed everything else.

When other subjects palled, Mrs. Selby was fond of conjecturing what Fane's grandmother would say when she met Alicia, who was a nobody, after all, although a rich one.

As the days passed and they attended countless routs, concerts, and plays, the main participants in the false engagement found it less and less enjoyable.

Alicia was bored. She hardly saw St. Clair, who was forced to meet her in shops in districts where their friends would be unlikely to be. When they met, St. Clair would use up much of their precious time in complaining.

"When will those damned Stornaways come to town! I feel like a spy, meeting like this."

They were in a small antique shop, pretending an interest in some Chinese lacquer boxes.

"Well, if you think I like having to go everywhere with Fane! He is terribly civil, polite, but he often looks as though he is being forced to swallow some vile-tasting medicine. He makes me feel that I am nothing but a burden to him."

"Why not end this farce, then?"

"Oh, St. Clair! Think of Harriet and Laurence!"

"Think of me! I am suffering from insomnia, I drink until dawn—"

"You have always gone to bed at dawn—don't try to blame me! It will not be much longer, really. The Stornaways are due at any time now. Once the permission is given, they'll get married right away—"

"I don't believe it," he said in comic anguish, "Lady Cecily, I shall never have your hand. The villains are separating us." He kissed her quickly, so that the shopkeeper would not see. When they walked out of the shop and went their separate ways, neither of them paid any attention to the ragged individual who had been watching them from the doorway across the street.

Alicia returned home unhappy, as she always did from these brief meetings, and found Charlotte crying on her bed.

"What has happened?"

Charlotte raised her head and angrily dashed the tears away.

"I have been such a fool! You can't imagine!"

"I certainly can't, if you don't tell me more than that."

Charlotte tried to smile, unsuccessfully.

"I have been an absolute idiot about Worthing. I thought I was being careful, that it would all come right—but it has not."

"What did he do?"

Charlotte sat up and said in a very quiet, very angry voice that he had asked her to become his mistress.

"Oh, is that all? My dear, he is just trying to be noble," said Alicia calmly.

"What do you mean?"

"I told him about Stanford, you know. This is his way of driving you into the arms of a more proper suitor."

Charlotte shook her head.

"No, I don't think so. He is incapable of that sort of nobility. No, Alicia, he meant it. And when I said no, he *laughed* at me! Said I should go back to my family, settle down with someone who would be better for me . . ."

"There, don't you see, he's just trying to give you a chance to leave him—"

"No, I tell you, that is not what it was! He—he insulted me, and he *meant* to—and we are not to see each other again."

Alicia did not know what to say to comfort her friend and they sat in silence for a while. Then Charlotte got up and wiped her face, saying she would be all right.

"It is so stupid, Alicia. I have never loved anyone as I do him, even with all his faults. I know all of his defects, and they make no difference at all."

Alicia was immediately tormented by the thought that she had caused these problems by telling Worthing about Stanford.

She was in such low spirits the next night that Fane was moved to ask her if she were feeling well. They had just been to see Kean in *Richard III*, and he remarked that she seemed to have gotten very little out of what was considered a remarkable performance by the actor.

"I know," she said pensively, "but I am feeling rather down, and this is not precisely the play that would cheer me up, you know."

"We should have seen *Trip to Scarborough*, then."

"Yes, you laugh, but that would have done very well."

In an effort to distract her, Fane suggested that they attend one of Webb's soirees.

"Webb? I have heard the name, but I don't remember . . ."

"He is an eccentric man who has a great deal too much money. His is one of the few private houses where there is play. Perhaps his faro table will entertain you, since the Shakespeare did not."

"But will it not be tedious for you?"

"No, I enjoy a go at the roulette table now and again, and some friends will be there."

When they arrived at the Webb mansion, the house was overflowing with guests, most of them very gay from the wine. Fane hesitated at the door, but Alicia declared that the drunken condition of the guests suited her exactly and that she herself planned to equal them, if she could manage it.

She had imbibed a good deal of champagne by the time she saw Lucien de Rohant playing faro. Fane had gone off to the roulette table, and she felt free to talk to him.

Lucien congratulated her on her engagement to Fane.

"Thank you, Monsieur de Rohant, very kind. I believe you do not know Nick very well, however."

"True, mademoiselle, but I do know this *canaille*—this St. Clair—and I had heard the rumors that you were to marry him."

Alicia wondered if she had heard him correctly, and asked him to repeat what he had said.

"I say he is *canaille*, and this is true. To be engaged to the young Miss Stornaway, and now to claim he is not—only a *cochon* would do such a thing! All before he meets you. So as to have the most fortune, he changes his story—but do not upset yourself, Miss Tierney! What have I said?"

She had gone even paler than her natural coloring and looked as if she might faint.

She agreed to go riding with de Rohant the next week, and

then she went to look for Nick. On the way she drank three more glasses of champagne in quick succession.

With no memory of how she got there, she found herself on the main staircase, holding carefully onto the side, taking one step at a time.

Fane was waiting at the bottom of the staircase. He was surprisingly solicitous, and wrapped her cloak carefully around her.

When they were in the coach she felt a strong desire to lean her head on Fane's shoulder. She looked at it and was gradually leaning in that direction, when Fane asked her something.

"So sorry," she said carefully. "Didn't understand. Drank, you know. Poor Charlotte."

"I asked what you talked of with de Rohant."

"Ah. He told me that *he* is a deceitful wretch, who—" Alicia suddenly realized what she was saying. "My own problem, not yours. Could you ask your driver to stop on the bridge? Must get out, feeling sick."

She got out and took several deep breaths of the icy air. A moment later, he caught her as she began to fall.

He carried her to the coach, and when she became conscious, she was lying in his arms.

"You are sometimes very kind," she murmured into his chest. "Harriet was right about that."

"Did you drink so much because of whatever de Rohant said?"

"No, other thlngi, too . . . don't ask me, you shouldn't take advantage of me when I am foxed. . . ."

Without waiting for his answer, she put her head against his shoulder and fell asleep.

Stilton was astonished when he opened the door and saw Lord Fane standing there with Miss Alicia in his arms.

"Please don't wake her," whispered Fane. "I'll carry her to her room. She's not been well."

"But I cannot—you cannot—Miss Jellicoe—"

"I *am* her fiancé," said Fane in the firm tone which had always been effective with butlers.

A worried Stilton followed Fane up the stairs, and showed him into the bedroom, where he gently laid her down.

The next morning Alicia had difficulty in remembering every-thing that had happened, but she knew she had a headache. She rang for Jellicoe and requested one of her restorative drinks.

"I should say you would! I've one all ready. I don't know what your poor mother would have said! Shocking, I call it. Carrying you into your room!" Jellicoe was actually upset, not just pretending, and Alicia began to fear that whatever had happened was very bad indeed.

"What are you babbling about, Jelly? I'm a grown woman. If I wish to get unhappy and then drink too much champagne, it is well within my rights—and don't try to tell me that half our acquaintances don't do the same!"

"It's the gentlemen that does it, miss, not so much the *ladies*," sniffed Jellicoe in her best Scots schoolmarm manner. Her round little face had such an expression of haughty disdain that Alicia laughed out loud. This was a mistake, she discovered, since it made her head hurt even more.

"All I have to say is that it's a blessing you're to be married to him! Imagine, carrying you to your own bed!"

Alicia began to have a horrible feeling. Maybe the dream she had had was not a dream—but reality?

"I collect you mean Stilton . . ."

"Don't try to bamboozle me. I know it was Lord Fane himself! Imagine, such a gentleman, having to catch you fainting! I've never been so mortified as when I heard the servants talk of it! Of course, his coachman spread the tale—no doubt he colored it some. . . ."

As the details of the previous night came back to her, Alicia flushed, causing Jellicoe to jump to the conclusion that she had contracted a dangerous fever.

"No, no, Jelly! Never mind the doctor! If you wish me to get up, go and have Eliza bring me a decent breakfast," she said, remembering her Cousin Freddy's advice about hangover.

She rose and examined her mirror. She had huge purple shadows under her eyes. Even after washing up and dressing herself in a becoming lace morning gown, she still looked like someone who had been foxed the night before. It all began to come back. The dazzling dandy, Lord Fane, had been forced to deal with a drunken female. His words came back to her— the words he had said the night of the Silver Tree. *But you will never make a lady!* and she had proved him wrong—she had impressed him at her card party, she knew she had. And now she would have to apologize. Alicia abruptly sensed that there was something black and ugly swimming to the surface of her memory of last night, something she did not really want to remember. . . .

She was halfway through her breakfast and the solicitous Eliza was pouring hot tea when she remembered.

"St. Clair!" she said involuntarily.

"What is it, miss?" said the alarmed Eliza, who was watching Alicia's face.

"Nothing, dear, nothing. But don't ever let a man ruin your breakfast, Eliza—promise me that."

When Charlotte got up Alicia told her everything she remembered of the conversation with de Rohant and the evening with Fane.

"Well," said Charlotte, "we can hope it is not true." Charlotte felt like a perfect traitor, not telling Alicia what Lady Mary had discovered, but she knew Alicia had to find out for herself.

That morning Alicia sat down and wrote two notes. One, to Fane, requested him to call on her the next day, the other begged St. Clair to arrive in Curzon Street as soon as he could.

Some hours later she was picturesquely reading by the fire in the library when St. Clair was announced.

"I was delighted to receive your summons. What is the reason for the charming note—you are longing for me? You have decided to end this pretend engagement to the so-respectable Fane?"

Now that he was here, it did not seem so easy, or so simple. He stood looking at her, a warm smile in his eyes. For a moment she considered not asking him. He had always needed money, and there might have been a time when Julia Stornaway would have seemed the only way out . . .

"Robert," she said with an effort, "just how *well* do you know Julia Stornaway?"

He made a gesture of impatience. "Oh, is that what this is about! I wondered when the stories would reach you. I had a brief flirtation with the child, but that is as far as it went. What she may have imagined, I don't know. I know the gossip—I am not well liked here." His anger got the better of him. "Of course I will understand if all of this causes a change in your sentiments!"

"Is that what you wish, Robert?" She was very upset, and was twisting the rose cut diamond ring, remembering how everyone had congratulated her on her engagement to Fane and her escape from St. Clair. She now saw them all as vicious gossips, who would ruin a man for little enough reason—their own enjoyment. No, as long as he wanted her, as long as he was honest with her, she would stand by him.

"No, Alicia," he said. "It is not what I wish. If this story has changed your feelings, I will destroy myself and have done. You are the only woman I have seen who could make me change my ways, save me from myself."

The look on his face frightened her: she could almost believe that he would destroy himself. But at the same time a small voice whispered that it was all drama, a show.

"I am not a good man," he said quietly. "So perhaps you had better have done with me now."

"Stop," she said weary of it all. "This is over. I believe you. We shall never refer to it again: we shall go on as before."

This interview drained her, and she was reluctant to describe it to Charlotte. She merely said that it had all been exaggerated—St. Clair had flirted with the girl, nothing more—and that as far as she was concerned, the matter was ended.

Charlotte comprehended that there was more to it than this, but she did not press her friend for details. Whatever had happened, Alicia was not completely satisfied with her St. Clair, and this was all that mattered. If only other disillusionments could follow soon enough, the marriage might be prevented.

The two friends stayed home that evening, playing cards. They played so badly, however, that they had to give it up.

"I suppose we are not concentrating enough."

"I certainly am not. What are you thinking of, Charlotte?"

"Jack, of course. I can't seem to think of anything else. It's terribly stupid. I know that I will get over it, I know that there will be someone else, but right now it does not seem that there will ever be someone like Jack, to laugh with. . . ."

Charlotte said nothing more about it, but Alicia knew that her friend would cry herself to sleep once again.

Alicia went to bed, but could not sleep. She looked at her

clock and saw that it was only one in the morning—Worthing would be awake, if he were home.

Giving in to the overwhelming impulse to do something for Charlotte, she decided to go and see Jack. She dressed quickly and tiptoed down the stairs to Jim Taylor's room. He was not asleep and was only too happy to set out on a venture that would certainly not find favor with either Stilton or Jellicoe.

It was a bitterly cold night, and Alicia was grateful for the lap rug Jim had thrown over her. She waited outside in the coach, as Jim went in to the Crescent Street house to see if Worthing were home.

He came hurrying out a second later, Jack behind him.

"What's this, my girl? Late-night visits?"

"I didn't leave the coach, so your servants haven't seen me. I have to talk to you. Get in and we'll take a drive."

Alicia told him everything that Charlotte had said since the night he had offered to make her his mistress. He listened in silence, but Alicia thought she saw a lightening of his countenance when she finished.

"I am grateful you came. This requires some managing, but I can tell you that I've been pretty low myself, missed her like the very devil! The only thing is—what's that!"

Thumping sounds came from the driver's box.

"Foodpads! And someone has a pistol."

"Have you anything with you?" asked Alicia.

"No. I'll get out and take a look."

Worthing climbed up on the side he judged to be the farthest from the noise and was immediately struck by a club. His assailant succeeded in knocking him off the moving coach. In horror, Alicia heard him calling to her, telling her to jump. She was about to do just that when a strong arm wrapped itself about her throat.

"Here, there, missy! Don't want you to be hurt!"

He smelled of gin, and Alicia's first impulse was to push him away, but he was very strong and merely tightened his grip. He had apparently entered from the other side just as she had been trying to get out.

He took a length of cord from his pocket and tied her wrists behind her back. After he was satisfied that she could not get free, he returned to the box, leaving her alone to imagine what was going to happen to her. It could be a ransom demand; it could even end in white slavery. But it was not simple robbery; they had fought Worthing and Jim Taylor, but they had not tried to take her rings from her.

Worthing lay on the road for a few minutes, trying to get strength enough to rise to his feet. He heard someone running towards him and was half-afraid it was a street thief who would finish the job the abductors had begun. With joy he recognized the voice of Jim Taylor.

"I'll get you home, sir, don't worry. We'll get them, I know who to go to—"

"Lord Fane—and only Lord Fane. Just get me to Nick's house on Cavendish Square. All right, Jim?"

It seemed to Worthing that it took hours to find someone who would agree to transport them to Cavendish Square, but the clock in Fane's room showed that it had only been an hour since Alicia had been taken. Fane was in his dressing gown, settled in for a good night's drink at home, from the looks of it.

"What is it, man? What has happened to your clothes?"

"I am afraid that Mercier's people have got Alicia."

The expression of vague affability disappeared from Fane's face in an instant. He quickly went to change, giving various orders to his man, Jerry Daws. A note was sent to Laurence with a brief explanation, requesting him to stay at Fane's house until his return and to accept and open any letters that might arrive. A Bow Street runner was to be sent after him if he didn't return in forty-eight hours.

In fifteen minutes he and Worthing were riding in the fastest carriage he owned. They returned to the street the attack had occurred on, and began to interrogate the linkboys as to the direction of the fashionable cream and brown coach. A half-hour of inquiry produced evidence that it had gone towards the Brighton Road. Jim Taylor was sent back to Cavendish Square with this information, and they were on their way, with Jerry Daws driving at breakneck speed.

"They will want an exchange, I think," said Fane.

"Most likely. I should have known that they might come after her—she being your fiancée, after all. Never should have driven around at that time of night, but she didn't want to come in—the servants, you know."

"Afraid of how it would look? The daring Miss Tierney?" Fane's voice was flat.

"Nick, I'm not free to explain, but she had come to help a friend—and that's all I'll say. She's a regular crackerjack, that girl, and I pray we get there before they scare her too much."

"It takes rather a lot to scare that one," said Fane, taking a bit of snuff and offering Worthing some. "Try this, my new blend. Quite nice, really."

32

THE MISSING COUPLE

Laurence Terbury was too used to following Fane's orders without question to allow what he knew of the events of late Saturday night to upset him greatly, but he began to be worried when his friends were not back by Sunday evening. He had sent word to Charlotte, so that Alicia's household would not be up in arms over the absence of its mistress. Charlotte had discussed the matter with Stilton and Jellicoe, who along with Potts and Jim Taylor, were the only servants to know that Alicia was not safely in her bed. Worried communications were kept up between the two houses, and it was decided that the Terburys should not be alerted until matters had become clearer.

At seven o'clock Sunday evening Laurence heard someone at the door, and Fane's butler came into the sitting room with an envelope.

"Rough-looking young person brought this, sir. Didn't wait for an answer. I imagine him to have been a hired delivery boy and nothing more."

Laurence read the ransom note, as it turned out to be, and wished he knew if Fane had been successful. The abductors were Mercier's people—now there could be no doubt of that—and they wished to exchange the life of Lord Fane's fiancée for that of one Jean Delahaye, now in a British prison.

In some ways this was a relief, for if Fane had been wrong, and the abduction had not been politically inspired, it might have been worse. Mercier would certainly keep Alicia safe until he had his exchange. The note included directions for a meeting of emissaries, to be held in a London coffeehouse the next night. The details of the exchange were to be worked out then.

Laurence was puzzled by the fact that Alicia had gone to Worthing's at such an hour, and he was beginning to feel that Alicia had brought a good deal of this on herself. He thought of Harriet with satisfaction—she'd never lead him such a dance of it, that he knew. But, he quietly acknowledged, if Alicia weren't so unusual, Georgiana would still have his letters. . . .

In Curzon Street, Jellicoe had also drawn a number of conclusions, all of them distressing, about Alicia's visit to Worthing. Charlotte merely laughed at her when she hinted that Miss Alicia might have lost her morals in London.

"Now, do not be absurd! It is no such thing! I think I know why she went, and it was to help me, if you must know. I am worried about only one thing—that wretched Frenchman de Rohant will come calling to take her riding tomorrow, and she won't be here. He talks like a magpie, and it will be all over London that Alicia's not at home."

Jellicoe's round ruddy face took on an expression of cunning. "We'll say she's sick."

"I told everyone that she fell from her horse, but I'm not sure he'll believe it—Lady Holland didn't. Of course, what can he do if we all say it's so?"

This settled, they turned their minds to what they would say if St. Clair happened to visit—the truth or not? Charlotte decided not. She still felt that he was not completely trustworthy. Who knew what he would say while drinking? The most serious problem had been Alicia's absence at Lady Holland's that afternoon; Lady Holland's invitation was one which no Whig would refuse. Charlotte had gone and had explained to all and sundry that Alicia had suffered a nasty fall from her horse and could not walk.

Lady Holland, sharp and eccentric, was a very bright woman, and she immediately knew that something was amiss. Charlotte was certain of it.

"I daresay I shall see the chit another time," was all Lady Holland said, surprising those who expected a withering remark.

Charlotte was saved from having to explain Fane's absence as well by his quick wits. He had written a note crying off, and had told Laurence to have it delivered in the afternoon. Miranda, high color in her cheeks, remarked that it appeared that the engaged couple wished to be together, "and not at Lady Holland's," a remark which expressed her ill-nature so well that Charlotte almost laughed aloud.

The only other person who had wanted an explanation was Anne Dunstan. She had been away at her country estate and had returned to hear the news of Alicia's engagement to Fane. She had expressed her shock and dismay at this match and declared her intention to visit Alicia at the earliest opportunity.

"Although I expect she does not wish to see me, now that she is to be married to Lord Fane. I can imagine what stories he has told her. Tell her she needn't see old friends, Miss Marlowe, if they interfere with her domestic happiness."

All in all, it had been a trying day, and Charlotte was glad to be in bed—but she could not sleep. What had happened to Alicia? Fane's note to Laurence had been brief and uninformative. They were not to worry, everything would be all right, but if they weren't back by Monday night, a Bow Street runner was to be sent to Brighton.

Alicia woke with a start, and at first she did not remember where she was. The room was a small one, the house appeared to be a fisherman's cottage. She could smell the sea and guessed that it was very near. The windows were nailed shut, but through a crack she could see a cart throwing no shadow in the sunlight It was noon, then, and she had been asleep a long time. She must have fallen asleep in the coach, and then been carried in here. It made her shiver to think of that ginsmelling lout carrying her.

She found a pitcher of water and was washing up when there was a knock at the door.

"Yes, who is it?"

"Something to eat, mum. A little porridge."

The door opened, and a little white-haired old woman came in, carrying a bowl.

"You are very kind, but I never eat porridge. I detest it."

The old lady gave her a sweet smile.

"Dearie, you'd best eat it anyway. Who knows when you'll be having such food again?" With that she left Alicia and the bowl alone together. Deciding that the old lady was no doubt right, Alicia overcame her distaste and managed to eat a little of the porridge. Then she tried to put some order into her appearance, cleaning the spots off her dress, wishing that there were at least something to read in the room. She had made up her mind not to imagine what would happen. Major Trilling had once told her that the only way to face something really unpleasant, like a battle, was to banish it from your mind until you were actually involved in it. She tried to hypnotize herself into thinking nothing was very wrong. Any moment they would come and save her. Worthing was *not* lying hurt on the road. Jim Taylor was fine. They would tell St. Clair, and he would come and find her. This was all going to be over, very soon, very soon. . . .

But it was not very soon. No one came; no one spoke. She decided against screaming: she would not give her abductors that satisfaction. The cracks in the boards seemed to indicate that the cottage was very isolated, at least from the side she could look out of. . . . How would they ever find her?

Fane and Worthing were having very little luck. The coach had not gone into Brighton, as far as they could tell. They began a slow search in the neighboring towns along the seacoast Finally they came upon an old man who had spent the day sitting by his window, which looked out on the crossroads where the Brighton Road intersected the Coast Road. The old man was fond of proverbs, however, and it took Worthing almost a half-hour to get any useful information out of him.

To their first question, the man replied that "He that pryeth into every cloud may be struck with a thunderbolt." Fane turned away, but Worthing persisted, and after hearing many unusual turns of speech, finally deduced that the cream-and-brown carriage had gone in the direction of Seaford.

Fane congratulated Worthing on his abilities.

"Yes, I was afraid that his cockloft was unfurnished, as he himself would say, but then I saw that he wanted to know what we were after. Before he would tell his story, I had to tell mine."

"And what was your story?"

"Runaway heiress, underage, evil French dancing-master. He immediately imagined the rest. Says if he doesn't see us come back he'll get the riding officer out. . . .

They rode towards Seaford, and half way there they saw a carriage being painted at a carriage maker's. It was all black, with silver trim, but just to be sure Worthing stopped and examined it closely. Underneath, the main body had not been painted yet, and it was a dark brown. They asked the workmen where the carriage had come from, but they swore they knew nothing of it—a local gentleman had bought it last week. Worthing was frustrated; he knew they were lying.

"They are afraid that we are investigating smugglers. I imagine that many of these families have something to hide. Best, in their view, to tell nothing to a stranger."

"Very admirable," said Fane in a bored tone. "You know, I think I shall go and have a drink in that tavern. You stay here with Daws."

Worthing thought this a strange way to go about finding Alicia, but shrugged his shoulders; in any case. Fane would do what he wished.

Little Polly thought that the gentleman was very handsome, and much more polite than her customers usually were. He invited her to have a drink with him, which she did. She saw that he became tipsy almost immediately, and she felt almost protective toward him. He told her the sad story of his young sister, who had run off with a worthless gamester. They were somewhere in the neighborhood, but the poor gentleman was afraid to ask anyone about it, because folks here were suspicious of strangers.

After some ten minutes of friendly discussion, punctuated, it must be said, by friendly kisses, Polly found herself offering to find out what she could for him. She went to the kitchen to talk to the serving-boy, who always knew everything. Bertie was his name, and he did indeed know all the doings up and down the coast—he was so undersized and young-looking that none worried about what he heard—he seemed such a child. The child was seventeen, however, and knew how to get the most from his knowledge. He told Polly to ask for five pounds. Polly turned to go and talk to Fane when she discovered him standing behind the kitchen door.

"Five is rather too much," he drawled. "Here is two pounds to split between you. Although Polly did get the price of a drink as well, I feel she was worth it, Bertie. Thank you for your help, and before you feel too bad about it, remember that I could have paid nothing since I had already heard what I needed to know."

Polly watched him go. A right fool he'd made of her—he hadn't been drunk at all.

Worthing was in bad humor and demanded to know what had taken Fane so long.

"The kissing, old man, the kissing. But I know which house now. It's the one at the far end of the next cove."

If Bertie's information was correct, there was no one tending her except an old lady.

"They did not expect us so soon," said Fane. "I imagine that they felt they had covered their tracks very well. Indeed, if it had not been for that proverb-spouting gentleman we might well not have found it."

When they drove up to the little cottage, the old lady came to the door, obviously terrified.

"What can I do for you, gentlemen? There is no one home but myself."

She looked so frightened that Worthing almost felt sorry for her.

"We have been sent for the girl, madam," said Fane calmly. "I shall go in and get her."

The old lady was torn. She half-believed that they might be the men who were supposed to come; but on the other hand, they were clearly gentlemen, and she had not expected gentlemen. She protested that they were not allowed to enter her house just like that.

"Madam, I would not talk about what we are allowed to do," said Fane in a cold tone. "If you come and let her out quickly, I may not bring charges against you."

Now the old lady became even more frightened. Her hands shaking, she gave him the keys. While Fane went inside, Worthing tried to calm her.

"You can tell them that we threatened to kill you. Will these men hurt you?"

"No, no, they won't. It is my son and his friends; it was just a job to them, your honor. They did not know what it was about. . . ."

Worthing chose to believe her. It was very possible that everything had been done through a third party. Considering Mercier's abilities, it was very likely.

Alicia heard the carriage drive up and expected that now she would come face to face with her abductors. The long hours of staring at the wall and trying not to think of what they might do to her had almost worn her down, but she was determined not to show weakness. She heard the door open, and a moment later was looking into the face of Nick Fane.

"How lucky you came in time," was all she said, oddly unsurprised.

He handed her a packet containing clothes and other things she might need. "Here, you must change into these as quickly as you can."

He went outside and Worthing asked him how she was.

"Calm, very calm. Not a very feminine reaction, but I'm glad of it—no scenes of hysteria, thank God."

She came out a few minutes later, dressed in a coat and buck-skins, a hat covering the red hair. Her groom Potts had done well, she thought, to remember the clothes—and her small pistol as well, concealed so that even Fane would probably not have felt it in the packet.

"Looking very fit for a girl as was abducted," joked Worthing. "Did Nick tell you what we are to do? I am to return by stage, you and he in the coach—so observers will see two men leave, just as two men arrived. Until we get to the stage stop you will have to lie on the floor."

She smiled her agreement to the plan, but Fane, who had put her down as a woman who had no nerves, saw with surprise the effort it cost her to smile. Just like a soldier, he thought. She did not wish to give in to her fear.

"It is really all over now," he whispered, as he helped her into the coach.

He saw that she was close to tears.

"Please do not be comforting just now," she said with difficulty. "It will be easier if you are not—otherwise I shall not be able to control myself."

She sat on the floor and turned away, as if looking out the window.

"But you need not, you know. You might feel better if you did cry—most women would, in your situation."

"I am not most women," she said stubbornly, wrapping herself in the lap robe.

Jerry Daws started off at a smart pace for Brighton. Just outside the city they let Worthing off not far from the stage station, so that he might walk in unnoticed. Fane was worried that his friend was too well dressed for the traveling stage.

"I'll make out I'm a gamester down on my luck," said Jack brightly, enjoying the prospect of flirting with pretty country girls. "And you, Alicia, remember to keep your voice low."

Alicia waved to him, feeling a little abandoned. Worthing

was so companionable, someone she could talk to. Now she was alone with Fane, her rescuer once again, and the last man with whom she would have wished to be alone in a coach.

It became clear in the course of their conversation that although Fane was not particularly forthcoming on the subject of the abduction, he knew more than he was prepared to tell her. Alicia was ready to swear that he knew precisely who had hired the men, and why. She surmised that it had to do with his missions in France and did not press him. After a while, their conversation trailed off, and they settled down to silence, each busy with private thoughts.

Remembering the times when she had thought Fane was many different men in one, Alicia came to the conclusion that she had been right. There was a subtle but definite difference in Fane today: perhaps he was too tired to put on the show, perhaps he no longer needed to. He looked different, attired in his now-crumpled riding clothes, and even his voice had changed—soft, firm, matter-of-fact, even when making attempts at his usual set-downs with her.

They traveled on, and Alicia, who had not seen anything on the way down, observed the changing landscape.

"It is a very prosperous land, isn't it?" said Fane, who had marked her interest in what they had passed.

"Yes . . . I had never really thought about it, but it is. . . . I have read that other countries are not so fortunate—is that true?"

"Yes . . . other countries are physically beautiful, but signs of prosperity you see here—the way the workers in the fields are dressed, for example, are strikingly different from France, Italy, or Spain. If it is true, as the historians write, that countries have cycles of affluence and poverty, then we are now in our affluence."

"And what of Napoleon and France—are they not affluent?

There are many in England who are in love with Napoleon and secretly wish him to win. What would happen then?"

"I do not think England would enjoy being under French rule—it is not a thing which would be endurable for most in this country. If England chose it, that would be one thing, but to have it imposed must always be repellent."

They passed the day quietly, stopping to refresh the horses and themselves. When it became dark, however, there were no distractions to be had. Alicia was uncomfortably aware of Fane's presence. She felt suddenly shy with him. She put it down to the impression Fane made of being a different man, but he was the same man who had seemed frivolous, who had several times humiliated her, irritated her, kissed her when she did not give him leave to. . . .

They drove on, passing fewer and fewer coaches. Alicia felt as though she were in a small boat, moving through the night, a sensation not at all unpleasant. She felt very tired, but she could not fall asleep. She was too aware of Fane sitting in the other corner, his hat over his eyes, his long legs stretched out to the side in what appeared to be a most uncomfortable position. She began to feel that she was a great burden to him, although this particular escapade could hardly be considered her fault— even though she had impulsively gone to see Worthing so late at night. This aspect of the problem struck her—what had Worthing said to Fane? Had he explained why she had come? She flushed, thinking about what Fane might have assumed. She wanted to tell him about Charlotte, but she could find no way to begin. Being alone in the coach made personal conversation difficult, somehow.

She was just beginning to think that at last she would be able to sleep when the coach came to an abrupt stop. Fane called up to Daws, who informed him that one of the wheels had hit a sharp object on the road. He was afraid that they would have to stop at the next inn to have it looked at. They were an hour past Redford, and the surrounding countryside looked very unpromising to Alicia. As the coach began moving, very slowly, she felt some of her fears return. What if the men who had abducted her were following? Now they would be able to catch up. She said nothing, but Fane seemed to sense her disquiet.

"I know this road fairly well," he said casually. "There is a place not far from here—I won't dignify it by calling it an inn—but it will do to give us some food and drink, and take care of the wheel. You may see some members of the High Toby as well."

Alicia was startled by this last remark.

"The High Toby? Highway men? But is it so safe?"

"Oh, I see that the daring Miss Tierney is afraid of meeting the gentlemen of the High Toby. Do not worry, I shall protect you."

"I am not *afraid*, your Lordship," she answered icily. "It is just that I do have common sense, and common sense tells me that you would be no protection at all in a room of such men."

"No, I neglected to tell you that these are *retired* members of that noble profession. After they had robbed enough persons they opened this hostelry. The Blue Man. They like to talk of the past, however, and make themselves out to be far worse than they were. Most amusing fellows."

By the time they arrived at The Blue Man, Alicia did not care who ran it—she was tired and hungry, and the roaring fire in the dining room was just what she wished. The landlord did not look at all frightening. He had the appearance of a half-pay officer who was a little the worse for wear. He had seen the fatigue in her face immediately.

"Come in, young fellow. Look pretty well knocked up, you do. A little meat and beer will bring you around."

The dining room had bright little boxes to sit in; they were quite cozy and gave a sense of protection. She sat there after she had finished eating, listening to the conversation of the men in the next room, which was the taproom. She had begun to think that Fane had been amusing himself at her expense with his story of the highwaymen, but as she sat there listening, the conversation did indeed begin to take on a reminiscent character.

They discussed who had gumption, whose blarney was most effective, how to get women to yield their jewels with the greatest alacrity, and other such fascinating subjects.

After she had eaten and drunk her fill, she began to be bored, and wish Fane would return from the taproom. She rose and walked to the windows, looking out at the moonlit countryside. She watched as a coach drew up and disgorged three men. She wondered why any other people would choose to stop here if they could go on to the next large inn. She returned to her seat and sipped the last of her beer. The new arrivals could be heard going into the next room to join the others, who were now singing what was apparently an old drinking and robbing song.

The song ended and they now became very loud as they argued over who had drunk more brandy, and who couldn't hold his drink.

The new arrivals had apparently had some difficulty getting served, for one of them began to call the innkeeper. Alicia went rigid as another voice seconded the first:

"Hey, there, innkeeper! Serve us some ale!"

The same voice had said "*Here, there, missy! Don't want you to be hurt,*" as he tied her arms behind her. Alicia made herself be calm. She must think what to do. Fane was there with them. Did they know him by sight? Would they deduce which one must be Fane? Did they know his carriage, or was it simply an awful coincidence? They would hardly stop here, she reasoned, when five miles further on was a bigger and better inn. The odds were

too great against its being an accident, and they were undoubtedly prepared for resistance. She decided that it would be best
to go and find Jim and whoever was fixing the wheel. The men
in the taproom were most likely too drunk to be of much help.

She was near the front door when Fane came out of the
taproom.

"Nick! Those are the men—" she began, and then stopped.
Behind him, a knife in his hand, was one of the three men.

"And who might this be?" the man said slowly. "Step into the
light, young man, so's I can see you clear."

Alicia saw through the window by the door that the other
two men were already out in the yard, standing by the coach. A
million thoughts raced through her mind.

"And who you might be is of no interest to me," she said in
an imitation of an annoyed young flower of the *ton*. "My boots
give me more concern than you do, you filthy vermin." With
that, she bent down as if to flick the dirt off her boottops. The
footpad was disconcerted by her aggressive tone; he did not
move quickly enough when he realized there was a pistol in her
hand as she came up. She shot him in the right hand, causing
him to drop the knife. It took a few seconds for her to see that
she had also grazed Fane's right arm. It had been a calculated
risk, since he was standing a little in front of the footpad. The
hall was soon filled with drunken men, demanding to know
whose pistol had gone off. Fane said nothing as she wrapped
a handkerchief around his arm. The footpad was collapsed in
a corner, looking very surprised. After she had finished with
Fane, Alicia had the innkeeper send one of his friends for a
doctor, for the man in the corner. She asked Fane if he wished
to be seen to as well.

"No, I think we had better get to London. It is but a scratch,
after all."

Alicia looked out the window to see what had become of the other men and the coach. They were gone, no doubt frightened by the shot and the general commotion.

But Fane was not so sure. He told the innkeeper that footpads had just escaped, a bad piece of business for an inn full of such fine hearty fighters. The innkeeper felt his honor had been questioned and immediately sent the rest of his friends to search them out and get them to a constable.

Alicia went to find Jim Taylor, who was with the wheelwright of the village. He was much amazed by recent events, expressed admiration for Alicia's "pluck." They were just finishing the repairs, so Alicia waited with them until all was ready. When she came to get Fane, she found him looking very white. She noticed his bandage was soaked with blood.

"Perhaps you should stay and see the doctor," she said diffidently, feeling that it might not have been to his taste to be rescued by a woman.

"No, I know about these things. Had a score such in the Peninsula—Badajoz. I'll have to have a little brandy to make me forget it, however."

She could see that it must be extremely painful, and she did not at all agree that a man in such condition should travel in such weather; but she was in no position to order him about.

In the coach, Fane began. "Alicia, I must thank you. I should have been taken by Mercier's men if you had not been there."

"Who is Mercier?"

"I have never seen him, but he is one of the most highly placed French spies in England. What name he uses here, I do not know. Of course I have my suspicions, but there is as yet no evidence. They wanted you so that they could then blackmail me into giving them one of their men, who is now in prison here. It did not occur to me that they would involve you, for which I must beg your pardon."

"No need to beg pardon—if I had not been so muddleheaded as to visit Worthing at that hour of the night, I daresay it would not have happened."

"Perhaps," he said. "But the fact remains that you have saved me. Where did you learn to shoot, or did your cousin Freddy teach you that, too?"

"No, my groom Potts taught me. He was a great shot in the army."

Alicia felt very hollow. The intense emotions and nervous energy of the past twenty minutes were now making themselves felt. She had shot a man—how many women could say that?

"Why don't you have some of this brandy. Make you feel better."

She stretched out her hand to take it from him, but he kept it in his own, and put an arm around her as he held it to her lips.

"There, it's going to be all right. You will forget it. At least you didn't kill him—you don't have that to have nightmares about. You really are a most shocking girl. Alicia. What would Mrs. Selby say? Oh, I can imagine how she'd begin: 'Lucilla, you will never guess! Who shot whom on the Brighton Road, and why were they abducted in the first place?'"

This was so accurate an imitation of that lady's slightly nasal voice that Alicia began to laugh, spilling some of the brandy on both of them.

"Oh, dear, now I've ruined this coat, too. I hope you have many more."

"I have a few to spare," said Fane dryly.

He did not remove his arm from around her shoulders, but took a cloth and, with his right hand, which must have been painful for him, wiped them both off as best he could in the dark. Alicia did not at all mind his arm about her, but she began to wonder if he himself remembered that it was there. Perhaps he was drunk on the brandy, weak from the loss of blood.

She brought the conversation back to an earlier remark.

"Did you have nightmares after you killed your first man?"

"Yes, many times, even with the third and the fourth. It is not something pleasant, even if war is the excuse. . . ."

He fell silent, as if thinking about something called up by this conversation. He took another sip of the brandy and lay back against the cushions, still with his arm around her.

"But this is not something I wish to talk about with you," he said softly.

Alicia took another drink of the brandy and was warmed by the stream of fiery liquid pouring down her throat.

"What is, then? That you wish to talk about with me, that is."

"I don't wish to talk about anything with you." He was very firm.

"Very well, then." She did not care in the least. She would go to sleep. If only he would move this very uncomfortable arm.

"Please take your arm back, Fane," she said angrily.

"It feels better that way."

"It is not that arm that I hit."

"True, too true. I'm afraid I have lied. That means I must be punished," he said, smiling sleepily.

He kissed her, but not at all like the last time, after The Silver Tree. It was a warm, lingering kiss, which left her out of breath. She felt his fingers touching her hair, and then her face, in the dark. He kissed her again, and she felt all the tightness in her body drain away. He kissed her again, with a force that shocked her out of her lassitude. "No," she murmured. He stopped but gently turned her so that she was lying against him, her head on his chest, her feet up on the seat. He wrapped his arms around her, giving her the peculiar sense of being small, next to his largeness, and told her to go to sleep, which she found very easy to do.

She awoke only when she felt him gently moving her.

"We are at your house," he said tonelessly. "Your butler is waiting to help you out. I shall come and see you soon, when I am recovered from this. . . . Good-bye, Alicia."

It was early morning, and there was enough light for Alicia to see his face, but it told her nothing. Impassive and impenetrable, he was once again Lord Fane, bored man of fashion. She felt thoroughly confused.

33

DE ROHANT

Overjoyed to see her friend unharmed, Charlotte did not ask too many questions, for which Alicia was heartily thankful. Alicia related everything about Mercier, her captivity and rescue, but said nothing of the coach ride from Brighton. After Charlotte had told her of events at Lady Holland's, it was decided that Alicia should sleep as late as she wished the next morning, and that if de Rohant came to call, Charlotte should put him off until the afternoon.

At eleven o'clock the next morning, Lucien de Rohant desired to see Miss Tierney. Stilton was just explaining that Miss was still indisposed when Charlotte joined them. She told him that Alicia had asked if they could meet at one, if that suited him.

He did not seem at all surprised, but agreed to return then.

Alicia woke at noon, wondering if she had dreamed the abduction. She looked at the peaceful landscape on her wall and wished she could walk into it and never return.

What would the very proper Nick Fane say to her when next they met? Of course he had been drunk, and weak from the loss of blood, but it did seem to her that he owed her an apology. After all the times she had been put in the wrong by him, it would be pleasant to see him on the defensive. She found herself hoping that she would see him very soon, to enjoy his discomfort. Of course he could be abominable, if he wished, point out that she had responded to his kisses, but she had been exhausted and a little inebriated herself, that was all there was to it.

Alicia looked at the clock and resolutely put these considerations aside. She changed into her riding habit, a new one of black trimmed with silver. She looked in her glass and decided that no one would have been able to tell how she had spent the past two days.

Charlotte came in to say good morning, and asked if Alicia had been told that de Rohant had not seemed surprised that she was indisposed earlier.

"Yes, Eliza told me what you said to her. I confess that my mind is running along the same lines. It is ridiculous to fix upon the only Frenchman one knows, but still . . ."

"I am not so sure that you should go riding with him."

"Come, Charlotte, I am not frightened by that French man-milliner. I doubt he can do anything with me while I am on Douro—he is a very fast horse. Not to mention Potts, who'll be watching the entire time. We are probably quite wrong about Lucien—he is far too obvious a choice, and too young to be a master spy, as Mercier is supposed to be."

When Alicia greeted de Rohant, she could detect no sign of surprise or discomfiture. He appeared genuinely glad to see her.

"Ma belle Mademoiselle Tierney! You are in wonderful looks today! I was so sorry you were not at Lady Holland's—it was my first time there, and I would have been so much more *comfortable* had you been there."

"Yes, it was quite silly of me to fall from Douro. And I had always fancied myself *such* a good rider."

He seemed quite satisfied with this, and he did not refer to her absence again.

They rode through the park, saluting many friends, including Anne Dunstan, who was taking a drive with Sir Reginald Warren, whom Alicia remembered meeting before. He still powdered his hair, and a trace of rouge could be detected on his cheeks. Alicia had always found him repulsive in manner as well, and wondered why in the world Anne was out driving with him. After they had spent a few minutes with this ill-assorted couple, de Rohant offered an explanation for their being together.

"It is that the so very lovely Lady Anne wishes money, and who can blame her? But Sir Reginald, he is not the man to settle for such a bargain as she will offer."

"And what kind of bargain would that be?" Alicia's eyes were hard. She did not like his sneering tone.

"Well, let us say, that she will wish to do as she likes. And what she likes is what *such* women usually do—freedom from restrictions that . . . ah . . . marriage may impose. . . ."

"I do not think you have the right to say such a thing, Monsieur de Rohant. You can hardly know very much about Lady Anne."

"You must not assume so much, dear Miss Tierney. I know a great deal about her—it is not difficult. Of course you English have such very strange rules of behavior. I think it is far safer to know about a woman like Lady Anne than to be ignorant."

Alicia spurred her horse angrily and rode off at a gallop, in a part of the park where this was not done, and heads turned as she went flying by. De Rohant suddenly found Lord Fane riding alongside.

"Do look at my new snuffbox, old top. Damned fine intaglio

on the lid. Who was that riding off like the wind? Looked a bit like Miss Tierney."

"It was, Lord Fane. She felt the need for a gallop." Here de Rohant gave a wide smile. "She has been shut in these past few days, you know."

"Yes, do believe I heard something of it. My fiancée, you know. Not sure I like it above half that you are riding with her. She didn't ask my permission. But I see you've lost her. Become a habit?"

"What do you have reference to, monsieur?"

"Losing things, old man, losing things. No matter, she is riding back this way now. I should tell you that I'm frightfully jealous and unsporting when I'm angry. Might find yourself with a bullet in your teeth if you continue seeing her. Just a friendly warning."

This was said in a flippant manner, but de Rohant had no illusions—this man would indeed kill him if he had to.

"What have I done to earn this, Lord Fane?"

Fane looked at him in surprise. "Why, I should think that is clear. Stay away from my fiancée. Don't even accompany her back. I shall do that."

Fane rode off, leaving a very disturbed young man behind him. De Rohant was so taken up by the dangerous undercurrents of this conversation that he was not as vigilant as usual, and did not see the man on the roan horse who was following him as he left the park.

Fane caught up with Alicia and Potts as they were riding back.

"Good day, Alicia. I am sure you were told not to ride like that in the park; what induced you to do it?"

"Something he said. A rather nasty tongue he has at times." Alicia did not look at Fane as she talked. She found that she did not wish to look in his eyes, just as she did not wish to tell him what Lucien had said about Anne Dunstan. Fane did not seem at all apologetic.

"Has he gone?"

"Yes, I sent him away with a warning. I do not wish you to ride with him, or to have anything to do with him in general."

"You think he knows Mercier?"

"I am not sure, but I do not want to have to rescue you again so soon."

This was said in a commanding tone which made Alicia's hackles rise.

"I do not enjoy being ordered about. I think you would do well to remember that this is not a battlefield, and I am not one of your soldiers!"

He smiled at her and said that she was certainly nothing like any soldier, especially in her black and silver riding habit. "But it is possible, Alicia, that this is more of a battlefield than you think."

She scanned the riders for de Rohant, but did not see him anywhere. Fane laughed and said that he thought her escort had been scared off.

"By you? In those clothes?"

"Don't you like mustard-yellow riding clothes? I am told they are all the crack in France." This was in such a seemingly injured tone that Alicia began to smile.

"You are far too . . . *large* to wear such colors, my dearest Nicholas. You will make yourself ridiculous."

"Just like to splash about a little color in this drab town," sniffed Fane in good imitation of Sir Reginald Warren, who also preferred the brighter tones for his riding clothes. Thinking of the casual clothes Fane had worn on the trip from Brighton, Alicia wondered why in the world he played the dandy.

As they rode, she asked him if he thought Worthing and Charlotte would make a match of it.

"Can't say yet. I don't approve of love matches, in general—they are bound to disappoint, don't you think?"

"I don't know . . . it depends on the people, I suppose. I think they will be happy."

"There's Kendalford, coming over, it looks like. Is he still languishing for you, Alicia? There's a good match."

His ironical tone made her decide to break the vow she had made to herself that she would be polite to Fane.

"Yes, rather like Miranda and *you*. I do hope Lady Terbury will invite her to dinner Saturday, so that you may enjoy some genuinely *rational* conversation."

He did not rise to this, however, but waved to friends who then came to join them, putting an end to all personal conversation.

A happy Charlotte met Alicia when she returned from her ride. Worthing had come to visit before he left London to visit his uncle. They had made up and were to resume their friendship.

"I know it is not what you would have wished, Alicia, but it will do very well for me. I do not think of marriage yet."

Alicia remembered Wycherly's words about Caroline Parr, and prayed that that young lady was not visiting Worthing's uncle.

When Alicia read her mail, she was horrified to discover that her brother and Amelia were planning to visit her in three days' time. They wished to meet her fiancé, Lord Fane.

"My God, they want to boast of the acquaintance," she wailed. "Half of London will be on the stoop to see them taking tea with Nick! What shall I do?"

"Nothing. Leave it up to Nick. He'll know how to manage them, I am sure."

This struck Alicia as true. He had saved her so many times, he could certainly do it once again.

"It has to be a hellish time," said Charlotte pensively. "That Stornaway woman is due, the shrike and the daughter. Come to see if you and Fane are really as one. And, supposedly, to finally give permission for Harriet to marry."

"I should like to go to sleep and not wake until they are all gone," said Alicia with a laugh.

"You laugh now, my friend, but just you wait. Edith and Julia are not going to be deceived by pleasant looks exchanged at concerts. You and Nick will have to be surprised in something a good deal more interesting."

Alicia did not seem to be at all disturbed by this prospect, a change which Charlotte duly reported to Lady Mary some days later.

"Perhaps they began to like each other better after the business of the abduction," said Charlotte. "Not that I am suggesting—"

"Anything improper. No, this generation doesn't have the gumption for it! Now if it had been me . . ." Lady Mary smiled reminiscently.

"But I am afraid this is not enough to stop her marriage to St. Clair."

"No, she is in a corner. Just look at the situation: she is a very willful, determined girl. Fought everyone's opinion to get engaged to St. Clair. Threw it in the teeth of what she imagined was conventional society. Now she discovers—although it is possible that she has not yet, but let's say she does—she discovers that he is not what she really wants. I'm not saying she knows he was involved with Julia—you say she excuses him on that account. But the point is, it's quite unpleasant to have to excuse such behavior. So even if she comes to like Fane—and we have no way of knowing how much either one of them likes the other—how can she abandon St. Clair . . . after all the noise she's made defending him? What would Miranda say?"

"She'd say I told you so, and Alicia would rather die than hear that from her. I see your point. But oh, I would love to see her with Nick!"

"But Nick himself is a problem," said Lady Mary thoughtfully. "He was a young blood. He rushed into the army and it changed him. He came back after those years hard, cold, a friend of Prinny's, a dandy ideal. It don't please me to see a man like Nick spending all morning tying a neckcloth! How did a perfectly intelligent young man return from the army and turn into such a fribble, with no ambition? I know, he goes on these missions, but that is purely out of boredom, I am positive—and he is become intolerably cynical about women!"

"All of these things are to be met with everywhere among our acquaintances," said Charlotte, thinking of Jack. "The question is, can he make her forget St. Clair?"

"No," said Lady Mary with a sigh. "I suppose he can't, and perhaps he wouldn't even want to. But we can hope; they are being thrown together constantly now."

34

DISILLUSIONMENT

The subject of these discussions was having a miserable day. She did not know what to do with herself. The most unwelcome thoughts were tormenting her, and she could not get rid of them. She wondered what Kendalford or Fane would say if they knew about the man in the inn; she tortured herself with the idea that St. Clair would break off with her if he knew; she even thought of going to Lady Mary for advice. At the end of the afternoon, she found herself longing to see St. Clair—he would get her back her sense of confidence. But the Stornaways would arrive at any time now, and she was under strict orders to avoid being seen with St. Clair.

She tried to read, but gave it up as impossible: what she needed was action. She looked longingly at the jacket, buckskins and waistcoat in her dressing room. . . .

Twenty minutes later, with Eliza's help, she crept out of the house by the servants' door while Jellicoe was drinking tea in the servants' parlor.

As soon as she and Potts were among the crowds on the street, Alicia began to feel better. There was so much energy and life on the streets of London that no one could remain dispirited for long. They rode through the fashionable section and into Fleet Street where the printshops, coffeehouses and hawkers were to be found. Clerks and messenger boys filled the streets, which were kept clean by the sweepers at every crossing. This was a street she would not have been able to walk down as herself, Alicia thought. It was certainly not a fashionable shopping district, and there were very few ladies to be seen in any direction.

The traffic was heavy, and she and Potts were moving very slowly through the tangle of coaches, hacks, brewers' drays and pedestrians. As she was looking at the bookstall fronts, she saw a familiar figure come out of the door of one of the shops. There could be no mistaking the set of the head and shoulders—it was St. Clair. She was about to call to him when she remembered she was in masculine dress—she would have to make sure there was no one with him before she approached him. A second later she saw another figure join him—a woman in a dark blue cloak. It was hard to see her face, but there was something familiar about her walk.

"Potts," said Alicia, "please hold my horse a moment. I wish to see something in that shop window." She lied automatically, her years of protecting herself against her brother and his wife standing her in good stead.

She sauntered over to the shop and looked in the window, watching out of the corner of her eye as St. Clair leaned into the lady's hackney. He held a little gloved hand in his. Alicia watched in fascination as he took off the glove, turned the hand over and kissed it lingeringly. Alicia gripped her riding whip tightly. St. Clair walked down the street as the hack pulled away. Alicia walked to the very edge of the curb so that she could get a glimpse of the woman as she passed. It was with a sense of fatalism that Alicia recognized Julia Stornaway. She stood there after the hack was out of sight, just gazing blankly at the street. Potts called to her, and when she did not answer, led the horses to her.

"Miss Alicia! Are you not well?"

She looked up at him blindly.

"I don't know, Potts, I don't know. . . ."

With an effort she made herself mount her horse. Potts asked her whether she wished to go home.

"No, I'll be quite all right. Let us ride a little more. I'm in great need of diversion."

Potts worriedly observed her tense unhappy face, but said nothing—he knew from experience that silence was best with her at times such as these.

Alicia saw nothing of the buildings and people they passed. She was completely engulfed by the pain of knowing that St. Clair had lied all along, that he had been seeing Julia from the first, that undoubtedly he *had* been secretly engaged. Gossip turned out to be right on all counts. And she—what kind of a judge of men was she? Everyone had told her, and everyone had been right. He had seemed her ideal, the adventurous pirate, the unconventional man. It was very funny, she thought bitterly. She could arrange everyone else's affairs but her own. She began to think of what she would say to St. Clair, how she would explain to her friends, how Miranda Drayton and the others would crow. And then there was the fact that she herself was just as much a liar and a cheat as St. Clair. Had she not gone to the man in the inn of her own free will? No, she had no leg to stand on, she could not pretend to be better than St. Clair. But it was clear that if it was St. Clair's very honesty she had valued in him, she was now undeceived: he was not fit to associate with her friends. He was playing a double game so that he would be sure of having a rich wife whether she cried off or not. A pretty coil, Alicia thought, her sense of humor beginning to return. They did appear to deserve each other. But she would not have him now, not a man who belonged to someone else. She remembered poor Julia's face when she saw the present from St. Clair. He deserved punishment, one that was at least as painful as what she herself was going through right now.

By the time Alicia and Potts got to Curzon Street, it was after six o' clock. Alicia had Potts find Eliza, who warned him that Alicia would most likely not be able to sneak in without Jellicoe's knowing.

"Well, Potts, I think I'm going in anyway. After all, she's my maid, not my mother."

"Yes, miss," was all Potts would say, but there was a definite twinkle in his eye. His money was on his mistress, but Jellicoe was going to give as good as she got, if he was any judge.

Alicia got to her room without incident, but as she was changing, Jellicoe knocked on her door.

Alicia took a deep breath and then told her to come in.

"May I help you change—"

Jellicoe's eyes widened in horror.

"I was afraid of this! I knew that if I let you drive that coach to London, you'd do it again! What would your poor mother say!"

"Nothing, since she is dead. Jelly, you will *not* have a fit of hysterics! I am your mistress, not your child, and I will not tolerate interference!"

But Jelly was not to be faced down so easily this time.

"You have a responsibility to your name, to your background! How could you make a spectacle of yourself! You have no modesty, Miss Alicia! I will—"

"You will leave this room and give me some peace," said Alicia, "and if you don't, I'll have Stilton carry you out! Make no mistake about me, Jellicoe—I am not a child, and what I do is my own business!"

Alicia went into her dressing room, and when she came out, Jellicoe was gone. Alicia decided she would play the role of the loving fiancée, and then cry off at the very last minute, by which time Julia Stornaway would be sure that all was lost. St. Clair would be so sure of her that he would have to finally let Julia go. It was a cruel thing to do, but even Julia deserved better than St. Clair.

35
MIRANDA

Miranda Drayton had been quite dissatisfied with Lord Fane's explanation of his absence from Lady Holland's dinner. She suspected that Alicia Tierney had a good deal to answer for, no matter what Nick said about "government matters," and "unavoidable delays." Nor did Miranda like the easy way Fane conversed with Alicia now, and the unsuitable way Alicia joked with him. Miranda was beginning to wonder if having Prinny at her engagement party was worth the discomfort of putting up with the comments of her friends. Her parents knew the truth of the false engagement, but her friends did not. Her only consolation was the company of Viscount Carberry, whose fortune could not be compared to Lord Fane's, but whose family pedigree was even more impressive.

They spent their time discussing family history, illnesses and the latest advances in the science of mathematics—Miranda was counted quite a mathematician, although she would never have tried to make it a profession. She enjoyed discussing the new articles with Carberry, who was most complimentary on the subject of her talents. She had been tempted to tell him that she was still to be engaged to Lord Fane, but had decided against it.

Carberry was therefore surprised when Miranda's former suitor was announced in the drawing room of the Draytons' house. He knew Lord Fane slightly and had no very high opinion of him. Viscount Carberry referred to all members of the dandy set as "man-milliners." He felt such attention to clothes and manners to be unfit for a man who was a real man, such as himself. He thought his name and lineage were sufficient recommendation to the world's good opinion, and he did not have to descend to such fripperies as ornate neckcloths and skin-tight coats of Bath suiting.

It was with a look of disagreeable civility that he exchanged greetings with Fane. They passed an uncomfortable five minutes together before Carberry took his leave, seeing that Fane and Miranda wished to talk privately.

Fane asked Miranda if Carberry was often to be found in her drawing room.

"Yes, I suppose so . . . but mamma is always home when he is here. You need not fear—"

"Of course not. It was not that, I know you would never be guilty of a moment's impropriety," said Fane.

"I am glad you understand me so well. My mother brought me up to understand the moral code a lady must live by. I am afraid that Miss Tierney's lack of a mother during her formative years had a disastrous effect on her character. I have something to tell you that I daresay will shock you. But I feel you should know—after all you are engaged to her in the eyes of our acquaintants, and her behavior reflects upon you."

Nick looked at his fiancée and saw that she was very happy to have something to tell against Alicia.

"And what is it, Miranda?"

"Carbeny was driving along Curzon Street a few days ago when he saw Alicia's horse—that dreadfully high-spirited, showy beast—and her groom as well. But there was a gentleman riding Alicia's horse—a gentleman who looked very like Alicia herself."

"Perhaps a relative?" inquired Fane with a bored expression, as if this were all infinitely unimportant.

"I do not think you quite understand, dear Nicholas. Carberry is certain that it was Alicia herself! In men's riding clothes! On the street. In daylight!"

Miranda's somewhat protuberant pale blue eyes expressed amazement at Fane's composure.

"It is possible, of course, but I rather think Carberry's made a mistake. It may very well be a relative. I shall ask Alicia in a roundabout way."

"I am afraid Miss Tierney would not scruple to tell a false-hood," said Miranda with a small sigh which indicated the regret she felt about such a character flaw. "The Viscount was most shocked by such a thing! Of course Caro Lamb does such things, but she is *mad*. I do hope Miss Tierney is not mad."

Miranda proceeded to give a critique of Alicia's manners, a critique Fane found singularly tedious.

"Nicholas! You are wool-gathering. I am only saying all of this so that you may perhaps influence her for the good. I would do it, but Miss Tierney would not accept anything from me! She would say that I was a jealous female, or some such thing." Seeing that Fane smiled at this last, Miranda was piqued.

"Nicholas, you cannot think that I would be jealous of that underbred creature, or of anyone else!"

"You are never jealous, Miranda? That is rare among women."

"No," said Miranda, who was now thoroughly nettled. "I pride myself on never giving in to such emotions—although to tell the truth I do not think I have ever actually experienced jealousy. For example, if my husband kept a mistress, I should not be disturbed in the least."

Fane's attention was caught, Miranda noted complacently.

"Very interesting. And why do you think it is that you are not disturbed by such things?"

"I pride myself on understanding the ways of the world. I think a truly elegant marriage is one in which a civilized breeding predominates. Jealousy is for the vulgar, as is marrying for love. What does it mean? I consider, frankly, that Laurence Terbury and Harriet Stornaway are doomed to disappointment. They are not thinking of common interests; they are merely under the temporary impression of what the poets call 'love.' I should consider myself ridiculous if I were to behave in such a way. I am sure that *you* of all people must understand how offensive such a conception of life must be to someone born to a great name."

"Of course I understand you," said Fane, wondering why he found it unpleasant to hear his own views on the matter from his future wife. He was grateful a few moments later when Mrs. Drayton came in to join them. He really had nothing to say to Miranda. As he took his leave, Miranda coyly reminded him to be attentive to Alicia at Lady Terbury's dinner.

"I shall be there watching, you know, I received an invitation today."

The invitation to Miranda had been an afterthought on Lady Mary's part. She had examined the situation from all angles, and it seemed to her that Miranda and St. Clair should both be at the dinner. Of course Alicia was not to know that St. Clair was coming. Lady Mary wished to observe her goddaughter's reaction to St. Clair. Charlotte had agreed that this was desirable.

"Perhaps Nick will see what a dreadful girl Miranda is if she's at the same table with Alicia, although I'm afraid that Nick only sees the superficial traits of Alicia's character."

"I wouldn't underestimate Nick; his understanding is sound. We shall see. It will be quite a little group!"

Lord Terbury found his wife's high spirits suspicious, but she swore that there was no special reason.

"Don't like it when you have that bright, expectant look, my love. Like the mother sparrow who's thrown baby out of the nest, and wonders if he'll learn to fly."

"Such a naturalist you are, Henry. Never would have suspected. Sparrows. So charming."

Charlotte and Lady Mary had planned everything with great care, including the seating arrangements, which placed the couples near but not next to each other. Fane and Alicia would be able to talk and hear Miranda and St. Clair. But Miranda and St. Clair would not be able to hear what Fane and Alicia said to each other if they spoke softly.

Charlotte's part of the plan consisted of making sure that Alicia was at her most beautiful. She went through Alicia's dresses several times before she found the one she liked.

"What does it matter?" asked Alicia. "Why do I have to look especially well for Lady Mary's dinner?"

"Because the oh-so-wonderful Miranda will be there, and I want you to outshine her."

On Saturday Alicia was calm about the prospect of seeing her archrival Miranda. Alicia felt that all of these things were unimportant now. What was important was St. Clair, how he had lied to her.

Over the days since she had seen him with Julia, Alicia had come to see that her reaction was caused more by wounded pride than anything else—which of course did not make it any less painful, but at least she did not feel that she'd lost the love of her life. He had always fascinated her, but she had not been in love—perhaps she was incapable of love. . . .

Charlotte was finally satisfied with Alicia's clothes, and so was able to devote some attention to her own. They were both to wear very simply plain mull muslin gowns which had demi-trains edged in lace. But as *La Belle Assemblée* reported, this season the "bosoms and shoulders are very exposed," and Charlotte had made certain that she and Alicia would follow the trend closely.

When they arrived at Grosvenor Square it was late and the house was ablaze with lights. Music could be heard from the street.

Cranmer welcomed them, and directed them to the drawing room, where the guests were just about to go to dinner. Charlotte had torn her hem when alighting from the carriage, so they went to find the housekeeper to get some needle and thread. On their way they passed a room from which the familiar voices of Worthing and Fane could be heard.

"Do let's go in," said Charlotte happily. "I want Jack to see the dresses first."

But as they stood at the door, they heard part of the conversation.

"Well, I can tell you what your uncle will say," said Fane. "He'll say that if you marry a girl whose grandfather was in trade, he'll cut you off. Are you prepared for this?"

"I don't know," said Worthing. "I simply don't know."

"Do nothing until you are sure, Jack. Nothing. Let the proposal wait."

Charlotte pulled Alicia away.

"Come, we must repair my gown. Why listen any longer? It is a conversation one can imagine without the slightest difficulty." Charlotte did not speak until they reached their destination.

"Don't feel pity for me, Alicia, it is a conversation I am used to—although not usually from *friends*. But of course Jack must consider what his uncle would think—all his prospects rest with the duke."

"But Jack did not sound so very sure that Nick was right. You must not assume anything. Of course Nick has ever been a supercilious proud peacock! The only woman who fits his requirements is Miranda Drayton! There's something to think on!"

"Alicia, I wish to forget this entire matter. The pity of it is that I like Nick very much. One should never eavesdrop. As my mother always said, one is sure to hear something unpleasant. But I don't want Lady Mary's dinner ruined for us. Let us try and forget it."

Alicia wanted to comfort her, but saw that the best thing would be to pretend it had never happened—the best thing for Charlotte's pride. Fane was simply abominable, and she should never have thought him otherwise! Of course, this fit perfectly with his character as it was known to her. Even now she could remember how, after rescuing her on the way to London, he had referred to her as a country nobody.

By the time Alicia and Charlotte had mended the hem, Fane and Worthing were back in the drawing room, just in time for their entrance.

"Dear Alicia! That gown is most becoming. Do come, we are about to go down to dinner." Fane smiled at her warmly. For a moment in her desire to give him a set-down, Alicia almost forgot that they were supposedly an engaged couple—but the sight of Mrs. Selby watching them attentively made her control her reaction.

"La, sir," she said with obvious insincerity, "I vow that you outshine *me*! That brocaded waistcoat is far more important than my gown! Not to mention the cravat—the mathematical, I believe? So becoming." She smiled up at him fluttering her long lashes.

Fane immediately felt the insincerity of her remarks. The underlying hostility apparent in her intonation pulled him up short. So, Alicia was angry about something. She would undoubtedly get over it after a glass or two of champagne.

But when they had passed through the courses of mulligatawny and turtle, the salmon and turbot, and were starting on a saddle of lamb—Lady Terbury had announced that this was to be an *English* dinner—and Alicia had continued her imitation of civility, Fane began to show signs of exasperation, she noted with satisfaction. His every attempt was rebuffed or turned into a parody of social discourse. She solemnly asked his advice on snuff, which he knew well interested her not at all; she asked him if he didn't think Miranda looked just lovely in her new gown (which she knew drew attention to Miranda's poor figure), and she refused to be herself for even a moment.

The conversation at the table turned to the current political situation, the surrender of Paris to Blucher, and Bordeaux to Beresford. Fane saw that Alicia forgot herself enough to take an animated part in these discussions, but as soon as he addressed a remark to her she changed immediately. He finnally lost patience with this game and asked her in a low tone what he had done to deserve such treatment. She answered that she did not know what he meant. Nick could not imagine what was bothering her.

One of the things bothering her was sitting across the table, flashing her dark gypsy smiles as he pretended to talk to Mrs. Selby on one side, and Miranda on the other. Alicia enjoyed the sight of Miranda in conversation with a man she thoroughly disapproved of: Miranda assumed an expression of distaste every time he addressed her, rather like someone who had eaten a bad oyster, as Charlotte later said. But Miranda had been brought up strictly and knew that well-bred persons did not converse across a table, but only with their partners to the sides. Since Lord Terbury was on the other side of her, sitting at one end of the table, and he was involved in a spirited discussion of a race at Newmarket with his old friend Mr. Curran, she had no choice: either she would talk to St. Clair or be silent. No such constraints were felt by Charlotte and Alicia, who freely talked to whomever they chose, without the least evidence that they realized they were committing a social sin. Miranda noted with disapproval that even Lady Mary did not always observe the social rules, but addressed remarks to Laurence, who was at the other end of the table. Miranda decided to be polite to Mr. St. Clair and demonstrate what a woman of good breeding was capable of. After a time, she discovered that he really was most personable, although it was quite easy to believe he had done a good deal of what was ascribed to him. She was watching him when everyone arose from the table, and saw him exchange a smile with Alicia.

"Be careful, Mr. St. Clair," she hissed. "We are being watched, you know. Please remember your role!"

"But is it not hard to camouflage one's real emotion?" he asked, smiling charmingly.

"When it is my duty, I am able to conquer my feelings," Miranda said calmly.

"That," said St. Clair with a bland expression, "would certainly not be the case were I the man in question. Too bad, really, always had a weakness for yellow hair."

Before Miranda could express her shocked anger at the

impertinence of this remark, St. Clair moved off with the other gentlemen to the library, where they would smoke and talk of matters not fit for ladies.

It was in no very good mood that Miranda settled herself in the drawing room with the other ladies. She sat down in a chair and made a show of taking up a book of verse from the side table. Lady Mary tried to include her in the conversation going on around the card table, but Miranda answered only in mono-syllables. After a few minutes, she was left alone. However, she became interested in the conversation which was going on about whether Charlotte's and Alicia's dresses were too revealing.

"I do not know," said Lady Mary. "I am of another genera-tion—of course, we had very décolleté styles ourselves at times, but they were not combined with these clinging fabrics which leave very little to the imagination. I do not know whether I would wear that dress."

"Well, *I* certainly would not" said Miranda from her corner.

Alicia looked up from her cards, an icy expression in her eyes.

"Such a style is not suited to every figure, of course."

It was a moment before Miranda understood. Then she flushed as she comprehended the insult.

"Is it not enough that you are pretending—"

"Do be quiet, Miranda—before you say something you will regret." This came from Charlotte, who looked over in the direc-tion of Mrs. Selby. Miranda caught herself, but she was deter-mined not to remain in the same room with Alicia. She begged Lady Terbury's pardon, and said that she had the headache and would go home immediately.

When she left, there was a moment of embarrassed silence in the drawing room.

"I imagine poor Miranda is upset because Alicia's got Fane," said Lady Mary calmly. "Can't say I blame her. Didn't think about it when I invited her." This was said with an air of innocence that convinced everyone but Alicia. Miranda had been invited for a reason—but what was it?

Miranda had no intention of letting Alicia get off so easily. She sent a servant into the library to get Lord Fane. He came out with a bemused look on his face and desired to know how he could be of help.

"Miss Tierney needs to be taught some manners! She insulted me in front of all the others, and I must say I cannot bear this comedy any longer! You must end this fictitious engagement, or—or—we shall not be engaged! I will not endure such behavior!"

Fane saw this his fiancée was extremely upset. She was actually beginning to cry. He had been in the middle of an important conversation, and he resented the fact that Alicia had once again caused him trouble.

"Don't worry, I will say something to her. Now, you just go home, Miranda, and be patient—it is only this week, and then it will be ended. Please, I do not wish to see you cry."

Miranda was sniffling and clinging to him, getting his new waistcoat wet, he noticed with irritation. Sibylla Crawford, for example, would never have given in to tears in this particularly unbecoming way.

When the party broke up. Fane waited until only a few people were left, and took Alicia aside.

"I must ask you not to upset Miss Drayton. I daresay that you were merely joking, but—"

"I certainly was not joking. The woman is insufferably pompous, and I felt I had a right to say what I did."

"I don't know what you said, Alicia, but it genuinely upset her."

"I can't say that she genuinely upset *me*, but I am rather tired of her condescension. She has no heart, only manners."

"Thank you for your evaluation of my fiancée," he said coldly. "Shall I give you one of St. Clair?"

"I wonder why we always bring out the worst in each other? No, I already know everything there is to know about St. Clair. Kind of you to offer, however. Not quite consonant with your usual lofty detachment."

"*Touché*. But you really must apologize to Miranda. She'll be quite impossible otherwise."

"Dear Nick, don't you see that we took each other in dislike the first time we met, and all else is merely repetition? Nothing will make me like her, and she was wrong in what she said to me. I am puzzled that—oh never mind!"

"Do continue. Speak your mind, Miss Tierney. It is always so bracing."

"It is just that I do not think you can precisely love Miranda. She is far too cold. I think you must think it does not matter, as long as she is well bred and so on."

She knew she should not say such things to him, but what he had said about Charlotte had made her wish to hurt him. But he answered very calmly.

"You may have something there, but love is not something that makes a marriage, at least in my view. Are you sure that you are not suffering from the opposite disease? Taking passion over the score of other things that matter?"

Alicia laughed. He could not know, of course, why this question was so amusing, now that she had decided not to marry St. Clair.

"Perhaps, Lord Fane. But it is so difficult to find all things in one person, that we may be excused for being satisfied with only a part. I had not planned to bring it up to you, but since we are having such an open tête-à-tête—why are you bent on ruining the happiness of Worthing and Charlotte by imposing your views about her family on Jack?"

Fane did not express a flicker of surprise, he did not question how she knew.

"Right to the heart of the matter. Since you ask, I will answer frankly. I do not think unequal matches fare well. If this makes me seem a snob in your eyes, there's nothing for it. But it is merely that I am a rationalist. But if Jack loves her enough, what I say will not matter much. I like Charlotte, of course, but. I do know that if he does not get some money settled on him by the duke, Worthing won't have much to feed a family on. And Worthing is sadly unreliable about women. His family favors Caroline Parr, you know."

"You consider all these things more important than the fact that they will be miserable without each other?"

"I suppose I do. They will both get over it, at any rate. Love is not such a lasting thing as young girls think."

And who gave him the bitter experience that made him say that, wondered Alicia. But aloud she said only that she disagreed, and that she had no intention of apologizing to Miranda, to return to their original subject. Fane laughed and said he had tried, and nothing more could be asked of him than that.

When they returned home, Alicia told Charlotte of this conversation.

"Of course he is right: if Jack loved me enough, he would know what to do . . . so I suppose this means that he does not."

"We did not hear the rest of the conversation. Perhaps there was something else that would ameliorate the impression you received. . . ."

"No, I know Jack. He respects Nick immensely. Oh, why do I love such a man!"

Alicia did her best to comfort her friend, assuring her that Jack would find out what he wanted most, but she was far from being sure herself.

"Charlotte, the last time you were apart. Jack was quite miserable—and it was only a week. Suppose you were to deny him the possibility of seeing you alone for several weeks, and during that time you were courted by someone else . . ."

Charlotte immediately saw the possibilities.

"Oh, he would be miserable! I know him. But the other gentleman would have to be someone really quite unexceptional, or it will look as though I am simply trying to make him jealous."

Alicia tried to think of a suitable gentleman, but other than Kendalford, who would never agree to it, no one came to mind. She thought of Wycherly, whom she had not seen in many weeks, but he disliked social gatherings so intensely that he would not be suitable. She made a mental note to go and call on the artist, however, and see how the draped portrait had turned out. Perhaps he would know of a possible *cicisbeo*.

The only thing to be said about Charlotte's problem, Alicia reflected bitterly, was that it helped distract her from her own. She was glad that no one, including St. Clair himself, would guess how many tears she had shed over him.

36

A DIFFICULT WEEK

Stilton recognized the somewhat beefy face under the beaver brim as Mr. William Tierney, come to call once again on his sister, and this time with a determined little woman beside him—his wife, no doubt. Stilton's air of formal condescension was so powerful that Amelia remarked to William that he was what she thought a butler should be, and why wasn't their own Martin that polished?

Before Stilton had time to inform his mistress that her brother was in the salon, Jellicoe had rushed to her with the news.

"Oh, Charlotte, this is the last thing on earth I wish to deal with today! I feel a cowardly desire to have Stilton tell them I am unwell."

"You are such an unconvincing coward, Alicia. I do not believe it. And besides, if you do not deal with them now, they will only return to plague you another time."

"Too true. I shall go and play the great lady. Why don't you enter after about ten minutes, to break the tension."

Alicia found her relatives studying the painting that hung over the settee.

"Do you like it? It is a portrait by Jacques-André Aved. I purchased it from a dealer who had acquired it from an *émigré* family."

"I do not care for French art" said Amelia.

"He is Belgian, not French. And I think there is a Flemish look to the portrait, but of course he is not to everyone's taste."

"We did not come to discuss painting, dear sister," said William ceremoniously. "No, we have the pleasure to congratulate you on the news of your engagement to Lord Nicholas Fane. A worthy man, a credit to his country. Father would have been most happy at the news of this alliance of the Fanes and the Tierneys."

Alicia found this speech ridiculous, but she mastered her amusement enough to ask them if she could give them some tea.

Tea seemed to last forever, with discussions of how and where Alicia should be married, who was to be invited, and what the sister-in-law of the bride should wear.

For the hundredth time, Alicia wished that Charlotte would join them, when Stilton entered and announced the arrival of Lord Fane.

Alicia was glad of the interruption, but she was not sure that he would know how to deal with her brother.

But when Nick joined them, Alicia found that he was more of a godsend than she would have believed. Very delicately but firmly, he depressed all of Amelia's pretensions, and made William feel that he was a very small fish indeed. The end result was that they left a good half-hour earlier than anyone would have expected. William became positively nervous, and Amelia became sullen, both states being especially noticeable as they left.

"Wonderfully entertaining people," said Fane dryly. "I think you owe me a glass of sherry."

"You may have a bottle! I must thank you—you took in the situation at a glance."

"No, it was Charlotte. When I arrived, she caught me in the hall and gave me instructions. Which I followed rather well, I think."

"And where is Charlotte, herself?"

"She said to tell you that she went to deliver a message, in person. She was looking quite beautiful, in a fur-trimmed cloak."

This cloak belonged to Alicia, although it did really suit Charlotte better; Charlotte borrowed it whenever she wished to make an impression—in this case on Worthing, Alicia was certain.

"Why do you have that *planning* look on your face, I wonder."

"Oh, planning our wedding, at Carlton House naturally."

"Oh, no, my girl. Gretna Green for you, not Prinny's palace!"

"But then Amelia would not be able to wear her satin and diamonds! Think of the loss to the fashionable world." She found herself almost liking him again, but the thought of Charlotte prevented her from relaxing completely.

"You must not let it bother you," said Fane seriously. "One cannot help one's relations, and it does no good to be nice to the ones that dislike you."

"Very true, but what am I to do? Cut them dead?" Like you do Anne Dunstan, was Alicia's unspoken thought.

"No, but I fancy that I could make them so uncomfortable that they would bother you very little."

"I have no doubt you could. But you will not always be my official fiancé, you know. I shall have to develop some of your—"

"Disagreeable ways, is what you wish to say, I believe. Just so. But of course I do it much more successfully, having had so much practice.

"But I am not come to save you from the dreaded William and

Amelia. I have the unfortunate duty of announcing that Edith Stornaway has arrived at Lady Mary's, to view our engagement at close range."

"Such a week for unpleasant persons! What is it we are to do?"

"I am to spend as much time as possible here, hanging about—with Charlotte always present, of course. We are to let ourselves be observed dancing dance after dance at Almack's. We are not to venture into the Terbury house until the end of the week. Must make it look real. So you must not grant any interviews to your beloved."

"Nor you to yours."

It was with a sense of relief that Alicia wrote a note to St. Clair, warning him that they were not to meet until the Stornaways had left. St. Clair and she had been able to exchange only a few words at the Terburys' dinner, but Alicia knew that he would have seen that she had changed toward him if he were alone with her for any lengthy period of time. Just seeing him across the table had upset her. She felt foolish and ashamed beyond words.

She still saw his charm of manner, and the passion in the dark eyes, but now they made her think only of poor Julia, a child of nineteen, promised marriage by him.

It was almost time for dinner when Charlotte returned, in surprisingly high spirits for one who had just given her true love a farewell interview.

"Alicia, it was beyond anything! His heart was broken! He told me I was too beautiful. How could I leave him? What could he do?"

"And what did you say?"

"Nothing, really. I said that I could not talk, that it was better this way for everyone, that he would have a new flirt within a week. But you know, I think it will take less than two weeks for him to decide. I almost didn't go through with it, he looked so unhappy."

"Is that why you are in such high spirits? Because you made Jack suffer?"

"No, no. I have solved our problems. I went to Wycherly's afterwards, since he lives so near Jack. Told him we'd come to see him in a few days. And an old friend of yours was there— Major Trilling. I immediately requisitioned him to be my new admirer."

"A miracle. Now if only you could arrange for my relations to be magically transported back to the country, along with Miranda Drayton."

Charlotte's countenance darkened. "Well, there is something to tell about her as well. I saw Lady Terbury this morning in the park, and she says that Miranda is doing her best to convince everyone she knows that you have been involved in some unsavory adventure, and are not the sort of person who should have been given a voucher to Almack's. Of course it looks like she's simply jealous—since Fane is your fiancé—but when the charade is over, I'm afraid she can do some real damage. The story of the charade itself will be used against you—"

"But Fane himself took part," Alicia pointed out.

"Miranda will excuse that on the grounds that he was misled by you. And men are allowed a greater degree of eccentricity than women."

"Well, I can't say I really care," said Alicia.

Some nights later, while attending Almack's with Fane, Charlotte, and Trilling, Alicia had to admit to herself that she cared more than she thought she would. When they had entered the main room, she had noticed several of the dowagers talking behind their fans, and a few of the gentlemen turned to watch them enter. When she discerned Miranda sitting with her brother at one end of the room, she thought she knew why people were talking. Alicia discovered that no matter how much one might hold such persons in contempt, it was very unpleasant to know that the gossips were watching every move. Despite the welcome presence of Trilling, Alicia was not relaxed. For the first time, she detected undercurrents of animosity toward herself in this gathering of the socially prominent, and it disconcerted her a little.

"Do not let them see you cast down," said Charlotte, who saw that her friend was taking things to heart. "You must throw it back at Miranda by being *especially* attentive to Fane. Pretend he is one of your flirts. He is quite attractive in his way, you know."

"Yes, he is, I suppose," said Alicia, watching her escort as he brought her some punch. She had to admit that he looked quite handsome in his faultless clothes, and if his face was still a little too tanned for the general taste, it suited her. No, physically, she had to admit, he was quite attractive.

Fane came and sat beside them, making light conversation. Alicia was distracted, and he asked her what the matter was.

"It would be better to ask Miss Drayton," said Charlotte tartly.

When he asked with a certain hauteur what she meant, Charlotte told him.

"I can scarcely believe it," he said. "Miranda is far too well brought up to—"

"Never mind. It is of no importance." Alicia did not wish to bring Fane into a battle between herself and Miranda, he had done enough rescuing.

Fane dropped the subject then, but Charlotte noticed him talking to Miranda while Alicia danced with Kendalford. The interview was very short and seemed unsatisfactory to both parties, judging by their expressions.

Charlotte explained what was happening to Trilling, who was fascinated by all the recent events.

"What do you wish to happen, Charlotte? I do not quite understand what your stake in this is."

"Dear Stephen, you are so dense. Do you not see that Miranda is a poisonous creature, and you surely cannot wish Fane to marry her. As for St. Clair, he is thoroughly untrustworthy, and it is taking Alicia a dreadfully long time to discover it What I wish is that they both would become disenchanted with their choices."

"But is that not up to them, you meddlesome girl?"

"Yes, of course. But one can hurry an inevitable process along, don't you think? Of course it would be capital if Alicia and Nick could make a couple themselves, but they are always at daggers drawn, so I have little hope."

"They do make a handsome couple, by God," said the major, watching them whirl around the floor in a waltz.

Alicia thought that if she could waltz this way enough, she could endure any miseries that might be in store. Fane was a surprisingly light dancer for one so tall, and she felt that she was floating across the floor.

"Alicia," he said, smiling down at her, "your Stomaways have arrived. You must smile beguilingly at me."

"Is this beguiling?"

"Yes. Very. Tell me, how long have Charlotte and Stephen been on Christian-name terms?"

It was obvious that he had been struck by the easy camaraderie between the two. Alicia hoped that Worthing, who had not yet arrived, would react the same way.

"Oh, he was always at Hansdown when we were there at Christmas. They deal extremely together."

"I am glad she is recovered from Worthing so quickly. Most encouraging," he said.

She was unusually silent during the dance, and Fane thought he knew why.

"You must forgive Miranda," he began. "I spoke to her. She had no idea that people would distort what she said about you in that fashion. I have arranged for you to go riding with her in the morning—that way all the tongues will be stopped."

Alicia smiled at the prospect of a friendly ride with Miranda. Fane did not seem to find it humorous.

"Please forgive me, Nick. It is just that I am sure she does not wish to be seen with me—in Hyde Park, of all places!"

"You misjudge her, Alicia, as she does you. I wish you to try and see her good points. She has led a very—proper life. She does not precisely understand your ways."

Alicia could not tell whether Fane really believed this, or was just trying to smooth things over. She decided to go along with it, and ride with Miranda the next day. At least it would be amusing.

"I shall most certainly come, and hang upon your every word," said Charlotte when she heard. "It will be the most entertaining thing since Prinny and Brummell."

Charlotte had been watching nervously for the arrival of Worthing, but the proposed public reconciliation between Miranda and Alicia amused her so much that she was laughing gaily when Worthing finally arrived. He immediately sought her face in the group, and when he saw that she was talking with great animation to a very distinguished-looking officer, his expression changed from one of expectation to one of unhappiness. Alicia watched him closely, and was in turn watched by Fane.

"Why does it make you happy that Jack is low?"

"It does not make me happy. It is just that I do not wish him to be so quickly 'recovered' from his passion, as you would say."

"Very nice, but not an answer to my question. You are up to something, and I warn you, you should not meddle here."

"I am grateful for your advice, and should I ever wish to please you, I shall follow it."

Fane's only answer to this was to drag her out onto the floor for the next dance.

"Smile, you termagant—the Stornaways are looking!"

Alicia smiled through her teeth.

"All I have to say to you, sir, is that if you actually believe that Miranda meant nothing by her slander, you are a sap-skull, and I never thought you that."

"No, but you thought me many other things," laughed Fane. "And it is not polite to call your fiancé a sapskull. Wherever did you pick that up?"

"Cousin—"

"Freddy. Of course. Your chief educator. I long to meet him and thank him for what he did."

Alicia made a provoking face at him and asked to be taken back to Charlotte and Trilling.

It was not to be supposed that the Stornaways would leave without approaching Lord Fane and his fiancée.

Mrs. Stomaway was attired in a dowager cape of purple satin and a purple and white striped gown, which made her look ten years older than her actual age, as Lady Mary joyously remarked.

"Dear Lord Fane! So nice to see you! I believe you are acquainted with my daughter Julia . . .

Fane bowed and said all that he ought, but he managed to inject an air of distance into his remarks, not unlike his manner had been with William. Alicia was thankful for his presence—all she had to do was make polite answers. The conversation between Fane and Mrs. Stomaway forced Alicia to try to talk to Julia, however, with less than successful results.

"You don't have to pretend, Miss Tierney. I know how you must regard me!" said Julia in a low voice, her eyes flashing a look of dislike. "I have spoiled your plans, I admit, but then you have complicated mine."

"That is all behind us now, Julia, and I wish to assure you that I wish you well."

This was true, Alicia thought, even if Julia didn't believe it. She wished the poor child nothing but happiness—although she doubted that she'd find it with St. Clair. It was hardly likely that he'd make a good husband for a jealous young girl.

Looking at the feverish spots on Julia's cheeks and the restless way her eyes swept the room, Alicia felt sorry for her. The girl loved him—there could be no doubt of it. Would she still love him as much when she discovered that he would gladly sacrifice her for Alicia's greater fortune? Julia's attention was directed to a gentleman who had just entered the far end of the room, a gentleman who was smiling in their direction. The dark eyes held Alicia's blue ones for a second, but she did not smile or nod. He was the last person on earth she wished to speak with. She turned to where Fane was talking to Mrs. Stornaway and gave him a beseeching look. He came quickly to her side.

"What is it? Are you feeling not quite the thing?"

"I am feeling rather faint. Do you think we could go now?" She was thankful he made no joke about the last time she had fainted.

Without further discussion, Fane made their excuses and they were down the stairs before St. Clair, who had been detained by his friends, could see that Alicia had left.

"Now, what was that? Was Almack's boring you?"

"Well, the bohea and weak lemonade are not precisely *exciting*, and all those poor girls looking for a 'suitable connection'!"

"It is quite clear that you were not in the least faint. I think I have been used, and that the least you can do is tell me the truth about why we left before everyone had time to inspect us."

"Someone had arrived, someone I particularly had no wish to see. You have saved me from a great deal of boredom and unhappiness."

"Boredom and unhappiness! What can you know of them? *You* were not talking to Mrs. Stornaway."

Mrs. Stornaway, it seemed, had been most tenacious in her inquiries. She had asked about the honeymoon, the bride-clothes, and even had been so vulgar as to wonder about the dowry. Alicia was certain Fane had known exactly how to deal with that.

What she had been thinking must have been easily read in her expression, for Fane said, "You see, there are certain advantages to what you would label an arrogant character." But if he thought to confuse her, he was disappointed.

"Oh, I have always known that there are *advantages*."

"Termagant!"

"Yes, I am, I suppose. Which makes me wonder, dear Nick, why you ever made that strange proposal." Alicia had long waited for an opportunity to ask this question, and something about the ease of their relations at the moment made it seem possible to, but she knew she was treading dangerous ground. But if she had thought to catch him out, she was wrong. He gave a surprised laugh and said that he had his reasons.

"Confess, it was a bet of some sort—I promise, I won't be shocked!"

"That I can well believe. But the Fanes, contrary to your beliefs, are not in the habit of jesting about such things. No, it was something else . . . someday, when we are old and doddering, I shall tell you."

Alicia felt reckless and a little vexed by his refusal to disclose what could now have no effect on their relations.

"But you can at least tell me one thing, Nick. It had nothing to do with any feeling of affection for me, did it?"

"No, my dear Alicia, it did not. We had not yet shared a coach ride," he said, as he handed her out of the carriage.

37

TWO ENGAGEMENTS

St. Clair knew that there was something wrong. Alicia's eyes no longer sought his in any gathering. Indeed, she looked more at Fane than at anyone else. It sometimes seemed to him that this false engagement was in danger of turning into a true one. Not that there was any obvious sign. No, it was the little things: whenever there was something comic going on, they would exchange looks, as if they understood each other very well. He did not like it at all. And God knew what rumors had finally made their way to Curzon Street. But would a high-stickier like Fane marry a nobody like Alicia—*he* didn't need the money, after all.

"No," said Sybilla Crawford when he asked her. "He wouldn't. Won't. I have enough to worry about with that Drayton chit trying to catch him—don't give me another to worry about! No, really, it is out of the question. He talked about the Tierney a little, in the beginning. Didn't like her sort at all, said she should have been disciplined more as a child, was stubborn, unfeminine, and so on. Hardly complimentary." Robert was comfortable on the gold couch, and felt soothed by Sybilla's pronouncements.

"The only thing is, that was a long time ago. And I can tell you, Alicia has something provocative about her. You have not seen her since she got some town bronze. Not a great beauty, but striking, damned striking."

Sybilla patted her golden hair, which matched the gold salon.

"It sounds to me, Robert, as though you have conceived a passion for your fair victim, rather unlike you."

He poured himself another drink. "Perhaps. She does interest me more than she did in the beginning. A challenge . . . but now I am afraid that someone has told her about Julia. She has grown cold—I am certain of it."

"And you think this is bringing her closer to Nick?" Sybilla was interested in his problem only insofar as it affected her own.

"Well, my dear, she is spending an inordinate amount of time with Fane. It wouldn't be the first time that propinquity resolved everything."

Sybilla yawned and said she did not think either of them had anything to worry about She was positive that Fane loathed the Tierney girl.

"But if anything comes to my attention which shows you to be right. Robert, believe me, I'll take steps."

At that very moment the subjects of this discussion were together at Grosvenor Square. The Stornaways had finally left London, and Mr. Stornaway had given his permission for the marriage of Laurence and Harriet. Lady Mary had gathered Alicia, Fane, Charlotte, and Worthing, and the young couple together to celebrate this wonderful news. Alicia wondered what Charlotte and Worthing, off in a corner, were talking about. Charlotte had been seen everywhere with Trilling for the last week, and until now had granted Worthing no time at all for private conversations.

Fane led Alicia over to the window and smiled at her gaily.

"Your fondest wish is being realized," he said. "Your friend is being proposed to by my friend. I think we have done rather well by them."

She looked at him in wonder.

"Never say you have been *for* this match, Nick!" She thought of the words they had overheard.

Fane seemed not at all put out, but amused instead.

"Not for it, not against it. I like Charlotte—a wonderful girl. But you must know that Worthing has broken a score of hearts, caused divorces, and so on. Hardly the man I'd trust with *my* friends. I pointed out to him all the objections to the match, made him see his uncle the duke to find out just how opposed the old man would be."

"And was he opposed?"

"Of course. But I found out what I wished to know."

"Which was?"

"That Jack was serious about her. When his uncle came the ugly over the girl's background, he told him he was going to propose anyway."

Alicia surveyed him with a half-disbelieving look.

"I can't understand—I thought you—well, I don't know what I thought, but it certainly wasn't this!"

"Ah, but *I* know what you thought!" he teased. "You thought that I was a mere popinjay who wished to spoil your friend's happiness. But you must have seen that I liked Charlotte very well."

Alicia felt very uncomfortable. She had indeed seen that he liked Charlotte, but she had assumed that his reputed snobbishness would win out over any feelings of friendship, when it came to the granddaughter of a merchant marrying his best friend.

Lady Mary drew them back into the general merriment, so

she was saved from having to answer him, but she felt that she had seriously wronged him.

In the course of the next few days, Alicia spent a good deal of her time thinking about Nick Fane's character. There were many sides to him which were quite unbearable—his mocking air of superiority, for one thing—but she now knew that he was not the empty dandy he had seemed at first. It had not required a great deal of logic to deduce that he was no mere courier for the army, but something much more important—a spy, she concluded. Once this was assumed, his behavior took on a different light, his actions were subject to other interpretations. He was still autocratic, he had a way of snubbing that was most unpleasant, and he always made her feel that he disapproved of her. But despite all of this, she saw that he was more worthy of admiration than she would have ever believed, and that his interference in the Worthing-Charlotte affair had been all to the good.

She was given further food for thought when Lady Anne Dunstan met her in Brook Street at a draper's. Still very puzzled by Anne's preference for the company of Sir Reginald, there was a certain constraint in her greeting.

Anne, in her turn, also seemed different.

"You must be readying your bride-clothes," said Anne with an arch smile. "Such an exciting time!"

"Anne, I cannot tell you about it here, but it is not as you think—"

"My dear, I understand! One must be practical. The marriage mart is a slave auction, and one must get the best price! Which is why I am with Sir Reginald, truth be told."

So de Rohant had been right. What a fool she had been not to see it, Alicia thought.

"I have just seen your friend Charlotte Marlowe in the

company of Major Trilling, and I must tell you, I do not at all like it."

Alicia looked at her coolly. "And why is that?"

"My dear, did I never tell you?" It was obvious that Anne was enjoying this. "These army men, you know—really, I can't tell you, but at a ball he made the most improper advances to me, in the conservatory. Some years back, of course, but I doubt such men change."

Alicia got away from her as quickly as she could, and returned home to tell Charlotte.

"No, how dare she!" was Charlotte's reaction. "Not the major—anyone else, but not the major. The woman is obviously a liar."

Alicia agreed, and thought of Fane's snubbing of Anne Dunstan. If she lied about this, what else had she lied about as well?

38

THE DRAPED PORTRAIT

Jem Cobb looked in no way remarkable, except perhaps in the very ordinariness of his clothes. He was indistinguishable from a hundred others who crowded through the streets the second week in April, when Napoleon abdicated. He was good at his job, but the news of the abdication made him wonder if it was worth continuing with it. His subject seemed to have done nothing for the past week but stay in the little inn near Billingsgate, going out each day to walk, muffled up in his blue coat, but never meeting anyone. His subject's slight limp made it easy for Jem to locate him quickly. But no word had come to the Darkhouse Inn, where Jem got his mail, so he continued to watch his man, expecting no particular excitement.

It was therefore with surprise that Jem found himself being shaken by the boy he had put on watch while he slept.

"What's it, lad?"

"The gemmun's going away! In a hack! Best hurry, Mr. Cobb, or he'll be out of sight."

Cursing his failure to sleep with his boots on, Jem hurriedly got dressed and ran out to look. The hack was turning the corner at the end of the street. Jem quickly found a hack and set off in pursuit.

It was four o'clock in the morning, and in most parts of the city there was little traffic. In the Billingsgate area, however, the main hour of the market day was beginning. Boats were unloaded, fishmongers readied their wares, and the salt-fish shops were already open. Buyers and sellers were choking the street near the Darkhorse, and progress was very slow, it seemed to Jem. Up ahead, still in sight, was the hackney containing his man, but he did not know how long it would be there. After twenty minutes, he decided it would be faster to give chase on his legs. This was more successful, and he made up some of the distance before they were out of the market area.

Once the hackney cleared the crowded areas, it began to move with unusual speed. This alarmed Jem, who realized that the driver must have been paid for speed, which meant that something was up. As luck would have it, he had difficulty in finding another hack for himself, but the other man was still in sight when he did. He followed him to Crescent Street, where he disappeared, as if into thin air.

Mercier, for it was he, the shadowy spy who had eluded the British in their own country, made his visit to the address in Crescent Street, and left after twenty minutes. He next went to the White Hart and booked passage on the stagecoach to Dover, which he took when it left some hours later.

Jem's interview with Fane was brief and uncomfortable, chiefly because His Lordship made no reproach.

"Bad luck, Cobb. I expect he is our man, however. Moving now is just too much of a coincidence. I imagine he's gone to Dover, and I'm sending Will after him. He'll have to get the fastest horses he can to get there before Mercier does. I want you to watch Crescent Street, find out if anyone new has been seen there."

After Jem had left. Fane sat down to consider. The man was Mercier—he had no doubt of that. They had finally located him, after a great deal of trouble. Now that Napoleon was off the throne, and the fat Frenchman who had been in exile in England was the king, all of Napoleon's secret agents would be going not home, but to safer destinations. But who had Mercier seen in Crescent Street? If it were not for the fact that de Rohant lived in rooms at the Albermarle Hotel, he would have thought it was he.

During his morning business affairs. Fane's mind turned on this problem, but he realized he was missing essential information; he could not do anything as it was.

A few days later Alicia and Charlotte were visiting Wycherly, to see the draped portrait which was at last finished.

They arrived in high spirits, and settled down to tea and a discussion of the Czar's sister (nice, but unattractive) and the latest horrors perpetrated by the Regent's tailors, now that he had broken with Brummell (pink jackets).

Finally it was time to examine the painting, which was on the easel. With a flourish, Wycherly removed the drapery.

It was a portrait of a young and beautiful woman. She was ethereally fair, but her eyes were brown, an unusual combination. But it was her expression that gave the painting its fascination. She looked greedy for life—a look of passion about the mouth, an expression that seemed to demand everything.

Alicia was reminded of someone she knew, but it took her a few moments to realize who exactly.

"It looks like Anne Dunstan, the coloring . . . she looked questioningly at Wycherly.

"Yes, it is. But she was Anne Jessamy in those days."

As they moved closer to the picture, Charlotte noticed a scene in the darkly colored background.

"It is a duel. How cunning—but there is a blotch here, where there should be ground."

Wycherly smiled slightly.

"This, my dear young ladies, is known as an anamorph. It is an ancient device in painting, rather like a hidden message. You see, you must look through this edge of the frame to see what it is—like this."

Alicia looked through the edge and discovered the blotch to be a skull.

"How horrible! Why a skull in a picture of a beautiful woman?"

"Beautiful women have more to do with skulls than you might imagine," said Wycherly.

"Do stop being so mysterious and tell us what it is all about," said Charlotte.

"The duel is between two friends. The skull, the symbol of human vanity, is there to point up the fact that the woman was responsible for the death of one of the men.

"She was faithless, and the victim's friend tried to tell him. But he did not want to believe it; he preferred believing her. Such youth and beauty could not lie, he thought. Far more likely that his friend was jealous—and Anne swore to her fiancé that his friend had made advances—when actually she had made the advances, and indeed had already been intimate with yet a third friend! Who could believe that such a young girl would lie and scheme until she found the greatest fortune? Although I must admit that it now seems less surprising, the world being what it is."

Disturbed by a number of things in this story, Alicia asked

how he knew that what Anne had told her fiancé was a lie, and what the friends had said was the truth.

"Men have been known to lie, Tony," said Charlotte in support.

"So they have. But in this case I believe I have the advantage of you—you see, I was the man who killed Anne's fiancé, Francis James."

There was a silence.

"Come, ladies! It was years ago—I have had time to get used to it! But it is this that makes me say my youth is in that picture, for when I left England after the duel I had aged ten years in a morning. The pistol threw left, and though I aimed for his arm, the bullet found his heart. I was stupid—I had not tested the pistol."

"And who was the third friend?" asked Charlotte, her dark eyes sympathetic.

"Nick Fane. He was the one who told me Anne was not the delicately reared child she seemed. It took experience with her to prove it to me, of course: I, like Francis, was blinded at first."

When they returned home, Alicia sat down by the window and gazed out at the street, seeing nothing. She felt a searing mortification. How wrong she had been about everyone. She had believed Anne Dunstan because she had wanted to, after having already conceived a prejudice at her first meeting with Fane. She had ignored virtually all of the evidence which indicated that he was not the empty fop she had labeled him. Even when she found herself warming to him, she had tried—actually *tried*—to remember all his faults.

Of course, his pride was still great enough—he had not wished to stoop to an explanation about his dislike of Anne Dunstan. He cared so little for what anyone thought—including herself, perhaps especially herself—that he had not bothered to lower himself and denigrate Anne Dunstan. What a fool she had been! She blushed to think of how she had spoken to Anne Dunstan, commiserating with her, discussing Fane's many defects. . . .

She was in an uncommunicative mood the rest of the day, and all of Charlotte's efforts to cheer her were unsuccessful.

"I am afraid that I have to get myself out of this mood, Charlotte. No one can and no one should help me—it is a web of my own making."

Alicia refused to come down for meals, and asked that a tray be sent up with Eliza. Eliza reported to Charlotte that Miss was eating hardly anything. Charlotte shrewdly surmised that it was all to do with Fane and Anne Dunstan.

After a day of self-recrimination, Alicia wrote Fane a note, requesting him to come to Curzon Street for tea. On the day he was to come, she banished Charlotte and told Jellicoe not to interrupt Jelly protested that Alicia was not married to him yet.

"I am his fiancée, however, and I shall do what I like in my own house." This was said in such a forbidding tone that Jellicoe held her tongue.

Fane found this invitation rather unexpected. Since they saw each other so often—the Stornaways' spies were still watching— they did not bother about such things as tea.

He found Alicia in the library, with the windows open onto the garden.

"It is not such a warm day as that!" he protested.

"I know, but I am so longing for the countryside, and this is the closest I can get to it."

They talked of flowers and fields for a quarter hour, and not once during the whole time did Alicia look Fane in the face. Finally she felt ready to begin the real conversation.

"I wished to say something to you, Nick . . . I wish to apologize . . . for my attitude . . ." Here she stopped.

"For your attitude . . ." Fane prompted. He saw she was twisting a handkerchief in her hands, a very uncharacteristic gesture.

"Toward you. You see, I did not know what Anne Dunstan was really like until very recently—I should have, by a thousand things—she disliked Eliza's learning to read, and—"

"What has *that* to do with anything?"

"I saw Wycherly's painting, and he told me about the duel and Francis, your friend."

Fane was looking at her with a slight smile around his mouth.

"And what is it you thought—that you need apologize for?"

It was harder than she had anticipated. She could not look at him.

"I thought that your only reasons for cutting her . . . were . . . due to your pride . . . and that, as she maintained, she had once . . . discouraged . . . your advances . . ."

"Do stop this, Alicia! I cannot bear it. Not your style at all," he said with an expression of boredom.

"That is so like you! I try to behave decently and apologize for thinking the worst and you criticize me for it!" Devil take the man! He put her in the wrong even when she was doing the right thing.

"That's much better. You've no need to apologize. I see that my airs of self-consequence, or whatever it was, led you to believe Lady Anne's tales. She is a marvelous liar, I must say. Don't be an idiot, Alicia—let us forget this matter!"

"It is not very nice to refer to your fiancée as an idiot," Alicia said with difficulty, moved almost to tears for reasons she didn't understand.

Nick touched her arm and looked in her eyes which were bright with the unshed tears.

"What is it? Why are you so overwrought? Do not take it all to heart—it is not so important as that."

"But I have been such a fool . . . about everything and everyone . . ." she said haltingly.

He was prevented from asking what she meant by the intrusion of Laurence, come to announce that a date had been set for the wedding. When he had finished telling all about the elaborate plans for the great day, and had gone to tell Charlotte all about it, they were left alone together once more. Alicia felt inexplicably shy with him and could make nothing but the most conventional answers to his comments about Laurence's obvious happiness.

She walked to the door with him, wanting to say something that would explain everything, but not sure how to go about it. She went outside onto the stoop with him, breathing in the air which held the first hints of spring.

He was just leaning toward her slightly, as if to say something, when a shot rang out. Turning quickly. Fane saw de Rohant across the street, struggling in the arms of Jem Cobb.

"Got him, guv'nor! Look to the lady!" shouted Jem.

Puzzled by this advice, Fane turned to look at Alicia and saw that she was upset.

"Do not be frightened, it is over with," he reassured her.

"I think that a bullet has grazed my arm," she said.

She took her hand away from her left arm, and Fane saw the blood oozing through her sleeve. Without a word, he picked her up and carried her back into the house.

"You don't have to do this," she protested. "It is only a scratch and Jelly will be hysterical . . ."

He did not answer, but carried her upstairs to her room, and with Charlotte's help, arranged her on her bed. Jim Taylor was sent for the doctor, and Jellicoe for bandages.

"Nick! Charlotte! It is nothing, I tell you." Alicia smiled at them. "I do not know what the fuss is about!"

"It may be nothing; she has not fainted," said Fane to Charlotte, as if Alicia were not there.

"Yes, but we must be careful. I shall fetch some brandy, I am sure I could do with some myself!"

Fane came over to the bed and pushed her hair back from her face.

"I am very sorry for this. I should have considered this possibility." There was an unreadable expression in Fane's eyes.

"It is nothing. Freddy and I *wrecked* our bodies daily when we were young—falling out of trees, off horses. I am quite used to blood."

The strange expression left Fane's eyes, and was replaced by his more usual one of ironic amusement.

"I have a feeling that de Rohant was not so used to blood. I don't think Mercier ordered this. It was his own idea. But he missed so badly he merely nicked *you*! Mercier would hardly be proud of him."

Alicia was beginning to feel weak, but even in this state she managed to accuse him of not being the dandy he pretended to be. He laughed at her.

"I am hurt, Alicia. Is this an oblique criticism of my coat, or perhaps my snuffbox? I assure you I *am* a dandy! Whether I am other things as well—that is another question. Now, you try to do what the doctor advises—though I am quite sure you won't—and tell *no one* how this happened. I shall invent a tale, and you shall remember nothing. You are too upset to know how it happened."

While the doctor took care of Alicia's arm, Nick consulted

with Charlotte. It was decided that they would say Nick had been showing Alicia his pistol when it went off unexpectedly. Since the servants had apparently seen nothing, there would be no problems, Fane thought. De Rohant would be sent back to his country to stand trial after the restoration of the King, as would Mercier, if he had been caught at Dover, which Fane rather thought he had been, considering the abilities of the man sent after him.

"Do you think Alicia will recover quickly?" asked Charlotte.

"I do. She is a very strong young woman. You are not to worry about her. A remarkable girl," said Fane, absently putting on his riding gloves. Charlotte had the feeling that he meant far more by the last phrase than was usually understood, and when Lady Mary came to visit the invalid (who was being most difficult and insisting on getting up), Charlotte told her that she thought there was hope.

"But my dear, what good does that do? Fane is not the man to simply break off an engagement—or rather a presumed engagement—to a girl of good family, like Miranda. Even if he wants to, it's rather difficult." Lady Mary looked pensive. "If he doesn't think up something, I suppose I will have to. It's so boring being the only person one knows who is *resourceful*. But we must find out how they really feel about each other first. It may be that they are still blind to it."

Alicia lay in her bed, reviewing her plans for revenge, all of which seemed pointless now. Why spoil St. Clair's life just because hers was? No, she would let him go.

She had planned to wait until she was recovered, but when St. Clair came to visit, she found she had no taste for the game.

"Robert, it is over. I release you from the engagement. Go and marry Julia, which is what you should have done in the first place. You may wait to tell the world of this, if it will help you."

He saw at once that no lying would get him out of it now, and gave in with grace.

"But there is someone else, isn't there?" he asked as he left.

She raised her tired eyes to his, and wished that he still had to power to excite her.

"Yes," she said, "yes, there is someone else."

When Jellicoe came in with her medicine some minutes after he had left, she found Alicia crying into her pillow.

"There, there, you'll be better soon. Don't cry, don't cry." Jelly patted her head sympathetically, at a loss when confronted by a crying Alicia, something she had not seen since her mistress had been a child.

"It's all right. Jelly, it's all right," murmured Alicia, quite sure that it never would be.

39
LADY MARY INVESTIGATES

While Alicia lay in bed for a week, Fane tried to find out where Mercier had disappeared to. The tenacious Will had lost his quarry halfway to Dover. The trail had suddenly run out in Maidstone, and no one had seen anything of the stranger with the slight limp after that. Will came with his report the day following the de Rohant incident.

"Gone into thin air, Lord Fane! Never have believed it, if I hadn't seen it meself! Thought he might have disguised hisself—with that limp it'd still be easy to spot him—but there weren't even anyone else he could have been! Course there's a deal of movement through Maidstone, he could have gone on in any direction."

"No, there's something strange here. I would have bet my last penny that he was off to Dover. Somehow I've miscalculated. No fault of yours, Will! You did your best, I'm sure. Let me think on this a bit. I'll get in touch when I need you."

Jem Cobb had reported that de Rohant had left from Anne Dunstan's house in Crescent Street. The young Frenchman was not talking, and Fane was quite prepared to believe that whoever

Mercier was, he was not stupid enough to reveal his plans or real identity to de Rohant. It was possible, of course that Mercier had gone in a different direction, gotton onto a smuggler's craft, gone to Ireland or a hundred other places. After turning matters over in his mind for a few days, Fane came to the conclusion that it would be best to forget Mercier for the present and turn his attention to other problems which worried his superior. But not before he spent a little time in conversation with Anne Dunstan. He had no wish to see her alone, but the de Rohant matter would not be finished until he talked to the woman who had seen him just before the attack.

It was a most unsatisfactory interview. Lady Anne had no intention of helping Fane in any way.

"De Rohant is merely an acquaintance. I know nothing of his political convictions. Of course I am shocked that he should have tried to kill you." This last was said in such a way as to leave Fane in no doubt as to her real meaning.

"Did you ever hear the name Mercier from de Rohant?"

"No, I do not think so. But then my memory is quite unreliable. If I recall anything, I shall let you know."

Fane maintained his calm demeanor, but he was seething inside.

"I must thank you for your time. I shall be going now, I have pressing matters to attend to. It is too bad about de Rohant. He may be executed, you know. A rather serious matter, espionage during war—and although Paris has surrendered, the situation is still unstable. We are not about to let anyone who has helped the French get off easily."

He saw that she was struck by these remarks. Perhaps the reference to the possible death of de Rohant had affected her. She no longer appeared so sure of herself, and Fane sensed that she was hesitating. But then the moment passed.

"Lord Fane, I had not thought *you* to be involved in such a business! So unlike you!" Her smile held not an ounce of warmth.

"Yes, I find I have to associate with the most disparate persons. But you know, I am quite happy to be of service to the Crown, even as a mere errand boy."

She stopped him as he was leaving the room. "There was a time, Nick, when I actually cared for you," she said with difficulty.

"Of course. Every fortune in the *ton*, was it not? You gave me a valuable education, Anne."

Fane knew that his usefulness to his superior was over for the moment. He would have to go to his house in the country and rusticate for a bit, until his role in this affair had been somewhat forgotten.

His superior had other plans, however, as he discovered when he reported the fruitlessness of this interrogation.

"No, m'boy," said the older man, "can't let you go yet. I know that your position is now dangerous—if Mercier is still here, which I think is possible, he will be very interested in you. It has been decided, on a higher level, that you are to let him find you. We shall give you some false documents to carry."

"Ah, you do not think that this peace is the real thing?"

"Never know, Nick. Boney's on his way to Elba, but who can say? The French have been used to his tyrannical ways. Won't know what to do without him telling them when to jump. Don't trust them at all. Also—damned interesting that Mercier decided to stay here—our agents who work for the French report that he has not been seen or heard of—and *no one is expecting him anywhere.* Strange, don't you think? Almost every *émigré* here will be going back, and those who stay will be quite easily observed, so why would he stay?"

"I begin to have an idea," Fane said slowly. "I have been turning it all over in my mind. No one ever really saw Mercier—he was just a name. But we know he has been in and out of England because our agents on the other side have reported it. When Will lost the man we had deduced to be him, it struck me as odd that he would have even a slight limp—too good to be true. Now I think he had no limp! He was in disguise; he was always in disguise. And now *he is no longer in disguise*."

"What do you mean precisely?"

"He is—"

There was a knock and then the door to the library opened.

"Dear Henry, dear Nick, why are you being so tedious? Dinner has been ready this half hour! When will you finish your boring discussions of sport?" Lady Terbury smiled, but her listeners knew her to be quite upset.

"Be along in five minutes, Mary. Go ahead and start. Having a quarrel, and it would be a shame to bring it to the table."

When she left, Fane asked Lord Terbury if his wife suspected what his duties had really been for the past fifteen years.

"I rather think she knows. Intelligent woman, you know. But we have never discussed it, and we won't until everything is over, and I've left my post. But, my boy, back to Mercier! Go on!"

Although his days were spent poring over reports on Mercier—some dating back five or six years—Fane went every evening to visit the patient in the Curzon Street house. He made a special effort to bring new bits of gossip to entertain Alicia, as well as new books and journals he thought she might find amusing. His attitude was that of a good friend—nothing more, nothing less.

Alicia longed for these visits, but found them disturbing at the same time. Soon, she knew, Fane would become Miranda's financé once again. Then she would see him only on social occasions. The banns for Harriet and Laurence had already been posted, and now was the time for the *ton* to hear rumors of a quarrel between Alicia and Fane. But Fane kept postponing this event, saying that they would wait until Alicia was quite well again.

Alicia discovered that Nick's solicitousness was infinitely more painful than his irony had ever been. If he were not so continually kind, it would have been easier for her. As it was, she was constantly reminded of her blindness. The man she had once refused came every day with presents, told her of his travels and showed her sketchbooks, and never made any reference to their past misunderstandings.

Charlotte, alarmed at Alicia's mood of self-castigation, tried to make her see that it was not all her own fault.

"He was dreadfully proud, Alicia, a shocking snob. That much was true. And if he has changed, I am sure it has to do with you, with the things you said to him—no one else ever has, you know. And it is perfectly understandable that you should have taken him in dislike after that first meeting on the way to London. And of course he no doubt thought you a hoyden. But now it is all sorted out, you have both learned something. Why not start over? The poor man is going through quite enough with Miranda—no need for you to be in the blue megrims every time he comes."

"I am not so with him. I make light conversation and pretend to be gay . . . but what do you mean? Is Miranda complaining again?"

"Well, you know she considers your wound to be a direct result of your bad upbringing—wanting to see Nick's pistol! Lady T. heard all about it from her maid, who is close to the Draytons' maid. It seems that Fane did not take this too kindly, and told Miranda what a remarkably cool head you had, and that he'd rather have you along as a companion on a mission than any other woman he knew. Miranda said that was all very well if one was a soldier, but she thought it all highly unsuitable for a female. Miranda was completely overset, and actually let him hear her voice in its upper range—screechy, as the maid says. I'd give anything to have heard hear. Must be jealous as a cat!"

"I can understand her feelings; she is worried that I may supplant her. I wish I could tell her how ridiculous such a supposition is!"

Charlotte made no comment, but she made a point of telling Lady Mary of this remark.

"That signifies that he has not let her know how he feels," said Lady Mary sagely. "Very bad. Matters are proceeding more slowly than I thought they would. Well, we shall just have to think of something to speed them up. I have had a thousand plans, but they all seemed wrong in one way or another. But do noi worry, Charlotte, I shall think of something—I always do. I think it is time for you to bring the matter up with Worthing. As his friend, he must have some idea of how things stand, and I shall interrogate Major Trilling. We must be sure that Fane is not desirous of marrying Miranda, despite everything."

Worthing did not think that matters would be easily resolved.

"I understand your view, Charlotte, and of course I should like to see Nick saved from the Draytons, but you must remember the influence Nick's grandmamma has had. She raised him to be a Lord of the Castle, and he must have a chatelaine who suits it. And Alicia is too unconventional—he don't know *what* she may do next. That girl's up to everything, awake on all suits, which is not necessarily what one wants in a wife. He ain't said a word to me, of course, but this is just what I know about him. Takes the family name very seriously."

This information gave even Lady Mary pause.

"Very discouraging. But I have thought of something. But I must investigate further before I begin."

Lady Mary consulted Major Trilling next.

It was Major Trilling's opinion that Fane had never felt anything remotely like love for Miranda Drayton, and that now he did not even feel affection. Nick was impenetrable when he chose to be, and there was no way of knowing what he really felt, but it seemed to Trilling that no man of average common sense could wish to marry Miranda. On numerous occasions the major had observed conversations between Miranda and Nick. He had seen Nick's negative reaction to Miranda's incessant gossiping about Alicia.

Miranda finally received her comeuppance, but from an unexpected quarter. One afternoon at Mrs. Selby's, she was placed directly across a tea table from Harriet, who was waiting for Laurence and Nick to return from an errand. Miranda was giving full vent to her obsession with Alicia and her sins, talking in a low but audible voice to Mrs. Selby herself, who was drinking in every word.

"Really, I can't imagine what her family must have been. No doubt the shop is in there somewhere—not, of course, from her mother, who was a Latham. But the girl simply needs to be educated in the ways of society."

Nick and Laurence arrived, just in time to hear Harriet lose her temper.

"Miranda, you are the most spiteful person I have ever known. It is you who lack breeding. You remind me of some—some fishwife at Billingsgate!"

This was so unexpected, coming as it did from the normally quiet Harriet, that Miranda could not answer immediately.

Laurence patted Harriet's arm proudly, and Nick asked languidly if he could escort Miranda home.

"Why did you think I wished to go home?" she asked pettishly. "Mama will come fetch me in an hour!"

"I rather thought you might like to leave, but if not, it's just as well. I am off to White's."

"In the middle of the day?" Miranda was icy.

"Do you dislike gambling, Miss Drayton? My *fiancée* feels that it is a good relaxation for me."

Miranda bit back her reply, remembering that as far as the people in this room were concerned, she and Nick were not engaged.

The people in the room who knew that Fane's engagement to Alicia was false found this scene highly absorbing, and reported the conversation to Lady Mary, who said that she had known it would be this way—familiarity, in Miss Drayton's case, must certainly breed contempt.

40

WYCHERLY

When Alicia went out into the world after a week in bed, she found that the tempo of London life had increased with the news of the return of Louis to Paris and the expected visits of the allied sovereigns to London in June. Everyone talked of how the Russian Czar's sister had arrived and taken over the entire Pulteney Hotel—some one hundred and fifty guineas a week, and two guards at her door. Caught up in the excitement, Alicia and Charlotte went to see the illuminations. Carlton House was resplendent in fleurs de lys, with a transparency representing the triumph of the lillies displayed prominently, as well as *Vive les Bourbons* placed in front.

Now that they were no longer in danger of invasion, many of the English upper class found kind words for the genius of Napoleon, and expressed their contempt for the way in which the French had so hastily defected from their great leader. When the Prince Regent buckled the Garter around the incredibly fat leg of the newly restored French king, no one could resist satiric remarks. Lady Mary, who read the radical press for amusement, quoted Peter Pindar's verses on the Regent and King:

And France's hope and Britain's heir
    Were, truth, a most congenial pair;

Two round tun-bellied, thriving rakes,
    Like oxen fed on Linseed cakes.

Alicia, however, found little to like in Napoleon, even now.

"I am rather tired of hearing what a great man he is. If he is such a genius, why then did we not let him conquer? (Surely his little finger holds more intelligence than Prinny's whole body!) But we would not have him, a brilliant tyrant; surely we had our reasons."

Wycherly, to whom these remarks were addressed, said that 263 he was of a mind with Byron, who referred to the French King as Louis the Gouty.

"You see, Alicia, Napoleon seems to some of us to be preferable to the Bourbons. They have always been a certain evil."

"I suppose so. But I would not have wished, or believed—as did many of the merchants on the 'change, who sold cheap, sure that Wellington would lose—that Napoleon could rule England half so well as we do ourselves."

"Of course, of course. But still, one can see that lesser men will now replace Napoleon."

Alicia looked around at the studio, searching for the portrait of Anne Dunstan. She asked where it was.

"Sold it. To one of Louis the Gouty's courtiers, as a matter of fact. He went into ecstasies over it and offered three times what it's worth."

Alicia thought this a great shame.

"Tell me, did Nick Fane ever see that painting?" she asked.

"No, I don't think he did. He's not terribly interested in portraits, unless they are Renaissance ones. Terrible snob about art—although in this case, he's probably quite right."

"No, really, I'm sure he—"

He smiled mockingly at her. "No need, Alicia. I don't take myself too seriously, you know. Life has at least taught me that. But tell me; how goes the false engagement? I have heard nothing these many weeks. Is it almost over?"

Alicia told him all the latest developments, and he was so sympathetic, drawing her out with practiced expertise, that she found herself telling him about her farewell scene with St. Clair.

"And what will you do after the engagement to Nick is all over with?"

Alicia's high spirits deserted her. "Why must you ask that? I don't know, of course. I have painted myself into a corner, as Jelly would say."

"And is there nothing you can do?" asked Wycherly gently. "Perhaps a suitable gentleman will be found."

"I am afraid that even then . . . You do not know the whole, and I cannot tell you, but there are reasons why I could not marry anyone, even if we were both willing and free."

Wycherly looked skeptical.

"You know, Alicia, I cannot imagine you as an old maid. Let me know if the possibility arises, and I myself will take care of it."

"How very obliging of you, Tony," said Alicia beginning to laugh. "Rather unromantic—as if your only aim were to prevent old maidishness!"

"Precisely. An abomination to be prevented where possible. But do not take your situation too hard, Alicia. Fate has a way of taking care of the coils character gets us into."

Something in the way he said this made Alicia suspect that be was talking about himself as well.

"Is it fate that gave you the scar, or character?" she teased.

"A bit of both."

Alicia looked around at his disorderly studio, and wondered that no woman's hand could be seen.

"Have you no romantic connections, Tony? I am amazed if not."

"Oh, I am like the man in the poem:

Out upon it, I have loved
  Three whole days together;

And am like to love three more,
  If it prove fair weather.

My philosophy exactly."

"Suckling. The Cavalier poets were rakes to a man, I fear."

"Most improper for you to know it, Alicia. Do not tell me they are teaching you ladies such verses nowadays."

"No, they do not. My father's library was very well stocked, and he let me read anything that took my fancy."

"That explains it," said Wycherly cryptically, and after a pause he went on, "Poor Nick, I wonder if he would have found something better to do with his life if his father had lived."

"How did he die?"

"It was a terrible thing. Quentin Fane was caught in Paris during the Terror, in '94. Guillotined, under another name."

Alicia looked at him in astonishment. "Why is it no one ever talks about him? And what a terrible thing for Nick—he would have been about twenty then."

Wycherly looked uncomfortable. "No one talks about it because his father was some sort of spy. They're related to some of the best families of France, the Fanes are, and he had cousins who were being killed. But the circumstances of his capture were most peculiar, and His Majesty's government wished to have nothing to do with it. Made Fane's mother very bitter, I can tell you. She died three years after his father's death."

"But why did the government wish nothing to do with his death? I don't understand. Surely they would take care of their own agent . . ."

Wycherly looked down at his boots. "Thing is . . . they weren't sure that he *was* one of their own."

It took Alicia a few moments to understand the enormity of this, and when she did she became afraid. What would the son of such a man feel about England? Would he really be able to forget what had been done to his father, abandoned to Madame Guillotine?

This line of thought terrified her, and she refused to consider it. He could not, he would not . . .

She had put on her cloak and bonnet and was standing by the door, lost in these unwelcome speculations, looking so unhappy that Wycherly was touched by it.

"Now what is this?" he said, tilting her face up. "What have I said to cause this unhappy look?" He looked at her for a second, and then bent down and kissed her gently.

Neither of them saw Nick Fane standing in the hall. He turned quickly and went out the door.

"Someone just left," said Alicia.

"It does not matter—he would have seen nothing but a kiss between friends, is it not so?"

As they were leaving, Wycherly found a note in his front door.

"I am afraid that Nick has rather gotten the wrong idea," said Wycherly, handing her the note.

So sorry to have missed you, Fane wrote, *but I saw that you were occupied with more interesting matters. Yr obdt svt, Nicholas Fane.*

At first Alicia felt at fault—she had been alone with Tony,

although Potts was just outside. But then she began to be angry. What right had he to write the note, to behave in such a manner after the liberties he himself had taken on the Brighton Road (no matter if she had allowed them).

She did not see Nick for some time, and knew that he must be trying to find Mercier, but she resented his absence nonetheless.

41
THE EMERALD RING

The note was brought to her early in the evening, as she was dressing for Almack's one Wednesday. After reading it, she dismissed Jellicoe and Eliza and collapsed into the wing chair. Her heart was pounding and her brain was whirling. The green domino had found her.

Dear Miss Tierney, the note read, *the time has come. I shall be at Almack's tonight, and will claim the last dance. Please believe that I have nothing but your welfare at heart. Your svt, I remain, The Green Domino.*

Alicia immediately went to Charlotte, sure that she could not bear to deal with this alone.

Charlotte immediately saw the problem.

"He knows precisely who you are, and where you live. But if he can get into Almack's, you know he must at least have social standing."

This last had not occurred to Alicia, so upset was she.

"But that makes it worse! It means he must belong to the *ton*, since the patronesses are so snobbish!"

"Oh, it's possible he is not rich or well-placed—they have

let in those who are not—Tom Moore, for example. But he must have *something* to recommend him. Oh, Alicia, this is so exciting that I don't see how you can bear it! The last dance will not take place until three o'clock, and we have to arrive by eleven or we shall be denied entrance. That is far too long a time for you to be on tenterhooks!"

But Alicia began to feel better.

"You know, I think I am relieved. It is something I have been dreading, but at least it will finally be over."

"Well, you will have to change your dress," said Charlotte with some asperity. "You can't go to meet your fate in that yellow thing—who in the world encouraged you to purchase it? It is exactly wrong for your coloring."

"As you say, Charlotte, I will change it. I am just so tired of all these white gowns," said Alicia meekly.

"White is right," said Charlotte severely. Then she saw Alicia laughing. "You wretch! You are taking me in!"

"This is my hairdressing gown—it does not matter if Jelly musses it. Can you not see that it is *ancient*?"

"Knowing you, Alicia, I thought you were about to bring in a new fashion for unpleasant colors."

At ten-thirty when they left for Almack's, Alicia thought she could manage her emotions. But as they made their way through Mayfair, which was filled with an endless procession of carriages, and the noise their wheels made on the cobbled streets, she felt that she was only an observer of this world of houses lit from top to bottom, gold-laced servants standing on steps, the women in their jewels and feathers. It seemed to her that she was watching the social life of these streets from a great distance, as if she had never seen them before.

The great palace of intrigues that was Almack's was in full bloom when they entered. The rather dull, unostentatiously decorated rooms served as a contrast to the gowns, jewels, and beauties that were to be seen in the crowd.

Alicia caught a glimpse of a young girl who looked desperately unhappy and frightened. It was most likely her very first time at this temple of exclusivity. As she greeted acquaintances and looked for the Terburys, Alicia saw that all of the patronesses were present, even Lady Castlereagh and Princess Esterhazy, who had been rumored to have left for Paris. As she looked at everything with new eyes, she thought of Wycherly, who had always been most satiric on the subject of the Marriage Mart. He had never been given a voucher, but then he had never requested one. His reputation would have made it extremely unlikely that the patronesses should grant him one. He claimed that when he was younger, before the elopement, he had gone to Almack's—to look at the beauties and make their mammas nervous.

Alicia was of two minds. Of course it was a hypocritical and snobbish institution; but she did enjoy dancing there. But she enjoyed it less now than she had in the beginning.

The hours passed slowly, or so it seemed to Charlotte and Alicia, who were discussing who the green domino might be every time they were together. Sometimes Charlotte would nod to Alicia while they were dancing, as if to say, "This might be the one." It began to seem so ridiculous that they started giggling every time they even looked at each other.

"We are like silly schoolgirls," said Charlotte. "But at least you are in high spirits."

"I am not so sure; perhaps I am in hysterics and don't know it," replied Alicia, distractedly. "And here is His Lordship, come to favor us with his presence."

Fane did not diverge in any way from his usual behavior, and Alicia could almost have believed he had seen nothing at Wycherly's if she had not read the note. She had to admire his control: he was waiting until they were alone to give her a lecture. After telling them the latest story about Poodle Byng (so named because of the dog he carried with him in his curricle, and because of his curly hair), he excused himself and went into the other part of the establishment to gamble.

The Terburys had not come, and neither had the Draytons, much to Alicia's relief. She felt she could not have endured Miranda this night. Major Trilling, Worthing, and others kept them entertained, but both Charlotte and Alicia were unable to keep their minds on even the lightest conversation. Their eyes examined every newcomer, looking for an uncut emerald ring.

It had crossed Alicia's mind that the domino could be St. Clair. Given his character, he might have lied earlier when talking about their first meeting—to deliberately mislead her. It was therefore with the most unpleasant sensations that she observed him sitting with some men in the other room. He did not come up to talk to her, but he gave her a glance of unmistakable passion. Identical, no doubt, to the ones he gave Julia Stornaway, Alicia reflected coldly. She was surprised at how little she felt.

Finally the last dance was announced. Charlotte was across the room with Worthing, but her eyes were fixed on Alicia and the empty chair beside her.

To Alicia's irritation, Fane chose this moment to ask her for a dance.

"I *am* sorry. I'm already engaged for the last dance."

"I know. To me."

"I don't think you understand. Someone else requested it earlier."

"You don't understand. You are dancing with me."

He pulled her to her feet and led her into the crowd of dancers.

"Of all the impertient—" began Alicia.

"Be quiet. Look at my hand."

There, on Fane's left ring finger was the uncut emerald. Alicia almost cried with vexation.

"How do I know you did not receive the ring from someone else?" she asked after a long silence.

His arm tightened around her, and he pulled her closer, so that she would hear every word.

"Did Wycherly, your so very good *friend*, never tell you where and when the duel took place? It was in Lincolnshire, near Grantham, and the inn I stayed at was the Carlton Arms. You wished to know once why I had offered you marriage. It is because I am an honorable man, despite my behavior that night. Until this year I had no idea who the girl was."

Alicia thought she would go mad. She made a great effort to regain control of herself. This man, whose gray eyes expressed nothing but cold contempt, had done what he wished with her body. She felt both humiliated and shamed. As she danced with him, each touch of his hands seemed to burn.

She was not calm enough to say anything until they sat down.

"So that is what you wished to do by offering for me—make an honorable woman of me? How very kind of you. But was it not *unsuitable*?"

He looked at her, an angry light in his eyes.

"Of course, at that time I did not know how many strings you had to your bow—I had the idea I was behaving honorably. I was actually afraid you might not contract an eligible connection. And since I am to blame, in a sense, for your . . . er . . ."

"Loss of innocence," Alicia supplied. "Just so. But I find it does not matter now that I have money. Men are willing to overlook such a small thing if there is enough money. *That* is what London has taught me."

"Well, I daresay you'll do very well. Kendalford, Wycherly, St. Clair—you have provided yourself with so many choices."

So that was what he thought of her, thought Alicia, surprised at how it hurt.

"At any rate," continued Fane, "the charade will be over next week. I sent a notice to the Gazette today, saying that the engagement was at an end. Next week I shall accompany Miranda to Carberry's rout for the Czar's sister—a perfect opportunity to announce *our* engagement." He paused, as if waiting for her to say something, but she could not. "I wish you to know that you have nothing to fear from me. No one shall ever know. And no one will blackmail you."

"I did not think you needed money . . . I appreciate your sentiments, and I—I must now take my leave of you, my lord."

She walked slowly across the floor to Charlotte and Worthing, suffering from the worst headache she had ever had in her life. She had noticed everything when she arrived, but when she left Almack's she was conscious of nothing but pain.

Charlotte took one look at her friend's face and quickly ordered Worthing to get their cloaks and to send for the carriage. Alicia told her everything as soon as they were safely in her bedroom.

"I understand that it was a shock—that Fane was the man—but why are you so upset? Surely it is better that it be a man of Fane's standing, a man who would do you no harm."

Alicia looked straight ahead, staring at nothing. "It is hard to explain . . . but as hard as I tried to dislike Fane for everything, I could not . . . and the truth of the matter is that I care very much—for—for his good opinion. And now he has nothing but contempt for me."

Charlotte did not ask why his opinion should matter so much to Alicia.

"You would feel better if you had a good cry," she said gently.

But Alicia's dark blue eyes were dry when she looked up.

"This is not something I shall be able to cry about," she said bleakly.

42

CARBERRY'S ROUT

Lady Mary smiled with satisfaction when she heard about the scene at Almack's. Charlotte did not feel that she could reveal anything about the matter of the green domino, but she said that there had been a misunderstanding involving Wycherly, which Alicia regretted far more than she normally would.

"And Fane was jealous of Wycherly—that is clear. What was she doing kissing him in doorways, anyway! These modern misses! But I am very happy, Charlotte, because I have already Taken Steps. The letter is even now on its way to Bayhall."

"To Bayhall?"

"Never mind, dear. Just trust me, I shall get them both out of this coil they have gotten themselves into. I imagine that Alicia has no desire to see Nick?"

"None. She is in constant fear of meeting him somewhere, and has refused all invitations as a result."

"Well, she needn't worry. She has only one thing to attend: Carberry's rout for the Czar's sister. After that she is to go to my sister Lucinda, in Brighton."

Charlotte demanded to know what was going on, but Lady Mary would only smile, her bright eyes merry.

"Not going to tell you, Charlotte. I am sure there is a great deal that *you* have not told *me*! A general does not reveal his plans ahead of time—even to his aide."

"But Lady Mary, suppose Fane wants to marry Miranda, or doesn't want to marry Alicia—you can't just assume these things!"

Lady Mary was offended.

"I am not a *meddler*! I am merely going to make certain things *possible*—and if Alicia and Nick decide to choose them, very good, and if they don't—I wash my hands of them!"

When Lady Mary suggested the visit to her sister Lucinda in Brighton, Alicia made no objection. She was very listless, and it could not be said that she showed any particular enthusiasm for the idea, but neither did she say no. It was agreed that she would leave the day after Carberry's rout.

Carberry's rout for the Czar's sister was being held in a house that would not hold above six hundred, but which on this night was forced to contain upwards of fifteen hundred persons.

Alicia and Lady Mary found themselves stranded on the main staircase due to the crowds.

"We shall not move an inch for a half hour, and these women will begin fainting like flies, you'll see. Lady Carberry is an absolute fool, always was. As is her son. Now there's a man for Miranda! I doubt we'll even get to see the Grand Duchess Catherine!"

Alicia was searching the crowd for Lord Terbury, who had gotten separated from them, when she met a pair of gray eyes over to her left.

Nick was standing with Miranda and her mother on the landing.

There was an unreadable expression in his eyes, and his glance was so hypnotic that she could not look away. Then Miranda turned to him and said something, laughing. He bent down to talk to her and Alicia turned away, the tears that had refused to come before filling her eyes now, at the most inconvenient moment.

As the crowds began to move, he made his way to her side and seized the opportunity to turn to her when the Draytons were talking to someone else.

He looked at her questioningly, why she did not know.

"I am going away tomorrow," she said with difficulty. "I must say good-bye to you now."

She thought he understood her completely, because he raised her hands to his lips in that mocking style she knew so well.

"Good-bye, my dear disaster," was all he said.

A welcome numbness enabled her to get through the rest of the evening, and she did not look at him again.

She should be grateful, she decided finally. Now she knew what it felt like to be in love: it was pain, nothing but pain.

43
LADY MARY TAKES ACTION

Charlotte missed Alicia terribly and demanded to know when she would return.

"I don't know," said Lady Mary sunnily. "Soon, I should think. Fane has just left to go and visit some property of his, so I think it is time for the plan to take effect."

"Are you going to tell me anything?" Charlotte was annoyed. Surely now that Alicia was gone she could be told things.

Lady Mary understood perfectly.

"Yes, dear child, I have tortured you long enough. And besides, I want someone to admire my strategy. Lady Sarton is coming to visit!"

"Lady Sarton?" The name was familiar, but Charlotte could not quite place it.

Lady Mary was shocked at this ignorance.

"Fane's grandmother!"

"Ah. But what good will that do?"

Lady Mary sighed a long-suffering sigh.

"So tedious, when one's companions don't know things. Arabella Sarton was at Miss Pinckney's with Henrietta Drayton.

They positively hated each other. Haven't seen each other for years, Arabella stays in the country."

"I fail to see how this can affect Nick's marriage to Miranda. He will not care if his grandmother hates his mother-in-law."

"Oh Nick won't care at all," said Lady Mary calmly. "But Miranda and her mother will!"

Charlotte gave up. Lady Mary obviously wanted to keep an element of surprise in the campaign, even for her aide-de-camp.

A week later, there was a small card-party at Lady Mary's, for ladies only. Among those present were Miranda Drayton and Lady Drayton.

"Dear Arabella is due any day," said Lady Mary as she casually discarded.

"I am so anxious to see her again," said Lady Drayton with a false smile. "Such a charming girl she was! It has been years."

Miranda was listening, with no particular interest, or so it seemed to Charlotte.

"Of course she has changed a great deal," said Lady Mary after winning the hand. "Having to be the sole administrator of the Fane fortune has been a heavy responsibility. Such a lot of documents and signatures . . ."

Lady Drayton seemed to lose interest in the cards.

"And does she have anything to do with Nick's portion?"

"Rather a lot," Lady Mary gave a laugh. "She has complete control. His father left it that way, the boy being young, the mother chronically ill. And Fane has never bothered to change the agreement—he goes off to Europe and happily leaves everything in her hands."

"Everything?" repeated Lady Drayton in accents of disbelief. "How very singular of him, to be sure. I expect that when he and Miranda are wed, the arrangements will change."

Lady Mary did not answer this, but became very absorbed in the game.

Charlotte could barely keep from giggling aloud. The Drayton women had had the idea planted in their heads. But what if Lady Arabella Sarton liked Miranda, despite her mother?

"*Don't* be ridiculous! She'll take her in immediate dislike." Lady Mary was very confident on this point.

She lost some of her confidence, however, after the first skirmish, when Lady Arabella was presented with her grandson's fiancée.

"A most charming girl," said Lady Arabella. "A little drab, a little too good, I daresay a bit of a bore—but good breeding there."

Lady Mary did not look up from the tea she was pouring, and Charlotte had to admire her composure. A defeat, but she was still upright in the saddle.

"Yes, I daresay. And her mother seems charming as well," said Lady Mary, lying beautifully, Charlotte thought. But where would this lead?

"Now that's coming it rather too strong, Mary," said Lady Arabella forthrightly. "She's a tedious woman who can't ride or produce children. She's good only for *ton* parties. Hate to see her in the country."

"Yes? How very difficult things will be then," said Lady Mary with a vague air.

"What do you mean?" Lady Arabella was suspicious.

Lady Mary, a mistress of timing, did not answer at once, but daintily consumed a scone.

"Why, Arabella, surely Nick has told you that Miranda wants her mother to stay with her whenever she is at Bayhall. I daresay that sort of companionship is just what you have been missing at Bayhall. As I recall, you have no dower house? Nick wishes you to stay on at Bayhall."

"Yes, he does," said Lady Arabella grimly, visions of the loathsome Henrietta running about her house depressing her.

Lady Mary said nothing more about it, but a week of visits with the Draytons made Lady Arabella see that the last thing she wanted was an alliance with the Drayton family. The girl Miranda was a cold little thing who would want to run everything her way—she had seen drawings of Bayhall, she had heard about it, and she had every intention of living there and giving gracious entertainments. The mother talked about decorating schemes and renovation. She was driven to confiding in Lady Mary by this bleak picture of what her waning years would be like.

"But what can I do? Nick wants the girl . . ."

This was Lady Mary's moment. She heartily regretted that Charlotte was not present.

"But dear Arabella, surely you know that Nick does not care a bit for Miranda. It is all duty—he got engaged ill-advisedly (you were not there to help), and now he cannot get out of it. I have every reason to believe that he wishes this engagement terminated. But of course he can't do it."

Arabella gave a little bark of laughter. "Mary Terbury, what are you up to? I'll wager you have been machinating!"

"Of course I have, and so would you, if you knew everything."

Glossing over the details, Lady Mary proceeded to give an admirably logical explanation of the relations between Nick and Alicia, and Nick and Miranda.

"Well, I don't know if Nick wants to marry this Tierney chit, but I see that he don't want Miranda. But what can be done? It is his affair, after all."

"*That*," said Lady Mary sternly, "is always what people say when they are too lazy or too unimaginative to help. *I* never say things like that!"

"That's because you are a born meddler!" retorted Arabella, who had suddenly remembered all the trouble Mary had gotten her into when they were young. "Well? Tell me what role you have assigned me."

"We shall not deprive Nick of the choice—we shall just make it possible for him to have one. All you have to do is the following: find a pretext to fly into a rage against the Draytons and say that Nick may marry, but he won't have your blessing—or the money from the main fund!"

"But Nick has a fortune of his own," objected Arabella.

"Yes, but they don't know that!" crowed Lady Mary. "And when Nick finds out, he has the choice of telling them that it doesn't matter, or letting Miranda cry off because he'll be less rich than she supposed."

"But are you sure she'll do that? Perhaps she loves him."

Lady Mary looked at her friend derisively. "Really, Arabella, you have been in the country too long. Henrietta Drayton is incapable of producing a loving child! Miranda is just as cold and egotistical as her mother!"

An first Lady Arabella was doubtful of the propriety of this action, but when she saw Miranda prosing on with Carberry about the joys of geometry, she decided. This was no woman for her grandson.

"But I agree only because Nick will still be able to decide if he wants her or not."

"Yes, of course. Tomorrow you will have your temper tantrum—I think it would be nice if you accused Miranda of flirting with Carberry while Nick is gone. *That* will do nicely, I think. Now if only Nick would return . . ."

44

MERCIER

Lord Fane and Jem Cobb had been riding for days through the spring rains and muddy roads, on the trail of Mercier. It was Will, drinking in a gin shop near the London docks, who had seen the hands. The body and face were different, but the hands—Will had memorized those oddly shaped fingers. He followed the man to Colchester and sent word back by special courier that it looked as though the man had settled in for a few days.

Twenty minutes after receiving this note at White's, where he was dining, Fane was on the road with Jem, mounted on the swiftest horses at their disposal. When they reached Colchester, they stopped at the main inn and found Will in the taproom.

"Very good, sir. He's at the Red Lantern Inn, plain as day, sitting in the coffee room. Like he wasn't at all worried."

"I begin to see," said Nick, lighting a cigar after sniffing it slowly. "He wants us to find him. He saw you, Will, and decided to have the meeting now. I think I shall go over there alone. There is something strange here, and I don't wish to throw our Mercier off his stride. I shall play by his rules. For now, anyway."

The innkeeper swore that there was no "Mr. Mersey-ay" at the Red Lantern. Fane took a look at the register and found a name which he recognized. Over the landlord's objections he went upstairs to the front room and knocked.

"Come in, it's unlocked," said the familiar voice.

Fane entered and sat down.

"And where are you bound for, Tony?"

Wycherly smiled but did not reply immediately. He poured them both some wine.

"I don't think I shall tell you that, Nick. Wouldn't be terribly intelligent of me."

"I don't see how you are going to get away, old man. The ports are being watched. And I'm disinclined to walk away."

Fane was still smoking his cigar, but did not touch his wineglass.

"It's not poisoned, or drugged," said Wycherly, nodding at the glass.

"I'm sure. But I find I am not thirsty. Why did you lead me here? I'm very curious—a new profession for you?"

"It is not new. When I left England, after the duel, I went to live in France. Naturally I became enamored of Napoleon. There's a man for you! At the time it seemed likely that England would fall to him."

"And you thought you would help it happen more quickly," said Fane dryly.

"No, it was not like that. At least not until the end. It was rather enjoyable, walking among my old friends, not having them know me. But it is all over. Nick, all I want is to go to the Americas. Europe has nothing for me anymore, now that he's gone to Elba . . .

"And why did you think I'd let you get away? You are Mercier, after all. And as long as Napoleon is alive, we can't trust France or her agents."

"Never think I am defenseless, even in England, Nick. I may kill you this moment, if I wish, and your pistol would not stop me."

"But why have you led me here? Why leave a trail?"

"Well, I did not know it was you; I must say I am surprised, although now that I think on it, I shouldn't be. After that business with your father, I should have guessed you'd try to finish his work. But I wanted the men who were chasing me to understand, before I left forever . . . I have not killed one Englishman in seven years of this work; surely that shows you something. I believe in the French cause, but I did not wish to destroy England."

"You could not have, even if you had wished to, Tony. It is not so easily done. Not by *you*, at any rate." Fane showed his contempt for the first time.

"The proud Lord Fane. You know, your pride cost you dearly. You have lost Alicia Tierney because of it."

Fane looked bored. "Do not be so tedious, old man. Your views on women are to be respected, of course; there have been so many of them in your life. Am I to understand that Alicia excited your interest, beyond the kiss I saw?"

"The kiss was nothing, Nick, at least to her. I swear on the body of Francis James, she is not false. You see all women as being like Anne. She marked you for life, I think."

Fane actually yawned. "You know, Tony, I am one of that rare breed: I find talking about myself quite uninteresting. And please don't tell me about Alicia Tierney. I feel in no need of information *there*."

Wycherly was watching Nick carefully, never taking his eyes off him.

"Well," he said abruptly. "I believe it's time to go. Say goodbye to Charlotte and Alicia for me. I may even write."

The pistol had been lying in the soup bowl which was on the table in front of Wycherly, covered by a napkin.

But as he stood up, Wycherly saw that Nick was holding a pistol as well, aimed at his heart.

"Not very sporting, Nick. You had it out the whole time." He reached as if to pick up his glass of wine, but in a swift and practiced motion threw it in Fane's eyes instead.

Fane fired, but realized as he did so that his reflexive reaction would cause him to miss. Rubbing his stinging eyes, he dimly saw a shape come down toward his head. He fell heavily to the floor under tht impact of Wycherly's pistol butt.

By the time Fane regained his senses a moment later and pulled himself up, Wycherly had disappeared through the window, and the clatter of his horse's hooves was fading in the distance.

Fane smiled ruefully. Wycherly had beaten him at the game, and that was why he had been allowed to find him. Wycherly wanted his pursuers to know that the only way they could capture him was if he let them. Nick had to admire the style of the man. Of course, Mercier-Wycherly had had seven years of practice to perfect his speed and ability to analyze a situation, especially when he chose the ground. He had known that Fane would bring a gun, and he had almost seemed to know when he would bring it out. The wine had been set up expressly for the purpose of throwing it in his eyes. Wycherly had not really drunk any of it; he only seemed to. All in all, it was an instructive performance.

Nick had to admit to himself that he was just as glad his friend had made his escape. Mercier could have done much worse than stun him with that pistol. Fane could never forget that. Mercier would no doubt turn up in America next, looking for whatever kind of work an unemployed spy was good at.

Nick returned to Will and Jem in a cheerful mood, for reasons which he could not explain to his subordinates.

"Well, he got away—but he's leaving England. We won't see him again. That I am sure of."

Jem looked puzzled, and Will downright dubious. But they were both accustomed to following Fane unquestioningly, so they said nothing.

"Shall we spend the night here?" asked Will, who was longing to sleep.

"You certainly may. But I have to get back to London. My fiancée expects me to accompany her to a dinner tomorrow night." said Fane in a flat voice.

Within half an hour he was on his horse, cantering toward London.

45
MIRANDA'S DECISION

The invalid lay on the green-striped Egyptian sofa, sighing periodically, when she was not drinking her bohea. Miranda was pacing up and down the salon, bright red spots burning high on her cheekbones.

"Nick will twist her around his finger, I have no doubt about it! You must not take on so, mamma!"

But Lady Drayton, vanquished in the battle with Arabella, could derive no comfort from this idea.

"No, no, she is going to ruin your life. You'll have to live in a little cottage somewhere, I daresay without even a town house to come to in London!"

"Mother," said her daughter tartly, "I shall *not* marry Nick if there is to be no money. It would make no sense! And if that—that harridan continues to stay at Bayhall, refusing to let us come visit—well, I shall just *do* something!"

Her suffering mother sat bolt upright at this.

"Not marry Lord Fane?! My dear! What are you thinking of? Our plans—the marriage celebration—"

"Can be done just as easily with Viscount Carberry! In fact, it might even be better!" said Miranda, thinking of how Fane had defended that Tierney chit.

Even Lady Drayton was astonished at this example of cold-heartedness.

"You don't mean that," she said weakly. "You are simply upset."

But Miranda was more than upset. Lady Arabella had not only accused her of flirting with Carberry while Nick was gone, but also intimated that the study of mathematics was not feminine. Such coarseness of mind, Miranda felt, could never be overlooked.

Despite her remarks to her mother about Carberry, Miranda was reasonably certain that Nick would be able to manage his grandmother to her satisfaction. Carberry was, in some ways, more to her taste than Nick. Still, she had no evi denco as yet that Carberry wished to marry her, and it woud require a great deal of work to get him to that point.

If she had heard Nick's conversation with Lady Mary, Miranda would have been far less sure of herself.

It was early Monday afternoon when Nick arrived at Grosvenor Square, to see his grandmother, who had unaccountably decided to stay there rather than in his house in Cavendish Square.

Lady Arabella wasted no time in telling him what she thought of his fiancée, and the scene of the previous day. Nick listened in silence until she was finished, and then asked Lady Mary why she had done it.

"Done what? What on earth do you mean, sir?" The merry blue eyes were wide with innocence.

"Really, Nick," interrupted his grandmother, "it means nothing if I cut you off—you have your own money. Of course the Draytons do not know that. Now you will discover if you are loved for yourself."

But Nick did not even look at Lady Arabella. His eyes had remained on Lady Mary.

He stood up and told them he had to see his fiancée.

At the door, he turned and said to Lady Mary, "You are the *wickedest* woman of my acquaintance, Lady Terbury."

Lady Arabella was a little frightened. "What are we going to do, Mary? He's very angry—he'll fix it all up again!"

Lady Mary bit a length of silk thread off and looked at the panel she had been embroidering. "Don't worry, Arabella. He's not as stupid as you think. And besides, I've already told everyone about Kendalford. That will do it, if nothing else does."

Lady Arabella found this last reference puzzling, but she was too tired to interrogate her friend.

Nick's welcome at the Drayton mansion was decidedly restrained. Miranda was at her most peevish, demanding that he "manage" his grandmother.

"But I can't do that. She has a mind of her own," he said mildly. "And I have a little money of my own, you know . . . we shouldn't starve."

Miranda looked at him in disgust. This posing dandy, taking snuff at this very moment (how she hated snuff!), what did he know of the expenses a household would incur!

"I am very sorry, Nick, but it would break my mother's heart if I married you under such conditions! Living in a small cottage, perhaps without a town house of your own . . . No, I must ask you again: can you persuade your grandmother to put aside these ridiculous plans to cut you off?"

He wiped his snuffbox with his handkerchief and restored it to his pocket. He had never noticed before how predatory

Miranda's finely boned face could seem. But now he saw it clearly.

"No, m'dear, sorry, but she runs the family. No opposing her. A matriarch, in fact."

In freezing accents, Miranda bid him good-bye, and said that there was no need for any further conversation on this subject. They would both be happier with other partners, she was sure.

He returned to Lady Mary's in a happy frame of mind—exactly, he recognized, as if he were a prisoner released from jail.

He told them what had happened in a very understated form, and they congratulated him. He was invited to dine along with Charlotte and Worthing, and they had a very happy dinner together. Lady Mary looked around the table, very satisfied with her work. One thing bothered her, however. Nick had not once mentioned Alicia, not even to ask where she was. Perhaps they had been wrong—perhaps he did not care for the girl?

She shook herself. No, one must never indulge in depressing thoughts. Generals must plan the next campaign and not regret the failures of the preceding one.

46

AT AUNT LUCINDA'S

If one was unhappy in love, Alicia discovered, spring was like any other season. Or perhaps worse: every bold new flower that burst through the soil, every budding green leaf, every singing brook, reminded one that all was lost. Nature was happy, but the lover was not.

Brighton had much to offer in the way of distraction, but the first week she remained indoors, deliberately cultivating each depressing thought. But she was too active to remain in such a state for much longer than that. The second week she began to go riding, taking lonely jaunts along the seacoast urging her mount to gallop at full speed.

Lady Mary's sister, Lucinda Hall, had proved to be some thing of a surprise. While Lady Mary was tall and commanding, Lucinda was short and tentative. She looked years older than her sister, but was actually younger. Lady Mary had warned that Lucinda would not be the best company.

"Lucinda is rather fluff-headed—she can barely take care of a cat, never mind a guest. So you be prepared to take care of yourself. But you'll see, she's very restful."

She was a thoroughly kind woman, however, and she adored her sister, whom she viewed as a sort of deity who had descended from Mount Olympus and gone straight to Grosvenor Square.

"And would you believe it, Alicia," she said one day, "even when we played dolls, she was the one who made up all the stories. Wonderful stories, too. But our cousin Jane stoppped playing with us after a while, which was the greatest shame."

"Why did she stop?" asked Alicia curiously.

"She said that Mary's dolls always had the best parts, and she was sick of it. Which," said Lucinda with feeling, "was really too bad of her! It was just that Mary was able to make whatever part her doll had *seem* the best. Why should she not?"

Just when Alicia was beginning to wish she could enjoy some rational conversation, she received a most unexpected visit from the Duke of Kendalford.

"Fitz!" she cried happily. "I am so glad to see you! What goes on in London? Tell me everything!"

Kendalford was in high spirits and told Alicia all about the latest events within the government circles. Starved for news, Alicia was utterly absorbed by all the things she had missed, including the wedding of Laurence and Harriet, which had just taken place.

"And how are our friends," she asked, making herself pronounce the name. "Nick, Charlotte, Worthing . . ."

"Well," twinkled Kendalford, "things have rather changed with Nick. He is not to marry Miranda!"

Alicia listened with eagerness to the story, laughing at Lady Mary's role, surprised that Lady Arabella should have gone along with such a scandalous plan. They talked for several hours, and then he left, promising to come the next day.

"Oh, I almost forgot—here is a letter for you, from Charlotte."

Alicia was delighted, and immediately tore open the envelope. Charlotte wrote:

It will come as no surprise to you that Harriet and Laurence made a wonderfully happy couple, and quite bored everyone with their joy. It was a quiet wedding, in good taste. I find that I prefer vulgar display, to tell the truth. But enough of this.—I will spend the rest of this letter (Lord. T. says you have to cover every inch of the paper, because franking is so dear—*this from a man who has two horses in the money) on gossip.*

Dear Robert St. C. is seen everywhere with little Julia, who is crowing about how she knew he'd come back to her. But St. Clair has a slightly hunted look, and I predict that their marriage will be perfectly miserable. Edith is aux anges. She is under the impression that old Alexander is going to leave Robert everything. Most amusing. Lord T. is a bit unhappy—says he doesn't even want that bounder slightly related to him.

Worthing and I are thinking of eloping. More exciting, don't you think? But we'd have to take his valet along (Worthing can't even dress himself, I suspect). And he would be de trop.

For weeks no one has seen Nick. Miranda and he, as Fitz will tell you, are done. She is much seen with Carberry. At church. With all the parents present. How does that suit you? Really, Alicia, your silence on this is quite trying. There are several divorces in the ton *this month. Spring, you know. The reports of conjugal infidelity (as Lord T. insists on referring to them) are increasing daily, and riding in the park grows in importance. Do not plan to be in the countryside until after our honeymoon—Paris, of course; Worthing had some strange idea about going to Turkey.Can you imagine? I couldn't. Told him it wouldn't smell nice.*

Oh, I have saved the best for last. Your brother and sister-in-law came to visit. I said you were visiting some friends and wouldn't be

back for a while—didn't know their address, but their name was Smith.
Your brother looked ready to murder me. Your sister actually thought
I was serious! Most pleasant interview with them. They predicted a
Dark Future for you—result of your wild up-bringing, which was all
your father's fault, even though he "was a saint. Too bad of you to have
missed them. Would have cheered you no end.

The Great World: Byron is as he was. So is Caroline. But it's too
repetitious to even write about. Prinny is fat. So, I hear, is Louis. Must
indicate something.

Your loving Charlotte

P.S. I finally got around to writing Stanford. Told him I thought we
shouldn't suit, even though our lands do march. My mother said I had
no sensibility. I said that it was contagious and that I contracted it
after prolonged exposure to you.

P.P.S. You sly creature, we all know why Kendalford is gone to see you!
Confess: you and he have been corresponding, haven't you? Miranda
will be consumed with jealousy if you become a duchess! I can't wait.

C.M.

Alicia found much to amuse and cheer her in this letter, but
Fane's absence from society disturbed her. Perhaps he was
involved in something to do with Mercier . . .

Alicia's first reaction to the story of Miranda and Fane had
been one of euphoria, but then she began to see that it really
made very little difference in her situation. Fane might be free
of Miranda, but that did not mean that he would ever think of
her, Alicia, with anything but contempt.

She sat in the small parlor, absently twisting the rose-
cut diamond on her finger—his ring, she wore it constantly

now—wondering how much she would have to suffer before she was happy again. She stared out the window, looking at the carriages going by, but not really seeing them. She heard a carriage pull up outside, and she rose, thinking it was Kendalford come back for something.

"Oh, dear, oh, dear," said Lucinda, peering nervously into the hall, "it is some man I don't know. Who can it be? To be sure he looks like a perfect gentleman, but he *is* very brown."

Alicia fell back into her seat, unable to think. He was there, he had come to see her, he would forgive her, he—

But Nick's first words were hardly those of forgiveness.

"What do you mean by this, you little fool? Haven't you done enough?" He jerked her out of her chair, in the presence of the stunned Lucinda.

She knew she would cry at any moment. After all her joy at seeing him.

"I don't know . . . what . . . you mean," she said haltingly.

"Kendalford!" he spat out, holding her arm so tightly that it hurt.

"He came today, yes . . ." She would cry this very moment. The tears were already spilling over a little; she hoped he could not see them.

"Are you to marry him or not? Answer me!"

Suddenly she was angry. How dare he treat her like this! "No, I am not, but it is certainly none of your affair!"

The tension drained out of his face immediately, and only then did she realize just how upset he had been—so upset that he had actually shown it.

In another moment he was smiling slightly.

"The wickedest woman in the world," he murmured half to himself.

"Who?"

"Lady Mary. She led me to believe that you were going to marry Kendalford . . ."

She moved away from him and then whirled to face him.

"And I might! Why should I not? Do you think I am not good enough for him?"

There was an unreadable expression on his face as he said that no, he did not think she was good enough for Kendalford.

"If you have come here to insult me, I would be quite happy to see you go, Lord Fane," she said through clenched teeth.

He passed his hand over his face in a weary gesture.

"No, I did not come here to insult you," he said, moving toward her, as she backed into a corner. "Please leave us, Mrs. Hall. We have something to discuss."

Poor Lucinda was grateful for the chance to get away from this disturbing and largely incomprehensible scene, and she quickly scurried out the door, dragging her three cats after her.

"I hate cats," said Fane. "I do hope you don't like cats."

"Are you mad, Nick? Why are you talking about cats? You were about to tell me why you came. And why I am not good enough for Kendalford."

"You are not good enough for Kendalford. You are good enough for me. And I came to do this," he said, embracing her and then kissing her several times with a thoroughness that made her weak.

"If you are going to do this, you must let me sit down. I cannot stand in this corner very much longer."

"I'll catch you when you fall," he murmured. "I'm not letting you out of this corner until you agree to marry me. I think I have been rather patient and deserve a reward. Several rewards, in fact."

After he had taken these rewards, which consisted of kissing her many times, she made him stop.

"And you did not think of me as a—an—easy woman, because of the inn, and St. Clair . . ."

"And Worthing, and Wycherly, and Kendalford. No, my dear disaster, you are the least easy woman I know."

Later, after all had been explained and reexplained, she sat beside him on the couch and began to giggle.

"What is funny, Alicia?"

"Lady Mary. She's going to take credit for all of it. You and I were just talking dolls to her!"

"Dolls? No, I don't want to know what it means. But you have to give me another reward, for not asking."

Two months later, two gentlemen went into White's and asked for the betting book.

There, under the entries for the fourth of October was:

Lord Fane bets Lord Worthing 300 g that a certain lady understood between them will change her opinion of a certain party, before nine months are up.

"You just made it under the wire," said Jack grudgingly, as he handed over the money.

Fane laujhed. "You are a sore loser, Jack. You should pay me double—I didn't merely make her change her opinion, I *married* her."

ABOUT THE AUTHOR

Alix Melbourne is an admirer of both Jane Austen and Georgette Heyer and wrote her novels as an homage to these two women.

ALIX MELBOURNE

FROM OPEN ROAD MEDIA

INTEGRATED MEDIA